MW01165834

timbuktu chronicles

Aida and the Chosen Soldier

Anthony Nana Kwamu

authorHOUSE®

AuthorHouse™
1663 Liberty Drive
Bloomington, IN 47403
www.authorhouse.com
Phone: 1-800-839-8640

First published by AuthorHouse 5/3/2010

ISBN: 978-1-4490-9138-5 (e)
ISBN: 978-1-4490-9136-1 (sc)
ISBN: 978-1-4490-9137-8 (hc)

Library of Congress Control Number: 2010905621

Printed in the United States of America
Bloomington, Indiana

This book is printed on acid-free paper.

For Emmanuel

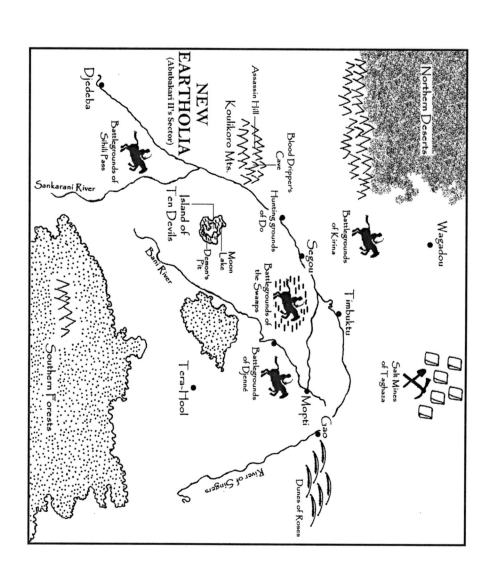

The Traveler's Account

chapter 1

The Famine

IT WAS IN DJEDEBA, FOUR summers ago, that I was misfortuned to witness the most appalling and fearsome sight that any of you is ever likely to set eyes upon. It was a sight so unbelievably horrid that I can hardly find words appropriate enough to describe it. I can only state that it demonstrated for me what man can become in times of bitter desperation. While I will do my best to describe it to you, I must warn that should you be of a weak nature or of a soft stomach, favor yourself by skipping this portion of my account, for herein describes, as best as I can put to paper, the sinking of man to the very depths of abomination through the most shocking and repulsive scene ever to have been presented before the very eyes of man.

Not far from the imperial garrison in Djedeba, a starving boy with a sunken face and his aging father disputed over the ownership of a half-rotten banana they had found on the roadside. Rather than share the banana as they had agreed in a bid to end their dispute, the boy punched the old man in the stomach and grabbed the fruit. While the man doubled over and wheezed, the boy quickly peeled and ate the banana, then laughed at the desolate old man. With amazing speed, the man grabbed a dagger and slit the boy's neck, then hacked open his stomach, plunged in his hand, clawed out the mashed and swallowed remnants of the fruit, and heartily gulped it down.

***

THEY CALL ME ABDEL EL Maliki. I am a Moor from Fez. My unending quest for knowledge has taken me to the farthest realms of the known

1

world. And for each of those realms I have taken upon myself the task of putting to paper an account of my adventures therein. But as for Timbuktu, from where I now put these words to paper, I will give you not an account of the city, but a tale—one which they say is true, and from which you will learn the truth about our world and what it might have become. It is a tale of a girl child and a soldier. I urge you to believe me when I tell you that its events are true, for what is about to be revealed to you comes not from my imagination, but from three of the very souls who were fortuned or misfortuned to find themselves in the thick of the said events. In the following you will read the account of a girl child as she told it to me; the account of a wizard of utmost importance to this tale as he, too, told it to me; and the account of the soldier, written by his own hand.

What has the famine in Djedeba to do with my tale, you might ask? To understand it all we must begin the tale at the very beginning, during the Breed Wars of ten thousand generations ago…

THE BREED WARS

ACCORDING TO THE BREED LEGENDS, the species began to change when some of their young started being born without the brown fur that covered their parents' bodies, without the two horns that adorned their parents' heads, and without the third eye in the back of their parents' heads used to watch for the evil behind their backs. These offspring were of a new breed, much weaker than their fathers and their mothers. They were like you and me. They were human!

Some in Eartholia Proper believed this new breed was a curse, a punishment for the evil their parents were doing to the land and its creatures. But the oracle, Bi-li Baba, disagreed. He believed the species was changing—evolving into a new breed—and that all the newborns would soon be of the new breed. The old breed was dying out, he said.

But the oracle's prophecy was flawed, for though many were born as the new breed during the next few centuries, many others were born as the old breed. The new breed members, who saw themselves as true humans, referred to the old breed as *raw-breeds,* or those who had failed to evolve. For many a century, man and raw-breed shared the realm of Eartholia Proper and lived in peace, until the Breed Wars. These were wars fought among the raw-breeds, sparked by the desire for some among them to turn man into slaves of Eartholia Proper; to be used by the raw-breeds to fulfill whatever needs arose in the realm.

The first of the Breed Wars was won by those who wanted man enslaved. And man indeed was enslaved, doomed forever to be forced laborers in a realm that no longer respected their existence. Yet, not all among the raw-breeds found comfort in the enslavement of man. So it was that a slave colony was founded in the outer world dimension, a desolate mystical world where all humans were transferred against their will, to be brought to Eartholia Proper only when their labor was desired. Entry into this slave colony was only through the Portal of Gorgida, the supernatural doorway that shielded the colony from Eartholia Proper and prevented man from escaping the torment of eternal servitude. The magical key to this portal remained in the hands of the raw-breeds, beyond the reach of any human.

But alas! Then came the second of the Breed Wars, fought among the raw-breeds over control of the magical key to the Portal. This war led to the loss of the key, a loss that kept the raw-breeds out of the outer world slave colony, a colony that the raw-breeds called New Eartholia, but which the humans simply called Earth.

The closing of the Portal of Gorgida, its key lost in the chaos of war, freed man from the evil of the raw-breeds at last, until...

The Soldier's Tale

chapter 2

1310 A.D. THAT WAS THE year I stopped teaching philosophy at the University of Sankoré in Timbuktu and joined the army.

I am Commander Gyvan Drabo of the Imperial Army of Mali. I have spent twenty-nine summers on this Earth.

Two years after I joined the army, I found myself leading 503 battle-hardened foot soldiers against rebel archers who were three times our number and who had nearly stopped the charge of my army's first cavalry assault against their battle lines. This battle to control the salt mines of Taghaza had raged all day, yet no end to the carnage lay in sight. As we charged at the archers I cringed as an arrow flew over my head. A soldier behind me cried in agony and dropped. His quilted armor padded with the fiber of the silk-cotton tree had provided little protection. Would the next arrow find its mark on me? I wondered whether like my father, who twenty-eight years earlier had been killed in a skirmish to retake the gold mine of Tekrur from northern invaders, I, too, would meet my end in battle.

Awed by the raw courage of our charge, many rebel archers fled in terror, while those who were left dropped their bows and drew their swords to engage us at close quarters. We clashed, body and soul, filling the air with cries of death all around, on my side and on the other. I felt secure with my mastery of the sword as I hacked my way through the enemy lines, bringing down many a rebel. Those who got too close for my sword to be of any use had a nasty surprise waiting for them—my wrist knife. This was a circular knife which I wore around my left wrist like a bracelet. The edges were housed in a sheath made of a strip of lion skin leather. At any moment the strip could be yanked off, revealing the deadly blade capable of delivering a fatal slash across an enemy's throat.

Before the rebel archers could use their numbers to overwhelm us, our emperor himself, Abubakari II, led a cavalry charge to reinforce our ranks. This brought the tide of battle clearly in our favor, for all around us the rebel ranks crumbled as many a rebel fled to save his skin.

The battle for the salt mines was crucial, for Fadiga, the rebel warlord, was himself leading the defense of the mines. For a reason that was not explained, Emperor Abubakari II had given orders that Fadiga was to be taken alive. The emperor himself had marched with us to Taghaza to make certain of this. Unfortunately a stray arrow slew the rebel leader, causing his men to flee in panic. Victory was ours. The warlord, an exceptionally brutal and atrocious character who had inspired so much fear throughout the empire that it was rumored that he had cooked and eaten four of his sons and two of his granddaughters just to demonstrate how nasty and ferocious he was, was dead at last.

Though the emperor and his generals regretted the death of Fadiga, the imperial soldiers were joyous at the prospect of victory in this war that had raged for two years. After all, we were one step closer to winning the war and could now look forward to returning home to our families.

Later that day, as we feasted and made merry, all I thought of was returning home to meet the woman I planned to marry. Little did I know that this battle would be only the beginning of much bigger trials to come. It had not been fought only for control of the salt mines. Something more sinister festered behind it. Something only the emperor and his commanders seemed to know. Something that had to do with the unintended death of Fadiga, a grievous error that would lead to consequences far beyond my wildest imagination—to a task which not even an army could accomplish, but which would rest almost entirely on my shoulders! And you, too, will judge for yourself that it was too great a task to befall a single man.

Sobo Ha-Ha Speaks

chapter 3

I AM SOBO HA-HA. I was the high eeid of Tera-Hool, appointed by the warlord, Fadiga, in the year the troubles began.

It was a dark cave hidden deep within the mysterious mountains of Koulikoro. These were the mountains where rested the notorious Assassin Hill. Here, some fifteen summers past, a confederation of fourteen kings had battled and defeated a heavily outnumbered but fearsome band of assassins people called Paipans. The confederation was led by the Emperor Sakoura of Mali, who despite facing only 102 assassins, lost 2132 of his 6000 men. And though the Paipans had lost, one survived, causing a frightening alarm among the emperor's troops that continued for many years after. As my account unfolds you will understand why so important a battle raged on Assassin Hill some fifteen summers past, and why the survival of a lone assassin caused so disturbing and horrifying a mood among the confederation of kings, their troops, and the empire.

I was on the mountains for an important task—to visit the creature or being that rested in the darkest, innermost corner of the cave that lay hidden within the mountains. It was a creature that as yet did not exist, but that would exist in due time. My task was to administer certain charms and potions of a dark nature to this creature that would help us accomplish our designs for this Earth—this cursed Earth.

The Soldier's Tale

chapter 4

I ENDED MY DAYS OF teaching philosophy at the University of Sankoré because I needed the thrill of a good adventure. What better way was there to seek such a thrill than by joining the army, in which I could chronicle my adventures so that generations to come would know me and my grand accomplishments? So I joined the army, where I was made an infantry commander with 503 men under my command. After the battle for the salt mines of Taghaza, only 274 of those men remained.

My love for adventure was known to most who knew me. My only concern so far was that I had been in no military ventures unique enough to be worth chronicling or boasting about. Had I known what awaited me, I likely would have reconsidered joining the army, for this adventure was one like no other, one I could never have imagined even in my wildest dreams.

After the battle for the salt mines, I soon left the merrymaking of our victorious army and retreated to my tent, to determine how best to inform the mothers of the fallen soldiers in my regiment that their sons had died. We were to return to Timbuktu in a few weeks and I had to be prepared for the grieving mothers. Many of them had hoped their sons would excel in the army and perhaps one day be made officials in Timbuktu or wealthy governors in some distant province.

I could hear the singing and dancing outside as I lay in my tent, cleaning the sword, dagger, and wrist knife that had served me so well in many a battle. Suddenly all the merrymaking stopped. I stepped outside. The soldiers were all staring at something. It was only a covered wagon that was being pulled by six horses and heading towards the emperor's tent. Yet a rather eerie feeling floated through the air. About ten mounted Red Sentinels, members of the emperor's own personal guard, were escorting the wagon. These elite soldiers wore their distinctive red turbans, were armed to the teeth, and were suited up in chest armor composed of silver, iron, and brass. Though no one could tell what exactly was in the wagon, it was quite clear that all understood that it contained something mysterious, something which emitted a nervous air.

In a few minutes that seemed to last forever, the wagon reached the emperor's tent. We watched closely to see who or what would come out of it. The tension was even more heightened than before, and heightened even further when Emperor Abubakari II himself stepped out of his tent to meet the wagon. He was dressed in a gown made of the finest cotton and patterned with intricate colorful designs as if to impress a stranger. Had he been expecting this eerie visitor? Who or what was it that created so disturbing a mood, but that the emperor wholly welcomed?

Our curiosity was about to be settled when Gans, the commander of the Red Sentinels and the leader of the wagon escort, dismounted his horse and spoke a few words to the emperor. Gans then turned to address the curious soldiers.

"Into your tents," he barked. "There is nothing to see."

We were disappointed, but heeded Gans's order, for as commander of the Red Sentinels, when he spoke it was as if the emperor himself had spoken. Gans had once been an ordinary Red Sentinel of no special value or rank. But this position had changed several years ago after he saved the emperor's life during a night ambush, during which he realized that the emperor was suffering from night blindness, which rendered him incapable of properly defending himself that night. For his actions, Gans was rewarded with the vacant position of Commander of the Red Sentinels. They were the elite group of soldiers responsible for the personal protection of the emperor. He also had the distinction of having fought in the famed Battle of Assassin Hill.

Gans was not well liked in the army, for after attaining his new rank he had lost favor with many military commanders because of his arrogance. Once quite sociable, now he was rarely seen associating with other commanders or even smiling, except for those few moments when he was charged with executing disciplinary actions against other officers. He was so despised that once, a commander who lay dying after a battle was asked if he had any last words. The commander said: "Commander Gans, there is something I have always wanted to tell you but have never had the courage to do so: You jackass!"

As I lay in my tent, my mind continued to marvel at the mysterious cargo that had been in the wagon. Why had the hated Gans ordered us into our tents? What was the emperor hiding?

By morning the mysterious wagon was gone. While riddled with curiosity, I was yet left with a single truth that comforted and brought some ease to my person—Fadiga was dead. That meant it was now only a matter of time before his last and most formidable stronghold, Djenné, would fall to us. For thirteen months the city had been under siege by our forces, yet its defenders had shown no signs of giving up. Each attack we mounted on the fortified city was beaten back even more ferociously than the one before it.

But now an end lay in sight, for our generals hoped that as soon as the defenders got word of Fadiga's death, their will to defend the city would weaken, forcing them to give in to the imperial authority of Mali. However, there was yet some part of me that refrained from such a hasty judgment, for our generals had made the same judgment after Djiouf, Fadiga's son and Djenné's high lord, was snapped in half by a hippopotamus as he and his forces retreated from the frontlines. Our generals had judged that Djiouf's death would force the city to surrender, but such a development had failed to come to pass. The will of the defenders had only been strengthened—an unexpected consequence which the generals had been quick to attribute to the fact that Fadiga was still alive to encourage the city's defenders. But now, with father and son slain, no one remained in the family to continue the insurgency save Mai-Fatou, Djiouf's mother and Fadiga's widow, who certainly was deficient of any military experience. The war would be over in a few weeks, we convinced ourselves.

***

I WALKED OVER TO MY commander, Tigana, to find out if he knew anything about the wagon. General Tigana had often told me that he cherished having me under his command because my quest for glory and adventure made me the only officer stupid enough to accept assignments that no one else would. I was his most able soldier and officer, he had often acknowledged. We had been on many a battlefield together. He was a good officer with a good sense of judgment. Once, for example, when he was a judge in Gao, a case was brought before him that concerned a merchant who had been stabbed to death while he was alone with a business rival known to have hated him. The business rival claimed the merchant had killed himself, a claim most actually believed. That was until Tigana insisted on examining the body of the slain merchant. Upon concluding his examination, Tigana had the rival brought before him. And Tigana asked him, "Do you expect us to believe that while you were alone with the merchant you loathed, he committed suicide by stabbing himself twelve times, three of those times through his heart, and nine times through his back; then went to his garden, dug a hole, buried the knife, returned to his shop, gave you a sack of gold, and then laid himself down very neatly behind his counter, and died?" The lying, murdering, thieving man was promptly dispatched to meet the axe man's fury.

Tigana and I were old friends who often competed on our combat skills. In answer to my wrist knife, he had made for himself a rather formidable weapon—a throwing knife like no other. It was meant to be thrown horizontally from left to right and was designed with multiple blades in order to increase its chances of hitting its target. I had seen him use it to chop off the leg of a fleeing rebel from a distance of about seventy paces. The rebel had been scouring the battlefield, stealing teeth from the dead to sell to the local teeth doctors. Tigana called this deadly knife his weapon of vengeance, which he had made to be used on a certain foe he hoped to meet, an old enemy he usually referred to only as the traitor of Sihili Pass.

"What do you know about the wagon?" I asked Tigana upon our meeting.

"Absolutely nothing," he responded.

***

SEVENTEEN DAYS AFTER OUR VICTORY at Taghaza we rode back into walled Timbuktu with the emperor at the lead. It was a relief to be home again. The perfect arrangement and order of the city's clean streets, and its houses that included a countless number of multi-story buildings made of earth brick and limestone, contrasted sharply with the chaos and mayhem that characterized the battlefields of Taghaza. The welcoming, proud citizens of Mali's greatest city cheered as we rode in, full of pride and pomp, pleased to be rid of Fadiga at last. It seemed all 90,000 of the city's residents had come to meet us, for not only were the streets packed, but the rooftops, windows, and balconies were also filled with jubilating citizens. A third-floor balcony even collapsed from excessive weight, injuring two men and a boy. Both were immediately attended by the emperor's physicians.

Most of the citizens were clothed in their fanciest and most colorful outfits as if on a festive day. The dazzling sunshine caused the many colors of the garments and vivid jewelry to create what seemed like a glittering rainbow of moving masses. Women and children sang songs and men played instruments of various types, more than I had ever seen in any single place.

The citizens had good reason to cheer and be merry, for it had not yet been a year since Fadiga's forces had managed to bypass imperial troops and suddenly arrive at the gates of Timbuktu, slaughtering several hundred and laying siege to the city. The city was only saved by some old retired soldiers who organized and manned a stiff defense that held the rebels back for seven terror-filled days. The siege only ended with the timely arrival of a thousand Red Sentinels dispatched from the frontlines. These elite soldiers instantly put to maximum use their smaller numbers by disrupting Fadiga's supply lines and forcing him to make a hasty retreat to his own lines lest his besieging army be trapped deep within imperial territory without provisions.

I had been away from Timbuktu for six months and I was elated to be home again. To look once again at the flowery city was a desire that could not be satisfied, not even if I stared at the city for a hundred years. Even more desirable was my longing to see Lili, the woman I was to marry one week after my return from the war.

After our grand entrance into Timbuktu, the generals dismissed us, granting specific permission that we go out and make merry of all that the city could offer. But the general under whose command I was, my friend, Tigana, was known to be a strict disciplinarian. Without a doubt his men were the best and most successful soldiers in all of Mali, and I was prouder than an ugly maiden on her wedding day to be one of them. He always maintained that the key to his success was the strict discipline he encouraged his soldiers to observe. He tolerated nothing that could lower their exceptionally high standards, both moral and physical. While most of the other generals in the army usually engaged their soldiers during dismissals for breaks such as this with long, senseless, and shockingly boring speeches about how proud they should all be and how well they should conduct themselves and live up to the good name of soldiers in the imperial army, General Tigana's speeches to his soldiers almost always consisted of a short, single phrase: "Do not do anything stupid."

But somehow, as fate would have it, even if I was not looking for trouble, trouble was always looking for me.

Lili, the woman I was to marry, lived in the southern section of Timbuktu. As I rode to her place, I noticed a few things that shook me up quite a bit. These things portrayed a Timbuktu that was quite different from the one I had left just six months past. Many agreed that before the war Timbuktu had been a decent city, where most were comfortable and most were merry; where many were willing to share with their neighbors; where all had a room to stay and plenty to eat; where fast friends were made and distrust among neighbors was kept to a minimum. That had been the nature of our city for centuries past, as far as I could tell. But now the city seemed slightly changed—a subtle, yet disturbing change. I received the first hint of this troubling circumstance when I noticed a member of the Emperor's Poor who seemed to have waited an eternity before he could receive any help. The Emperor's Poor were the blind and the maimed of Timbuktu, who survived mostly as a result of an edict passed by the imperial court some five decades past. Under this edict the empire retained certain lands and revenues for their subsistence, and when they traveled through territories within the empire, food, drink, and a guide for the blind were to be provided to them at public cost for a period of fifteen days. All in the empire had always been willing to assist these Emperor's Poor. But now it seemed there existed some hesitance among some to extend even a small amount of charity to so needy a misfortuned bunch. The second hint of the troubling circumstance occurred when I noticed that where a small marketplace had stood before the war, an uncomfortably suspicious building now stood. Several beautiful young women stood in front of it, waving at all the men who walked by, beckoning them to come inside. I could hardly believe it. Whoring had reached Timbuktu! What was happening around us?

As I rode past the front of that house of shame, I barely looked at the young women as they flocked towards my horse, advertising their shameful services to me. I was about to take up speed when a glare suddenly caught my eye. It was from one of the wild women. It was a bracelet she wore that was made out of the purest gold. It occurred to me at that moment that I had promised Lili a gold bracelet upon my return from the war. After inquiring of the woman where I could buy a bracelet such as hers, she bid me follow her into their building, where she claimed to have some she could sell to me. I reluctantly did as she bid, whereupon she led me into a room and opened a wooden box containing several bracelets even lovelier than the one that adorned her wrist. I spent some time trying to select an appropriate one for my Lili, after which I paid for it and scuttled out of there as if the building itself was a contagious disease.

When I emerged outside I was instantly upset by the sight that confronted me. There stood three soldiers from my regiment. How dared they come to dabble in this house of shame, lowering our standards thus, an act of such base immorality that could cost them their place in the army? Obviously these three had not heeded Tigana's warning: Do not do anything stupid. As I walked towards them to confront them about their actions, I was surprised that they made no attempt to hide themselves from me.

But they were the ones who had a surprise for me.

"Commander Drabo," one of the soldiers called, his white garments turning brown from the dust kicked up by the strong winds that were beginning to pummel the city, "the general wishes to see you immediately."

Why did Tigana want to see me? Whatever it was, I hoped it was not going to keep me from seeing my Lili for even one more day. I rode with the soldiers back to the camp, and as we got in I noticed a beautiful woman saddling a horse. She was dressed in a single tight-fitting sleeveless brown garment that covered most of her upper body but ended just above her knees, exposing much of her long, shapely legs, which sported a pair of leather sandals. I decided to sneak up behind her, to jerk and give her a fright, just for the boyish pleasure of hearing her scream at my prank. I dismounted and stealthily walked towards her from behind. But just as my hand was about to touch her shoulder, she suddenly and unexpectedly spun around, grabbed my arm in a painful twist, and threw me over her shoulder so forcefully that I crashed on my back and thought I heard it crack. Before I could get up and collect myself and my bruised honor, her sharp sword was already waiting for me, inches away from my neck.

"Shang," I called her name, "sometimes I think the only thing more alert than you is a viper on the warpath."

"I am just doing what you taught us, Gyvan," she said with a mocking grin. "Alertness is the greatest virtue of the true soldier." I offered my hand and she pulled me back to my feet.

Shang was the only woman in the entire Malian army, an exception having been made for her because she possessed extraordinary scouting abilities which she had acquired as a little girl accompanying her father on hunting trips in the famed hunting grounds of Do. It was rumored that she could smell an enemy fart from 1500 miles away, a rumor no one had really cared to verify.

Babayaro, an officer and immigrant from the southern lands, and One Eye, an albino infantry officer, had seen Shang throw me to the ground. They walked over to me, laughing at me. One Eye and Babayaro were both officers in a regiment I had once belonged to. They were some of the finest swordsmen I knew. One Eye was an even better bowman, despite having the use of only one good eye; the other eye having been lost some years ago, where now rested an eye patch. The manner in which One Eye had lost his eye was one too disturbing to relate, yet too incomparable to ignore. Some summers past, during an expedition sanctioned by Emperor Abubakari II, One Eye, who at the time had the full use of both eyes, was part of a detachment of merchants, diplomats, men of science, physicians, and soldiers charged with making useful contact with the kingdoms that lay in the mysterious eastern land of Abyssinia. Along the way to these lands, he was misfortuned to contract a rather destructive sickness that proceeded to slowly ruin the vision in one of his eyes. Upon learning from the physicians in his company that this crippling sickness could spread to the other eye, blinding him permanently, and that nothing known to medicine could rescue him from this predicament, he decided to take matters upon himself. All I can say is that what happened next was not for the faint of heart. The men in his company woke up one morning to discover that this bowman commander, in order to prevent the spread of the disease to his one good eye, had completely torn out the diseased eye himself, with a fish hook! During times of peace, One Eye usually earned some extra gold dinars working as a caravaneer, hiring out his skills to help protect trade caravans across the treacherous northern deserts and even across the perilous southern jungles used by traders and other travelers making their way to the lands of Kano, Sokoto, and Katsina, to obtain precious spices and clothing.

A short moment after my embarrassing tumble by Shang, Jeevas, a cavalry officer and close friend of One Eye, Babayaro, and Shang, walked over to us. Their close friendship was known to all, for where you found one you were likely to find the others. Jeevas and Shang were closer still, fueling rumors that they were secret lovers and would soon be married.

"I thought you went to see your woman," Jeevas said to me.

"Tigana asked to see me," I responded.

"He very likely wants to give you the news."

"News?"

"They are sending us to Djenné," Jeevas broke the news to me. "The siege of the city is not going well."

"Djenné will not fall," said Shang. "No army has been able to lay a successful siege on that city for two centuries—ninety-eight times to be exact. This is the ninety-ninth attempt and it's not looking very good."

"We will succeed," Babayaro declared. "It is the only way we will flush out the last of the rebel rabble. Fadiga is dead. They cannot hold out for much longer."

Jeevas looked at Babayaro and said, "As we speak the rebels are regrouping, preparing to launch another offensive."

"How?" I asked. "Their leaders are slain."

"That is correct," Jeevas said, "but Fadiga's widow, Mai-Fatou, has taken charge of what is left of them. She now gathers a fresh new army in her husband's city of Tera-Hool, where she is now the high lady."

This bit of information was troubling. As much as I would have loved the chance to do battle again and perhaps find in it a fitting adventure for my intended writings, I was also just as eager to stay with my wife-to-be for at least a few months before being dispatched again to the frontlines to kill or be killed.

So all the jubilation and merrymaking after the death of the rebel warlord, Fadiga, had been for naught—a perfect example of what some call wishful thinking. The empire would remain at war! One Eye, Shang, Babayaro, and Jeevas did not seem troubled at all. They seemed revived, for war to them was a necessity, essential to their well-being.

***

I MARCHED INTO GENERAL TIGANA'S quarters in the camp. He was alone, feeding his tits—a blue tit and a great tit—both housed in a splendidly decorated brass cage. These beautiful birds had been given to him as a present by a Tuareg chief as a measure of gratitude after the general had his soldiers help the people of a Tuareg village dig a well.

"It appears we are heading back to battle," I said to Tigana. But he did not respond. His focus remained on his tits. Something troubled him, I sensed. It was not the war. That could hardly trouble this seasoned soldier. It had to be something of a more personal nature.

"What troubles you, my friend?" I inquired. He hesitated. Then he turned to face me before he finally spoke.

"You are the finest soldier in this regiment, Gyvan," he said softly.

"That's what they say," I responded with a smile.

He breathed deeply, and then said, "We are above all other regiments, Commander Drabo, both in morals and in battle skill."

"Of course," I responded, getting impatient. "Look, friend, favor me by telling me what hides in your mind and why it is you have so suddenly requested my presence."

Tigana hesitated before responding. "You are the best soldier in this regiment, yet today you have chosen to lower its standards to the lowest possible level."

"I do not get your meaning," I said, quite mystified.

"You were seen walking into the house of the wild women, Gyvan."

Ah, the house of wild women, where I had purchased a gold bracelet for my Lili. That was what this matter was all about. As mentioned before, if I was not looking for trouble, trouble certainly was always looking for me. But I had to defend my honor.

"I deny that accusation," I said most vehemently. "I went into that house to purchase a bracelet for Lili."

Tigana then added, "That is not all, Gyvan. There are also reports that while in Taghaza you engaged in alcohol on a certain night, got drunk, and made quite an idiot out of yourself."

I remained quiet about this charge. I had been under some assumption that my drunken incident with palm wine some weeks earlier, which had resulted in a civilian's broken nose, had slipped by unnoticed.

"I do not care much about the alcohol," the general continued, "but seeing wild women is something I cannot back you on."

"I told you already, Tigana, I only went there to purchase this bracelet." I showed him the bracelet.

"I believe you," the general said sincerely, "but many of the men may not."

"What does that mean?" I asked, not even daring to think of the implications of his statement.

Tigana looked away from me, not wanting me to see his face, the way an executioner covers his face to hide it from the man he is about to behead. It pained him to say what he was about to say, and I knew what he was about to say. Then he looked straight at me before delivering the volley of arrow-tipped words to my ears, spoken so softly, yet striking so deeply. "I will have to relieve you of your command, and of the regiment."

My friend, General Tigana, was discharging me from the army. His words hit me like a raging thunderbolt. I managed to convince myself that the general was only joking about my discharge from the army, so I erupted into near uncontrollable laughter. But after a few seconds, during which I noticed that he was not even smiling, I understood how seriously he took the matter.

"I am sorry, Gyvan," he said. "Too many men saw you walk into that house of shame. I cannot let you be responsible for lowering the standards of this regiment."

"You cannot do this to me, Tigana."

"I have little choice. This regiment has existed for longer than you and I have been friends. I cannot risk destroying its reputation. I deeply regret the circumstances, but the rules must bind everyone, officers and common soldiers alike, or they would not be rules."

I stared at my friend in speechless puzzlement. So this was it—the end of my days in the army, the institution I had made my life. I felt my sword at my side, knowing it would never again be wielded in defense of the empire.

"And my sword?" I asked the general, for only military men and active caravaneers could bear arms.

"You may keep it," he declared. "After all, it was your father's. But you must strip it of its regimental markings."

Keeping my sword was some relief. In my hands, this sword had saved my life and even Tigana's more times than I could remember. I was about to storm out of the room in anger when Tigana called out.

"Gyvan," he began, "extend my greetings to Lili."

I felt more like extending the knuckles of my clenched fist to his cheekbones. I hated him. I wanted to do something to hurt him, like killing his tits, especially his great tit, which he seemed to love more than the other. I stormed out and I could tell that he knew that he had just made an enemy out of me. How could he do this to me?

So that was it. I had quit teaching at the University of Sankoré in order to join the army, from which I had hoped to write about the great adventures it would bring my way. But this life had just slipped away from me simply because of the glitter of a wild woman's bracelet. My world was crumbling around me. As for my upcoming marriage to Lili, how was that to happen now? I had lost my job and I was not certain I would be reaccepted to teach again at the university. I had not exactly parted with it on pleasant terms, for I had deeply criticized many of the teachers there for their religious, historical, and poetic writings, which I often found archaic, redundant, and almost fatally boring. I had told them that I would show them how to write something that everyone could enjoy—an adventure story full of vigor and life, something to entertain.

As I rode to Lili's house, I could not bear to think that the good news of my arrival would quickly be marred by the bad news of my discharge from the army. I did not know if she would like it or hate it, for she, after all, had always complained of my long absences ever since I joined the army.

She must have seen me coming, for when I approached her house she was standing outside, waiting for me with a big but peculiar smile on her face. I ran to her and was about to hug her when she unexpectedly greeted me with a rather nasty slap across the cheek, taking me by complete surprise. What on Earth could have brought such unforeseen calamity upon my person?

"What did I do this time?" I demanded, bewildered.

"Wild women, eh?" she spat.

Bad news traveled fast around these parts. I could not believe she had already heard of my visit with the wild women.

"I can explain. Listen—" I attempted to explain.

She shot into her house and banged the door behind her. I opened it and walked in, where she sat frightfully furious. She looked me dead in the eyes, expecting an explanation—my side of the story, thankfully, which I gladly provided, including how it had gotten me discharged from the army.

Lili had no quarrel with my discharge from the army, an occurrence she actually welcomed, though she blamed herself for that misfortune since it had resulted partly on her account. Yet she was pleased to know that never again would I be sent away to fight in long and uncertain wars for the empire. And best of all, she said, I would not be going to Djenné, now known to many a soldier as a widow maker, where so many young men throughout the empire had met their end.

By the end of my visit with Lili, we had decided that I would return to the university to attempt teaching again, and, whether I was successful or not with that venture, we were to wed the following week.

***

As I rode to my home from Lili's, all the happenings of the past few months flashed through my mind—the battle of Taghaza, the killing of Fadiga, the mysterious wagon visitors to the emperor, the unending siege at

Djenné, and the regrouping of the rebels under the Widow of Tera-Hool. Sadly, I was leaving all that behind. But by the end of the following week I would be married to the most caring and beautiful woman in Timbuktu. That was the one thing that gave me some solace in this cruel life. Lili was a merchant who did business with the traders who came from across the great desert of the North and even with traders from as far south as Kano. Although she was not terribly wealthy, she made enough from her trade to live a life of moderate comfort. She had even built for herself a two-story house out of limestone with copper-lined windows and doors, complete with a balcony and hedged terraces.

I walked into my spider-web-filled earth brick house and went straight to sleep. I needed to rest and think things over. I thought of my aunt and grandmother who had raised me, and wished they could have been here to see me get married. My lifelong thirst for wild adventure had led them to predict that I would die in some far-off territory before I could turn sixteen, perhaps eaten alive by some wild animal in a forest in some remote place no one in Timbuktu had ever heard of.

My grandmother had been the first to go, dying some two summers earlier. My aunt, Jama, had been next, passing a few weeks after my grandmother, and after an unbelievably agonizing illness which no doctor could determine or cure, not even the cataract-removing doctors from Gao. Aunt Jama and Grandmother had been the only other relations I knew, my father having left me with them because he was always away fighting for the then-emperor, Manding Bory. My father had been a soldier right to his bones, putting the army and the empire before everything else. His justification for this was that too many good men had already died building the empire, including his father, who had fought alongside Sundiata Keita in 1235 at the Battle of Kirina. Perhaps my decision to join the army was partly influenced by a substantial but previously suppressed desire to continue this long family military tradition.

As for my mother, who was Aunt Jama's sister and my grandmother's daughter, I never knew her or anything of her. She was still alive, I knew, though my grandmother and aunt always refused to speak of her, claiming it was for my own good not to know. I always wondered why I could not be told about my own mother, a woman whose very existence they seemed to loathe. As a little boy, whenever I did something silly, like when I attempted to set a live chicken on fire just to see what would happen, I remember often overhearing my grandmother excusing such misdeeds on my part with a phrase very similar to, "It is not the boy's fault. It is the bad blood from his mother."

After the passing of my father, my grandmother, and Aunt Jama, I resolved to find my mother, for she was my only living kin, after all. What could she have done to deserve such scorn from her own mother and sister? I do not know if it was my supposed love for a mother I did not know that made me determined to find her, or whether it was just a matter of curiosity, but I was going to find her, or she was going to find me.

***

TIGANA, MY DEAR FRIEND, HAD devastated my spirit by discharging me from the army one week before my marriage to Lili. I was happy for the marriage but ravaged within, for I was no longer a proud soldier of Mali, but was condemned never again to ride into Timbuktu and be welcomed by cheering and adoring crowds. How I despised Tigana. The brute had wrecked my life. But if I thought my termination from the army was my biggest problem, I was dreadfully mistaken, for as I lay on my bed, through the window I saw mounted men riding towards my house, carrying gold-coated wooden shields and swords. They were the emperor's guards, Red Sentinels, led by the detestable Gans. Red Sentinels at my home? Could having prohibited dealings with wild women, even though such a misdeed never did occur between me and the other party, have become so despicable an offense as to merit the interest of the emperor? Surely he must have had more important matters to worry about.

I met Gans and his Red Sentinels outside to learn what fate awaited me.

"The Table summons you, Gyvan Drabo," Gans said to me, contempt in his eyes.

My heart skipped in horror when Gans mentioned the Table, the imperial council composed of the most important officials of the empire, including the emperor himself.

"I have already lost everything. What more can the Table want of me?" I asked Gans.

"You will know when we get there."

I went back inside my house and came back out wearing my sword, expecting the Red Sentinels to seize it from me. Gans glanced at the sword but said nothing. I mounted my horse and rode with the Sentinels towards the emperor's palace. As we got closer to the palace gates, my heart jumped when something peculiar in front of the palace gates caught my attention. I stopped and stared at it, then at Gans, and then back at it.

What was going on here?

I continued staring. Gans urged me to move on in as rude a manner as he could. I was too baffled by the presence of this thing to mind the Red Sentinel's rudeness. I flashed one last look at it, then moved on as urged. It was the mysterious wooden wagon that had been brought to the emperor after our battle in Taghaza.

"So what was in the wagon?" I asked one of the Red Sentinels escorting me.

"I do not know," he said. "We were ordered not to look inside. But what—"

"Quiet, Bei!" Gans ordered the Sentinel, who immediately ceased talking.

Gans was still determined to conceal the contents of the mysterious wagon. But whatever or whoever had been in it had to be in the emperor's palace at that moment, and perhaps at the Table, and I was being led to the Table.

They say a man's fate can be altered in a single day. That may be true. But the events that happened next did not alter the fate of one man. They altered the fate of all men!

***

MY HEART POUNDED AS WE walked into the emperor's palace. I tried to peer through the glass windows that dotted the palace walls but saw nothing that could help answer my questions about the mysterious wagon or my summons. Why was I, a simple and disgraced former soldier who had lost his honor, being brought to the Table?

"Wait here," Gans ordered as we approached a door.

I stood where I was while he went into the room. A moment later he emerged.

"The Table will see you now," he said. His face indicated in no way whether I should expect good or ill from the Table.

Eighteen Elders made up the Table: the emperor, the twelve representatives of the twelve provinces, and five advisers to the emperor, among whom were his brother, Musa the Elder, and Kouyaté the Elder, a Tuareg from the Northern provinces, easily recognized by the blue robes characteristic of his people.

The Elders sat at a semicircular table facing the door so that as Gans and I walked in, they were looking right at us. I bowed before the Table. Gans walked to the side of the room to keep watch.

What could the Table possibly want of me?

Six bloodthirsty guard dogs that wore spiked collars of gold and silver lined the wall closest to me. Their handlers stood nearby. Gans was the only human guard in the room, but he was not the only other individual. As I turned to see who else was present, I saw two others who made my heart explode with absolute horror. I could not believe it! Was I losing my mind? I instantly reached for my sword to destroy these horribly grotesque beings that had infiltrated the palace grounds. Instead of aiding me in this fight as I hoped, Gans seemed to be coming after me instead. And, unbelievably, the Table Elders remained calm. Were they all blind to what stood in the room? They were raw-breeds—those vile creatures that still plagued our nightmares—the ones the Breed Legends say were once slavers of man. I had never believed they ever existed, until that moment. They loomed before me, hairy as baboons, with two horns protruding from their horrendously deformed skulls. I shuddered when one turned and I saw the eye on the back of his head.

It was clear that these beings had taken the Table hostage. Though a lone human stood little chance against two raw-breeds, I was determined to go down fighting. When six Red Sentinels burst into the room, I felt relief, but it was short-lived, for I soon noticed that the guards had not drawn their swords, but were also coming after me. Along with Gans they quickly seized me and held me to the ground.

"Calm yourself!" Gans snarled at me.

I glanced towards the two raw-breeds, who surprisingly stood as still as they had been when I had walked into the room. They had made no attempt to fight me back. What was going on here?

I calmed myself and the guards released me. I stood up and took a long, hard look at the raw-breeds, both dressed in dark green coats of an unknown cloth that covered their bodies from head to foot. So these were the occupants of the mysterious wagon. The emperor had been right to keep their identities concealed, for if the army had learned of their presence in their midst, the result would have been either mass desertions out of fear of the creatures, or a mutiny started by soldiers trying to destroy the creatures. I was dying to know why they were here in New Eartholia—our world, the lost outer world dimension of Eartholia Proper, according to the Breed Legends. But most importantly, I was dying to know what it had to do with me.

For a short while nobody uttered a word, until the emperor broke the silence.

"Soldier?" he addressed me.

"Your Highness," I answered.

"What you will now hear is for your ears only."

"If that is your wish, Your Highness." I pledged my secrecy to whatever was about to be revealed to me.

"We do not have much time left so we will get right to the point," the emperor said.

Why were they running out of time, how could I help them, and why me? But in the middle of all these questions I immediately saw an opportunity and I wasted no time in taking it. If the Table could use my help then I could also use its help.

"Your Highness," I addressed the emperor, "you address me as *soldier* but I regret to inform you that I was lately discharged from the army this very day."

"Hold your tongue, Commander!" Gans screeched at me. "You will speak only when spoken to!"

"Let him speak," Emperor Abubakari II calmly said to Gans. I could see a visible feeling of stupidity on Gans's face. He must have really despised me, jealous because the Table needed my help and not his.

"Soldier," Musa the Elder, the emperor's brother, began, "we are aware of your alleged dealings with the wild women. We sent word to General Tigana. He agreed to let you return to your regiment. Now let us talk about more important matters."

I was pleased to hear this. My military aspirations were again alive.

I took another look at the raw-breeds, whose existence was disputed by many, though they were the villains talked of in the Breed Legends and in countless fireside stories meant to frighten children. It was terrifying to learn that they truly existed. Now the presence of two of them on New Eartholia—Earth—meant only one thing: the key to the Portal of Gorgida had been found. Why were they in Timbuktu? And what had it to do with me?

"Fret not over the raw-breeds," Musa the Elder assured me. "They mean you no harm."

"Pardon my rashness, my lord," I apologized. "I had always believed raw-breeds to be fictional creatures in tales of horror meant to frighten children."

"And you are now involved in a tale of equal horror, Commander, but one that is true. And how it ends will depend on you."

As I stood in front of the table trying to understand how I could possibly be of such importance to the empire and to raw-breeds, Musa the Elder introduced the creatures to me. They were called Shokolo-ba and Tin-zim.

"Soldier of Mali," Tin-zim addressed me, "you alone stand at the crossroads of the survival or destruction of both the human and raw-breed civilization. For two thousand years Eartholia Proper was at war, which recently came to an end when clearer minds prevailed to prevent our own doom. There has been peace and quiet for ten years now. But some have been displeased with the return of peace, for they had learned to profit from the war, to profit from the death and anguish of countless others. One of those war profiteers was a warlord named Lord Venga. His attempt to seize control of the government of Eartholia Proper failed, making him a fugitive and forcing him into hiding, where he found the long lost key to the Portal of Gorgida, the doorway into New Eartholia, your world.

"Along with two followers, he escaped to New Eartholia some two years past. It is not by chance that that was when your own civil war with Fadiga began. Lord Venga came here to raise a human army to help him make war against the government of Eartholia Proper—another civil war."

"But humans cannot wage war against raw-breeds," I protested. "It will be a slaughter!"

"True," Shokolo-ba affirmed, "but Lord Venga possesses the blood dripper!"

"The what?" I asked.

"The blood dripper is a spell of mysterious dark origins. No one knows exactly how it works or how it is to be deployed. But we do know that it would aid Lord Venga's cause, destroying man in the process. If Lord Venga succeeds, his human army may help him win the war he seeks in Eartholia Proper, but when that war is over there would not be enough living among the human race to bury the dead. It would be the biggest and most destructive war of all time, bigger and more destructive than all wars ever fought in Eartholia Proper or New Eartholia put together. When it is over, only a few scattered villages here might remain, but nothing more. And if the surviving raw-breeds do not return to destroy them, the people of these villages would very likely run out of food and suffer a slow and painful death brought on by disease and starvation."

Sobo Ha-Ha Speaks

chapter 5

I WAS NOT ENTIRELY CERTAIN what the blood dripper was, nor was I party to the knowledge of how Lord Venga intended to use it to complete our task here on New Eartholia. But I was pleased to be doing my part to prepare it—this creature, being, entity, or whatever it was—for its eventual maturity and awakening. So it was that I again found myself in the dark caves of the mountains of Koulikoro to administer to the blood dripper the potions prepared by Lord Venga himself to bring it to maturity and make it ready it for our use.

I peered into the cave where the blood dripper rested, hoping to catch a glimpse of the creature so as to build in my mind some image of the mysterious being. But I could see nothing, for the mouth of the cave was covered in a mist that shielded whatever lay within it, which was unknown to all but Lord Venga. Then I heard something. I listened closely. They were hisses, coming from within the cave. The blood dripper was hissing! This was the creature or being that would secure Lord Venga's domination of Eartholia Proper and New Eartholia, though it was not ready for its purpose yet. But it was growing, maturing slowly but steadily.

I chanted the incantations for the relevant spells and administered the potion into the mist as Lord Venga had directed. Though he had declined to reveal how the blood dripper was supposed to aid our task, I was not very eager to find out. As cold and as dark-hearted as many swore I was, this creature in the mist, whatever it was, terrified me to the core. What did it possess that even Lord Venga did not allow it to stay with him on the Island of Ten Devils? What unimaginable horror could it unleash on the world? How much longer did we have to wait before this secret weapon could come to our aid?

The Soldier's Tale

chapteR 6

ACCORDING TO THE RAW-BREEDS, LORD Venga's gruesome intentions for Eartholia Proper and New Eartholia were feasible because he was in possession of the being they simply knew as the blood dripper. Its true structure and manners were known only to Lord Venga, though its immense and highly destructive powers were not underestimated by the raw-breeds. Yet if this blood dripper was indeed a force capable of such catastrophe, how then was Lord Venga able to control it, I demanded of the raw-breeds.

"The answer is simple," Tin-zim responded. "Lord Venga's Third Shadow is a White Shadow."

That was no matter to be taken lightly. To understand the White Shadow, you must understand certain matters that link some humans and raw-breeds. According to the Breed Legends, in the days before man, when raw-breeds alone inhabited Eartholia Proper, many of the three-eyed creatures were naturally endowed with the Third Shadow at birth. The Third Shadow is that which we humans now call black magic. Just as many a raw-breed failed to evolve into a human, so too did the Third Shadow fail to be lost by some humans. The Third Shadow therefore was retained in a few humans and could be passed on to their offspring. These human witches and wizards became more influential and powerful than other humans, for they were used by the raw-breeds to control the other humans enslaved in the outer world colony of New Eartholia. The raw-breeds called these witches and wizards *eeids*. These eeids, being the enforcers of the slavery of man, soon attracted the scorn and hatred of the other humans in the slave colony, for many considered them traitors.

When the key of the portal into New Eartholia was lost during the second of the Breed Wars, man became free of the raw-breed peril, and all were joyful, even the eeids. But soon after, these eeids began to miss the power they had once wielded over the rest of humanity while serving the raw-breeds. Their lust for power therefore led to another war. Only this time it was a war among eeids, the most destructive and demoralizing war ever seen on New Eartholia, with each eeid clan fighting to be the sole ruler of the slave colony. Eventually they killed each other off. They lost their war and man survived, becoming once again master of his own destiny.

The Eeid Wars ended and man was pleased. But many young offspring of the eeids did survive. Man worried little about this, for he could always teach the young eeids to use the powers of the Third Shadow for good. So the sons and daughters of the eeids were raised and taught to use the Third Shadow for the good of man, leading to a long period of peace in New Eartholia.

But little did man know that the greatest evil still lingered. It was man!

If man could teach the eeid offspring to use their powers for good, man could also teach them to use their powers for evil. And as was later to come to light, there soon was no shortage of men willing to teach the eeids to use their powers for evil.

And so there soon existed evil eeids on Earth once again.

***

LORD VENGA'S THIRD SHADOW WAS a White Shadow, the most fearsome and most formidable mold of the dark arts, known to have been possessed by only a few raw-breeds. In the wrong hands, none could be safe from its wrath, for it was a Third Shadow so powerful that it alone could possibly be used to control and deploy a being as catastrophic as the mysterious blood dripper.

According to Tin-zim, in order for Lord Venga's designs for our world to come to pass, he had to find a human who could gather a significant following, a human he could make a host of his Third Shadow by endowing him with a dormant mold of his White Shadow. Through this human, Lord Venga could turn all men into dedicated and diabolical slave soldiers in his army of doom. And for such a human, Lord Venga had found Fadiga, a disgruntled imperial general with thousands of men under his command. But now Fadiga was slain, and though this had delayed Lord Venga's designs, he had wasted no time in choosing another host—Fadiga's widow, Mai-Fatou, the high lady of Tera-Hool. Upon her, Lord Venga had endowed a dormant mold of his White Shadow, which gave her no powers, but could be used by him to control his intended slave army through her. He had ensnared her with promises of riches and greatness to come, as he had also done to her misfortuned husband.

So Mai-Fatou, the high lady of Tera-Hool, was now a host of the White Shadow. That was why she had been able to rally her slain husband's forces to her side so quickly. That was why the rebels continued to fight.

I held my breath as this tale of horror and its shockingly terrifying possibilities unfolded.

"So how do you intend to save us all from Lord Venga?" I asked the raw-breeds.

Shokolo-ba looked into my eyes and smiled. "That is where you come in," he said coolly.

"Me?"

"You will stop Lord Venga."

How was I to stop Lord Venga? The raw-breeds could not stop him. The entire Malian army could not stop him. But I, a simple soldier, was expected to stop him? I was going to laugh at what I perceived to be a very bad joke, but seemed to forget how. So I just stood there, wide-eyed and open-mouthed, staring at the Table and the raw-breeds, waiting for some answers.

Tin-zim continued to explain, "During his escape to Eartholia Proper, Lord Venga was accompanied by two raw-breed disciples, Tichiman and Tsing-tsing. He may long ago have succeeded in his designs had Tichiman not come to his senses and tried to stop him. Tichiman was of pure heart. He came to understand the true nature of Lord Venga's treachery. So he betrayed Lord Venga and notified the Committee, the government of Eartholia Proper, of Lord Venga's intentions.

"Shokolo-ba and I are peace agents in Eartholia Proper, officials charged with maintaining the peace in order to prevent a repeat of the destructive wars of centuries past. We have been dispatched to stop Lord Venga. The only way to stop him is to capture or destroy that which gives him the power to choose a host and control the blood dripper, and that is his Third Shadow, the White Shadow. Its capture or destruction would cause the fugitive lord to lose his powers and would end forever his threat to the inner world or outer world dimensions. Tichiman succeeded in trapping Lord Venga's White Shadow in two magical orbs, but never completed the course necessary for its complete capture or destruction, for he was found by Lord Venga and Tsing-tsing.

"Simply trapping the White Shadow did not prevent Lord Venga from using its powers. Rather than succumb to Lord Venga's tortures of unimaginable cruelty, Tichiman hid the orbs and put an end to his own life. And even though he left us information on where he hid the orbs, the problem is that we still cannot find them."

"How do you mean?" I asked.

"His information was written in riddles," Shokolo-ba responded.

"Riddles?"

"Had Tichiman written down the location of the orbs in plain terms," Shokolo-ba continued, "and someone happened upon the information before we did, that person could have easily obtained the orbs and lost them to Lord Venga, not comprehending their true importance. But by writing the location in riddles, Tichiman ensured that only an individual with an understanding of the importance of the orbs would attempt to find them. Fortunately we found the riddles first."

"So what seems to be the problem, my lord?" I asked.

"We cannot solve all the riddles."

With the powers of the Third Shadow naturally afforded to many a raw-breed, I would have believed it highly likely that solving the riddles of Tichiman would be a task too easy for them. Yet I was wrong. There were four riddles in all, the first of which Tichiman had left an answer to, and the fourth of which the raw-breeds and the Table had been able to solve.

"What about the second and third riddles?" I asked.

"They are the most important. Each of them reveals a location for one of the orbs. Those we have been unable to solve."

"So what do you intend to do about them?"

"Not us, Commander Drabo. You!"

"Me?"

How was I to solve riddles that had baffled the Third Shadows of the raw-breeds?

Shokolo-ba continued, "The first riddle is a test riddle for which Tichiman provided an answer. Whoever is able to solve it may be able to solve the second and third riddles. We will give you this first riddle and you will search for an eeid capable of solving it."

"Why an eeid?" I asked. The Third Shadow was terrifyingly more powerful in raw-breeds than it was in eeids. If the raw-breeds had been unable to use their Third Shadows to solve the riddles, then humans certainly stood no chance.

"It will take both the supernatural powers inherited from raw-breeds and the superior intelligence of man to solve the riddles," Shokolo-ba explained, "and only eeids are so created. We therefore believe only the most powerful of eeids can solve this riddle. Your task is to find such an eeid and bring him before us, and we will give him the second riddle to solve. If he succeeds, it will reveal the location of one of the orbs. You will then protect him with your life, and with him you will retrieve the orb from wherever it may be. Upon the success of the task, your eeid will be given the third riddle, and if solved too, it will reveal the location of the second orb, which you both again will be charged with retrieving. And this is the part where you really come in, Commander Drabo."

There was a long silence as I waited to hear my part in this entire affair.

Tin-zim broke it to me. "You, Gyvan Drabo, are the only human capable of touching the orbs without bringing harm to yourself."

"How?" I questioned. "I am neither raw-breed nor eeid."

"We have endowed you with a charm to protect you from harm should you lay hands on the orbs."

"But why me and not another?"

"You will have your answer when the moment is right," the emperor himself responded.

So many things were happening very fast. First I had been discharged from the army, then I had been brought before the Table—with raw-breeds—and now I was being told that I alone could save the realms of Eartholia Proper and New Eartholia by finding, retrieving, and holding in my hands two magical orbs that ensnared a White Shadow, the most potent and absolutely terrifying supernatural force known to exist.

"Mai-Fatou, the widow, has to be captured alive," Shokolo-ba emphasized. "It is the only way the White Shadow can be captured from her. She will be no use to us dead."

"What about Lord Venga?" I asked. "Why not capture the White Shadow from him directly?"

"That would be best for all, for capturing the White Shadow from Lord Venga would not only enable us to seal it and deprive him of its use, but would also enable us to completely destroy it, ending forever his threat to Eartholia Proper and New Eartholia. He knows this, and that is why he currently resides on the Island of Ten Devils."

"The Island of Ten Devils?"

Lord Venga's current residence was reason enough to let him be. No one who knew the difference between life and death and preferred the former would go anywhere near the Island of Ten Devils. You will learn more about this island as my account unfolds, but for now, understand that the decision to pursue Mai-Fatou for the White Shadow was the wiser one.

Still, why had I been chosen to retrieve and hold the magical Tichiman orbs? That was one question that continued to nag me. Another had to do with the fourth Tichiman riddle. Though it had been solved by the rawbreeds and the Table, its purpose had not been revealed to me, heightening my suspicions of the existence of hidden intentions by the Table.

"What about the fourth riddle?" I dared to ask.

"Do not concern yourself with it at this time," Shokolo-ba responded.

I decided to inquire no further, at least for the moment.

Tin-zim continued, "After the orbs are found and retrieved, imperial forces will storm the widow's stronghold in Tera-Hool with the purpose of arresting her so that the White Shadow can be captured from her and sealed, saving both our worlds from doom."

"Forgive me for asking, my lords," I addressed the Elders, "but why wait until the orbs are retrieved? Why not storm Tera-Hool now to get the widow?"

"Because Djenné still stands," Musa the Elder explained. "It is the support base for Tera-Hool and that is why it has to fall before Tera-Hool can be attacked. If we abandon the siege of Djenné and attack Tera-Hool, rebel forces from both cities could have our forces trapped between them."

Djenné—a handsome city and once the prize city of Mali—had lately become a thorn to the empire. For seven months, imperial troops had laid siege to this rebel stronghold. Yet it stood as mighty as before, showing no signs of weakening, but growing stronger as the siege dragged on. Perhaps the empire should have taken heed to history's warning, that ninety-eight times the city had been besieged over the centuries, and ninety-eight times it had stood its ground. The engineers said this city's tenacity was mostly on account of the genius of its builders, who had built it in an area that was unapproachable on almost all sides and surrounded by treacherous and inhospitable moats and swamps caused by a tributary from the Bani River. These had left the city approachable from one direction only, one so deadly that on one occasion the empire had lost two hundred brave souls in less time than it took a man to count to sixty as they attempted to charge through it.

Over the months, Djenné had become a hell on Earth, growing costlier in lives by the day, becoming every Malian soldier's nightmare, and even earning a rather ghastly reputation as a widow maker. No soldier wanted to be posted there, for its conditions were so unbearable that commanders who had wronged the government were sometimes sent there as retribution.

But if humanity was to survive, this city had to be taken. Too many men had been lost there for the army to give it up now.

***

DESPITE THE PRESENCE OF THE raw-breeds, the actuality of what was being revealed to me by the Table sounded too fantastic to be true. Musa the Elder sensed my doubt. He rose, walked towards the alabaster window, looked through it, and pointed at the sky. It was darker than usual.

"See?" he said.

"Clouds of the rains, my lord," I responded.

"No. These are clouds of the evil to come. As Lord Venga's Third Shadow takes over more and more of his host, the darker the clouds and the land will become. So let the sky be a reminder of how urgently you must work."

It was soon time to present the test riddle, the one I was to use to find the eeid. Shokolo-ba pulled out a scroll from a small wooden box and read the riddle.

Could I provide an answer to the riddle? No, of course not. I lacked the powers of the all-powerful Third Shadow. This riddle had been made by a raw-breed, to be solved by none save an eeid well-trained in the dark arts.

Shokolo-ba then gave me the riddle's answer.

"The path of Daoda."

The path of an eeid's Third Shadow was his most guarded secret, for an eeid could destroy the Third Shadow of a rival eeid if the path walked by that rival's Third Shadow was known. Asking an eeid for the path walked by his Third Shadow was a very dangerous and daring deed, for such an eeid could believe the questioner intended to use the knowledge to cause some manner of harm upon his person. Such a mistake, without a doubt, could invite immediate and certain death upon the questioner, for threatened eeids were known to stamp out threats with little hesitation. Once, for instance, a mad fellow, though only in jest, demanded to know from an eeid if his Third Shadow walked the path of Daoda. The eeid smiled but did not answer, taking his leave shortly after. But moments later, the poor fellow shrieked in a most agonizing pain. Live maggots were eating him from the inside out, with some boring out from beneath his skin. He had been the victim of the precautious eeid. A soldier put the poor fellow out of his misery by severing his head.

I asked again about the fourth riddle, which the Table and the raw-breeds had solved, and again I was politely informed to worry no more about it. Only in due time, when the moment was right, would I be told the riddle, they said.

Why all the secrets? What were they hiding? Nonetheless, this was my chance to put to paper a great tale of a wondrous adventure, a piece of work that would baffle the archaic and mundane teachers and scholars of the universities, who only wrote and studied works on philosophy, politics, science, mathematics, medicine, and religion. I was going to be different. I was going to write simply to entertain, putting to paper an account that would be real and bigger than any other battle anyone else in the empire could have possibly been involved in.

If only I could have fathomed then the true cost of what was to come.

***

BECAUSE OF THE URGENCY OF the task at hand, I was to take my leave to search for a worthy eeid without delay. I spent the remainder of the day obtaining supplies and charting a course for my undertaking. The following day I was ready to depart. My horse was fed and my sword and wrist knife were polished and sharpened by the emperor's own sword smith. But most importantly, I was given one of the emperor's imperial rings to help with my passage through the empire during those dangerous times, to prove myself as the emperor's envoy. In addition, I was also granted a note that bore the emperor's seal.

"This is a note for one thousand gold dinars," Kouyaté, the Tuareg Elder had said to me. "If you need gold anywhere in the empire, take this note to any nearby treasury or government outpost and you can be given gold for up to the amount written on the note."

As I left the imperial palace my excitement grew. I could not help but catch the loathsome look Gans, the commander of the Red Sentinels, shot my way. He seemed totally hateful of my person, jealous that this honorable task had been given to me and not to him.

But why had I been chosen for this assignment? Was it because I was a good swordsman who could handle himself if danger came close? Not necessarily. I was a fairly good swordsman—better than most. But there existed in Timbuktu alone at least ten others who were much better swordsmen than I ever could be, the records of their accomplishments giving them such merits. Even the emperor himself had once been a reigning fencing champion, until his night blindness had prevented him from taking part in nighttime tournaments. So the reason I had been chosen for this task, which was certain to involve a great amount of peril, was not because of my skill with the sword. There had to be some other reason, one which I was yet to find out.

I could not have asked for something better to write about than this—saving the world in a battle between good and evil, in which humans and raw-breeds forged an alliance to prevent the greatest battle creation had ever known. I only hoped it would have a happy ending.

I wished that my aunt and grandmother were alive to see me embark on this mission. Even more, I wished that my mother, whoever and wherever she was, also knew that I was perhaps now the most important person in Mali. At the end of this whole affair I was determined to find her to let her know of her son's accomplishments.

***

I WAS GOING TO BE spending the next few weeks looking for an eeid and possibly even living with him as we searched for Tichiman's orbs. Having an eeid for a companion was not a prospect any person with his wits about him could want, for most eeids could not be trusted and could kill without warning. To make matters worse, an eeid who could solve the difficult riddles of Tichiman would have a Third Shadow that likely walked the fearsome path of Daoda, the test riddle's answer. But my sword, ever present at my side, gave me the assurance I needed to overcome whatever fear I had concerning my impending companionship with any eeid I was to find. I am faster with the blade than any eeid can cast a death spell intended to bring about my doom. And any eeid with such ill intentions would be sure to find his head neatly separated from his shoulders before he could complete a single word in casting such a spell. I did not like eeids. Few did, except those who used them for their selfish misdeeds.

As I rode away from the palace, I thought of Lili. I had postponed our wedding three times before on account of imperial duties. Yet here I was, about to postpone it once more. But I was certain she would understand upon learning of the importance of my task.

Mali was 150 days of travel long and 150 days of travel wide. I knew I would not have to travel the entire empire in order to find an eeid capable of solving the test riddle. It was going to be an easy task, for I was in Timbuktu, the city of knowledge and learning, where one could get all the answers from the numerous eeids (good or evil), wise men, and scholars who staffed the city's universities and libraries. My first stop was the University of Sankoré, where I had been a teacher. Would I find my eeid there?

Sobo Ha-Ha Speaks

chapter 7

I WAS THE HIGH EEID of Tera-Hool, in the service of its high lady, Mai-Fatou, known to many a misguided soul as the Dark Widow. I had served in the same capacity for her husband, and after his death I had worried little, for I knew Lord Venga would soon choose another host for his White Shadow. I was pleased when he chose Mai-Fatou, for I had been acquainted with her for some years and therefore readily extended to her the same invaluable services I had extended to her husband. The world would soon be ours, we knew. All we had to do was keep the emperor and his forces at bay long enough for the powers of the White Shadow to strengthen and speed the mysterious blood dripper to maturity.

I was the special advisor to the widowed high lady, and as such I had devised several ways of getting information about the emperor's actions against us. The most trusted way was through my trusty owl, Noo, a spy bird I could send to any place I desired, to be my eyes and ears from the sky. All it had to do was look at what I wanted to see or hear, and upon its return I could read its mind and learn of the events that had transpired in the domains it had visited. And so it was that I learned of the Table's designs after Noo returned one afternoon from an assignment over the emperor's palace.

Moments later I walked into the war room in the high lady's palace in Tera-Hool, where she was meeting with two of her military commanders, Lord Elcan and Commander Abdoulaye Malouda.

"My lady," I addressed her. "I bear some news. The emperor has dispatched a soldier to find the orbs."

"They solved Tichiman's riddles?" she asked, alarmed, removing her hands from the pouches of the magnificently patterned bright yellow gown she wore.

"No, the soldier is expected to find an eeid who will."

35

"Do we need to worry?"

"No, my lady. No eeid as yet has been able to solve the riddles, not even I, the greatest of them. I assure you that it is safe to assume that the orbs are lost forever."

"We should take no chances," Lord Elcan, the high lady's chief military commander, insisted. The sunlight coming in through the open window reflected handsomely from the tin helmet that protected his rather large head. "Send in the Horsemen of Diaghan to track the soldier and destroy him before he makes any progress."

"No, we will risk no Horsemen in imperial territory," the widow said. "If the riddles cannot be solved, we are safe. We will need the Horsemen for Djenné, when the time is right."

The Horsemen of Diaghan were absolutely terrifying soldiers, believed by most to be the best cavalry force in the land. It was said they could move their entire force across the empire in fifteen days, a journey that could take any other force of equal numbers no less than a hundred days. For centuries the Horsemen had served many a ruling dynasty loyally. But, lured by promises of rich rewards, they had joined Fadiga and his rebels when the war started. Their services in the rebel army had enhanced their reputation, making them the most feared outfit throughout the empire. It was a reputation well earned, for unlike most military outfits, imperial or rebel, the Horsemen of Diaghan often devastated their enemies with frightening efficiency, leaving none alive and taking no prisoners. Whole imperial armies were known to have fled battlefields upon learning of the presence of these Horsemen. A whole regiment facing the Horsemen was even known to have resorted to mass drowning upon finding themselves with no avenue of escape. The Horsemen's reputation for terror was so well-known that in some remote imperial outposts the Horsemen did not even have to fight anymore. They just circulated word that they were thinking of attacking a garrison, causing the soldiers there to flee in order to avoid being annihilated.

After Lord Elcan's request for the Horsemen to seek out and destroy the soldier was declined, he pleaded with me to lend him my support on another matter regarding the treasured Horsemen.

"Perhaps, High Eeid," he began, "you may assist me in convincing the high lady to dispatch the Horsemen and a relief force to break the siege in Djenné. Our men hold strong but reports indicate it may not be for much longer."

"No," Mai-Fatou, the high lady, said softly. "Let the siege persist. No army in history has ever succeeded in taking the city by force, and it will not now be taken. The siege provides a useful distraction to imperial forces. I need the Horsemen here to protect us should Tera-Hool come under attack." She then turned to me and asked, "So, tell me, great eeid who knows all, why did they choose this particular soldier to find the orbs of Tichiman?"

"You may not believe what I am about to reveal to you."

The Soldier's Tale

chapter 8

ONCE OUT OF THE PALACE grounds, before I embarked on my quest for a skilled eeid as desired by the Table, I promptly rode to the local House of Taxes and Tariffs. There I obtained a hundred gold dinars using the emperor's note that permitted me to withdraw up to a thousand gold dinars for any expenses. I purchased a sheepskin tent, a light blanket, a bronze oil lamp, some food supplies, and some ink and paper for the chronicling of the great adventure which I believed was in the making.

The clouds were getting darker, and I desperately hoped this would not last long. After all, I was in Timbuktu, the city of learning, where it was said one could find answers to anything—with the exception of who my mother was, I used to add, for that remained the biggest unanswered question in my life.

My first stop was the city's university at Sankoré, to consult its headman, a well-known doctor who had learned and taught others in matters as delicate as the removal of eye cataracts. But as I approached the walls of the university I was appalled by what I saw. Four men were being led away by soldiers. Could they have broken some law to merit the escort of armed soldiers? Such scenes were rare in Timbuktu, the city where most lived in harmony with each other and where quarrels were few. I walked up to one of the soldiers.

"What have these men done?" I asked him.

"They broke into the university's library and tried to steal books," was the response.

I could see now that Lord Venga's powers were indeed taking hold of the land, for too many strange things were happening too fast. First the wild women had set themselves up in town, and now we had armed robbers trying to steal books from a library, perhaps the most sacred institution in Timbuktu, a city of total security, where few had ever had to fear robbers and bandits, where many never even locked their doors.

Times were changing. The skies were darkening.

***

"Gyvan Drabo!" the university's headman cried out when I walked into his chambers. "Can you believe it? Armed robbery in Timbuktu?"

"But why steal books?"

"The book trade is becoming the most profitable in Timbuktu, even more profitable than gold or copper."

We exchanged greetings.

"So have you come back to teach again?" he asked.

"No. I've come for some answers. I seek the most powerful eeid known to be living."

"What for?"

"It is an affair of the state, the relevancies of which I dare not discuss."

The headman understood. Being a citizen in the free society of Mali, he was bound to assist the state.

"There are three eeids who can be of service to you," he began. "They helped us when Fadiga's eeids tried to destroy the city during the seven-day siege. Kubai-chek is the best of them. If any eeid can help you, it is he."

"Where is he?"

"In Segou."

"And the other two?"

"Sicama and the woman, Muoria. They live in Mopti. They are not as good as Kubai-chek but they may be helpful."

I thanked the headman and departed, returning to my home to prepare for the two-day ride to Segou to find Kubai-chek. But upon learning from two soldiers of increased rebel activities on the road to Segou, I decided to take no chances. I chose instead to take the longer route by sailing down the River of Singers from Timbuktu to Segou, a course which was going to add one day to my journey, but which was a worthwhile expense.

When I got to the river port of Timbuktu, I exchanged my horse for passage to Segou on a boat that was transporting salt to the hunting lands of Do. I was the only passenger in this small boat with a crew of five. For one whole day the boat sailed smoothly, the crew happy to have me on board, for I endlessly entertained them with perhaps slightly exaggerated tales of battles I had been party to.

All began well, until a really strange thing happened.

Sobo Ha-Ha Speaks

chapter 9

I RODE INTO THE FOREST where the high lady was hunting for wild birds. In her company were several guards and commanders, including Lord Elcan and Commander Malouda. It was Commander Malouda's duty to ensure the safety of the high lady, for he commanded the Watchmen of Tera-Hool, the centuries-old military order sworn to protect the rulers of the Malian dominion of Tera-Hool.

The high lady was taking aim at a dove with her bow and arrow when I rode in. My horse's neigh caused a stir that frightened the bird away, and I gained for myself a censorious stare from the high lady.

"What is it, eeid?" the high lady grimaced, displeased at my sudden interruption that had caused her to lose her sport.

"It has suddenly dawned on me," I began, but then stopped short when she suddenly raised her loaded bow, pointed it towards my head, and let the arrow fly, granting no more than a quick glance at her target. The arrow whizzed past the top of my head, grazed my hair, and flew towards the sky. The poor dove, which I believed had escaped the high lady's sport, squealed and dropped from mid-air with the arrow through its belly. I gasped in dazzling amazement at this remarkable display of archery.

"You were saying?" The high lady bid me explain the reason for my intrusion.

"It has suddenly dawned upon me, my lady," I continued, "that there yet may exist an eeid who may be able to solve Tichiman's riddles. He was one of those responsible for beating us back when your husband laid siege to Timbuktu."

"Who is he?" Lord Elcan, the widow's chief military commander, asked.

"Kubai-chek of Segou."

"I have heard of him," Lord Elcan said. Then he turned to Mai-Fatou. "Allow me to take a few Horsemen to Segou to dispose of this eeid."

"No," the high lady rebuffed. "As we speak, Abubakari sends reinforcements to the area. It will take more than a few Horsemen to break through and kill Kubai-chek."

"Then I will take as many Horsemen as needed, my lady," Lord Elcan pleaded.

"No, Lord Elcan, that won't be necessary," the widow declared and then turned towards me. "There is an easier way to dispose of this Kubai-chek, isn't there, Sobo Ha-ha?"

"Of course there is, my lady. I will destroy his Third Shadow. That will make him unable to help the soldier."

The high lady said to Lord Elcan, "Why risk my precious Horsemen on a task that one man can perform?"

A race was on. I had to find Kubai-chek before Gyvan Drabo did.

I later learned from Noo, my spy owl, that Gyvan Drabo was on a boat on the River of Singers, two days away from Kubai-chek. I was four days away. I could not possibly allow the soldier to get to Kubai-chek first. And although I could not use my Third Shadow to kill the soldier in an instant without first obtaining and using some body part of his, I could possibly slow him down. But how? Well, he was traveling to Segou by river. I could certainly do *things* with water.

The Soldier's Tale

chapter 10

I HAD JUST FINISHED TELLING the crew about the Battle of Taghaza, giving myself a slightly inflated role in it, with a rather pompous flair that was enough to impress even a one-day-old baby. I then decided to retire to one of the two cabins on the boat to resume putting to paper my accounts of what had happened so far during my quest for the orbs of Tichiman. That was when something strange began to occur. It was a storm, one that erupted unexpectedly—in a river! How could there be a storm in fresh water? The boat began shaking violently, with the crew just as baffled as I was. Wave after wave of water poured in as the crew tried desperately to balance the boat.

"Look!" one of the crewmen cried, pointing at the shore. We all turned and saw to our complete bewilderment that the weather on the shore was fairly peaceful, sunny, and calm, with no hint of any wild winds.

"Must be an ill omen," the crew captain cried. He was right. This storm was being caused by someone. It was meant to delay the boat. Who was on this boat that had to be delayed or stopped? I could think of only one person—me. I had therefore been spotted by elements working for Lord Venga and the Dark Widow.

"Leave the boat!" the captain yelled at his men. "Save yourselves!"

"No!" I yelled. "I alone will leave the boat. It is me they seek."

"You?" the captain questioned, a look of terror and confusion in his eyes.

"I have not time to explain." I dashed into the cabin, placed my belongings into my watertight leather bag, which I slung across my back, then scurried back outside. My only hope now was to make my way to shore and continue my journey to Segou on foot. I grabbed a flat wooden board from the deck and jumped into the screaming river. Upon hitting the water, I lay on the board with my belly and rode the waves to shore.

Upon reaching the shore, the winds and the storm on the river came to an abrupt end. I stood up, relieved that the ordeal had ended. The boat, which I could see clearly from the shore, was now in sailing order, its crew now emptying all the water that had poured in. I waved at them, a gesture they returned, pleased to know I was safe, or perhaps pleased to see that I was off their boat, along with the ill omen that had nearly cost them their lives.

Although the river incident was a major setback to my task, I was content to be alive. But now I knew that someone knew of my location and had tried to slow me down. Therefore, it was only safe to say that this person was also going to where I was going to, and wanted to get to Kubai-chek before I did. I therefore had to make haste, for the fate of man and raw-breed alike rested in my hands.

I ran at length without stop until I came to a small village, where I purchased a horse.

Sobo Ha-Ha Speaks

chapter 11

My Third Shadow had served me well. I had slowed down the soldier, and now I stood at Kubai-chek's door while the soldier was still one day away. I had just knocked on Kubai-chek's door and was waiting for him. If I found myself unable to destroy his Third Shadow, I was ready to put to use the deadly dagger hidden under my cloak. I had used it to kill on many an occasion before when my Third Shadow had failed me.

"Greetings to you, sir," Kubai-chek said after he opened the door. He was an old man with a long gray beard and serious black eyes.

"Greetings to you," I responded.

"How may I be of service to you?"

"It is an old wound of the mind that troubles me, sir," I said, in as genuine a tormented voice as I could fashion.

Kubai-chek let me into his house. It was just what I needed—to be alone with him, where no one could see me slit his throat, if it came to that. He was a gentle being, and I found myself wishing I could destroy his Third Shadow so that I would not have to kill him. After all, we eeids always have a certain respect for each other.

We sat on two stools with a table between us. My goal was to get him to delve into the plane of Shadows as he attempted to cast a charm to heal me of my ailment, so that I, an unsuspected eeid, could delve into that plane too, discover the path of his Third Shadow, and destroy it before he could realize his folly.

"So," Kubai-chek said, preparing to work on my ailment, which at my bidding had been cast on me by a lesser eeid in the high lady's services. "Tell me more about this wound of the mind."

"It is the work of an old eeid," I began, "who placed the curse upon me after I refused to give my daughter's hand in marriage to his son. I will never know peace of mind and I will always find trouble wherever I go until the day I die. That is my curse."

Kubai-chek threw a long and questioning gaze at me, straight into my eyes, a gaze that was getting more and more intense with every passing moment. I was a little shaken. Had Kubai-chek read my true intentions?

I put my hand under my cloak and reached for my dagger. I felt its hilt. I had no other choice. I had to destroy Kubai-chek in the old-fashioned manner—a well-aimed jab through his heart. But then he suddenly brought himself to a relaxing mood and smiled. "I have found the path walked by the Third Shadow of the eeid who placed this dreaded curse upon you," he said.

"Can you heal me then?" I asked. I pulled my hand away from my dagger, relieved that I would not have to kill this man.

"It will cost you."

I dropped a small sack of gold dust on the table in front of him. He picked it up and weighed it. He was pleased.

He then began reciting the incantations needed to bring my sickness to an end. Once he was fully immersed in the plane of Shadows, I silently began my own eeidic chant and snuck into that plane too. There, I detected the path of his Third Shadow, for he had failed to close it, being carelessly unaware that I, too, was an eeid. His was the path of Feung, a path based on the energy of the Earth. Mine was the path of Daoda, a path based on water, which I instantly used to flood and drown his Third Shadow. Kubai-chek ceased to be an eeid. His Third Shadow was no longer. He stood motionless, dazed and shocked, attempting to understand the happenings of the last few moments. I enjoyed seeing the horror on his face, for I had once again proven to myself the superiority of my powers over others.

Kubai-chek soon realized who I was. He fell back in fright, believing I was about to kill him, for my reputation preceded me. I had destroyed many a Third Shadow before, and many an eeid.

"Sobo Ha-ha?" he groaned in anguish and disbelief, his sudden misfortune now even clearer to him.

"At your service, sir." I grinned. I was not going to take away his life. I was in good spirits. I dropped another sack of gold in front of the frightened and distraught Kubai-chek and walked out. What exactly became of him after that I do not really know, but I did hear some months later that he had been spotted as a wandering dervish somewhere in the Dunes of Roses beyond the territory of Gao.

The Soldier's Tale

chapter 12

I FINALLY RODE INTO SEGOU after three days, for I had ridden as fast as my horse could carry me, bent upon getting to Kubai-chek before my competitor could, whoever he was. Kubai-chek sat on a stool in front of his house, a square building made of thatched sun-dried mud and protected from above by a grass roof.

"I salute you, Kubai-chek," I called to him.

He looked at me from head to toe, and then from toe to head.

"How may I assist you?" he asked.

"I seek answers to a riddle."

"A man came before you. I cannot help you or anyone else anymore." He walked into his house and closed the door behind him.

So my competitor had beaten me to the great Kubai-chek. My last hope now lay with Sicama and Muoria, the other two eeids in Mopti recommended by the headman at the University of Sankoré. They were nowhere near as powerful as Kubai-chek, he had stated, though their counsel was worth seeking. If my competitor could destroy Kubai-chek's Third Shadow, then certainly neither Sicama nor Muoria could mount a defense against him.

I looked at the clouds as I set out for Mopti. Most would not have noticed, but it was getting darker, even though it was daylight. The powers of the White Shadow were growing. That meant the blood dripper, whatever it was, was maturing.

When I arrived in Mopti, it was a relief to learn that Sicama and Muoria were still in business. The eeid who had destroyed Kubai-chek's powers had not yet gotten to them. Either I had lost him or he believed that Muoria and Sicama could be of no help to me. And he was right, for neither Sicama nor Muoria could solve my riddle, each one stating that there were certain times when every eeid faced a challenge that could not be solved.

"How can an eeid not be able to solve a simple riddle?" I protested in frustration during my consultation with Sicama.

"Eeids are not gods, you know," he said calmly, "for if we could find solutions to every problem, I would have found a solution to my eternal quest for riches. I would be the richest person in the empire.

"I suggest you return to Timbuktu. In the Birdman's Library you will find an eeid. She is young—only about eighteen summers she's seen—so she has little experience. There is little chance she can help you, but you have nothing to lose by consulting her. She is known to have helped a few people before, but nothing more."

"What do they call her?"

"Feidi."

I thanked Sicama, paid him two gold nuggets, and departed for Timbuktu, this time heading for the Birdman's Library to find Feidi, a girl eeid.

***

TWO ARMED GUARDS STOOD AT the doorway to the Birdman's Library, so named because its founder had thought he could fly, and so had made a set of wings for himself, strapped them on, and jumped from a cliff. He was buried on a rainy morning. The guards were posted there to help protect it from the recent upsurge in armed robberies against libraries, by shameless rascals trying to make a profit in the highly lucrative book trade.

There were three other men and a woman in the library who had come to seek the services of Feidi, the girl eeid said to have stationed herself here. I was informed that Feidi used the library to practice her art because her father was the head librarian there. She insisted that the library's quietness enabled her to delve into the plane of Shadows more easily as she serviced her clients. Though no one was certain from which of her parents she had inherited her Third Shadow, it was often said that it must have been from her mother, who had died some five years prior. It was also whispered that since her mother's death, her father had spent countless hours in the library with his daughters, forcing them to read every book that came in from different lands, hoping that they could perhaps learn of the mystery of life and death, whatever that meant.

While Feidi was in one part of the library using her eeidic powers to service the few people who came to her, her father and little sister were in another, reading as many books as they could lay hands on, supposedly trying to find elusive answers to that all-time mystery of life and death. The family's love for books and knowledge was so profound that Feidi, the practicing family eeid, even demanded payment for her services in books if gold was not available.

My turn to consult with her came after that of a woman who had had a painful swelling resulting from a spider bite. She had come to thank Feidi for curing the swelling with lemon juice which she had blessed with her eeidic powers. When my turn came to consult with her, I was not hoping for much.

"How may I service you, dear one?" she asked of me.

"I have a riddle."

"Riddles are what I am best at."

I provided the test riddle to her, as I had to Sicama and Muoria in Mopti. But as I expected, Feidi was blank, staring at me, definitely clueless. If only she could utter those elusive words, *The path of Daoda*, then we would be on our way to the Table and towards eternal glory, searching for Tichiman's hidden orbs.

As I also expected, she asked after a few moments, "Repeat the riddle."

But we were suddenly, yet pleasantly interrupted by a most unexpected person. It was Feidi's little sister.

"Eeids who walk that path are all powerful, soldier," Feidi's little sister said, cuddling a doll as she walked into the room. She had been listening to us. She looked about ten or eleven summers on this Earth, with black shining eyes and beautiful long braids with gold beads plaited into them.

"What did you say?" I asked, taken aback.

She then said to her doll, "The soldier wants to know what I just said, Naya. Should I talk to him?" She held up the leather doll as if waiting for some manner of response from the object. After a brief heart-wrenching moment of seeing the little girl play with her toy in the face of so serious a matter, she said, "Naya says it is okay to talk to you."

"Well, get on with it, little one," I lashed out, losing my patience.

"The answer you seek," she began quite indifferently, "is the path of Daoda, the most powerful and the most dreaded path in the plane of Third Shadows."

I just stood there, suddenly frozen, looking at the little girl, awed and in speechless amazement. She had answered the test riddle. I was stupefied beyond belief, yet pleased, but also disappointed, for I knew that there was little chance the Table would allow me to take a child so young on the quest for the orbs. They would make a mockery of me, or worse, think I was making a mockery of them. But then again, if she had solved the test riddle, then she could, according to Tichiman, solve the two needed to locate the orbs.

Before I could speak any further, there was a harsh cry from one of the guards outside, followed by the rushing into the library of twelve armed men who had just attacked and killed the guard.

"Book robbers!" Feidi screeched.

In a snap, my sword flashed out of its sheath, ready to defend my eeid. I pounced instinctively and ferociously onto the book robbers and was able to cut two down almost immediately before they realized their peril. The remaining ten stopped in their tracks to organize an attack against me, realizing their task was going to be tougher than they had predicted. They certainly had not counted on the presence of a swordsman in the library, and I was certainly going to give this scum a living nightmare.

They sprang at me with the true zeal of a determined enemy, hoping to use their numbers to overwhelm me. But I cunningly moved around the shelves and tables in the library, disrupting their offensives and launching some of my own. In the thick of the melee some of them managed to slip past me in order to fill up their bags with books, while the others engaged me, our swords clashing in this duel to the death.

As the fighting progressed, I soon heard a scream from a female. I immediately ran towards it, where I found Feidi on the ground bleeding heavily, and with one of the bandits about to jab his sword into her little sister. I could not reach the bandit from where I stood, so I hurled my sword at him, sticking him right through his neck, dropping him instantly. I then ran to him to withdraw my sword from his body, but as I stood over him he unexpectedly woke up and grabbed my throat. He pulled out a dagger and was about to thrust it into me when I surprised him with my wrist knife, slicing him across the chest. He dropped and I pulled out my sword from his lifeless body. I threw a quick glance at Feidi. She was dead. I picked up her little sister with one hand and began fighting my way out of the library with the other. But the robbers intensified their attack, determined to avenge my slaying of their fellow bandits.

"My father!" Feidi's sister screamed. Feidi was already dead, so my only concern now was to preserve the life of her sister, who had solved Tichiman's test riddle, and who I now needed to aid me on my quest. Yet she was already proving as annoying as children are, for she continued screaming about her father as I fought my way towards the door. Her screams became so annoying and distracting that I finally gave up and decided to battle my way back towards the room where her father was, after she had bitten me and would not let go. Three more dead robbers and six surviving and very angry robbers later, I finally made it into the room. But the man was already dead.

As my fight to escape from the bandits with the little girl intensified, I grew more and more tired and began to doubt if I could make it out of there alive. The bandits were skilled swordsmen too, very likely soldiers or ex-soldiers from the rebel army. But to my relief, several imperial soldiers soon dashed into the library, and together we finished off the remainder of the bandit lot.

"Just in time," I said to the lead officer of the imperial soldiers, expressing my gratitude for their timely intervention. I was slightly acquainted with him from the army training grounds just outside Timbuktu.

"We were on patrol when some students reported the robbery in progress, Commander," the lead officer responded excitedly. "It is the closest I have ever been to battle."

"Be grateful for that. You do not want to be in a battle. Believe me."

Then I focused my attention on the little girl, who was crying deliriously over the body of her sister, Feidi. I should have felt bad for her, but I did not. She had just lost her entire family and I could not empathize with her. After engaging in countless battles before, I had become so used to death that I was incapable of pity or sensitivity at the sight of the dead. Those were luxuries no good soldier could afford. My only concern was getting her to the Table so that she could solve the two riddles needed to find the orbs, earning eternal glory for me and securing my place in the chronicles of the empire.

"What is your name?" I asked the girl. She did not answer, the recent calamity too distressing for her to afford any attention to me. I was getting impatient with the child. I had never been particularly fond of children and even though I needed this one's help, I was not going to allow myself to be fond of her. She was a dangerous eeid after all, more dangerous than adult eeids, for child eeids, not fully comprehending the strength of their Third Shadows and not fully understanding how to control them, could unwittingly put them to deadly effect whenever it suited them, without giving a rational thought as to the possible consequences of their actions. And I was going to have to live with this one for the next few weeks during our search for the orbs, I reminded myself. Whether she was going to take a liking or a loathing to me was of little concern to me. My only concern was finding the orbs. But from the fiery manner she looked at me after I repeatedly asked her for her name, I understood that she had taken an immediate loathing for me. I therefore took it upon myself to have my sword ready at all times and not hesitate to use it in case she attempted anything suspicious upon my person.

"What is your name?" I demanded once again. Still she did not answer.

"You do not know her?" one of the soldiers present asked me.

"Who is she?" I asked.

"Aida. The Child Eeid of Traoré."

The Words Of The Child Eeid

chapteR 13

UNTHINKABLE STUPIDITY! THAT IS WHAT I thought of the soldier.

I am Aida of Traoré.

I had never hated anyone before. On that day in the Birdman's Library, uncivil men had just taken away from me everything I had—my sister and my father. But it was not them I hated. It was the soldier who had saved my life that I hated, not because he had saved my life, but because he had saved my life and was now tormenting it. Mali had just lost two of its most important citizens. Feidi was known to be a generous eeid who had bettered the lives of many. My father had perhaps been the most honest man in all of Mali, so much so that he was one of three Persons of Confidence in Timbuktu. These were men appointed by city officials to take care of the goods and property of foreign traders who died in Timbuktu, until the people with rights to the goods showed up to claim them. Yet this soldier of Timbuktu seemed not to give a care in the world about my father or Feidi.

Even in the midst of my tragedy, I could tell that he had other designs for me. Because I had solved his riddle he needed me, not for my own good, but for his own, and that was the only thing that concerned him, the deaths of Feidi and my father meaning little to him. If ever there was a time when I wished ill upon a person, it was at that time, and the soldier was that person. As I mourned my father and Feidi, the soldier simply stood and watched, not even offering a shoulder for me to cry on. Only the lead officer of the other soldiers present had the good sense to console me. He bent down and held me in his arms.

"I wish we had arrived sooner, Aida," he said.

"What is going to happen to me now?" I asked, sobbing.

"Do you have any other relatives?"

I shook my head. The officer did not know what to say next, struggling to search for the right words.

"Well," the hateful soldier who had saved my life saved him the trouble, "the girl will come with me."

I was startled. "I would sooner kiss a snake!" I spat out at him.

"You can do that if you wish, little witch, but that will not make me go away or bring your father and sister back."

I had scarcely been acquainted with such rudeness before. I was so astounded I could no longer cry or think properly.

"You have nowhere to go," the hateful soldier continued. "Come with me. You will benefit from it. I promise you."

The soldier was right. I had nowhere else to go, so I reluctantly decided to go with him. Whatever he wanted from me could be no worse than what I had just undergone.

"But we need to bury Feidi and my father," I reminded him.

"These soldiers can take care of that," he said, referring to the other soldiers. "Our task is too important and we have no time to waste on funerals."

How could he be so unconcerned?

"Please, soldier," I pleaded with him, "I beg of you."

But my pleas fell on deaf ears. The hateful soldier had to have his way. He turned to the lead officer of the other soldiers and said, "Should anyone inquire about this girl, you know where to find me." He then grabbed me by the hand and walked me out. As we stepped outside, I realized I had forgotten something very dear to me, and even dearer now, more than ever.

The Soldier's Tale

chapter 14

"WHAT IS IT THIS TIME?" I asked the child eeid as she attempted to return into the library.

"Naya, my doll," she said. "I cannot leave her by herself."

"Leave it be," I said, doing my best to be as gentle as possible with the annoying little creature. "I will buy you ten more dolls later. We need to go."

"Buy a hundred more if you will, but I want Naya! Feidi made her for me herself."

Before I could say anything more, she darted into the library. I walked in behind her. She found the doll, smiled, and cuddled it warmly, a look of relief passing over her face as if it was her father and sister returned to life. But as we began to walk out, one of the bandits sprang to life, grabbed Aida by her braids, and knocked her on the head. She fell down hard. In a flash my wrist knife was out of its lion skin sheath and the bandit ceased to exist as a living being. Aida lay motionless on the ground. Her eyes were closed. I feared the worst as I examined her.

"Is she dead?" one of the soldiers asked.

"She lives," I replied, relieved. I picked up the unconscious little witch and put her on my horse. I did not forget her doll. It was the cursed thing that had brought this new calamity upon her. It must have been a source of her Third Shadow, I thought. But whatever it was, if it was going to help her help me find the orbs, then it was coming with us.

I knew it could be hours before she regained consciousness, a major setback I could scarcely afford. I had no choice now but to wait for this to happen before presenting her to the Table as my undesirable but necessary companion on my quest.

I was going to be spending at least the next few weeks of my life with a child eeid—the most dangerous creature on Earth. With the very potent powers she possessed, no one could ever be sure what her next action would be. They say the bite of a baby viper is deadlier than that of an adult viper, for the baby does not understand the extent and strength of its venom. So the infant snake injects more venom than is necessary to disable its prey. What would I do if this "baby" eeid, who might not understand the extent and strength of her Third Shadow, turned on me?

I decided to take her to the home of Lili, to await her recovery there. As we rode I continued pondering why I, and not another, had been chosen for so important a task. We soon arrived at Lili's home. As usual, she was excited to see me. But excitement was not hers alone. It was mine too, even though it had been no more than three days since I saw her last. I was compelled, driven largely by the presence of the unconscious Aida, to explain the reason for my recent absence, and in so doing, broke my oath of secrecy to the Table and divulged to Lili all about the recent happenings. But did she believe me?

"You are an absolute idiot," she laughed, thinking it all a joke or some wild adventure I had made up for the book I intended to pen. "Why would anyone with a right mind put the fate of the world in *your* hands?"

Because she would not believe me on my word alone, I showed her the emperor's imperial ring and the note for a thousand gold dinars. The seriousness of the matter suddenly dawned on her. She almost fainted.

In the midst of all this, though, Lili's main concern was for the unconscious little witch, whom she had gently laid on her bed and whose face she had begun cleaning with a damp cloth, wiping away her dried tears. Lili did not think it fair to involve a little girl in so diabolical an affair as I was about to undertake.

"She is an eeid," I reminded Lili. "Her very existence is diabolic."

"She is but a child, not a soldier," Lili insisted. "Eeid or not, a child remains a child. You cannot get her involved in one of your big glory-seeking ventures."

It was useless arguing with Lili. She was always *right*, even when she was wrong, and knew that I knew that she was wrong. That was a beauty about her. So I decided to proceed no further with the argument. Besides, I had to take my leave, for there were other affairs I needed to attend to.

"Take care of the girl," I said, walking out.

"Be careful."

I walked out. I loved Lili. It was also for her that I was undertaking this venture. I sought glory for my person, yes, but it was because I wanted to impress her. I wanted her to be proud of me. And as sure as the devil's wrath, I could not let her experience the untold suffering that was sure to exist in a world under Lord Venga and Fadiga's widow.

Sobo Ha-Ha Speaks

chapter 15

I HAD BEEN SITTING ON a balcony in the palace of Mai-Fatou, the high lady of Tera-Hool. After a considerable amount of time, the object of my wait, my trusty spy owl, Noo, came flying to me, braving the red dust that filled the air. It landed on my arm, bubbling with information. It chirped to me all it had lately witnessed. I laughed after interpreting the information. Though it all seemed like a desperate joke on the part of Commander Gyvan Drabo, I took the information to the widow and her war council anyway.

"So what has that bird of yours got for us this time?" the high lady asked me as I walked into the room where she was present with Lord Elcan, Commander Malouda, and other officials of her dominions.

"The soldier has found someone," I began, swallowing hard. "An eeid of some sort."

"An eeid of some sort?" Lord Elcan questioned.

"His eeid is but a little girl," I continued, "ten summers on this Earth. They call her Aida, from the town of Traoré. I had never heard of her before."

The room went quiet, all staring at me like I was a strange being just dropped from the heavens. And then all of a sudden everyone burst into loud laughter. Lord Elcan found little humor in the matter, though.

"Could this little girl be able to solve the riddles?" he asked.

"Not likely, not at her age." I responded.

"What about the test riddle?" Lord Elcan asked. "She did answer it, did she not?"

"I could not get that piece of information," I said, quite disappointed with myself. "But we should worry about her no more. She will not succeed."

"We should take no chances," Lord Elcan blurted. "Again, high lady, I request you grant me some Horsemen to finish off the child eeid and the soldier."

"No," the high lady said. "We will need every Horseman we have if we ever hope to break the siege at Djenné. Worry no more about the girl, Lord Elcan. Leave her to Sobo Ha-ha. She is no threat to us."

The Words Of The Child Eeid

chapter 16

IT WAS NIGHTTIME WHEN I opened my eyes. I found myself in a strange place, lying on a bed with a mattress made of feathers and straw. A lady sat on the bed next to me, almost causing me to scream in fright. But her gentle eyes looked as comforting as she was beautiful. Her smooth, shiny dark skin was a perfect and lovely contrast to the bright white robes that adorned her slender body.

"How do you feel, child?" she asked me in a voice as sweet as a bird's whistle. I did not answer. I was still trying to understand my surroundings. "I am Lili," she said. "What do I call you?"

"Where is Naya, my doll?" I asked.

She handed Naya to me. I hugged it dearly, my first thoughts going to Feidi and my father, and for a brief gleeful moment, hoping that I had only dreamt of their deaths. But I had a rude awakening when the despiteful soldier walked in. I almost lunged for his throat, but held myself back out of respect for Lili, who seemed to be a companion of the soldier. He was a tall, lean man with skin as black as charcoal and teeth as white as cotton. He had a narrow face and a rigid posture that complimented his well-muscled arms.

"I see the little witch is up," he said, referring to me.

"What am I doing here?" I asked. "I want to see Father and Feidi."

"Relax, little one," the soldier said. "Nothing you do is going to bring them back. If—"

"Gyvan!" Lili scolded him, suggesting that he mind his words to me.

The soldier shrugged and took a deep breath, preparing to tell me something important, which I dearly hoped would be about Father and Feidi. He put his hand on my shoulder, which I angrily slapped away, yelling, "Don't you touch me!"

The soldier withdrew his hands, and though I was miserable and depressed, I felt good after shunning him. Then I waited to hear his information. Was it about Father and Feidi? No. I was not that fortunate. It was some insane story about me and him having to meet the Table and save the world from raw-breeds and evil eeids. Before, I had believed the soldier to be slightly unbalanced in the head, but now I was certain that he was not only completely unbalanced but also totally insane. What was his motive and what did he take me for? I might have been only a child, but at least I knew that there had been no raw-breeds here for thousands of generations. Yet I had little choice but to follow this incredibly stupid soldier on his supposed quest to save the world. After all, where else could I go?

I knew it would have been useless to ask the soldier where Feidi and Father were buried, for he cared little about my loss and therefore would have cared little to know where they were interred. So I let him be. He and I left Lili's house shortly after he returned, riding on separate horses, the harness of mine tied to his, likely to prevent my escape, which he surely expected. Although I felt quite sad leaving the graceful Lili behind, I was surprised that she believed in the soldier's story. She had even given me some milk and dried meat for the road. Along with Naya, she was the only other earthly creation that made any sense to me. On the other hand, the soldier was the only earthly creation that made me question the whole purpose of life—why such an exaggeratingly foolish person was put on this Earth in the first place.

To my amazement, not long after we left Lili we neared the emperor's palace. Several heavily armed Red Sentinels were at its gates, along with their terrifyingly aggressive guard dogs that wore spiked collars of gold and silver. Still mistrustful of the soldier's intentions, I crossed my fingers, understanding that this was likely my end on this Earth, for at any moment the guards would unleash their deadly arsenal on this mad soldier and his companion—two oafs riding up daringly to the imperial palace during these dangerous times of war. But I was astounded when one of the Red Sentinels, a commander, walked up to us. Instead of directing us to leave the area on pain of death, he asked a question of the hateful soldier, suggesting some familiarity between the two.

"So did you find what we all seek?" the Red Sentinel asked the soldier in a rather unfriendly tone. I could instantly tell he did not like the soldier very much either. For this reason I immediately took to liking the Sentinel, for we both seemed to share a scorn for the soldier.

"Stand aside, Gans," the soldier responded to the Red Sentinel commander. "I will discuss my findings only with those who matter. Not you."

To my surprise, the commander of the Sentinels reluctantly stood aside and let us into the palace. What was going on here? Was the soldier's story about the raw-breeds and everything else true? He and I were led into the building and into a large room where, unbelievably, I found myself in the presence of the Table and Emperor Abubakari II himself. I stood motionless briefly, attempting to fully grasp the idea of being called to the presence of the Table. It was an impressive sight. The emperor and the Elders were all dressed in white robes, except for the Elder representing the Tuareg regions, who was dressed in the blue robes characteristic of his people. There were guards present, all carrying beautifully engraved shields and gold-mounted swords. More bloodthirsty guard dogs were also at the ready, secured by their handlers, and ready to deal a swift and brutal death to intruders.

I bowed to show my respect for the authority of the Table Elders. And then I looked more closely at all in the room. When my gaze shifted to the right, my eyes widened and I yelled louder than the devil himself, and fell back with a dreadful terror as I saw two raw-breeds staring at me. The soldier must have expected this reaction from me, for he caught hold of me before I could hit the floor. I held him tightly for protection, my dread of the beastly raw-breeds temporarily overwhelming my loathing for him. But he quickly pushed me away with a feeling I had not witnessed in him before. Hate—pure hate for me. He hated me just as I hated him.

"Look, little witch," he sternly warned in a whisper which only I could hear, "let me make one thing clear. The only reason I am going to spend the next few weeks with you is because we have a task to accomplish. You will lay no finger on me unless I authorize it, and know that I will have my sword at all times, and upon any actions on your part that may endanger my life, I will not hesitate to use it. I hope you understand me."

I remained quiet. The soldier was right to be wary of me holding on to him like that. He knew that I disliked him and that I wished him ill, and if, as an eeid, I could manage to grab a single strand of hair from him or scratch off a little portion of his skin, I could use either of those to concoct a dark potion to cast a spell upon him that could bring him untold misery. I understood his worries. He did not trust me. Few people trusted eeids. But at least one thing was clear. The soldier and I deeply distrusted each other.

My attention now focused back on the raw-breeds. Although I had never seen any before, these two fit perfectly the frightening descriptions of these hideous creatures that every child knows so well, descriptions passed down through the ages, and as told in the Breed Legends. I quickly realized I had nothing to fear from them, for no one else in the room seemed bothered by them. I held Naya close to my heart, comforted that she was my friend in the room. As I looked at the Elders I noticed something slightly out of the ordinary. They seemed to be more bewildered at seeing me than I was at seeing them, their stares burning holes through me.

I had only seen the emperor once before, when he had visited the library in Gao. He had come there to find information on what lands possibly lay beyond the vast sea to the west. He had told the head librarian that if there were any, he was determined to find them. The emperor was an adventurous man who had previously sent a fleet of discovery into that sea, but it had been four years since and none of the ships had returned.

The stares at me continued in silence, eventually broken by Musa the Elder, the emperor's brother.

"Gyvan Drabo?" Musa the Elder spoke, "what is the meaning of this?" he pointed at me. "We task you to find the best eeid in the empire and you bring us a child?"

"The girl answered the riddle, my lord," Gyvan responded.

Fearful murmurs hissed through the room.

"Does the child eeid know why she is here?" the raw-breed I would come to know as Tin-zim inquired.

"She does," the soldier said.

"What is your name, little one?" the emperor asked me.

"I am Aida of Traoré, Your Highness," I responded. I then turned to the raw-breeds and addressed them in Breed, their language. "Chi cheena, cal hom." Their eyes glowed, stunned at my usage of their language.

"Chi cherere, gol bal," they responded.

"You speak Breed?" the bewildered emperor asked me. "No human, be ye eeid or not, is known to speak Breed, a language dead and buried on this Earth for countless generations. However did you learn it, child?"

"They say my Third Shadow is strong, Your Highness," I responded.

That was the end of that topic. No one dared inquire about my Third Shadow, as all knew not to cross that line with an eeid, not even an emperor. If I had solved that riddle, I had to be even more dangerous than most eeids, for enemies were likely to underestimate my strength on account of my youth and let their guard down.

"You do know that this is a dangerous task you are about to undertake, even for an eeid such as yourself."

"For the empire I will take the risks, Your Highness."

The emperor signaled the raw-breed, Shokolo-ba, who pulled out a scroll from a small wooden box.

"We will only read one riddle," Shokolo-ba said. "If you get it right and find the orb, bring it back here and we will give you the second riddle to find the second orb.

Shokolo-ba read the riddle. It was something about the Circle of Life, twelve pillars, a fire-breathing dragon, and its tooth. I stood quietly for a while after the reading. I closed my eyes and began my eeidic incantations, calling on my Third Shadow to unravel the mysteries within this riddle. But the answer would not come.

Sobo Ha-Ha Speaks

chapteʀ 17

I RETURNED TO THE CAVES of Mount Koulikoro to administer the sacred potions to this creature which Lord Venga called the blood dripper. It was a potion prepared by Lord Venga himself, and one which was concocted with the darkest forces and most diabolical intent that the White Shadow of Lord Venga could muster. I called upon my Third Shadow and recited the appropriate incantations needed to give the potion its desired potency. After the incantations were complete, I poured out the potion at the mouth of the caves as instructed by Lord Venga.

The mist at the mouth of the cave was now lighter than it had been on the occasion of my last visit. In time, Lord Venga had told me, with the regular applications of the sacred potion, the mist would clear and the blood dripper would be matured, visible, and ready to be deployed into our service. Though lighter, the mist remained thick enough to deny me even a glimpse of the blood dripper, though I believe I did hear a low ghoulish shriek from within the mist.

What exactly was this creature? What was its exact purpose? For a brief moment I pondered venturing into the mist to steal a quick look at what monstrosity lay within, but being an eeid, I knew better than most not to dabble with an entity not yet known or studied. I therefore reasoned it best to let the creature be. After all, in good time it would make itself known to the world.

As I rode away from the mountains, my guards, as usual, tightened their security when we rode past Assassin Hill, where the gang of assassins known as the Paipans had been slain some fifteen summers past by a confederation of fourteen kings. The guards feared that the lone assassin reported to have survived the massacre, who was now known to be terrorizing the empire and many small kingdoms, may have returned to wreak vengeance upon any who dared set foot near the sacred ground.

The Soldier's Tale

chapter 18

THE CHILD EEID CONTINUED HER eeidic incantations as if in some kind of devilish trance as she searched for the answer to the second riddle. Then she suddenly went silent.

"Would you like the riddle repeated, Aida of Traoré?" Musa the Elder asked.

"The Kamablon," she said hastily. "The orb lies somewhere in or around the Kamablon."

"How did you come to your answer?" the Emperor asked her.

"'The Circle of Life' is what the people of Niani used to call their town, for it is the birthplace of Sundiata Keita, the founder of our empire. The 'twelve pillars' within the 'Circle of Life' represent the twelve children of Maghan Kon Fatua, the Lion King of old Mali. The dragon that cast the evil ring of fire on the Circle of Life is Sumanguru Kante, the Sorcerer King of the Sossos. The only wooden pillar that survives the dragon's breath and chokes it to death represents Sundiata Keita, the only child who survived the terror of Sumanguru and slew him on the plains of Kirina three score and seventeen years past. The remaining tooth of the dragon represents the only building left intact after the battle—the Kamablon. It is within it, or around it, that the first orb we seek is hidden."

There was silence. Was she right? There was only one way to tell.

"Go with the child to the Kamablon," Musa the Elder commanded me. "If you bring back the first orb we will know she is right."

I certainly hoped the child eeid had rightly answered the riddle. I wanted to quickly be done with this whole affair so that I could reap the benefits of all the fame and glory that were certain to come with it, and return home to marry my Lili. But for now, I had to put up with the child eeid.

The following day, fresh horses and supplies were waiting for us. For good measure, Musa the Elder reminded me, "The Dark Widow and her forces have spies everywhere. They may try to stop you. Should you encounter her, she is not, and I repeat, she is not to be harmed."

I was aware of this already. Destroying the Dark Widow would send the White Shadow she hosted back to Lord Venga, making its capture and prevention of the blood dripper, whatever it was, impossible.

Although I had attempted and failed to get an answer on many an occasion before, I concluded that I had nothing to lose, so I asked of the Table once more, "My lords, I have brought forth an eeid worthy of this quest. May I now ask why I was chosen for this task?"

"You will know in due time why that is so, Commander," Musa the Elder answered. "But as of now you must take your leave. The clouds grow darker as we speak. Lord Venga's power grows over the land. May you find success."

Gans led me and the eeid out, his dislike for me giving me a strong feeling that he was a spy for the Dark Widow.

As the child eeid and I walked out, the emperor stopped her.

"Some here now say you may be the greatest eeid in Timbuktu," he said to her. "If it is so, you may be able to help me. I fear fighting may come to Timbuktu sooner or later. I want to be able to fight with my soldiers, be it day or be it night. But I suffer from an illness that renders me blind at night. That will do me no good should the fighting come at night. Can you heal me of this ailment?"

The little witch thought for a moment, murmuring an eeidic charm under her breath. Then she said, "Yes, Your Highness. But there is something you must eat once every week until your night blindness is cured. I have just cast a noble charm upon your palace so that all such items that are brought into it will be affected by the powers of my Third Shadow."

"And what is this thing I must eat once every week if I am to be cured?" the emperor asked eagerly.

"The raw liver of an ass."

The Words Of The Child Eeid

chapter 19

AS THE SOLDIER AND I rode away from Timbuktu to the plains of Kirina, where the Kamablon was located, my misery returned to me. The journey to Kirina was to last twelve days by horseback, all of which I was going to spend with the despicable soldier. I started thinking about my father and sister, and how the soldier had prevented me from giving them a proper goodbye and seeing them one last time. They had very likely been buried in some unmarked grave with no one to wish them well in the afterlife. I again pondered asking the soldier if he knew where they were buried, but I chose not to, for he cared nothing for them and little for me. He was only interested in using me to solve the riddles, becoming a celebrated hero, and writing an account of his adventures, all to add fame and fortune to his name.

But I forgot my misery for a while, when as we rode past the well closest to the gates of Timbuktu, I saw many a joyous child not much older than myself, playing in a sand pool they had created with water from the well, helping to temper the sweltering dry season heat. The children were merry, and I was happy for them. If the soldier and I failed in our task then all this would be over. There would be no happy children playing by the well.

The task at hand was what preserved the sanity in me, for it would have been lost when every single day, for the following few days, the last *thing* I saw before getting my sleep was the soldier, and the first *thing* I saw when I woke up was the same idiot, for he only took to sleep once he was sure that I was asleep. He feared that if he went to sleep before I did, I could work up a spell to cause his person some manner of grievous harm.

Most of our journey to Kirina was by the River of Singers, where we boarded a boat from Timbuktu and made two rest stops for a day each, first at the city of Segou and then at the city of Do. We could have continued along the River of Singers but received reports of rebel activities further down the river. So from Do the soldier purchased two horses with a note for 500 gold dinars that had been issued to him by the Table. We then continued by land towards the plains of Kirina.

The journey from Timbuktu to the plains lasted seven days, a period during which the soldier spoke very little to me, as had been his manner all along. He watched me always, suspecting I may turn to some unpleasant mischief at any time. That was okay by me. I was glad to know that he did not like me and knew that I did not like him either. He was as despicable a creature as there could be, and even though he was not exactly this, I liked to think of him as a cadaverous being that looked like something that had dropped from a dog's behind.

Sobo Ha-Ha Speaks

chapter 20

THE NEWS THAT NOO, MY spy owl, brought back was not exactly pleasant, and I trembled at the thought of having to deliver it to the high lady. But it had to be done. Her guards informed me that she was in her bathhouse, and so to her bathhouse I went. Lord Elcan, who had been consulting with some of his officers, noticed my arrival and stopped me. I gave to him what information I had received from Noo, throwing him into a panic. Together we rushed to the high lady, whose attendants let us into her bathhouse, where she was in a pool of steaming water, being bathed by three castrated menservants and attended by three of the prettiest maids you ever saw.

"The child eeid has solved the test riddle!" I broke the information to her.

She stood speechless for a brief moment. A terrifying chill crept up my spine for I knew not what she would do to me.

"You swore the child was not good enough, high eeid," the high lady scolded me in a cold, dangerously threatening tone. "You swore she could not possibly solve the riddle."

"It gets worse," I managed to blurt out, fearful of what she could do to me in her current state, but understanding that for my own safety it was best to provide all the information I knew. "She has also given an answer to the second riddle."

"And is her answer right?"

"If she finds an orb then we will know."

"Do we have to wait for her to find the orb?" Lord Elcan interjected. "My lady, grant me my Horsemen and we can end this now, killing her and the soldier before they get any further!"

"As I said before, Lord Elcan," the high lady responded, "your Horsemen are to be deployed for more worthy challenges at Djenné. The Horsemen of Diaghan will not be reduced to chasing a little girl and a soldier."

"But she is not just a little girl," Lord Elcan argued. "She is an eeid whose Third Shadow could destroy our cause."

"No. If the most powerful eeids failed, then what chance has a little girl got?"

And that was it. The high lady had spoken. All we had to do now was to wait and see if the child eeid would find the first orb of Tichiman.

The Soldier's Tale

chapter 21

THE MOST DANGEROUS PART OF my mission was not that I was very likely to encounter the forces of Lord Venga and the Dark Widow. It was that I now had to spend my next few days with an eeid. This was as dangerous and risky as cheating drunk soldiers in a gambling game. Just as they could easily draw their swords and slit each other's throats without hesitation, an eeid could, with equal ease, suddenly cast a spell that would bring unsuspecting injury and untold misery to anyone. I would not hesitate to use my sword on the child eeid should she try anything suspicious, I constantly reminded myself. And though she was but a little girl, she was just as deadly and as unpredictable as any eeid, good or evil. I trusted neither.

Had it been up to me I would never have exchanged words with her, but I had been left with no choice. We had to talk about matters that concerned our task.

"How are we going to know where exactly in the Kamablon to find the orb?" I asked.

"We could try looking," she responded rather harshly.

I hope somebody chokes her, I thought to myself.

When we got to the Kamablon I was relieved at being a step closer to completing my task. It remained a fine building made of sun-dried mud and straw, and with a smooth surface, despite having withstood the test of time for more than seventy-five years since the Battle of Kirina. This was the only building that had remained intact immediately after the epic battle.

There were about ten builders there when we arrived. They were members of the Keita clan, the descendents of Sundiata Keita, the soldier who had emerged victorious from the battle after defeating Sumanguru the tyrant usurper. Every seven years since the battle the members of this clan, to this very day, have been re-thatching and re-roofing the building in order to preserve its beauty and historic significance.

Presenting the royal ring to the head builder, I informed him that I was inspecting the building for the emperor. I told him the little girl was my daughter, a lie that instinctively and instantly caused me to cringe. The head builder was happy to let me and the eeid inside, where we started looking for anything that could aid us in locating the orb. We searched for a while but came up with nothing. Just when I thought things could not get any worse, she did what I hated so much. She spoke to her doll.

"Be patient, Naya," she said to the doll. "We will find the orb and we will go home, okay." She kissed the doll. I wished I could steal it and burn it, but I knew she would not let it out of her sight for any reason.

The child eeid walked up to the head of the workmen.

"What part of this building do you not often have to replace or maintain every seven years?" she asked.

"We replace everything," the headman said, "except the wooden bars that hold up the roof. Those were made from well-seasoned baobab wood. It will be about twenty more years before they will need to be replaced."

I immediately looked at the wooden bars. I looked at the side of them, at the top of them, and at the bottom of them, but saw no orb. But the child eeid was staring intensely at them, something having grabbed her attention. She soon walked towards the bars and pointed at one.

"Soldier of Timbuktu," she said to me, pointing at a bar, "pick that up."

I did as she had instructed. She examined the bar in my hands but did not touch it, arousing my curiosity. Then it suddenly hit me! Why would she not touch the bar herself? She had got me! She had cast a spell on the bar and had tricked me into touching it. What would now be the nature of the misery she had inflicted upon me, I wondered in fright. I cursed myself for my own folly. A rare smile glazed over the face of the little witch.

"It's the orb!" she said in a low, soft tone.

My fears of being afflicted with some manner of eeidic spell evaporated. I looked down even more closely at the wooden bar I held in my hand. It was no piece of wood. It was glass—the orb disguised as wood to protect it from the wrong hands. That is why she had asked me to pick it up, for the Table had decreed that only I could touch it and live, but instant death upon all others who might so lay a hand on it.

We had just found the first orb of Tichiman.

I glanced at the child eeid, who at only ten summers on this Earth, had solved what no other could solve. Maybe I felt a little respect for her, I do not know, but for a very brief moment I appreciated her. Her eyes seemed to glow as she looked at the orb, likely longing to feel it, I could tell. Should this object have fallen into the hands of an eeid as powerful as she was, there would have been no telling what manner of devilish use she could have put it to, had she been able to cast an eeidic spell to allow her to touch it without bringing harm to herself. I did not want the opportunity to find out, so I quickly shoved the orb into my bag and proceeded to warn her.

"If I see you around this bag," I began, "I want you to know I will waste no time in slicing you in half!" I made sure she understood me well, for I meant every single word I said. I believe she did, for she drew her doll closer to her heart and held it tight, as if protecting it from me.

For my part, I was pleased that this venture was progressing smoothly. If it ended successfully I would be a Malian hero. My aunt and grandmother who had raised me, as well as my father, would be proud of me as they lay in their tombs. I was hoping that by then I would have found my mother, whoever and wherever she was, and that upon my first meeting with her she could be proud and pleased to know that her son was a hero of Mali and a favorite of the emperor.

The child eeid and I soon mounted our horses and headed back towards Timbuktu with the first orb that held part of Lord Venga's trapped White Shadow.

So far it had been easy. I hoped that finding the second orb would be just as easy. But I should have known better. I was heading for a terrifying adventure beyond the wildest imagination of any living soul, born or unborn.

The Words Of The Child Eeid

chapter 22

OUR RETURN JOURNEY TO TIMBUKTU to present the first orb of Tichiman to the Table was not particularly pleasant. While the civil war itself had done its own share of the damage, there was something more sinister at work in the land—an evil not created by man, but by some diabolic being of unknown creation. It was an evil that meant only one thing: Lord Venga's Third Shadow, the White Shadow, was increasing its grip across the empire.

It started with the animals. Many had died where they had fallen, stricken by famine and diseases unknown. Next to be hit were people, a growing number of reports of the plague having broken out in some parts of the empire. Here was Timbuktu, a city that even in times of wars past had remained tranquil and blissful, where neighbor had always helped neighbor and where fast friends had always been made. But now the city had slowly changed into a place where no one trusted anyone anymore. It was now a dying city.

A most unfortunate event that occurred a few days before our entry into Timbuktu emphasized the severity of the times. Believing that the bag the soldier guarded so carefully contained food, a poor thief snuck into our tent to steal it. Upon touching its contents, the orb of Tichiman, the thief died a most painful death—his eyes popping out of his head and his bones cracking inside him one at a time—a painful demise that awaited all who laid hands on the orb, save the soldier.

"Poor man," the soldier said soon after. "If only he had asked me for a slice of meat, I'd have given him one."

The local authorities later identified this thief as a wealthy trader who had been ruined when one of his workers was accused of bringing the plague to his town after returning from a business journey. This accusation had driven away all the wealthy man's customers and reduced him to begging and thievery, a warning to many that misery of a sort never before seen in these parts was dawning on the empire.

Was our slowly decaying empire a result of the blood dripper? I could not say, for no one save Lord Venga knew the exact workings of the mysterious entity.

The blood dripper. What was it?

Sobo Ha-Ha Speaks

chapter 23

I HAD ONCE AGAIN BROUGHT myself to the cave on Mount Koulikoro, to administer the potion that would prepare the blood dripper for its awakening and for our use. The mist around the cave's opening had further cleared away, giving me some hope of eyeing the mysterious being that hid within its eerie presence.

As instructed by Lord Venga, I chanted the sacred words that would give the sacred potion its potency. I then emptied the potion on the soil at the mouth of the cave. It disappeared in a puff of black smoke which suddenly arose and eroded within what was left of the mist. I attempted to look beyond the mist but could see nothing. Yet as I turned to leave, I heard something, a hiss and a growl like that of no other beast or creature known to me. I looked into the mist again, and for a moment only as long as one can manage a single blink, I noticed two eyes staring at me, which then vanished into the mist of mystery as quickly as they had appeared. The eyes had almost looked like man's—white, with a dark pupil in the middle of each, but with something largely odd about them, something I could not quite put a finger on, nor quite describe.

So what was this blood dripper? What was this force or being that may have had eyes like a man but sounded like a beast? How was it to aid Lord Venga in seizing New Eartholia and Eartholia Proper? I could only wonder.

The Words Of The Child Eeid

chapter 24

THE SOLDIER AND I SPOKE very little on the way to Timbuktu, and I liked it that way, my only real company and source of some solace being my dear doll, Naya. In her I could still feel Father and Feidi. Wherever they had been buried, I only hoped that it was a place worthy of them.

The night before our arrival in Timbuktu, I secretly obtained and glanced through the soldier's journal while he slept. From it I was quite surprised to learn that, like me, he, too, felt a deep sadness after the death of his loved ones—his aunt and grandmother—and that he did not know his mother but had made it his goal to find her if she was still alive. But after I thought of how insensitive he had been to me after my own recent losses, I quickly lost whatever compassion I may have felt for him.

He had also written of me in his journal, not very pleasant things. I understood that he hated me because of fear—fear of eeids. I did not blame him for hating me, for most people feared and hated eeids, believing many to be the root of all evil on Earth. But I blamed him for hating me without knowing me.

When we arrived in Timbuktu, the situation was the same there as with many a village, town, and city we had passed through. All seemed darker—a gloomy darkness. The faces in the city had lost much of their happiness. Even the well, which had been blossoming with merry children playing with its water, seemed to have lost part of its glamour and allure. The water was running out, I was told. Children no longer played there. They fought—over the limited amount of water it now spurted. Even the golden swords of the Red Sentinels and the spiked golden and silver collars of the emperor's dogs seemed to have lost their charm and shine. All these changes could only mean one thing. The dark powers of Lord Venga were growing. They were very slowly turning the once happy and noble people of Timbuktu into savages.

Gans, the commander of the guard, met us at the gate. He seemed worried about my well-being, for it was me he addressed first.

"We are glad you are back, Aida," he said to me warmly.

"I'm hungry," was all I said.

"Worry not, child," he said. "The emperor's kitchen will serve you whatever may please you most." Then he turned to the soldier and said rather rudely, "So, did you find the orb or did you spend your time visiting wild women?"

"No, Gans," the soldier responded. "But I found a river I think you should jump into and drown."

It was clear that the two men disliked each other, and any man who disliked the soldier was a friend of mine. Gans led us to the Table, where I was ready to prove the strength of my Third Shadow to the Elders by presenting them with the first orb of Tichiman, safely tucked in the soldier's bag.

A sudden silence fell upon the Table when Gyvan and I arrived in its presence, its members and the raw-breeds all eager to learn the outcome of our venture. I bowed to show my reverence for the lot. We stared at each other for a moment, during which time not a word was spoken by anyone, until the emperor broke the silence with an unexpected topic.

"The raw liver of an ass touched by your Third Shadow, eh?" he said with a chuckle, referring to the remedy I had given him to cure his night blindness. "Couldn't your Third Shadow have touched something more acceptable, like figs or bananas?"

"I'm sorry, Your Highness," I calmly said, "but my Third Shadow pointed me towards the ass's liver."

"Well," the emperor said, "it is working. My sight gets better by the day."

"I am glad, Your Highness."

The awkward silence returned, each group waiting for the other to comment on the orb. I decided to break the silence this time.

"Your Highness," I addressed the emperor, "we have the orb."

The soldier reached into his leather pouch and pulled out the orb. At this the Table stood up in awe and disbelief. Tin-zim and Shokolo-ba, the raw-breeds, walked over to the soldier. They examined the orb closely without touching it. Then after chanting a spell understandable to them only, Tin-zim picked it up. No, his eyes did not pop out, nor did his bones crack within his body, nor did he suffer some grievous manner of death as had befallen the poor thief who had touched the orb last. No harm came to Tin-zim, his Breedish incantations having averted that. The raw-breeds continued their examination of the orb. There was a nervous silence among all. Even I was nervous, for I can tell you that some doubt existed in me as to whether I had found the right orb. The raw-breeds exchanged some words among themselves in Breed. Then Tin-zim put the orb away safely in a wooden challis.

Shokolo-ba turned to the emperor and said, "Your Highness, the girl has found the first orb of Tichiman!"

There was an instant air of relief in the room. We were one step closer to ending Lord Venga's threat. All the attention soon turned on me, the Elders showering me with praises, with the soldier being largely ignored at first. And though I took delight in my newfound status, at the back of my mind one thing dampened any joy I could possibly feel.

Would I be able to solve the next riddle?

The Soldier's Tale

chapter 25

THE CHILD EEID WAS RECEIVING all the praise for finding the first orb of Tichiman, with little thought being given to the fact that it was I who had battled the forces working against us. It was I who had found her. It was I who had protected her to the Kamablon and back. Yet no one paid any heed to me, until Musa the Elder finally spoke to me.

"Commander," he called to me, "we must commend you for your assistance in this matter. We stand corrected on our doubts about the child."

"Anything for the empire, my lord," I said, and bowed to him, glad for my own role in the matter to be recognized at last.

The emperor turned to the raw-breeds and said, "Peace agents of Eartholia Proper, time is not on our side. I believe the eeid is ready to hear your next riddle."

Aida cleared her throat as Shokolo-ba opened up the box that contained the riddles. He unfolded a scroll from it and read. The riddle was something about fruits, rivers, bees, a rotten town, and the moon blocking the sun. But could the child solve it? She stood speechless for a while, stroking the gold beads plaited into her braided hair, perhaps using them to invoke an eeidic charm. Then she closed her eyes, chanting her spells and calling upon the powers of her Third Shadow. She clutched her braids and pulled them tight, fixated in some manner of eeidic trance. She soon opened her eyes and was ready to speak. She had solved the first riddle, so I had every reason to believe she would solve this one too. Easily.

"Your Highness," she spoke, "some riddles are harder than others."

"Can you solve this one, child?" the emperor questioned.

"The 'tree that yields many fruits' is the River of Singers. The towns that are sustained from this river are the fruits it yields. The fruit that 'sprouts at the point where two branches meet' is the town of Djedeba, which is located at the point where the River of Singers meets the Milo River. It is no ordinary town, because it is from here that they mine the metal iron, which is stronger than all others. This iron is the seed the fruit produces. The birds that live on this tree and 'extract its seeds' are the people who extract its iron and make a living in the iron mining and trade of Djedeba. The fruit 'without a tree' where the iron is taken to is a town which does not sit on a river. My Third Shadow tells me there are three towns without rivers that receive the raw iron: Tabon, Wagadou, and Sibi. The 'bees that defend a hive' that the seeds are transformed into are weapons, the most potent being the ones made of the strongest steel.

"To find out which of these towns makes the strongest steel we have to go to Djedeba and learn from the miners. And when we learn of the town, we will go there and find out from the weapon makers what giant weapon, a 'bee as big as ten,' was dispatched—on the day when the moon blocked the sun, a phenomenon which men of science call an eclipse—to a town that was 'rotten.' In that giant weapon, in that town, is the second orb of Tichiman."

Then there was silence until the emperor declared, "Child, you must rest before your departure for Djedeba on the morrow with Commander Drabo."

Perhaps now that I had proven my loyalty by helping to find the first orb, the Table could grant me answers to the three questions that pressed upon me at every turn: Why had I been chosen for this task; What was the mysterious fourth riddle; and Why was it being kept secret? I dared to ask again, but Gans, the commander of the guards who despised me to the bone, made a move as if to shut me up. A stern look from the emperor made him hold his ground and his tongue.

"It is okay for the soldier to ask his questions," the emperor said softly. "After all, it is he who risks his life to save us all." He turned to me and said sincerely, "But Commander, it is the belief of all here that for your task to succeed certain things must be kept hidden, even from you. But I assure you, Commander, that should the need arise, the Table will divulge to you the contents of Tichiman's fourth riddle and the reason why you were chosen for this task."

I was pleased with the emperor's honesty. I trusted his judgment and decided to question the Table no more. But I did have one request of him, and it was that I be allowed to spend the night out of the palace grounds so that I could visit Lili, the woman I was to marry.

"All right, Commander," the emperor agreed to my request. "You may visit your woman after you and the child eeid are fed and rested. But on the morrow you must leave for Djedeba, for time remains our enemy."

"I am grateful, Your Highness," I responded.

"And one more thing," the emperor continued. "You will be taking the eeid with you to your woman's house."

So I was stuck with the eeid once again. I had believed I could at least be rid of her for a day while I enjoyed what could easily be my last day alive with Lili, my wife-to-be. I did not blame the Table for making me keep Aida. They certainly would not have been thrilled to have a dangerous child eeid under the same roof with the emperor. I could control her, they believed. After all, I had found her.

After a hefty meal fit for a king and a brief period of resting, Aida and I were escorted to Lili's house by a troop of Red Sentinels led by Gans.

"Be ready to depart before the cock crows," Gans said to me after we arrived at Lili's. Then he departed with the Sentinels after having handed me another imperial note for a thousand gold dinars.

Lili opened her door after I knocked on it. She looked even lovelier than ever, though the sadness she faced because of my absence and the emerging torments of the troubles sweeping across the empire had caused her to lose some of her glamour.

I was a little jealous when, instead of welcoming me first, Lili went for the child eeid and lifted her up in the air, delighted to see her. They seemed to have taken quite a liking to each other, and I could actually feel the little witch wondering how such a gentle woman like Lili had ended up with a scoundrel like me. It was a moment or two before Lili even acknowledged my presence, whereupon she hugged me and expressed her gladness in seeing us again.

"The dark clouds grow," she said softly after we had settled down. "Most do not notice it yet, but that will soon change."

There was the gloominess in the air that meant nothing was the same anymore. Times were getting tougher. Trading had slowed and the harvests had been poor, the evil of Lord Venga and the Dark Widow having been hard at work. Lili understood quite well the difficulties of the times. She had made a living by trading with merchants who ferried goods across the empire. Few had arrived during the last few weeks. No one knew why. Inquirers had been dispatched to look into the matter, but none had returned. There were reports that the situation was just as bad in the lands across the eastern Dunes of Roses, across the northern deserts, on the far side of the southern forests, and beyond. Some from those lands had even fled to Timbuktu, hoping for better times, only to find Timbuktu no better, or even worse, than their own lands.

But I was glad to be home again. The child eeid and Lili spent most of the time together. I just watched them, reflecting on what the morrow might bring. Sometimes the child eeid played with her doll while I simply rested in Lili's arms, trying not to think of what troubles possibly lay ahead.

Our search for the first orb had been easy, without much intervention from the Dark Widow or her forces. Would the search for the second orb be just as easy? Why had the widow not sent assassins after me or the child eeid? Why had she not sent out the Horsemen of Diaghan, the most feared and fiercest horsemen in the land? Why had the child eeid, who loathed me beyond description, not resorted to some manner of grievous evil against me? I began to believe she was hiding a deep, dark secret of her own.

Sobo Ha-Ha Speaks

chapter 26

THE HIGH LADY WAS NOT going to like the news I had just obtained from my spy owl. I burst into her war room, where she was conferencing with her commanders, discussing plans to relieve her besieged stronghold at Djenné.

"The dark clouds grow, High Eeid," she said to me. "I hope the news you bring does not spoil that spectacle."

"My lady, I'm afraid it does." I nervously replied.

"Talk."

"The little girl, the child eeid. She found the orb!"

The high lady and her commanders flexed in disbelief.

"My lady," Lord Elcan lamented, "we can wait no longer. Grant me my Horsemen—"

"Quiet, Lord Elcan!" the widow scolded, then turned to me. "You are certain of this?"

"I trust Noo more than I trust my own eyes, my lady," I said. "The orb was found in the Kamablon. Right now it rests with the Table."

"And the second orb?" the high lady inquired.

"The soldier and the child eeid will soon take leave to search for it."

"Where will they search?"

"I do not know. But Noo will follow them until it is found. Then Lord Elcan and his Horsemen can be dispatched to destroy them, and I will bring you the orb."

"No," the high lady shot back. "We cannot risk having the orb found. We are too close to our goal to take that risk. In a few months the blood dripper will be ready and the clouds will be darker than the night itself."

"So what would you have us do, High Lady?" I asked.

"Not us, High Eeid. You!"

"Me?"

"You will destroy the child eeid's Third Shadow," she said, "as you did to Kubai-chek of Segou."

I had given some thought to this idea myself, but so far I had been unable to determine the path of the child eeid's Third Shadow, which I needed to know in order to destroy her powers. But she was only a girl of little eeidic experience, bound to be careless at some point in coming, I convinced myself. I had destroyed the Third Shadows of far greater eeids, so I had little cause to worry. The fact that she had solved two Tichiman riddles must have been only some cruel twist of fate, I consoled myself. I could destroy her powers. But there existed just one little worry.

"My lady," I said to the widow, "just how do I get close enough to the eeid and her guardian soldier? They say he is quick with the sword."

The widow turned to me, surprised at my question. "You are the high eeid of Tera-Hool. Find a way."

"I'll do my best, my lady."

"What if the high eeid fails, My Lady?" Lord Elcan asked. "Then my Horsemen can—"

"I will not fail, Commander!" I interrupted, reiterating my worth to the high lady. I turned around to walk out of the room.

"Sobo Ha-ha?" It was the high lady who had called to me. She pulled me into a corner for a private word out of earshot of her war commanders. "Does the soldier know yet why he was chosen for his task?" she asked.

"No, my lady," I said. "Should I let him know?"

The widow thought for a moment, then sighed and responded, "No. No. Tell him nothing. We cannot be sure if that would help or hurt us. Just destroy that little girl's Third Shadow. And kill them both if you have to."

The Soldier's Tale

chapter 27

I THOROUGHLY ENJOYED MY TIME with Lili. The only thing that almost ruined it was the child eeid, who seemed to be competing with me for Lili's attention, and winning. But in a few weeks, I reminded myself, we would solve the riddle, find the second orb, and the eeid would be out of my life for good.

The night was short, made even shorter by the accursed Gans, who arrived at the twinkle of dawn's light to make certain that the eeid and I left for Djedeba in good order. The very idea of Gans ached me to the marrow. Few people liked him. He was the only soldier I despised, second only to Tigana, my former commander and friend, who had relieved me of my command and thrown me out of the army after the rumors of my mingling with wild women began circulating. I looked forward to the completion of this venture so that I could return to my unit and let him know that I, Gyvan Drabo of Timbuktu, had been chosen above all others, even him, to carry out the most important military assignment the empire had ever known.

I also thought of my four friends in the army, the finest soldiers I ever knew. I had last encountered them in Timbuktu after we returned from the campaigns in Taghaza. There was One Eye, the albino archery commander and part-time mercenary who, during peacetime, sold his military skills as a caravaneer, helping to protect the countless caravans that traversed the treacherous northern deserts. There was Babayaro, the immigrant from a southern kingdom, who had been recruited as a mercenary along with a thousand others, but had been asked to stay in the army by his commander as an infantry officer. There was also Jeevas, the cavalry officer. Lastly, there was the beautiful scout, Shang, who was the only female in the military, and who was also rumored to be the lover of Jeevas, though no one knew for certain.

***

"Commander Drabo?" Gans interrupted me as the child eeid and I readied to depart for Djedeba.

"What do you want?" I asked.

"You take good care of the child," he said.

I looked at the child eeid. Everyone seemed to like her but me. And she appeared to like everyone but me.

"I'll try," I said.

Aided by the Red Sentinels, the child eeid and I loaded our supplies onto our horses, freshly provided from the emperor's stables. The supplies were light, consisting mostly of food and a portable tent made of cloth and sheepskin coated with tar and bee wax.

It was soon time for me to say goodbye to Lili. I did not know what to say to her. I felt a sadness that put me at a loss for words, for there was a possibility that this would be the last time I ever saw her. She hugged and kissed the child eeid. But I could not say goodbye to Lili. I could not bring myself to do it. We stared at each other for a while, our eyes seeming to say it all, that we were two people who cared deeply for each other but feared to admit the possibility of a future for us that might never come. The child eeid and I then rode away towards Djedeba, and as we did so, I looked back and saw Lili fade away into the horizon. So it was that I parted from her, my Lili, without a word.

As I examined the growing misery all around me as we rode through Timbuktu, I sensed that the quest for this second orb would be different. Not like the first. It would take us into a world of its own.

I could never have imagined the perils that awaited us.

***

The child eeid and I said very little to each other during our travels, speaking only when our task demanded it, our distrust for each other ensuring such a mood. After three days of riding we arrived at the town of Do. Do had been a nice little town before these harsh times, famous for its excellent hunters and rare meats. Most buildings in the town were circular brick houses with conical-shaped thatched roofs. A large bread-making oven stood in the middle of every compound, with each compound consisting of three to ten houses depending on the wealth of its owner. The inns, most of which were story-buildings constructed out of limestone and mud bricks, had served the most delicious meals, packed with the finest wild meats that the hunters could find. Deer, wild fowl, grass cutters, and rat moles were only a few examples. We arrived at the town on a market day, when it would have been packed with traders and buyers. But now it was different. The number of people present at the market was almost halved, for there were fewer people to buy and even fewer goods to be sold, the crops having been hit hard by the harsh times. But still there were some here who had decided to go on living, who had so far managed to ignore these rough times. Some of these were traders in metals who were also heading to Djedeba, as we were.

We decided to spend the night at an inn in Do, where I hoped to eat some wild meat, if any could be found. We were served with a meal which looked and tasted quite strange, yet was wholesomely delicious. It was raw viper served on a plate of well-boiled pig intestines and fried camel testicles. It cost me sixteen gold dinars.

As I enjoyed my meal, what I thought was a brilliant idea hit me. Many of the traders here in Do, and at the inn, were going to Djedeba to trade in metals. Surely they could tell us what town produced the best steel used in weapon making. That way, we could cut our journey short and not have to travel all the way to Djedeba. Many of these traders bought raw iron and took it to the steel-making towns to have it purified, made into weapons, and sold for profit.

"Waste of time," the witch said to me when I suggested my idea. "No steel trader would tell you the best steel-making towns. There are already too many traders in business. They would not like to see you become another competitor."

She was right. The production of steel was a closely guarded secret, having been learned, according to the witch, from the kingdom of the Abyssinians, who live far to the East and worship the Nazarene prophet. They, too, had learned this rare skill from others—from a tribe of people known as the Haya, who reside many leagues to the south of their kingdom. So our best course of action remained going to Djedeba to talk to the miners themselves, who would sell information to anyone willing to pay.

A few moments later, as we continued our meal, I noticed something quite troubling, but I chose to ignore it. It could not possibly be true. It was someone who was not supposed to be there. He was watching the eeid and me, but quickly disappeared behind a pillar upon realizing that he may have attracted my attention. So I pretended not to have seen him at all.

He was one of Gans's Red Sentinels.

But what was he doing here? I recognized him because I had seen him among the emperor's guard detail before. Why was he following me? Was the emperor or the Table keeping an eye on me? Or was Gans the one behind this? I considered confronting the Red Sentinel to demand answers. But I chose to exercise restraint, resolving to know how far he would follow me and how many others he had with him. So I ignored him for the moment, dismissing his presence as a coincidence of little significance and choosing not to let his presence worry me. The only people I worried about who could be following me, and I was quite surprised not to have encountered any yet, were the widow's Horsemen of Diaghan—the fiercest and most fiendishly efficient butchers in these parts, known to have a voracious appetite for death. Why had they not come after me and the child eeid yet? Where were they?

***

WE MET MANY PEOPLE ALONG the way to Djedeba—traders, farmers, fishermen, and even miners heading to or from Djedeba. I remained highly suspicious of the child eeid, and I hoped that she was not leading me into a trap, and that she did not have any nasty designs of her own on what to do with the White Shadow if we captured it. She was very bitter towards me for not giving her time to mourn her father and sister after their slaying in the Birdman's Library. But who cared? She was an eeid, and as far as I was concerned, she was a diabolical fiend not deserving of pity from me or anyone else.

Three days before our arrival in Djedeba, the eeid and I stopped for a rest by a drying well where many a traveler usually stopped to rest and water their horses. This was also time for me to update my journal and reflect on other matters that bothered me. Besides the constant state of fear I lived in because of my close company with the child eeid, I continued to wonder why the Table had chosen me for this task, and even more why the Elders had declined to tell me the reason. What were they hiding? What was the fourth riddle of Tichiman, that which the Table had solved but would let neither the child eeid nor me know what it was?

At least I was alive, but for how much longer? Would the child eeid, who hated me like no other, suddenly cast a death or crippling spell upon me Or would I be slain or captured by the Dark Widow's forces in the ongoing civil war? My only comfort and escape from worry was my journal, which I continued to update daily, determined to write about my adventures and entertain future readers, and prove to the scholars in Timbuktu that not all writing was supposed to be about religion, philosophy, the sciences, or some other treacherously boring subject. People could also read to be entertained.

But all the while I thought of the only two people besides Lili whom I had loved in the world—my grandmother and my aunt, Jama. I wished I could share my story with them. I wished I could make them proud by letting them know that I was now in the direct service of the emperor and his Table. Most importantly, I wished they were here so that I could unravel the secret they had taken with them to the grave—the secret of my mother's identity and why they had kept me from knowing her. But one way or another I was going to find her. As soon as my assignment was completed, I intended to use the fame and fortune that was certain to come to seek her out, whether she was dead or alive.

***

MOST TRAVELERS, LIKE THOSE AT the rest stop, traveled in caravans, packed together in order to safeguard themselves from the increasing numbers of bandits who roamed the area like never before, searching now not for gold, but for food. Lord Venga's evil was on the move, sweeping across the land and changing people for the worse, both in mind and body. One of the caravans that came through was composed of traders returning to their homes in Kangaba after a fruitless search for goods to buy. The child eeid talked to one of the traders and learned that when the traders had gone to the market town of Sibi, they found that most of the residents there had contracted some kind of plague and therefore no business could be conducted. They had turned away in panic.

The plague. As terrifying as Lord Venga himself, this peril had slowly been spreading across the empire for some weeks past. The child eeid was always confident she was not going to contract it. She always ate a special root she had blessed with charms from her Third Shadow, claiming that that helped to prevent her from catching the dreaded illness. Because she did it, and I really had nothing to lose, I ate this root too. Since the first reports of the plague had reached Timbuktu, she had also asked the emperor to issue a declaration asking citizens to eat as much of this root as possible, wherever it could be found. I ate so much of it that the mere sight or thought of it made me nauseous, but still I ate it, because the sight of plague victims was even more nauseating. Although I despised this little witch, I still trusted in her powers. After all, the emperor's night blindness seemed to be getting better ever since he had started eating the raw liver of an ass as instructed by her.

So I, too, decided to eat this odorous root wherever I could find it in order to prevent myself from catching the plague.

The root was garlic—simple, ordinary, raw garlic.

For our rest I set up our tent under a huge baobab tree. We both sat outside the tent in order to enjoy what little amount of sunlight was left, the dark clouds covering up more and more of the sky as the days rolled by.

Not long after we had begun our rest, another trade caravan came through. The child eeid was always in the habit of talking to travelers about the lands they had visited, and even about their lives and professions. She always seemed eager to learn things about different peoples and different places. This puzzled me, because she was supposed to know most of these things naturally, through the powers of her Third Shadow. Maybe she was only a different kind of eeid. She talked to a party of goat herders about the habits of their animals; she spoke to a struggling, desperate farmer about the planting seasons; she spoke to a doctor about headaches; she spoke to a group of musicians who were keeping up the spirit of the caravan with what little music they could provide, wanting to know from them what their instruments were called and how they were made. She got her answers. But after she noticed that this caravan had an unusually high number of women and children, she thought something else was amiss.

This was not a trade caravan. It was an evacuation.

"From what do you flee?" she asked one of the men in the caravan.

"It's the flood!" a man traveling with his wife and two young children said. "The River of Singers, too, is angry with the times. It swept away our village and took many a man, woman, and child with it. Bandits and rebels from the Dark Widow's army have shown us no mercy either. They have looted and destroyed what was left."

"It is sad," the witch sympathized.

"Indeed it is. Nothing is the same in Mali anymore. We hear of plagues, diseases, banditry, and war everywhere. Yet the emperor does nothing."

"He, too, struggles," I said, trying to keep the child eeid away from any conversations with strangers. "He worries about himself and all others within the empire."

"He should do more," said the man, lifting one of his young children in his arms. "I want a world safe for my children."

"So where are you headed?" the witch asked him.

"Many of us do not know where we are going," the man said. "We just want to get away, to some place where peace can be found. But for me, I am going to Timbuktu with my family. I have a brother there working as a builder."

"Timbuktu does not look too good either, man," the child eeid said to him.

"So you are from Timbuktu?" the man said to the eeid excitedly. "I thought I recognized you. Are you not the little sister of Feidi, the eeid in the Birdman's Library?"

"I am," the child eeid responded, suddenly saddened. "She is dead—murdered."

"May she rest easy," the traveler consoled her. "Mali is changing for the worse. Once the safest place in the land, it is today no safer than a crocodile's jaws."

"Mali will again become what it once was," she said confidently.

"They say you, too, may grow up to be as good an eeid as your sister."

"Some say that, I've heard."

Then the traveler suddenly became excited. "May I bother you for a favor, child?" he asked. "I have gold. I'll pay you if you will help me with a predicament I have lately found myself in. You are the only eeid I may see before I arrive in Timbuktu."

"Keep your gold, traveler. You and your family will need it more. But I will help you with your troubles."

"You are as kind and as wise as your sister," the traveler said kindly, bringing a rare smile to the witch's face.

"Come into my tent." The child eeid led the man into our tent to help bring an end to his troubles. I had no worries with this. After all, she was an eeid and that was part of her work. But I thought she should have taken the gold. I followed them into the tent and stood by its entrance as the two sat down to face each other. The traveler's wife and two young children waited outside with the rest of the caravan, whose members were resting, watering their horses, and struggling to fill their gourds with water from the drying well.

"So," the eeid said to the traveler, "what troubles you?"

The man cleared his throat. "It is an old dream, young miss, begun after I committed a deed so grave. I killed a man on a lake thirty days past. I killed him because he tried to kill me. The village council cleared me of any wrongdoing because I had acted to preserve my own life. But every time I try to sleep I see his face. He haunts me in my sleep, in my dreams. I cannot sleep. I believe his mother has cast a wicked spell upon me to torment me to my grave. That is my predicament, child."

Sobo Ha-Ha Speaks

chapter 28

WITH THE AID OF NOO and some associates in my service, I had located the child eeid and her guardian soldier heading towards Djedeba. They were set up next to a caravan of several hundred villagers who were fleeing from the floods, bandits, and rebels who had ravaged their village. This was a caravan I had joined, pretending to be one of the villagers with a wife and two young children. My companions were actually a woman and her two children whom I had paid to accompany me. I was a false traveler pretending to be tormented by bad dreams and nightmares after murdering a man, and now seeking the help of the child eeid to rid me of that false ailment. She and the soldier had fallen for my trick, and I was about to find out the path her Third Shadow walked so that I could destroy it and be rid forever of the threat she posed to Lord Venga's cause. It was a perfect plan.

The child eeid had declined my payment in gold, so I paid her, as it was said her sister had preferred, with books—two books about an ancient conqueror beyond the northern sandy sea named Alexander. This payment she gladly accepted.

"When was it last that you had this dream, traveler?" the child eeid asked me, clutching a doll which she seemed to always carry with her, as she attempted to heal me of my false predicament.

"Last night, child," I said. "It destroys me."

"I will help you."

I was pleased that my plan was working. The soldier stood by the tent's entrance, keeping a close eye on me. I toyed with the idea of telling him why he had been the one chosen for the task he was undertaking, but decided against it in keeping with the high lady's wishes. Besides, I was about to destroy the child eeid's Third Shadow, ending the menace from her and the soldier forever.

"Do you know the mother of the man you killed?" the eeid asked me.

"I see her every day. I do not like the way she looks at me. But I believe she hired the eeid who cast this spell on me, to torment me to the end of my days."

In truth, I had gotten one of the lesser eeids in the widow's service to cast a minor spell of the mind on me. Just as the powerful eeid Kubai-chek had done in Segou, I hoped that in trying to heal me of my illness, Aida would expose the path of her Third Shadow, enabling me to infiltrate the plane of Shadows and destroy her Third Shadow.

The child eeid closed her eyes to meditate and call on the powers of her Third Shadow. That was my moment. I prepared myself.

She began her eeidic chant.

But something was horribly wrong.

Many a time I had been able to infiltrate the plane of Shadows seconds after the chanting and meditating began. But this time was different. I was unable to, even after several attempts. How could this be? I silently called upon the most potent of my powers. Still she did not react as I expected, my Third Shadow proving completely useless. So I tried again, but still failed to locate the path of her Third Shadow. I might as well have been trying to locate the Third Shadow of a dead ox.

Then the child eeid stopped her meditation. I had lost my chances of destroying her Third Shadow. This had not happened to me in years. Not to Sobo Ha-ha, the high eeid of Tera-Hool.

Then the child eeid calmed and relaxed herself, informing me that she had a cure for my nightmares and torments, a remedy for my ailment.

"Face your fears, traveler," she said to me. "Only when you overcome your fears will the dark spell that torments you be undone."

"I do not get your meaning, child," I said to her, trying to sound as legitimate as possible, and hoping she would again be forced to summon the powers of her Third Shadow, giving me another chance to destroy it.

"Your ailment is guilt," the child eeid continued. "Face the mother of the man you slew. Tell her you did what had to be done to preserve your own life. Tell her you wish the outcome could have been different. Seek her forgiveness, for it will end the nightmares that torment you so that you may go to your grave a peaceful man."

The child eeid had provided a remedy for my false predicament. She was right. If indeed I faced the torment I had described to her, her remedy would have healed me. She had not healed me, but she had summoned her Third Shadow to grant me a means of healing myself.

But why had I been unable to locate the path of her Third Shadow? Then a thought hit me. It had to do with the doll she had with her. The one she always took along with her wherever she went. Maybe it held a different mold of her Third Shadow, just like the orbs of Tichiman held the White Shadow. If I could get a hold of the doll for just a moment, I could destroy the Third Shadow in it with just a simple, silent chant. But how could I separate an eeid from the object that held her Third Shadow? Well, she may have been an eeid but she was still a child at heart, so I tried to appeal to her childlike emotions.

"My daughters," I said to her, referring to the young children whom Aida and the soldier assumed were mine. "I would like to make for them dolls as fine as yours. They will cherish that very much."

"Thank you," the child eeid said. "My sister made it."

"It is beautiful. May I see it?"

Believing me to be only a weary traveler, the child eeid gave me her doll, the object that certainly held a mold of her Third Shadow, putting it right into my hands. That was all I needed.

I was again ready to cause her demise.

I proceeded to utter a silent chant intended to wreak permanent destruction on the child eeid's Third Shadow. But this was not to be. Something was again amiss. I again could not locate the path of her Third Shadow in the path of Shadows. I could not even sense her Third Shadow in the doll. I returned it to her.

"Did you like the doll?" she asked.

"Y-yes," I managed to blurt, trying to hold myself together, my inability to destroy her Third Shadow almost unnerving me. I looked at the soldier and again considered informing him why he had been chosen to find the orbs, hoping that knowledge of that information would cause him to aid me in my current predicament and perhaps lead him to our side. But I dared not go against the high lady's wishes, who had perhaps rightly determined that giving the soldier such information could have unpredictable results, too unpredictable to be risked. So again I let it be, instead focusing more on the problem at hand—the child eeid's Third Shadow. Why was I unable to destroy it, even though she had exposed its path to me? I could find it neither within her meditation nor within her cherished doll.

Then the answer hit me like a thunderbolt. I suddenly understood why I could not destroy her Third Shadow. Neither I nor anyone else, eeid or raw-breed, could destroy her Third Shadow, not even with all the combined dark forces of all the eeids in the land. I could scarcely believe it! There was much more to this child than met the eyes. The high lady would be as baffled as I was, I knew, and would understand why the child was all-powerful.

But first I had to do what had to be done. If the child's Third Shadow could not be destroyed, she herself had to be destroyed. I had to kill her. I therefore put my hand inside my cloak, reaching for the dagger hidden beneath it. I felt the blade, itching to spill the blood of the little one who had caused the high lady so much worry and could cause much more if she was not destroyed now.

I was about to pull out the dagger when my eye caught the image of her guardian soldier, Gyvan Drabo, standing next to the entrance to the tent, his exposed sword threateningly glittering as he sharpened its menacing edges.

"Are you well, traveler?" Aida asked me, sensing my uneasiness.

"Yes. I am just thankful that my ordeal will soon be over."

"You may go now, sir. Do as I say, and your ordeal will end."

"I am grateful, child."

I once again tried to secretly reach for the dagger hidden under my cloak, but then I saw Aida's guardian soldier, this time looking straight at me, his eyes gazing at my every move as if suspecting my true intention.

I had to leave. I had failed. I now knew why I could not destroy Aida's Third Shadow. The high lady was going to be just as shocked as I was at the reason.

The Soldier's Tale

chapteʀ 29

I HAD BEEN STARING AT the traveler for a while as the child eeid helped him with his troubles. His voice and his looks were becoming more and more familiar as time went by. I soon began to suspect his intentions after I realized his beard was false. But I was able to recognize him only when he began to walk out. When he got to me at the door, I stopped him, my hand ready to put my sword to work within a split second.

"Sobo Ha-ha?" I called his name.

"Gyvan Drabo," he, too, called my name, and smiled. "I thought you wouldn't recognize me."

"I'll always recognize the eeid voice that called out the thunderstorms that routed the emperor's army at the frontlines of Selegugu two summers past, old man," I said to him, recalling his deed that had cost the emperor several hundred men, and had almost cost him a battle against the Dark Widow's husband, Fadiga.

"That was war, Commander," he said. "I was only trying to survive in this world like anyone else, with my family." He pointed towards the woman and young children he was traveling with, still trying to play the innocent traveler and hide his true intentions.

"Why do you, an eeid, need the help of another eeid to end your illness?"

"Because he suffers from no illness, soldier of Timbuktu," the child eeid jumped in. I turned around to look at her.

"What did he want, then?" I asked the child eeid.

"To destroy my Third Shadow," she said.

At this moment I instantly knew that Sobo Ha-ha was the eeid who had destroyed the Third Shadow of Kubai-chek. I was particularly upset about this because had Kubai-chek's powers not been destroyed, it would be him on this mission with me, and not this annoying little witch who spent half her day talking to a doll. I turned around to address Sobo Ha-ha, but he had simply vanished without a trace. I could not find him anywhere. I pulled out my sword and hurried to the family that had accompanied him. They said they did not know where he was. They barely even knew him. He had simply joined them on the trip and paid them some gold to let him accompany them. I returned to the tent, where the child eeid was busy playing with her doll.

"Your Third Shadow. Did he destroy it?" I asked.

"No," she said simply.

I left it at that, somewhat pleased that she still had the Third Shadow that I desperately needed to help me complete my task. But I feared her even more now. If Sobo Ha-ha had succeeded in destroying the Third Shadow of Kubai-chek, an eeid believed to be one of the most powerful, but then had failed to destroy that of the child eeid, then she was powerful indeed. What was the path of her Third Shadow? Where did her powers come from? She was to be dreaded.

Sobo Ha-Ha Speaks

chapter 30

I RETURNED TO THE WIDOW's stronghold of Tera-Hool in all haste. I had failed to destroy the powers of the little girl for reasons that the widow was about to find out. I had also failed to kill her because of the presence of her guardian soldier. As for him, I could not even for one moment consider killing him during our encounter without a substantial risk to my health, on account of his reputed quickness with the sword.

When I walked into the high lady's court she was planning an attack on the imperial troops besieging her forces at Djenné. Among the officials at hand were Lord Elcan and Commander Abdoulaye Malouda of the Watchmen of Tera-Hool, whose loyalties lay with protecting the ruler of Tera-Hool.

Once again I interrupted them as I had done many a time before.

"My lord, Sobo Ha-ha," Lord Elcan said to me, "you do not look in good spirits."

"My lady," I addressed the high lady, "we have trouble."

"Talk," she demanded.

I hesitated a moment, trying to conceive of the best way to relay to the widow what I had just learned about the little girl, Aida. I was most disturbed because the widow would now have to dispatch some of her precious Horsemen to hunt down and destroy the girl, diverting resources from her assault aimed at relieving her besieged troops at Djenné.

"Speak up, High Eeid of Tera-Hool," she scolded. "What has shaken you so?"

Yes, indeed I was shaken, uncertain of how the high lady was going to receive the information I was about to deliver about a deep dark secret the eeid held, a secret that made the destruction of her Third Shadow impossible.

"My lady," I began, somewhat nervously, "what I have learned about the girl is so grave it will have to be for your ears only."

With a snap of her fingers her guards, military commanders, and everyone else vacated the room in a flash.

"Come forward, then," the widow ordered me. I walked over to her and whispered to her what I had just learned about Aida, the child eeid from Traoré.

"It does not make sense," the widow commented, puzzled by the information I had just delivered to her.

"My lady, it makes perfect sense to all eeids."

The high lady clapped her hands, and her guards and military commanders returned to the room, a puzzled look on all their faces, surely wanting to know too what I had learned about the little girl and why it had made me unable to destroy her powers.

"That little girl is the only thing that stands in our way now," the widow thought aloud, pacing across the room.

"So, High Eeid," Lord Elcan began, wanting to know what I had just told the high lady, "by the look of things I see you have failed to destroy the child eeid's Third Shadow. What could be the path of her Third Shadow that defeats even our high eeid?"

I did not respond to Lord Elcan. The widow stopped pacing about the room. She raised her eyes and looked at Lord Elcan sternly. Then she uttered the words he had been waiting for.

"Unleash the Horsemen!"

The Words Of The Child Eeid

chapteR 31

THE SOLDIER SEEMED EVEN MORE terrified of me now that the great Sobo Ha-ha himself had failed to destroy my Third Shadow. He began to increase the distance he kept from me but did not keep his eyes away from me. Yet he had to protect me even more now since he knew that Sobo Ha-ha and others working with him could return. I was delighted that he feared me. Anything I could do to make his life more miserable was welcomed. A man who had whisked me away after my father and sister died, without giving them a proper funeral or letting me pay my respects, I had no love or forgiveness for. The only good thing he had done so far was letting me keep my dear doll, which was my only comfort, and I knew he hated it. Because he hated when I talked to the doll, I talked to it even more.

We were one day away from Djedeba when we rode through Bonshé, a small village where misery also presented itself on every possible corner. Vultures feasted greedily on what was left of the bodies of three children and a few dead dogs that had starved to death and were strewn about the streets. As we rode through, it was quite strange that no one came out of their stone houses to beg us for food. They seemed to be hiding not from us, but from someone or something frightening that was in their midst!

What was amiss? The soldier stopped his horse and mine. He would go no farther into the village until he understood the source of the terror that he sensed gripped the village. Our horses suddenly became unstable, mine almost throwing me off its back after letting out a deafening neigh. Shaken with fright, I clutched Naya, to protect her and to feel safe. Protecting her was like protecting Feidi, doing what I could not do for her when she was killed in the Birdman's Library.

I looked around and saw several hoofprints in one corner of the road that ran through the village. I touched the soldier and pointed at the hoofprints. He had seen them too.

"Horsemen!" he whispered, a slight tremble in his voice.

The Soldier's Tale

chapter 32

SO THE DARK WIDOW HAD finally unleashed her hordes on us. From the number of hoofprints I could see, I estimated that there were about ten Horsemen in all. I was not going to back down. I had to protect the child eeid, at all costs. After all, it was her they really wanted. This comforted me slightly. Perhaps I could just toss her out to them and be done with it all. But to achieve the glory, fame, fortune, and adventure that I hoped to write about, I had to keep her alive.

I dismounted. And without a word, I pulled her down from her horse and slowly backed away towards a wall, putting my back against it.

"Do you wish to live?" I asked the eeid. She nodded nervously. "Then stay behind me." She hurriedly stepped behind me and clutched her doll tightly.

With the eeid and me backing the wall, I could be sure that no one would attack us from behind. They could only come from the front, where I would be waiting with my sword. We waited for the Horsemen to come, for I knew they were out there somewhere, lying in wait for the right moment to spring a deadly ambush on us. But I was not going to go to them. I was going to have them come to me. Then a short while later, an elaborately dressed man whom I assumed to be an officer of the Horsemen emerged from a house.

"Gyvan Drabo?" the man called.

"What's your story?" I responded.

"I am Lord Elcan. Give us the girl and you may live." This was a tempting offer from Lord Elcan. I looked at the child eeid and briefly considered the offer, but quickly decided against it, for I still had a task to complete.

"I'm very sorry, but you will have to come here and get her yourself," I said.

Lord Elcan was not pleased. He smiled slightly and waved his arms around his head, prompting seventeen well-armed and dismounted

Horsemen of Diaghan to emerge from their hiding places within some of the buildings, not ten as I had believed.

"Before we kill you, child eeid," Lord Elcan taunted, "I am curious to know the path of your Third Shadow, so powerful that the high eeid himself could not destroy it."

"It is more than you or your high eeid could ever understand, Horseman," the child eeid shot back.

Lord Elcan smiled grimly. "You will be dead soon anyway," he threatened. He waved his hand again at the Horsemen, who immediately rushed at me with unimaginable ferocity.

I stood my ground and cut down the attacking Horsemen one by one, defending myself and the child eeid, each time rapidly moving from one house wall to the next, and making sure that my back and hers were always against the wall, so that we were sure that no one could attack us from behind, and that I was only dealing with a frontal assault. Because I could not fight all seventeen opponents at the same time, my success depended on my ability to separate them into small groups, isolate each one, and destroy it.

Soon only Lord Elcan and eight Horsemen were left. Eight were slain. Nine remained who, not having learned their lesson, continued to fight. After a short while another Horsemen dropped dead and the others backed off to reassess their situation, finally realizing the hazard I was posing to their health and understanding just who they were up against.

The child eeid and I were backed up against a wall next to a window when the Horsemen suddenly stopped fighting, lowered their swords, and began to stare at me. Then I realized that they were waiting for something, expecting something from behind me. It was almost too late when I turned around to look at what they were watching. I only felt it behind me. Through a window, one of the Horsemen who had slipped through was just about to jab his sword through my back, but I was quicker. I did not exactly turn around to look at him, but my sword was there to do that, pinning him right through his heart, by way of the open window, dropping him instantly. The survivors, composed of Lord Elcan and six Horsemen, scrambled, mounted their horses, and fled with their lives, another testament to my superior skill with the sword, even against the notorious Horsemen of Diaghan.

I sheathed my sword and uttered a sigh of relief. It was over! At least that is what I believed. But it was not so, for a sudden, terrifyingly loud shrill from the child eeid broke my relief. Believing she had been attacked, my sword was out of its sheath in a split second. But I saw no threat.

"They are gone," I assured her. "The Horsemen are not coming back."

But her worry was not the Horsemen. It was something else.

"They took Naya!" she continued screaming.

"They what?" I retorted, quite upset with the tumult she was causing over a doll.

"They took her. You have to get her back!"

"You must be crazed in the head, witch," I snapped. "I will risk my life for no doll."

Then she turned to me and said in a voice so stern it put quite a shiver through me, "She is not just a doll!"

But as far as I was concerned it was just a doll and I was not going to go after the Horsemen in order to get it, and that was the end of it.

"Forget that doll," I scolded the eeid. "I will buy you another."

"I do not want another. I want Naya!"

"Then you can go and get her yourself."

"Help, me, please. Help me, Gyvan."

Gyvan. That was the first time she had ever called my name. But I could not risk my life or the security of our task for a doll.

"There will be no more talk of the doll," I warned.

Giving in and realizing that her pleas were getting nowhere, the child eeid sank into a deep despair for the remainder of the night. I decided that we spend the night in the village where the Horsemen had attacked us, for I did not want to risk traveling at night in case there was another ambush waiting for us. But I remained mindful of returning Horsemen bent on leveling lethal vengeance upon us. The villagers could not help me with any defenses, for they had problems of their own, too insurmountable to worry about my safety or that of the child eeid. They were, however, willing to loan me two houses for the night in exchange for a rare and badly needed item—meat, horsemeat, from the horses left behind by the Horsemen I had just slain.

The famine was so bad here that it was said that a woman of the village had lately died after cutting off her own breasts and cooking them in order to feed her children.

***

I STOOD IN FRONT OF one of the two houses I had been loaned in the village of Bonshé, where I had just had my first encounter with the Dark Widow's Horsemen. There I harnessed my horse and the child eeid's. In the other house, which stood across the street from the first, the child eeid and I rested. Any returning Horsemen would be fooled by the presence of our horses in the first house, I hoped, and would search for us in it. There, I had placed an ingenious contraption of pots and pans, the slightest disturbance of which was to cause it to collapse into a noisy, clanking pile, alerting me to the presence of intruders.

The child eeid and I lay in the same room, each of us on a separate wooden bed. My sword and wrist knife were unsheathed, not only in readiness for the possible Horsemen attack, but also in readiness against the child eeid, now horribly cross with me for declining to retrieve her doll. For me, danger lurked beyond and within the confines of the room in which I lay.

But in the midst of all the danger, I began to feel something I had never really felt before—pity. It was pity not for me, not for the poor and starving villagers, and not for the countless plague victims dying across the empire. It was pity for the child eeid. She appeared lost and even more misery-stricken without her cherished doll. Surprisingly, I found myself trying to think of something to say that could appease her and lift up her spirits, much like a mother or father would want to say to a crying child. But I could find no words. She cried herself to sleep, very likely damning me in her dreams or nightmares. I looked at her in her slumber, her smooth, baby-like face partially visibly through the moonlight that came in through a crack in the closed window. I had never felt so bad about my actions before. For reasons I never could comprehend, I began to feel what my beloved Lili had said to me of the child eeid: "Eeid or not, a child remains a child." And like all children, she needed nurturing.

So it was that for the first time I put myself in the child's place and decided to forget that she was an eeid. I attempted to see only the little girl in her—the child in her. Her recent ordeal came to mind—the death of her father and sister, how she had been deprived of a chance to wish them farewell; the loss of her doll—the only possession and true friend left to her, snatched away by people who were trying to kill her. And worst of all, she was spending all of her time with me, a soldier who had made it clear to her that she meant nothing whatsoever, and would outlive her usefulness upon the retrieval of the second Tichiman orb.

The innocence of the child eeid had gotten to me. To this day I know not why I decided to undertake the actions that followed, but all I know is that I did undertake them for good reason, to bring some solace to a child under attack in a brutal and hostile world.

I made the decision to get her doll back.

It was the only friend she had, and although I had been alone with her for many weeks, she still did not consider me her friend, perhaps because I had not given her the chance. But all I can say is that I had a feeling such as I had never had before when I looked into her eyes before she went to sleep that night, for the first time without her most loved and trusted friend, Naya.

While she slept I informed the village chief that I was leaving for a short while and would be back before dawn. Should the child wake up, she was to be informed thus. I sharpened my sword and mounted my horse. This was a daring mission I was willing to risk undertaking if only it could make the child eeid happy.

As I tracked down the Horsemen using the hoofprints left by their horses, I also searched the roads for any signs of the doll had they happened to toss it away. But why did they want the doll? Perhaps to show the Dark Widow how close they had come to destroying the child eeid.

After a few hours I spotted the Horsemen, the six survivors of our skirmish. They were resting near a campfire they had built, roasting an unfortunate cat they had seized from a village girl. I dismounted and walked calmly over to them with my sword still sheathed. I made no attempt to hide myself or my intentions. These men were going to give me the doll and live, or they were going to give it to me unwillingly and die.

As I approached them, all six, including their leader, Lord Elcan, failed to notice my presence until I was about twelve paces away from them. Startled, they instantly stopped what they were doing and briefly stared at me in terrified perplexity, dazzled by my daring and baffled as to my intentions. They cautiously stood up, slowly drawing out their swords one by one, but none yet daring to step forward to face me, even though my sword remained sheathed. Only when Lord Elcan walked forward did the others dare approach.

"All I want is the doll," I said.

"It is right here," Lord Elcan said, pointing at it where it lay next to some saddles. "I'm very sorry, but you will have to come here and get it yourself."

"And that I will," I said, instantly drawing my sword, my blood now boiling.

The child eeid's fight had become mine. I had hardly ever fought in anger, but this time I was going to fight because I was extraordinarily furious that these cowards had made a child upset. The fight was a very personal matter. I unsheathed my wrist knife too, hoping to have these demons close and looking them straight in their eyes as they took their last breaths.

Without warning, and before giving them a chance to brace themselves for an assault, I charged at the Horsemen with all the intensity in the world. They were no match for me at all in my current state of extreme anger. Within moments, all were dead or dying except Lord Elcan, who had simply vanished, no doubt having slipped away in the middle of the butchery.

The Words Of The Child Eeid

chapter 33

THROUGHOUT THE NIGHT I DREAMT of my father and sister. I hoped they were now in some place better than this cruel Earth. I also dreamt of Naya, my doll, the last thing I had had to remind me of them. Like my father and sister, she too had been untimely taken away from me. And once again the appalling soldier had been unwilling to help me ease the intolerable pain that came with the loss. I thought of the Horsemen who had taken poor Naya away. I wished them no ill, but prayed they would treat Naya well.

I awoke at dawn, knowing not what calamity or grace the day would bring. The soldier as usual, was awake, keeping a watchful eye on me as he always did. But it was not he I concerned myself with at that instant. It was the object that lay on the floor beside me that suddenly caught my attention. Was I seeing what I thought I was seeing? Yes, yes, I was! My pains instantly faded away. It was Naya. She was back! But how did she get here? Then I looked at the soldier. He had a slight wound on his head that had not been there before.

"Thank you," I said sincerely. "Thank you for bringing Naya back, Gyvan."

"Anything that comforts you, comforts me, Aida," he said softly and sweetly as he had never done before.

Aida. That was the first time he had ever called my name.

The Soldier's Tale

chapter 34

THANK YOU FOR BRINGING NAYA back, Gyvan. That was the first time anyone had ever sincerely thanked me for anything. Looking at Aida at that moment, seeing her clutching Naya like it was the only thing that made life meaningful to her, seeing just a little girl who needed to be cared for, I was overcome by a feeling I could not immediately discern—love. I loved and felt loved like she was my own flesh and blood, like she was the daughter I did not have but perhaps needed. I was finally friends with Aida, the child eeid, my companion for these many weeks past.

She was crying, a happy cry, with little drops of tears flowing from her eyes. Maybe it was a spell she had cast on me, I thought. And if it was then it was a good one. We looked at each other, and for the first time, we smiled.

The Words Of The Child Eeid

chapter 35

FROM THAT MOMENT ON, I no longer regarded Gyvan Drabo as a selfish man out only to achieve glory for himself in order to be on the good side of the emperor, nor did I anymore think of him as something that had dropped from a dog's behind. I now saw simply a man caught up in the times and circumstances, and one who was going to be there for me in times of need. I felt bad for some of the troubles I may have caused him so far. However, I still had one question for him, and I hoped it would not now spoil the mood.

"Gyvan," I asked, "do you know where my father and sister were buried?"

He paused, and then responded, "While you slept at Lili's I returned to the Birdman's Library to see that they received a proper burial. They were buried right next to my grandmother and my aunt. I did that so that my grandmother and aunt could look after them and take care of them in the life beyond ours."

"Where are they interred?" I inquired.

"In Timbuktu. In one of the best areas of the city you can find. Seeing them properly laid to rest was the noble thing to do. I did not let you attend the burial because I did not believe you could handle the pain."

The Soldier's Tale

chapter 36

I WAS QUITE MOVED BY Aida's understanding of my actions after the slaying of her father and sister. Despite the great wrong I had done to her she chose to lay no fault on me.

Then I said to her truthfully, "I never told you I was sorry for their deaths." There was a long pause as Aida listened intensely to these long awaited words of condolence from me. "Now I feel like I knew them, like he was my father and she was my sister." I paused again, then took her hand in mine before continuing. "I want you to know that if ever you are in need of a father in your life, I will be here. I may not be the best father in the world, but I will do my best to be the best father to you. And if you are ever in need of a mother, Lili will be delighted to help you there." She threw herself into my arms in our newfound friendship.

It had been two days since the Horseman attack, but even though I now saw not the eeid in Aida, but the little girl in her, I still thought it better to know everything there was to know about her, so that I could protect her better. I had to know the path of her Third Shadow, partly for security concerns, and quite honestly, out of a curiosity aroused after the failure of the high eeid to destroy her Third Shadow. Even though we were now amicable, I understood that Aida was still an eeid and a wrong move on my part could lead to deadly consequences for me, for asking an eeid about the path of her Third Shadow could provoke immediate suspicion that the questioner wanted the information in order to harm her or sell it to a rival eeid. I was willing to risk asking her anyway, and I was ready to bear any consequences that could arise. However, I could not now bring myself to do any kind of harm to Aida, even if her response to my question became deadly, as could be expected. This was because in her I now saw only a little girl whom I loved as a father would love a daughter, and with whom I had shared all manner of misery and faced death these many weeks past. I therefore put my sword away so that I would be unable to use it on her in case her reaction to my impending inquiry became violent.

"So what is the path of your Third Shadow?" I asked abruptly.

A smile faded from her face. She shot me a look so diabolical only the devil could describe it. It was a cold, deathly stare!

Sobo Ha-Ha Speaks

chapter 37

THE HIGH LADY, COMMANDER MALOUDA, and some of her officials and engineers were reviewing plans for the defense of Tera-Hool, expecting an attack from imperial forces, when Lord Elcan walked in. His large, round face bore a low and humiliated look. The high lady took a single look at him and guessed his circumstances.

"Did your Horsemen fail at Bonshé, Commander Elcan?" she asked in a low, stern tone.

"The soldier was strong, my lady," Lord Elcan defended. "Neither I nor my Horsemen could best him or the child eeid."

"My high eeid failed to destroy her," the widow lamented, "and now my best soldiers also fail me."

"Maybe it was the power of the child eeid's Third Shadow."

"No, that could not have been possible!"

The high lady was right. It could not have been possible for Aida of Traoré to have used the powers of the Third Shadow to help Gyvan Drabo defeat the Horsemen. The reason for this was the same reason why I had been unable to destroy her Third Shadow.

"My lady," Commander Malouda cautiously began, "may I ask why that would have been impossible, why the child eeid could not have used her Third Shadow?"

"Sobo Ha-ha," the widow called, "why don't you tell the commanders?"

I had to find the right words to explain so that the commanders could fully understand our peril, understand how Aida got her powers, and how they made her even more powerful and dangerous than any eeid I had ever known. It was something about her that no one had expected, not even me. I hesitated before revealing it to the commanders, the deep, dark, and completely unexpected secret the little girl held.

"So, Sobo Ha-ha," Commander Malouda pressed on, "what is so special about this child that terrifies you so?"

I again hesitated, not sure of how to word my response.

"The little girl, Sobo Ha-ha?" Lord Elcan reiterated.

"An eeid can only destroy the Third Shadow of another eeid," I began.

"So?" Lord Elcan asked.

"Aida of Traoré is no eeid," I stated simply.

"What is that supposed to mean?" Lord Elcan asked.

"She has no Third Shadow. I cannot destroy that which does not exist."

A brief moment of silence suddenly hushed the room. It was a moment the commanders used to attempt a complete comprehension of what I had just revealed to them.

"From where then does she acquire her powers?" Commander Malouda managed to inquire soon after. A petrified look was plastered on his face.

"Her powers are not from the realm of the dark arts, but from that of human arts," I responded. "The girl uses the knowledge of logic and experience, such as may be the case with a sage. But she alone seems to bear the knowledge of a hundred sages. Where she obtained such knowledge, I cannot tell."

"It makes no sense," Commander Malouda said.

"I'll make it simple for you, Commander: she is simply intelligent!"

The Soldier's Tale

chapter 38

THE CHILD EEID STARED AT me with a look as cold as death itself. I had asked her the most sacred of questions one could ask an eeid—what the path of her Third Shadow was. Would she ignore my error or would she repay me with a ghoulish spell heaped upon my person? I was ready for the consequences, my sword safely tucked away to prevent my use of it upon the child.

"So what is the path of your Third Shadow?" I asked her again. She remained silent, her cold gaze still fixed on my person.

Then she blinked, smiled, and pointed to her head. "Up here," she said. "In my head."

"In your head?" I asked, puzzled. "I fail to get your meaning, Aida."

"I have no Third Shadow, Commander Drabo."

"Then from where do you acquire your powers?"

"Books, mostly. All I know I learned from books and scrolls of all kinds. And never do I fail to seize an opportunity to carry on a conversation with all manner of people from whom I can learn a thing or two."

I knew not what to make of it all. She was no eeid, she said. All she knew she had read, mostly. I was not fully convinced.

"And your sister?" I asked. "If you are no eeid, what then was she?"

"No eeid either. She and I spent more of our lives in libraries than we did at our home. Most of what we know we learned from the libraries with my father, who was even the head librarian at the Birdman's Library in Timbuktu. Frequent conversations with all manner of travelers, people with all manner of employment who came to my late mother's inn, or people we simply chanced upon, also added to what we know of this world and beyond. Many a traveler we did chance upon—merchants, doctors, soldiers from distant lands, envoys, politicians, and scholars; and many a conversation we did make with them, learning about their lands, countries, places they had visited, their trades, and even their families. Thus has my knowledge been built over these many years past."

"And Breed?" I asked, referring to the language of the raw-breeds, which she had used to address the raw-breed peace agents at least once during our meetings. "How did you gain the knowledge of a tongue so distant and foreign?"

"Two manuscripts in Breed survived here from the Breed Wars. They were destroyed in a fire set during the siege of Timbuktu before I could get a chance to master the tongue."

"And the garlic we have been eating to prevent catching the plague? The raw liver the emperor now eats in order to end his night blindness?"

"All cures I read about while studying the medicines of the pyramid builders in the northern deserts."

Aida was wittier and more intelligent than most indeed, perhaps even more than all. All her strength and knowledge had come from her readings and conversations with all manner of people, stemming from her voracious curiosity and insatiable quest for knowledge, a trend that had begun after her mother's passing, when her father had wanted to learn, along with his daughters, the ever-present mystery of life to death. The more little Aida had read and learned, the more she wanted to read and learn, a desire for knowledge so strong that it had led her and her sister to actually spend most of their lives in libraries. Her sister, after performing her "eeidic" services, had often demanded payment not in gold, as was the case with most eeids, but in books, if it was possible. Aida's love of reading and inquisitiveness had given her knowledge above all others, even eeids.

She was a walking library.

"So the scrolls you read are not eeidic?" I later asked Aida, referring to the scrolls she usually read, which I had once believed contained sacred spells for her Third Shadow.

"No, they are from my family's private collection. My father had over six hundred books and scrolls in his collection, including a few that date back to the eighth century. The book I last read from it was by Ibn Khaldun, a famous Arab traveler I once met when he came to Traoré with a trade caravan from Walata."

"I have read of him. You met him?"

"I have. He ate at my mother's inn and was kind enough to indulge me with knowledge of the fantastic places he had visited."

It was not easy to believe. This child had solved riddles no eeid could solve. She even knew of medicines known only to a few. Yet she claimed to be no eeid.

"So you have no Third Shadow?" I asked again to be sure I had not misunderstood her.

"No, I do not, soldier of Timbuktu," she responded, smiling cockishly, obviously satisfied with her ability at such masterful deception.

"Seriously?"

"Seriously. That is why the high eeid, Sobo Ha-ha, could not destroy my Third Shadow, for I have none to be destroyed."

"How did everyone, even eeids, come to believe you to be an eeid?"

"Because I am cleverer than most, even eeids," she declared loudly, boldly, assuredly, and confidently.

***

THE CHILD AND I ARRIVED in Djedeba some days later, reporting first to the local military garrison where I used the authority of the imperial ring to exchange our tired horses for two fresh ones. Djedeba was no better than Timbuktu. Misery had surfaced here too. Food was scarce and plants would not grow. It was here that a man was said to have killed his son, sliced open his stomach and retrieved and eaten the swallowed remnants of a banana his son had cheated him out of.

We were in Djedeba to learn from the miners what cities that received their iron ore produced the strongest and best steel used in weapon making. It was from that city that we were to find the second orb, according to Aida.

First we had to be fed and rested. We stopped at an inn where a bowl of food which had previously commanded half a gold dinar now commanded a hundred. Pounded sorghum and dried ass meat was all that was available at the inn. It was all that was available anywhere. The very idea of eating ass meat was repulsive to all, but the recent depletion of cattle, goats, and other food supplies had forced the people of Djedeba and elsewhere to begin eating their asses, horses, and even dogs and cats. As a result, we were left with little choice but to settle for the ass meal.

It was while we were eating that I again noticed something that I had noticed some days before but had ignored. It was a Red Sentinel, the same one I had seen at Do. Now he was also in Djedeba, conversing with some sandal makers and likely unaware that he had been spotted.

"There is a man following us," I said to Aida. "A Sentinel."

"I know."

"You know?"

"He has been following us since we last left Timbuktu. I have spotted him at every town we stopped in since."

"I do not believe we have to worry about him. At least he works for the emperor, not the Dark Widow. Or perhaps this is the work of Gans," I suggested.

"Why would he send a Red Sentinel to watch you?"

"He despises me. He hates it that I was chosen for this task and not him."

"I think Gans is a very gentle man," Aida commented.

"Really? Have you heard what people say about him?" I scoffed, not too pleased she had taken a liking to that raving brute.

"Have you heard what people say about you?" she defended that worm.

"People say things about me?"

"Oh yes, Commander Drabo, oh yes."

"Like what?"

"Something about a certain drunken incident in Taghaza."

***

THE TABLE HAD LEFT ME with more questions than answers during our last encounter. Why had I, an ordinary soldier, been chosen for this most important task? Why had the fourth Tichiman riddle, the only one the Table had been able to solve, been kept hidden from me? And now, why were Aida and I being followed by a Red Sentinel? In due time, I chose to believe, all would be answered. So once again I ignored the Red Sentinel following us and continued to enjoy my meal, especially the crunchy, tasty bones of a rat mole's tail.

After our meal, Aida and I rode to the iron mines just outside the city, where we hoped to find part of the answer to the third riddle of Tichiman. We decided that the best way to be sure that the miners were going to give us the right answers was to talk to several mine officials of different mines, asking of them the city that produced the best steel. If we got a similar answer from each, then we could be sure we had gotten the right answer.

Six iron mines operated in the Djedeba region alone. I let Aida do most of the talking, for she knew more of mines and geography than I could ever know. The first mine we came to was the largest in the region. Security was tight here, for it had not yet been one year since rebels under the Dark Widow's deceased husband had attempted to seize it with an army of several thousand. Now, several thousand of the emperor's forces protected the mine and others in the region.

"What place makes the best steel out of the iron you mine?" Aida asked the head mine official after we had introduced ourselves and displayed the imperial ring.

"There is no one place, little one," the official said to Aida. "Traders take the iron to whatever place pays the most at the particular time. It could be Dia, Wagadou, Segou, Do, or Mema." That was the answer we needed for now, at least, according to Aida.

During the next two days, Aida and I visited the five other mines and again were informed by their officials that there was not one single place that produced the best steel. I became slightly frightened. Maybe Aida was wrong this time, because according to her, Tichiman's riddle had pointed out that there could only be one town, but all the mine officials had mentioned Dia, Wagadou, Segou, Do, and Mema as the towns that produced the best steel from the iron mined in Djedeba.

"If there is one thing I am sure of, Commander Drabo," Aida said to me after I voiced my fears, "it is that I am always absolutely correct."

"But we have no answer."

"On the contrary, we now have the answer we need," she said.

"I am listening."

"All the towns that the mine officials have mentioned—Dia, Segou, Do, and Mema, all lie on, close to, or along a river. Or as Tichiman put it in his riddle, "fruits that sprout from branches.""

"They also mentioned Wagadou," I reminded her.

"Exactly. Wagadou is the only one of them that does not lie on, close to, or along a river, or as Tichiman put it in his riddle, it is "a fruit without a branch.""

I smiled. But was Aida right? There was only one way to find out

Next stop, Wagadou.

Sobo Ha-Ha Speaks

chapter 39

MY LOST BATTLE IN THE tent with the little girl had proven one thing: in the battle between the powers of the dark arts of the Third Shadow and the wisdom of man, the latter had prevailed.

Our failure to destroy Aida of Traoré and her guardian soldier weighed heavily on the high lady. The pair had been operating mainly in imperial-held territory, making it extremely risky for the high lady to send a larger force there to destroy them. But she was willing to wait, hoping that it would only be a matter of time before the soldier's quest brought him and the girl into territory her forces controlled.

The situation at Djenné had not changed much for the high lady's forces. But though they still held solidly onto their fortress, the imperial forces were showing no signs of relenting.

"Djenné may soon fall," one of the high lady's commanders stated during a meeting with her war council, which had representatives from all the territories under her control. "Reports indicate our forces may not be able to hold back the imperial troops for much longer."

"What of the imperial troops?" the high lady inquired.

"Their spirits are low," Lord Elcan stated.

"Now is the time to send in reinforcements—the Horsemen," a commander suggested. "If the emperor sees that we have more men to spare, his will to continue the fight may weaken."

"What makes you think he won't send in reinforcements of his own?" Commander Malouda asked.

"His forces are stretched too thin, trying to protect every scrap of land they occupy," Lord Elcan shot back.

"We should hold our Horsemen," another commander suggested. "They remain the only reserves we have. If we throw them into the field and the emperor also throws whatever reserves he may have left, then we may have trouble."

"When do you suggest we use the Horsemen then, Commander Marou?" Lord Elcan asked.

"When we are certain that the number of imperial forces is at their lowest, when our use of the Horsemen can bring us decisive victory," Commander Marou responded.

"Lord Elcan," the high lady called, "your Horsemen will be dispatched to Djenné. They will be put to use harassing the imperial troops besieging the city." With these commanding words the matter was closed.

The Horsemen of Diaghan were going to Djenné.

With the matter of the Horsemen settled, the military officials and other representatives were dismissed to their quarters, save Lord Elcan, Commander Malouda, and me, who were asked by the high lady to stand fast. She had matters to discuss with us regarding the soldier and the little girl. Lord Elcan and I blamed each other for the failure of the destruction of the two, and on this occasion, even raised our voices at each other when the high lady introduced the matter.

"If you, High Eeid," Lord Elcan attacked me, "had killed the girl when you had your chance then we would not be having this conversation."

I attempted a feeble defense. "You know she had no Third Shadow to be destroyed."

"It is not her Third Shadow I talk of, Sobo Ha-ha. I am talking about the dagger you hide under your cloak, the one they say you use so well."

"I intended to use it on the girl, but the glitter of the soldier's blade caught my eyes. And I dared not give him reason to use the weapon, since we have come to realize there may be no man we know, living or dead, able to wield the sword as well as he does."

"You are right," Commander Malouda said. "There may be no *man*, but perhaps there may be a *woman*!"

"Woman?" the widow asked, as baffled as I was.

"Yes, my lady," Commander Malouda stressed. "Woman!"

The Soldier's Tale

chapter 40

AIDA AND I WERE CROSSING the River of Singers on a boat that was ferrying soldiers to a province in the western sector of the empire in response to recent reports of increased rebel activity in the area.

"The empire is falling apart," one of the army officers on the boat said to me in the middle of a heated conversation concerning the empire's destiny.

"Not just the empire," another added, "but the whole world. Nothing remains the same. I've been all over the empire and there seems to be no end to the fighting. Desolation now looms where happiness once thrived. Death lurks everywhere."

"What about Djenné?" I asked the second officer, thinking of my friends—Shang, Jeevas, Babayaro, and One Eye, who were all stationed around the besieged city. "Have you been there lately?"

"Djenné, the widow maker," he lamented. "That was my last post. It is bad."

"What are its conditions like?" I asked.

"The rebels won't give in, the army won't give in. No one is certain whether the city will ever fall. The only thing certain is that men inside and outside its walls will continue to die there every day."

"Will you be going back there?"

"Going to Djenné is a death sentence. Nobody wants to go there. Haven't you heard? Troublesome officers now get assigned to Djenné as retribution for whatever it is they have done." There was a brief pause before he continued. "You see, out there we are not just facing the scourge of the rebels within the city walls. We also get attacked by rebels from the outside, the dreaded Horsemen of Diaghan, who try to distract our forces, hoping to relieve the pressure on the city. The first time those Horsemen appeared, the siege was almost abandoned. Red Sentinels had to be called in to even the odds."

"It's wild, eh?" I added.

"Oh, yes, it is," he said. "Twenty-one days ago I stopped an ambush and saved the life of one of our generals in Djenné. He was so grateful he asked me if there was anything he could do for me. I asked for a transfer out of Djenné without hesitation. He granted it, and now I am here. Poor general. He could not even transfer himself out, but he could transfer out anyone else he desired. He had been sent there for killing his wife's lover and forcing her to bathe in his blood."

The Words Of The Child Eeid

chapteR 41

AFTER CROSSING THE RIVER OF Singers, we parted with the soldiers and rode north to Wagadou. The soldiers had warned us of bandits known to have been prowling about this area recently, since many of the imperial troops who had once been stationed there had been sent to the frontlines.

From the point where the boat dropped us off, it would have taken us only half a day's ride to get to the nearest town, but because I was hungry and tired Gyvan decided that we stop for a meal and a rest. He pitched our tent next to a drying creek, where we enjoyed a good meal of dried beef and bean cakes, a rare luxury which Lili had provided on our last parting.

Some hours later we were ready to carry on. Gyvan pulled down the tent and loaded our supplies onto our horses.

But then something happened.

Just as I was about to mount my horse I heard a whizzing sound through the air, speeding towards me with terrifying speed. It was an arrow, heading straight for me! This was it! My end had come. My hands tightened around Naya tightly and held on to her. I stood motionless, unable to move. I waited for the arrow's sharp, deadly point to make its fatal penetration. But that was not to be. The strong hand of Gyvan Drabo was there at the last possible moment, catching the arrow dead in its path. I was saved!

Then almost instantly I heard another whizzing sound. This time a deadly arrow sped to Gyvan. He still held the first arrow with one hand and had just grabbed me with the other, and could not possibly catch this second arrow as he had done with the first. My heart pounded as the arrow flew closer to its target. With a swift jerk and turn of his body he dodged the arrow and it flew past him, almost grazing his ear.

I looked up and I saw the attackers. Bandits—eight of them. Gyvan did not give them time to send more arrows our way. In a flash his sword sprang out of its sheath and he charged at them single-handedly even before I could fully discern our peril. The bandits, all shirtless, with well-muscled bodies, dropped their bows, pulled out their swords, and charged at him too, all eight of them, towards the single imperial soldier. There was no fear in his eyes. If only those bandits knew what they were up against.

Within seconds two of the bandits were slain, all prey to the sharp sword and rare skill of the soldier. The other six did not give up, and neither did Gyvan. It took the death of one more of them, who fell victim to his wrist knife, for the rest to realize their deadly mistake and flee, understanding that despite their numbers, they were disastrously outmatched by Gyvan.

I ran up to Gyvan and held him tight, not wanting to let him go.

"Little girl," he said smiling, "before anyone gets to you, he will have to come through me. Anyway, you won't have to worry about any more bandits coming after us. I spared the other five so that they could warn their friends to keep away from us."

I caught sight of one of the slain bandits. His face bore unusual discolorations, made no better by the squishy, yellowish liquid that oozed from giant sores that dotted his face and hands.

"It's the plague," Gyvan said, "It's spreading."

***

A SHORT WHILE LATER, WE mounted our horses and continued to Wagadou. We rested that night in a village, where Gyvan informed the town officials of the slain bandits he had left behind. The officials showed little concern, not even bothering to dispose of the bodies. The days were gone when the slightest hint of ill will towards fellow man would have invoked an army of investigators and curiosity from the populace. The days were gone when the carcass of an animal or some hapless human found on the streets or roadside would have been promptly removed, properly cleaned, and disposed of by the authorities. Now so many dead and dying lay scattered along the streets and roads that they seemed to even outnumber the living.

The following day, we departed the village and continued to Wagadou. Just before nightfall, about one day's ride from our destination, we noticed something that stopped Gyvan dead in his tracks. Never had I seen him so horrified before. The terror in his eyes was real, even raising the hairs on his eyebrows. It was as if he had seen the devil himself. Perhaps even the devil would have been frightened by what terrified the imperial soldier. The dread he exhibited was not the type a soldier would exhibit before marching into battle. This was the type that would cause a soldier to turn his back and flee from battle. I looked at what he was staring at, yet I failed to understand what frightened him so.

"What is the matter?" I asked.

With his eyes fixed on what lay in front of us, he simply drew me closer as if to protect me from some unseen demon. Then he slowly and cautiously pulled out his sword and began to frantically scan the area—every single section, as if he expected someone or something of immeasurable strength and powers to pounce us at any moment.

"Gyvan," I whispered, trembling, "what evil troubles you?" If the soldier was terrified, then I leave it to you to imagine my own dread.

"The Dark Widow has unleashed a most vicious enemy," he said feverishly, fear and panic apparent in his voice, his eyes again fixed on what lay ahead of us.

I still did not understand his fear, for what lay ahead of us were only the bodies of the five bandits he had spared after they had attacked us. Now they too were dead.

"They are bandits," I managed to say, "likely killed by what is left of the army patrols in this area."

"Look closer at the bodies," he whispered fiercely, his eyes again wandering in every direction. I looked more closely at the bodies and then I saw what he saw.

My blood froze. I clenched hard unto Naya, the realization of our sudden incalculable peril causing these reactions. Only one word can describe what now boiled inside me—terror.

A Paipan had been dispatched!

That was the first time I had ever seen Gyvan Drabo, a commander in the emperor's army, afraid. His face had turned white, his body had stiffened.

"The Cross of the Paipan!" he exclaimed to himself in disbelief.

The bodies of the slain bandits were not what bothered us. It was the manner of their deaths that bothered us. All five of them had an X-shaped sword cut on their foreheads. This indicated only one thing: they had been slain by a Paipan—a battle assassin.

"He spared none," I remarked, referring to the assassin and horrified at the possibility of us confronting him.

"The Paipan spares no one who faces her," Gyvan said, "You cross her path, you die! She killed them as a warning to us, knowing that we were coming this way. She aims to frighten us and drive us into a panic."

"She?" I asked, alarmed. "You are afraid of a woman?"

"She is not just a woman, Aida. She is the deadliest assassin known to man, or woman!"

"But I do not understand," I said, puzzled, "I thought the Paipans were destroyed in the Battle of Assassin Hill some fifteen years past by the confederation of fourteen kings led by the then emperor, Sakoura."

"True, they were," Gyvan said. "But one survived."

One Paipan had survived the Battle of Assassin Hill some fifteen years past, and that lone survivor was now our mortal enemy, no doubt put to task by the Dark Widow to hunt down Gyvan and me and rid the Earth of our presence.

The Paipans had been a group of specially trained battle assassins who dedicated themselves not to the murder of kings, queens, princes, princesses, or people of government, but to the infiltration of enemy camps and battle sections during the heat and intensity of battle, to slay generals, commanders, and other military leaders. Their purpose was to sow the seeds of chaos and confusion among the now leaderless forces of their opponents. This was a trade the deadly assassins had hired out to various armies and warring factions for centuries, and with deadly consequences. These men and women had been the deadliest and best-trained combatants and sword handlers the land had ever seen. They were so terrifying that to this day it is said that even as far south at the trading cities of Kano and Katsina, parents often frighten their children with the phrase, "The Paipan awaits thee at the gates of hell!"

No one knew what had given the Paipans their skill and made them such extraordinary fighters, though some said it had all come from the anger they had against the world, for the Paipans were people who had suffered some unimaginable grief and turned their backs on humanity. They had suffered injustices so grave that only a hatred for life itself could provide a remedy for those injustices.

Such had been the case with Mandip, the lone surviving Paipan after the Battle of Assassin Hill, who now tormented me and the soldier. Before joining the Paipans, she had been a wealthy and noble Mandingo princess from the East. She was wedded to a young prince from the North, for whom she birthed a set of fine twins—a boy and a girl of noble prospects. A subsequent war with a usurping general left her dear prince slain and made her a prisoner of the usurper, along with her twins, who were each no more than four summers on this Earth. The usurper placed upon her two choices regarding her twins: they could be slowly put to death using all manner of torture in a process that could run from sunrise to sunset, or she could spare the twins the ordeal and dispose of them swiftly, herself.

The noble princess chose the latter, swiftly putting to the sword her own children by her own hand, but sparing them a torturous ordeal at the hands of the usurper's torturers. She was herself spared from the hands of the torturers after she managed to escape and chanced upon a Paipan troop who, after learning of her ordeal, readily accepted her into their ranks to make her one of their own. Yes, she became a Paipan and became well-schooled in the art of the battle assassin.

Some years went by before Mandip exacted a Paipan vengeance upon the usurper. He was found during a battle, tied to his tent post with his own entrails—alive, but wishing he were dead. The Cross of the Paipan was marked on his forehead. It took him twelve agonizing days to perish, his entrails having been placed back inside him by his doctors, but his stomach having been bloated with pus. He had rotted to death.

The story of the Paipans neither began nor ended with Mandip. Some fifteen summers past, the fourteen kings of the land, who had for many a century used the skill of the Paipans to make war with each other, came to see these deadly assassins not as tools but as threats to the power of the kings. So it was that a confederation of the kings, under the leadership of the then Emperor Sakoura of Mali, led a force of some 6000 to destroy the Paipan threat. This was carried out during the annual Paipan gathering at their mountain fortress known to friend and foe alike as Assassin Hill, where they were attacked and destroyed by the army of the confederation. It was a hard fight that lasted many days and nights. The Paipan army had only numbered 102. At the end of battle 102 Paipans lay slain. 2132 soldiers of the confederation had met their end as well.

One Paipan had missed this gathering and the battle, and was spared the hand of death, for she had been on a mission across the great northern desert.

Upon her return from across the northern desert, she learned of the ghastly treachery that had met the Paipans at Assassin Hill, and resolved to continue to trade her deadly services, not only for gold or riches as had been the Paipan way throughout the ages, but also to exact vengeance upon this Earth, a cruel Earth that had stripped her of all she had loved—her husband, her twins, and her Paipan family. So it was that she only accepted assignments that gave her the chance to create havoc and mayhem in this world. Yes, her name was Mandip, now set upon us by the Dark Widow. The widow was now one of the many kings, queens, and nobles who had for some years past come to see the last of the Paipans not as a threat but as an asset to be maintained during times of war.

The last of the Paipans could handle a sword better than any known man or woman, born or yet to be born. No one, living or dead, was known to have fought a Paipan in single combat and lived. Many a battle was won or lost on account of Mandip, a woman of rare beauty, who had seen no more than forty summers on this Earth.

***

THE CROSS OF THE PAIPAN. That was what had alerted Gyvan to the Paipan's presence when we stood at that road, feverishly staring at the bodies of the slain bandits in front of us. The Cross of the Paipan was the X-shaped sword cut on the foreheads of Paipan victims. Each of the slain bandits had been crossed before his death. Paipans used the cross to mark their opponents during a fight. The purpose of this was to ensure that if an opponent happened to survive a fight with a Paipan, he could easily be recognized by any other Paipan, who would then put all else aside and make it his or her duty to finish off the marked man or woman. Even Mandip, the last of the Paipans, was known to cross her victims in keeping with the terrifying Paipan tradition, an act meant to inspire fear and terror of the last Paipan. It was a signature of death, to let the world know who had brought death upon a soul, and death was what anyone could expect, should he or she be found bearing the Cross of the Paipan upon the Paipan's return for retribution. And death would it be for the bearer of the cross and all within sight of him or her.

Many sane minds heeded this fear. Some did not. An example readily comes to mind, when some sixteen years past a daring officer in the emperor's employ had wanted to find out for himself if the terror attached to the Cross of the Paipan was warranted. He therefore crossed his own forehead with the X-shaped Cross of the Paipan using his dagger. At dusk he left his garrison along with two female companions. He did return the following day, along with his companions, in twelve bags, dropped by a mysterious rider who disappeared as fast as he or she had appeared. The severed heads of the female companions now bore the Cross of the Paipan as well.

So here we were, awaiting the Paipan, this merchant of death dispatched across the empire to make a hasty disposal of Gyvan and me.

"The army has a rule for how to counter a Paipan," Gyvan said to me, "and that is, if you come across one, run!"

And that is exactly what we did. We mounted our horses and sped towards Wagadou to save our skins.

The Soldier's Tale

chapter 42

THE PURPOSE OF OUR HASTENING towards Wagadou was to ease Aida's fear. If the Paipan was after me, there was little I could do, save spend the remainder of my days within the protection of a military garrison, which in itself was no guarantee of survival from her. Sooner or later she was bound to find me. Had I been on alone, I would have stood my ground and waited for the assassin, but I had to save Aida. It was my intention to get Aida to safety and then to seek out the Paipan and possibly plead with her by explaining the importance of my task.

I scarcely had any sleep that night, staying up to keep guard over Aida for fear the Paipan would strike while we rested.

The following day we arrived in Wagadou, where we immediately reported to the local army garrison. This was an important trading city, the former capital of what was once Ghana. The garrison here housed several hundred soldiers—a safe place for Aida and me, safe from the Paipan, at least for now. I knew that I would have to face the Paipan in due time, for Aida and I could not hide forever. This meant leaving Aida at the garrison so that if I fell by the Paipan's sword, Aida would still remain safe, at least for a while.

First, we asked for and met the commander of the garrison, to whom we introduced ourselves. We were promptly meagerly fed and assigned a room to rest. I chose to stay in the same room with Aida for fear of leaving her out of my sight, though two guards were posted just outside the room at my request. The commander had chosen this room for us with Aida in mind. It was adorned with toys and with a glass window that provided a once-beautiful view of the city and of the garrison's once-magnificent terraced courtyard. The guards placed outside this room informed me that it had once belonged to the daughter of the garrison commander, a fine child who had been killed one year earlier during a rebel attack on a convoy that was returning from the Moon Festival in the Dogone cliffs.

Aida immediately went to sleep upon our entry into the room, fatigued by our escape from the Paipan. She lay on the bed as lovely as a newly formed spring flower, Naya faithfully tucked under her arms. For my part, I spent some time updating my journal as I readied to face the Paipan. I did not want to let Aida know of my intentions, so I thought of slipping away. But if this was my last day on Earth, I still wanted to look at those beautiful round dark eyes and that long, thick hair of hers which was curled up into the most beautiful braids with golden beads plaited into them. Upon updating my journals I took one last look at her, the sleeping beauty, and then attempted to sneak out to face the battle assassin.

"Where to, O soldier of Mali?" she said to me. She had suddenly woken up.

I was taken aback but managed to respond, being at a loss for the appropriate parting words and eager to distract her from my impending doom.

"Many a toy for one who is no more," I said, referring to the many toys of all sorts that the commander had in this room for his slain daughter. "He must really miss her. They say she was about your age when she passed on."

"It appears these are dangerous times for children. Many want me dead."

"Anybody who wants you dead, Aida, is going to have to come through me first." I smiled. I was trying to find the courage to just leave without hugging her but it was difficult, for she was only a little girl who had been cast into a horrible circumstance not of her choosing, and who needed all the protection she could get. But to protect her I needed to leave right then to face the Paipan.

"Aida," I called her name, trying desperately to hold back my emotions, "I hear there is an excellent sword maker in this town. I am going out to see if I can get him to make me one. If you need anything, just ask the garrison commander. I have spoken to him." I started for the door.

"Gyvan?" Aida called. I stopped. She walked over to me, seized me in a hug, and held tight. "Everybody knows the great Gyvan Drabo fights only with the sword his father gave him."

The clever little girl had caught me in a lie. The sword I used had been passed down by my father, who had received it from his own father, and I had used no other, ever.

"That is true, child," I said.

"I talked to the guards while you were with the commander," she continued. "They say Mandip the Paipan is the deadliest fighter there is. No one ever faces her and lives. But I also know that Gyvan Drabo is a

128

great swordsman. And as you face the Paipan today, Gyvan Drabo, use your *head* and your *sword* as if they are one, and then you will return by nightfall." Then she let go of me and I walked out.

But before I departed the garrison, I met with its commander and explained to him that I intended to leave the garrison for a few hours, and that if by nightfall I did not return, the guard around Aida was to be tripled and the Table notified immediately. I also informed him that in the likely event of my failure to return, whatever was left of my estate should be divided equally between Aida and Lili, a request which I put in writing. There was also a small share of my estate which I would leave for my mother whom I did not know, just in case she was ever to turn up.

"Suicide is against the law, you know," the garrison commander said to me, not knowing what I was about to engage myself in, but realizing that whatever it was, it could end with my demise.

"This will not be suicide by my own hand," I said.

"Murder is also against the law," he said.

"Only if you can catch the murderer."

"May I ask where you set forth, that death seems so certain?"

"To meet someone whom no man wants to meet," I said softly.

"Then why do you set forth to meet this person?"

"To save the people I care about—a little girl, the woman I am to wed, and a mother I still do not know."

"I do not know where exactly you are going or whom you set forth to meet, Commander, but I do hope for the sake of the little girl, for the woman you are to wed, and for the mother you are yet to know, that you return by nightfall."

I hoped for the best, as the commander hoped, but hope was but a fruitless dream when facing the sharp end of the Paipan's sword. The commander sensed a greater fear in me and inquired if he could be of any assistance. I declined. But upon his insistence on providing assistance, I chose to divulge my intentions.

"I go to battle the Paipan." I said.

The commander said nothing at first. His face was briefly overcome with a blank, speechless stare. Then he chuckled, believing me to be making some cruel joke on him. But after noticing no laughter from me he understood the seriousness of the matter.

"You are not yet married, are you?" he asked me.

"No, sir, not yet," I replied. "Why?"

"I was just wondering. They say married men live longer than single men, but married men are a lot more willing to die. And you are not even married yet."

***

USE YOUR HEAD AND YOUR *sword as if they are one*. Those were Aida's last words to me. What did she mean by that? As I rode out to face the Paipan, I continued to wonder. It was a riddle she had given to me, one I could not solve. But I quickly forgot about it, for I knew I would be dead by nightfall anyway.

I stopped at a grassy plain just outside Wagadou. I did not tie down my horse. I let the animal go, for it would have no rider to ride it back to the garrison by the time my meeting with the Paipan was concluded. There was a small river nearby from which I drank and cleaned my face. The river splashed into a small but steep waterfall a short distance away.

I stood, just waiting for the Paipan. I could not see her, though I could somehow feel her. I knew she was close. I walked towards the top of the waterfall and stood there, backing it, so that she could not surprise me with an attack from the rear. Even with the near supernatural skill she was reputed to have, she could not possibly swim up a waterfall. Like a loyal servant waiting to say goodbye to his master for the last time, my horse still stood where I had left it, watching me.

A moment later I turned towards the river and looked at it. I could see the reflection of my face in it, along with the reflection of the sky, growing ever darker. I was sweating heavier than usual, which I understood to be from my growing anxiety and dread. I dipped my head into the river, hoping to cool down myself and my fears. When I stood up and looked at my horse, it was gone, but in its place was death itself—the Paipan, the curvy, well-endowed harbinger of death!

The Paipan stood in front of me, watching me. It seemed as if she had been there for an eternity, studying the victim she was about to terminate. Words eluded me, the silence between us holding steady, interspersed only with the sounds of the rushing river and the splash it made as it tumbled into the waterfall. I was petrified.

By her looks the assassin had seen about forty-eight summers on this Earth, yet she remained one of the most beautiful women I had ever laid eyes upon, even lovelier than most young women in Timbuktu on a festive day. She was dark, smooth, tall, and with eyes as big and as round as oranges. Her hair was plaited into multiple spike-shaped locks pointing outwards, with two braids falling down her face, one on each side. A sword scar across her right cheek seemed not like a scar at all, but like some cosmetic touch that added a deadly touch to her dangerous beauty, to remind admirers that behind all that splendor lay the omen of instant death.

The battle assassin just stood there, looking at me, not saying a word, just looking forward to my death. As I watched her I knew that behind her cold, hard, expressionless look she was smiling at me, tormenting me and enjoying the misery she knew I endured as I watched my life vanish before my eyes. Her sword was not drawn yet, still resting in the sheath slung across her back, the same way all Paipans had carried their swords.

But despite my fear I had something to be proud of—a showdown with the last of them, the last of the Paipans. This would be quite a fitting conclusion to my adventures. Should Aida survive this entire ordeal through some stroke of good luck, I hoped that she could complete my written account with a conclusion similar to, "And so to save his true love, Lili of Timbuktu, and his true heart, Aida of Traoré, Commander Gyvan Drabo, the daring soldier of Mali, faced the last of the Paipans and fell by her sword."

The traumatizing silence between the Paipan and me continued until I decided to break it. I was at least going to attempt to reason with her and make her understand what I was fighting for, if it could save the empire.

"I am Commander Gyvan Drabo," I gently said to the assassin. "I serve Emperor Abubakari II." I waited for her to respond but she said nothing, her cold, deathly stare still fixed on me, as if she was waiting for me to wallow in misery during my last few moments on Earth. "I am on a very important mission for the emperor. The woman who sent you to kill me, the Dark Widow, wishes only to tear the empire apart and heap upon it a misery the likes of which has never been seen before. She aims to destroy us all." The assassin did not budge. She remained as silent as a desert viper, my words making no impression on her at all. "Should you kill me or the girl, the world you know will be no more." She said nothing still. "The empire needs me. The empire needs you too, Mandip, if you would join the emperor. Humanity needs you." Still there was no response from the assassin.

Yes, she had lost her humanity indeed, like all Paipans—the scum of this Earth who had nothing else to lose. Perhaps I could not blame her manner, for it was the cruel nature of this Earth that had caused her children to be put to the sword by her own hands.

"Assassin, you must stand down and let me be!" I scolded. The assassin remained still, silent, expressionless.

It was useless attempting to reason with her. I had to attack and perhaps bring a quick end to my misery by falling victim to the skill of her sword, a weapon which in her hands was reputed to possess a voracious appetite for blood. I feverishly pulled out my sword. Still the assassin made no move to pull out hers. She simply stood as before, her confidence terrifying me to the bones.

131

I decided to move first, suddenly darting towards the Paipan like a wild boar, my blade thirsty for Paipan blood, and my throat ready to receive her sword that would end it all for me. About twenty paces away from her, she still had not pulled out her sword, and I was drawing nearer to her. Fifteen paces away from her, and still she stood there, her sword still sheathed. Ten paces away and yet she just stood there, calmly watching me draw nearer. Five paces away and still she stood, sword still sheathed. And then when there were no more paces I struck at her, aiming straight for her heart.

But then I heard a clanking sound of swords clashing. Her sword had deflected my blow away, throwing me backwards. I could not believe her skill. With speed ten times faster than the blink of a squirrel's eyes, her sword had simply flashed out of the sheath that was slung across her back and deflected my blow that was aiming for her heart. She had pulled out her sword so fast that I had not even been able to see her do it. With such speed, any ordinary swordsman could not last ten seconds in a fight with her. But I was no ordinary swordsman. I was one of the best in the army. So I understood that I could at least last a full minute against the dreaded assassin before meeting my demise.

Before I could recover from her masterfully crafted defensive blow, she launched a ferocious attack of her own against me, swinging and thrusting her broadsword at me with such speed that it seemed as if I was fighting against six attackers. But I had fought ten men at once before, leading me to believe I could survive for a few shorts moments in a fight against the dreaded assassin. But what was different about the Paipan was the ease with which she fought. While I used all the might I could muster, she simply took it easy, as if toying with me, keeping me on the defensive at all times as I chaotically attempted to fend off her endless blows and thrusts that seemed to be coming at me from every direction. She easily parried and fended off the few blows I managed to throw her way. It was so easy for her that it seemed as if she was dancing, performing a well-mastered choreography.

I soon realized I had lasted about a full minute, and then another, and another, becoming quite surprised at myself and my tenacity. Even though I was on the defensive and understood that it was only a matter of time before the Paipan succeeded in running me through, I soon noticed something that gave me a pint of hope—the battle assassin was getting angry and impatient.

Yes, the assassin, used to disposing of her enemies seconds into a fight, was losing patience with me as our duel to the death dragged on. And that was not all. She was also beginning to fight more and more vigorously, losing the ease with which she had begun our fight. Yes, I was not the everyday swordsman, indeed, and even though I knew I would die in this fight, killing me was going to take more than just a few minutes. My father had started teaching me the skill of sword handling by the time I had begun to crawl. And for many years after he had fallen at the skirmish in Tekrur against nomadic invaders, I watched the soldiers practice at the local military garrisons in Timbuktu and even sometimes convinced them to show me a thing or two about sword handling.

With renewed assurance in my own skill as I battled the deadly assassin, I was determined to hold out against her for as long as possible, even though I knew that my death was imminent, for her ferocity and unconquerable skill became more and more difficult for me to withstand as the moments passed.

I thought of Aida and her fate should I not return, and as I did, her last words to me crossed my mind. It was a riddle I had given little thought to. "As you face the Paipan today, Gyvan Drabo, use your *head* and your *sword* as if they are one. And then you will return by nightfall." Those were her words.

And then it struck me. I broke her riddle and understood its meaning.

The clever little girl had been up to something.

Use your head and your sword as if they are one. It was a riddle that told me how to defeat the Paipan. I could not fight the Paipan with my sword alone. I also had to use my head to think, or study her skill, just like Aida had studied the ways of the world and learned to survive it. I, too, had to study the Paipan's skill, to learn what made her so deadly, and then find a way to survive it.

So as I continued to battle the assassin I began to study how her sword moved, how her body moved, how her legs moved, and how all these culminated into a lethal delivery of instant pain and devastation.

Then I got it!

The key to her skill was her legs. It was the skillful use of her legs that enabled her to seem to attack from many directions at once. She had mastered an art of skillfully coordinating the movement of her legs with the movements of her sword. The way she moved her legs made her body seem to be going towards one direction while it was actually going towards another direction, along with her sword, fooling her opponent into attacking her at the wrong part of her body while expecting an attack from the wrong direction.

I watched the Paipan's long legs carefully and saw how they moved in a pattern that could not be easily comprehended, but that was efficient enough to get her body and sword in exactly the position and direction she wanted. It was a game of the mind she played with her opponents. She was a master of her lethal art.

So I had identified the deadly skill of the beautiful assassin. But now I was faced with an even bigger problem—how to counter her skill within the next few moments, the amount of time I estimated I had left in this cursed world before her sword could finally put an end to me. I lacked the time to find an answer to this question. I needed more time to devise a countermeasure to her superior skill, a daunting task that could account for several hours, or even days.

I therefore had to escape. But how?

Was escape even possible?

Though my strength was beginning to fail me, the Paipan only seemed to grow stronger, showing no signs of slowing down, her self-assurance and confidence remaining just as resolute as at the beginning of our duel.

Then the splashing sound of the waterfall just about thirty paces away from me presented an idea of the hasty escape I so badly needed. I began to slowly fight my way towards the top of the waterfall, hoping to jump into it and swim to safety. Though the risk of being crushed to death on the rocks below the waterfall was great, it yet presented a far greater chance of survival than the risk of staying in the duel with the Paipan.

But this beast of a woman seemed to know what my intentions were, for she intensified her attack, attempting to block my path towards the waterfall. I, however, succeeded in getting to within one pace of the waterfall as I struggled in a violent attempt to free myself from her. But then it became quite impossible to jump into the falls, for each time I attempted this the assassin interrupted my jump by somehow placing herself in front of me in such a way that had I jumped, I would have been split in two by her sword and reached the bottom of the falls in two halves. I therefore decided that my best option was to simply freefall into the waterfall. Yet each time I attempted this she reached out and grabbed me by my garments. In one instant, after grabbing me as such, her other hand, armed with her sword, began to rise, ready to strike a death blow upon me. But with my free hand I reached into my garments and pulled out a dagger with which I attempted to strike at the hand that was holding onto me. To avoid my strike at her hand, the assassin had to let me go, finally allowing me to freefall to the bottom of the waterfall. As I fell I threw the dagger at her, hoping it would bury itself in her and make the luckiest kill in the history of combat. But I knew too well that that was not to be. As easily as a baby slumbers, she caught the dagger and promptly threw it back at me as I made my rapid descent into the waterfall. My own weapon had just been turned against me. It very narrowly missed my left ear and splashed in the bottom of the waterfall below me.

In an instant I, too, landed at the bottom of the waterfall, lucky enough to have stayed clear of any rocks. I was free at last. But I should have known better, that my freedom was not to be. I heard another splash at the bottom of the falls almost immediately after mine. It was the Paipan. She had jumped in after me.

I quickly disappeared under the water and swam away as fast as I could. After a short while I quietly emerged at the river bank, and to my horror, saw that the Paipan stood only about ten paces away from me. I could almost reach out and touch her. But fortunately she was looking in another direction as she searched for me. I stood very still, not wanting to submerge and let the sound it created alert her of my proximity to her. Most likely assuming I had drowned, she soon walked away, scanning the area, but having given up her search for me. I waited for what seemed an eternity before leaving, to be sure that she had completely cleared the area. I was thankful for my life. I had to be. I was the only person who had fought a Paipan in single combat and lived. I was proud of myself, another testament to my excellent combat skill, though I had just been bested by this woman.

Then I headed towards the city of Wagadou, back to the garrison, where Aida waited for my return. As I walked towards town I came across a man who suddenly changed directions and went another way as soon as he saw me. Though I found his behavior odd, I gave it little thought, convincing myself that he must have mistaken me for another. The next person I saw was a woman also walking from the opposite direction. She paid no heed to me until I greeted her, whereupon she let out a loud cry in terror the moment she laid eyes on me. She fled as if I was some wild beast from the devil's lair. That was strange, but I managed to convince myself that she must have mistaken me for some criminal or a ruffian known for misdeeds in these parts. Then I came close to the city gates, where six men were arguing over two scrawny starving cows and some shiny silver plates they were about to trade among themselves. As soon as these, too, laid eyes on me, they cried out and fled in several directions, terrified and leaving their cows and silver plates behind.

Now I understood something was terribly amiss. Why had these strangers fled upon my appearance? Then I felt something trickle down my nose, some kind of liquid. I touched it and looked at my hand. It was blood. I was bleeding from my head. But that alone could not make people terrified of me so. There had to be something more to this. I picked up one of the shiny silver plates and used as a mirror, to see the nature of my head wound that had aroused such terror in all who laid eyes on me. Then I saw what they had seen, the terrifying nature of the wound on my forehead. I wished I could flee as they had done, but I could not possibly flee from myself. There was death on my forehead.

It was the Cross of the Paipan!

***

I HAD BEEN CROSSED BY the Paipan, marked for death along with all those within sight of me upon the Paipan's return to complete her task. That is why all those people had fled for their lives the instant they had seen my mark of death. I tore a piece of cloth off my garments, wound it into a band, and tied it around my head, concealing the Paipan's dreaded death mark. I then walked into town, hoping to avoid being driven away or lynched by a mob determined not to have me bring the Paipan into their town.

As I walked, I understood that I would certainly have to face the Paipan again. This time, I knew, the assassin would take no chances with me. The death she would impose upon me would be swift and merciless. I was now even more horrified than ever. But somewhere deep within me I had a small glimmer of hope, for if I had survived the Paipan once, I could survive her again.

When I reached the garrison its commander was pleasantly surprised to see me.

"It is not nightfall yet, Commander Drabo," he said.

"And I am happy I still breathe," I responded, then slowly took off my headband, revealing to him the Cross of the Paipan etched on my forehead.

"You survived a duel with a Paipan!" the stunned commander exclaimed.

"I did."

Then the commander's mood sank. "But for how much longer?" he added, writing me off as a dead man walking.

"If I survived the Paipan once, I can survive her again. I fear her no more."

"It is not fear that keeps men away from fighting the Paipan. It is the certainty of death that does."

The commander was right, but all I could think of was Aida.

"Where is the girl?" I asked.

"She waits for you in my daughter's room."

I again tied the cloth around my head to conceal the Cross of the Paipan and then went forth to see Aida.

"I am happy you have returned," she said to me softly, not surprised to see me, as if she had always known I would return.

"If I have returned, little one, it is because I learned to use my head and my sword as if they are one," I said to her, quoting her riddle, her parting words to me.

She looked at my forehead wrapped in a piece of cloth. "But your survival has earned you the Paipan's mark of death."

"How do you know?" I asked.

"Why else would you wear the cloth around your head?" she asked.

Then she jumped off her bed and onto me, hugging me tightly. After my near-death experience I held on to her as if I never wanted to let her go.

***

AFTER HAVING WHAT COULD BE managed for dinner, as well as a short rest, I went to the garrison's armory to have my sword sharpened, ready for the eventful days that lay ahead. I had very little sleep that night, thinking about what had come to pass and what would come to pass. But most of all I thought about the battle assassin, and how I might devise a technique to defeat her skill. It had seemed so flawless. By dawn I had still found no solution, giving myself more time to think over it, and hoping desperately not to encounter her before I could devise an effective defense against her.

Aida and I woke up early the following morning. We had a long day ahead. With a piece of cloth still wrapped around my head to hide the Cross of the Paipan, Aida and I headed for the city's foundry, where iron was made into steel using the process learned from the Abyssinians, who themselves had learned it from the Haya, who resided deep beyond their southern borders. At this foundry we hoped to find out what "rotten" town, according to Tichiman's riddle, a huge weapon, or "a bee as big as ten," was sent to during the last occurrence of an eclipse. We were accompanied by about twenty soldiers to help protect us from the Paipan, though they knew nothing of the Paipan, otherwise few would have come. On our arrival, I introduced myself and Aida to the official in charge. I then left Aida inside with him to get the answers to her questions, while I joined the twenty soldiers outside to help guard the entrance.

Some moments later Aida emerged with a smile on her face.

"You have an answer?" I asked

"Yes," she said, "I now know where the last orb of Tichiman hides. And you are not going to believe where."

"Where?" I asked, dumbfounded.

Sobo Ha-Ha Speaks

chapteR 43

THE PAIPAN INFORMED US THAT Gyvan Drabo had drowned trying to escape from her. The high lady inquired of her if she had seen his body with her own eyes, to which she confirmed she had not, but asserted her certainty of his death. Lord Elcan and Commander Malouda advised the high lady to take no chances but to continue the hunt for the soldier or his carcass. Though neither the carcass nor the head of Gyvan Drabo was presented by the Paipan, as had been agreed to at the beginning of her service to the high lady, a manservant was ordered to present the battle assassin with ten thousand gold dinars, as had also been agreed.

For all the dread, the scorn, and the frightening reputation that accompanied the perception of Paipans, there remained at least one thing that many a man or woman admired about these feared assassins—their word. If Mandip promised to kill you, then you would be dead. If she said Gyvan was dead, then it was so. But if by some unfortunate stroke of ill fate the soldier had managed to evade death, it would come to the attention of the Paipan, who would neither sleep nor rest until she made true her word of killing the marked soldier, who undoubtedly must have carried the Cross of the Paipan, were he alive or slain.

And so it was that I again dispatched Noo, my companion of fifteen years, to scan the horizons for any sign of life from the imperial soldier.

The Words Of The Child Eeid

chapter 44

THE CLOUDS CONTINUED TO DARKEN, making life more miserable for many a creature in the realm—the bones of beasts and humans were scattered along the roads in equal demise. Gyvan and I continued our ride in haste, to find the second orb, the supposed location of which I had already revealed to Gyvan. It was the perfect hiding place for the orb, but one that created a problem so monstrous and unsolvable that Gyvan even briefly considered giving up the search. Getting this second orb was not going to be anywhere near as easy as anything we had done. But Gyvan insisted that we get to the location first and then decide on how best to retrieve the orb.

We were about two days' ride from our destination when we stopped by a spring to fill up our gourds and water the horses. A sudden urge caused me to look upwards, where I instantly noticed an owl perched on a dead tree, staring at us. It was a rather odd sight, for it was daylight, when owls are known to be at rest, awaiting the darkness. This was no ordinary owl, I concluded. Why was it staring at us, during the relative brightness of daylight? Only one answer seemed satisfactory—it must have been dispatched through some manner of incomprehensible eeidic force to keep a watchful eye on Gyvan and me.

"What worries you, Aida?" Gyvan asked me after taking note of my puzzled look.

"The owl," I said, tilting my head towards it.

As we spoke, the bird flew away, as if to report our presence. Did it know who we were? Then a sudden sense of fear gripped me. We were now within the realm of Tera-Hool, one day's ride from the city itself.

We stood inside rebel territory!

According to Tichiman's riddle, Tera-Hool, our destination, was where the last orb of Tichiman was hidden, right within the widow's palace, in the alarm bell of the palace watchtower, under the Dark Widow's own roof, where neither Lord Venga nor the rebels would have suspected. We

139

had come to Tera-Hool to assess its defenses so that we could return to Timbuktu, inform the emperor of our findings, and have him send an army to storm the city. But before we could get to the city our fears were confirmed: the spy owl had given away our position.

We suddenly found our path blocked by about fifteen Horsemen of Diaghan, swords drawn and ready to rip us to shreds. Lord Elcan, positioned in front of his men, was mounted on an armored steed, glad at last to have Gyvan and me within his grasp.

"Give us the girl, Commander Drabo," Lord Elcan commanded, "and we may let you live."

"As I told you before, Commander," Gyvan responded, "you will have to go through me to get her."

"And that we will, Commander. That we will."

Gyvan had to waste no time in launching a ferocious offense to take the Horsemen by complete surprise. He had to get us out of our peril and this required a sudden, unexpected, and lightning-quick strike against the foe that stood before us. He very swiftly yanked me off my horse and placed me on his own, behind him, all before I could even fully understand what was happening.

"Hold tight, and close your eyes," Gyvan instructed me. "You are too young to witness what is about to happen here."

Gyvan then attacked, charging at an enemy fifteen times his number. He had just survived the Paipan. He feared nothing anymore. I held onto him as he speedily galloped towards what seemed certain death, right into the middle of the enemy, chopping and hacking his way through them, defending not only blows intended for him, but those for me as well. Although my eyes were closed and I could see nothing, I knew that the screams I was hearing were not Gyvan's; they were the Horsemen's, many dropping dead from their horses like dead leaves from a tree in the middle of the dry season.

Then I was abruptly yanked off Gyvan's horse and flung onto another. I opened my eyes. I was on Lord Elcan's horse. He had somehow seized me and set me in front of him as he rode away as fast as his horse could gallop. Seized with terror and panic, I began to scream. Lord Elcan was speeding away while the surviving Horsemen busied themselves trying to hold Gyvan back with every bit of strength they could muster, preventing him from coming to my rescue.

"Aida!" Gyvan roared, a fiery look in his eyes. "I am coming for you!"

I was screaming and kicking, calling out his name and pleading to be rescued from this terrible man, Lord Elcan.

In almost an instant all the other Horsemen were slain but one, who broke out and ran towards my direction to protect Lord Elcan from Gyvan.

But Gyvan continued chasing after this rider and me. The rider pulled out a lasso, turned slightly around as he rode, and threw it at Gyvan, catching him right across the torso, causing him to fall off his horse. The rider did not stop riding. He continued, dragging poor Gyvan over the rough, harsh ground, as he was now trapped in the deadly grip of the lasso. But somehow Gyvan maneuvered his sword to cut the lasso in two and free himself.

As if neither his fall from his horse nor the crushing torture he had suffered while being dragged behind the rider's horse had affected him in any way, Gyvan immediately leapt to his feet and continued his determined chase on foot. His horse was running after him too, and with sword in hand, without even slowing down for a moment, he leapt into the air and onto his horse as soon as it got close enough to him. The surviving rider stopped, turned around, and charged at Gyvan, only to have his torso suddenly separated from the rest of his body by the now very angry Gyvan Drabo, who still did not slow down. He continued chasing after me, no doubt determined to also put an end to my captor in the process. Lord Elcan, certainly having no desire to face Gyvan Drabo, desperately galloped with me down a hill. Then I turned to look in front of me, to see what lay at the bottom of the hill. I was confronted with a terrifying spectacle. It only meant the end for me and Gyvan.

There was no way we could survive this.

In front of me, at the bottom of the hill, was a spectacle fit only for another army of equal disposition. But this spectacle had not been prepared for another army. It had been prepared for one man—Commander Gyvan Drabo. He had been led into a trap—a frightening army composed of at least one hundred well-armed Watchmen of Tera-Hool under the command of Commander Malouda, and two hundred armored Horsemen of Diaghan outfitted in coats of iron mail, ready to make mincemeat out of Gyvan and me. This small army had been assembled to face one man, no doubt considered to be a one-man army all by himself. But one-man army or not, there was no escape for us this time.

Gyvan stopped suddenly in his tracks when he reached the bottom of the hill, confronted with the army that awaited him at the bottom. Taken aback, he looked around in vain for a way out for us, the despair on his face apparent when he realized the odds were not with him. He simply dismounted, sheathed his sword, and awaited his fate, fearless in the face of death.

Seeing that Gyvan had given up the chase for him, Lord Elcan stopped his horse too, relieved at saving his skin. He dismounted, pulling me down with him. Gyvan was immediately surrounded by the rebel troops. I ran to him and he held me, trying to protect me from the vicious horde that was now slowly and cautiously closing in on us with weapons drawn.

"We will get out of this, Aida," Gyvan reassuringly said.

I knew, and he knew that I knew, that we had had it. No avenue of escape was open to us.

"Commander Drabo," Commander Malouda called with a smile, "welcome to Tera-Hool."

"I must say you have a rather impressive welcoming party, Commander," Gyvan responded.

"Only as befitting a guest with a reputation such as yours."

"So what now, Watchman Commander?" Gyvan asked.

Lord Elcan signaled to some Watchmen, who very cautiously walked over to Gyvan and snatched his sword, a deed that in effect also took away part of his being, for that sword had been bequeathed to him by his father and his father's father.

Then Lord Elcan and Commander Malouda walked to us.

"Gyvan Drabo," Lord Elcan began, "all we want to know is where the last orb of Tichiman is hidden. You are here in Tera-Hool, so at least we know it's in this part of the territory."

"Why do you believe I'll tell you, Commander?" Gyvan asked.

Lord Elcan looked at me, smiled, and said, "Because we could make things really unpleasant for the little one here." Lord Elcan was referring to me. I did not quite like the "unpleasant" part of his words.

"She is but a child," Gyvan protested. "Leave her out of this."

"You have till the count of ten to talk," Lord Elcan threatened, "or we will begin by plucking out those pretty little eyes of hers."

Lord Elcan pulled out a dagger and held it close to my eyes, waiting for Gyvan to reveal the location of the orb.

This was not good. Though I knew very well that Lord Elcan meant every word of what he said, for he was known for his extraordinary brutality, I truly cared little about losing my eyes. I was prepared to sacrifice them to save humanity. The loss of my eyes was not my worry. My worry was that Gyvan worried. I was about to face a most horrific torture and there was nothing he could do to save me, except reveal the location of the orb to Lord Elcan. I saw the pain he felt as Lord Elcan's sharp, pointed dagger drew closer to my eyes. Gyvan was going to talk and reveal the location of the orb, I was certain, and I could not let him do that. There was much more at stake, more important than the pain of losing my sight. I had to do something to prevent Gyvan from talking, but what could I do? I had to think quickly and act on it.

"Stop!" Gyvan yelled at Lord Elcan, whose dagger was just moments away from gouging out my left eye. "I'll tell you where the orb is."

"I am listening," Lord Elcan said.

"It is here, in Tera-Hool."

"Yes, I know it is here, you idiot. That is why you are here, isn't it?"

I had to interject before Gyvan could reveal the precise location of the orb.

"The orb is in the Dark Widow's palace," I hastily shot in before Gyvan could say any further.

"How do I know you tell truth?" Lord Elcan asked me, his dagger still threateningly close to my eye.

The fact is I had told Lord Elcan the truth, but I had omitted the precise location. And I had a trick in the works for him, so I continued. "Actually, on second thought, I just lied to you. The truth is that the orb is really hidden under a tree in Djenné."

"So which one is it?" Lord Elcan demanded. "The high lady's palace here in Tera-Hool or a tree in Djenné?"

"Come to think of it, it is hidden in a fisherman's shoe in the Bani River."

"The what?" Commander Malouda asked, baffled.

"Did I say the Bani River?" I continued. "No, I think it is the Sankarani River."

"So which is it?" Lord Elcan exploded in frustration, his patience growing thin. "The palace, the tree, or some river somewhere?"

"Now I know. The second and last orb of Tichiman is hidden in a tomb of a chicken thief who died of the pox while in Kita."

"Look, little girl," Lord Elcan scolded, threatening me with the dagger. "This is no game! Where is the orb?"

"You see," I said to the Horseman commander, "this is exactly my point. You can never be sure of any answer I give to you now, even if it is the truth. So you will have to keep us alive, for even under torture I may still provide a wrong answer." Lord Elcan reluctantly considered my proposal. "And I need both my eyes to find the orb."

The Dark Widow's commanders, as much as they hated to, reluctantly came to understand that they had to keep Gyvan and me alive at least for a while, if they hoped to ever find the orb. Lord Elcan sheathed his dagger, disappointed he had not had the chance to use it as he had intended.

"We will go to the Dark Widow," Commander Malouda said to Lord Elcan.

The small army began to move out, taking Gyvan and me with it. We were placed on separate horses and rode in the thick of the rebel troops.

Gyvan had his hands bound, and thirteen Horsemen rode around him with their iron-tipped spears pointing threateningly at him, ready to jab him to death at the slightest hint of trouble.

I, on the other hand, was neither bound nor surrounded by spear-waving Horsemen. I was allowed to ride freely beside Lord Elcan and Commander Malouda, understanding that I could not attempt an escape without Gyvan. As I rode beside the already infuriated Lord Elcan, I decided to further irritate him as retribution for the harsh treatment of my guardian soldier.

"The orb is actually hidden in the purse of a mad woman who—" I tried to continue irritating Lord Elcan.

"Shut up," he stormed, fed up with my tricks.

I looked at Gyvan and he smiled at me, wordlessly commending me on my quick wits.

***

THE WALLED CITY OF TERA-HOOL was heavily protected by two humongous bronze gates and thick mud walls reinforced with copper and limestone. As we rode into the city I was quite astounded at the small number of soldiers left to defend it—only a few hundred Horsemen and Watchmen scattered throughout the city. The Dark Widow's forces had been thinly stretched, leaving her stronghold dangerously unprotected and exposed to a major imperial attack. This, unfortunately, was a fact likely unknown to the imperial commanders, who still believed Tera-Hool to be heavily defended. Yet, perhaps the imperial commanders believed the strength of Tera-Hool's defense lay not in its number of defenders, but in its almost impregnable fortifications.

As for the poor people of Tera-Hool, they fared no better than people in imperial territories. Starvation, sickness, and death filled the air here as well, with no end in sight for their misery save death itself; and death itself was what the Dark Widow's forces were quick to deliver to many a soul who dared raise a hand in protest against the high lady or ask for a bite to quell his hunger. At least it was said that the Dark Widow had brought some dignity and respect to the women of Tera-Hool. Because shedding the sacred blood of women, considered to be the givers of life, was taboo in many other dominions, the Dark Widow had become the first ruler of Tera-Hool to outlaw the barbaric practice of beheading female prisoners.

Instead, they were boiled!

***

GYVAN AND I WERE WALKED into the Dark Widow's palace, where we quickly realized no expense had been spared in contrasting the conditions within the palace from the conditions outside. The palace was awash with plenty and all manner of luxury—food, gold, precious gems, water and drink, all seized from the poor people of Tera-Hool, who were still forced to pay high tribute to their high lady even during these hard times, or face the pain of a most gruesome death.

The palace at Tera-Hool—it was here that the last orb of Tichiman lay hidden in the alarm bell that hung inside the watchtower that stood above the four-story main building. Gyvan and I had only intended to scout the palace and the surrounding area so that we could inform the emperor of any useful intelligence gathered so that he could return with his army to retrieve the orb. But knowing Gyvan, I knew that now that we had been brought within the palace itself, he was going to try to retrieve the orb rather than wait for the emperor to open up another uncertain front in the war. But given our present circumstances, getting the orb was one thing; leaving Tera-Hool alive was quite another. We just had to wait and see.

We were brought to the Dark Widow's war room, where she was seated, surrounded by about fifty Watchmen, the protectors of the rulers of Tera-Hool. The large number of guards around her was no coincidence. Gyvan had dueled with the Paipan and survived, and was therefore not to be perceived lightly. The Watchmen of Tera-Hool and the Dark Widow had taken no chances. Next to the Dark Widow was the high eeid of Tera-Hool, Sobo Ha-ha, with the spy owl that had given us away perched on his shoulder. It was being fed with a juicy piece of flesh, no doubt a reward for a job well done.

"My lady," Lord Elcan called, pointing at Gyvan and me, "a most precious gift for you." The Dark Widow slowly rose from her throne and walked over to us, staring at Gyvan for quite some time without even throwing a single glance my way. She was a very beautiful woman, likely fifty summers and no more. She wore big gold earrings that matched her flaming red long gown that swept the floor around her feet as she slowly walked in a circle around Gyvan, examining him from head to toe, front to back. Then she suddenly turned her attention towards me as if she had just stumbled upon the realization of my presence.

"So you are the girl who fooled all you were an eeid," she said to me.

"I never once said I was an eeid, High Lady," I responded truthfully. "People only assumed I was one."

145

"You even outclassed my high eeid," she said, pointing at the hapless Sobo Ha-ha.

"I wasn't outclassed, High Lady," Sobo Ha-ha protested, "I was just—"

"Sshh," the Dark Widow silenced Sobo Ha-ha.

Then she turned to Gyvan, again examining him from head to toe, as if to see everything about him there was to see. She touched his face, seemingly pleased to make his acquaintance.

What was the meaning of all this?

"Commander Drabo," she said, "I must say it is really a pleasure to see you. I have waited a long time for this."

"So have I, Dark Widow," Gyvan responded threateningly, and dangerously softly, a burning anger in his tone. "So have I."

The Soldier's Tale

chapter 45

SETTING EYES ON THE DARK Widow filled me with such anger and loathing as few can feel. If I had had my way I would have instantly put her to the sword, but regrettably this had been strictly forbidden by the Table in the strongest terms, because the Dark Widow was needed alive for the White Shadow to be captured from her. So I chose not to concern myself with her much, but to worry about how to get the last orb of Tichiman from the watchtower and get myself and Aida out of a captivity that could otherwise result in a grisly fate.

"We have much to discuss, Gyvan," the Dark Widow said to me.

"I am listening," I said.

There was silence in the room as all waited to see what would happen next. I was worried for Aida, who was terribly frightened. I got down on one knee next to her and held her hand, to assure her that I would remain her protecting angel till the end.

"Don't be frightened," I consoled her. "Just hold on to Naya whenever you feel afraid."

"I am not afraid for myself, Gyvan," she said. "I am afraid for what these terrible people may do to you."

"They can do nothing to me, nor to you, you hear?"

Aida nodded.

"Well," the Dark Widow mocked, "how touching. Even the great Gyvan Drabo has a tender spot."

"You said we had much to discuss, Dark Widow," I said. "I am listening."

"The days of the empire are few," the widow began. "We have dispatched a relief force to Djenné, and the siege by the emperor's forces will soon be broken."

"No, Dark Widow," I said. "When Djenné falls to the emperor your days will be few."

"Djenné will not fall. No army in history has ever been able to seize it during the three hundred years it has stood. You know that."

The Dark Widow was right. Even the presence there of my best friends— Jeevas, Shang, Babayaro, and One Eye, had made little difference, despite their fine combat skills and expertise in military matters. I hoped they were faring well, for that had been their station during the many weeks past.

"There will be a first time, Dark Widow, when that city will fall, and the time is near," I teased the Dark Widow.

"You dwell on false hopes, Commander."

The widow abruptly changed the subject and went directly to a stunning proposal. "Join me, Commander Drabo, against the emperor and his forces."

"I don't understand," I said, mystified.

"Join me," she repeated. "Together we can achieve a power that is greater than any that this Earth has ever seen, or can ever again offer!"

"No, Dark Widow," I responded. "You join me. Join the empire against the evil that threatens to destroy us all. Join us against Lord Venga and his hordes. Help me capture the White Shadow."

"The emperor possesses no means to grant me the power Lord Venga offers," she responded.

"You fall prey to an illusion, Dark Widow. Wake up." I tried to persuade her as to the folly of her ways. "Should Lord Venga succeed, this world would be gone forever. There would be no one left in it over whom you could wield the enormous power you seek."

"I know that, Commander. There may be no one here in this world, but there would be in Eartholia Proper, the greatest and most powerful of all the realms, where my place is fixed, next to Lord Venga."

"Lord Venga can grant you no higher place here or in Eartholia Proper. He remains a fugitive there. Come to your senses, Dark Widow. So much death and misery has been brought upon this tender Earth already."

"But when I help him get what he needs, he will be the ruler of Eartholia Proper, and the current rulers there will become the fugitives. I ask of you again, Gyvan Drabo, join me. Make something of yourself."

"I would rather dine with a thousand pray-devils than join you, Dark Widow."

"I beg of you," the Dark Widow pleaded, a strangely genuine concern for me in her voice. "There is more to this than the Table has revealed to you. I again ask you to join me, Gyvan Drabo."

There was more to this than the Table had revealed to me?

Did the Dark Widow know something I did not?

Yes, at least on that front the widow and I were in agreement. The Table was hiding secrets from me. Why had this mission been mine to undertake? Why had the fourth Tichiman riddle been hidden from me though it had been solved by the Table and its two raw-breeds? And why had a Red Sentinel been lately following Aida and me?

But I chose not to let the Dark Widow's insinuations overcome me. I was a soldier of Mali and I was going to fight for the empire to the very end. I continued my verbal battle against the Dark Widow, hoping she would come to her senses and drop her evil ways.

"Are you willing to sacrifice everyone on Earth just to satisfy your quest for power, Dark Widow?" I demanded, walking closer to her, prompting some Watchmen to immediately rush towards me, keeping me at bay.

"You will no longer address the high lady as Dark Widow, soldier!" Sobo Ha-ha angrily commanded. "You will address her as High Lady."

"Why does she deserve my respect?" I demanded. "Because she offers me powers beyond even her means?"

"No, insolent soldier, she is your mother!"

***

SHE IS YOUR MOTHER! WHAT destructive words those were. The world suddenly stopped. The room suddenly went silent. I knew not how to react to so catastrophic a revelation. Aida walked up to me and held my hand as if she understood the intense and cruel dilemma I was about to undergo. I took in a deep breath and collected myself before speaking.

"The Dark Widow is my mother?" I managed to ask.

"Yes, Commander Drabo," Sobo Ha-ha emphasized. "Your mother."

I stood there, mystified, trying to make sense of it all. How could it be? Words alone cannot do justice in describing the torment and clash of emotions that raged within me. Was I to laugh or cry, rejoice or despair? How could the Dark Widow be my mother, the mother my aunt and grandmother had rarely spoken of, the mother I had searched for these many years past?

"You cannot possibly be my mother, Dark Widow," I protested softly, hoping desperately that I was being lied to.

"It was about twenty and nine summers past," the Dark Widow began to explain. "You were only a child. Your father, Mamadou-Bas, and the army had just returned to Timbuktu after a successful expedition against marauding Tuaregs. He took me to the victory festival that night, where I caught the eye of one of the generals, Fadiga, who at that time served the imperial regime under Emperor Manding Bory. I had to move up in the world. I had to make something out of myself as I now urge you to, so I left your father and you for him."

"And where has that gotten you?" I asked, not knowing quite how to react.

"I am the high lady of Tera-Hool, am I not?" she boasted. "And soon I will be the most powerful woman in Eartholia Proper and New Eartholia."

"You cannot be my mother. I refuse to believe it."

"Everyone who matters knows this, but you," the Dark Widow said. "Even the Table."

"The Table?" I asked, even more puzzled.

"Of course. Why else do you think you among all others were chosen to find the orbs, Commander Drabo?"

So the Table had had knowledge of my kinship to the Dark Widow. Why they had not informed me thus, I could not tell. Could the mysteries and secrets they held be any stranger?

"You tell me, then, Dark Widow," I demanded, "why I among all others was chosen to find the orbs."

It was odd how events had turned out. Here I was, a loyal soldier in the service of the emperor, about to learn from my enemies what I had been unable to learn from the Table, the institution I served. Would my inquiry help or hurt my cause? I could not tell. I only desperately wanted to understand more about my role in this entire matter.

The Dark Widow cleared her throat before speaking, as if preparing me for the unthinkable.

"I tell you this only because I believe it may help you join our cause," she began. "As you already know, I host Lord Venga's White Shadow, which can be captured through me or destroyed if captured through Lord Venga. But because Lord Venga hides on the Island of Ten Devils, where no man or woman with a clear head would dare set foot, your emperor has decided to capture the White Shadow from me." Then she paused, looked me dead in the eyes, and continued, "And now, listen carefully, for this is where you really come in, my son."

"I am listening," I said.

"The only human who can touch the orbs that hold the White Shadow of Lord Venga has to have my blood in his veins, someone with the same bloodline as me. And you are the only such person in the world, my son. Only I, Lord Venga, certain raw-breeds with specific knowledge of certain dark arts, and you can touch the orbs without falling victim to a most gruesome death. That is why the Table chose you for this task, my son."

So that was it. I had been chosen because I could safely touch the orbs, thanks to my kinship with the Dark Widow. But why had the Table kept this secret from me, I wanted to know.

"My son," the widow attempted to continue.

"Do not call me your son," I scolded. "No creature as beastly as you should be a mother of mine."

The Dark Widow had indeed become a beast. That was why my grandmother and my aunt, who had raised me, had rarely spoken of her, lest I seek her out and become like her.

"Gyvan, my son, I ask you one last time to join me. The world could be ours for the taking."

This fiendish woman, the Dark Widow, was hiding some other secret from me, for it seemed she had stopped just short of divulging to me what she had really intended to tell me, other than that I was one of the few who could safely touch the orbs. I decided to press her for her secret.

"I fear there is more to this than you wish to inform me of," I insisted. "Please, tell me all I need to know. Why did the Table keep the secret of my birth hidden from me?"

The Dark Widow smiled, then said, "I absolutely cannot tell you until I am certain as to where your loyalties lie, whether they be with the emperor or with me, your mother."

"I cannot give you my loyalty until I am privy to the secret you keep from me."

"That secret I cannot reveal until such time as your loyalties are fixed. All I can tell you is that it has to do with the fourth riddle of the raw-breed traitor, Tichiman."

The mysterious fourth riddle.

It was the one the Table had solved but would not reveal to me. Could the Dark Widow now end that mystery for me as well and put my mind at ease?

"What do you know about the fourth riddle?" I eagerly inquired of the Dark Widow.

She smiled, determined to keep me mystified until my loyalties could be determined. Then again she said, "Gyvan, my son, join me against the emperor."

"And, Mai-Fatou, the high lady of Tera-Hool, *my mother*," I said rather uncomfortably, "I ask you, in the name of Emperor Abubakari II, to give up the White Shadow and lay down your arms. With my intercession your punishment for high treason and crimes against the people of Mali would be light."

The Dark Widow laughed mockingly. "I am afraid that won't do, my son," she said. "You are just as naughty as your father."

"My father?" I asked, her words about him hitting a raw and painful spot in my memory, making me quite upset that a villainous creature such as herself had dared to speak ill of a man who had selflessly given his life for his people.

"Speak of him no more," I yelled at the Dark Widow. "You betrayed him, your mother, and your sister."

"Yes, my mother and my sister," the Dark Widow mocked. "They and you were the last of my bloodline. They had sworn they would never forgive me for leaving you and your father, you know. I heard they both died miserably a while ago. What a pity?" She smirked.

"Did you have anything to do with their deaths?" I demanded.

The Dark Widow chuckled. "After Lord Venga made Lord Fadiga a host, I was told to ready myself to be the next host, should Lord Fadiga meet an untimely end. It was then that I learned that only a person who shared my bloodline could ever capture the White Shadow from me should I become a host. I could not risk having them around any longer, especially with the way they hated me."

"You killed my grandmother and my aunt?"

"It is my understanding that they died quite painfully. Sad. You would have been done in too, had you not been away on one of the emperor's endless military expeditions."

By this time my anger against the Dark Widow had reached a point of no turning back. Before I had time to think clearly, I managed to seize a sword from one of the Watchmen standing next to me and leapt at the Dark Widow, despite my hands being bound before me. At the very instant, the three nearest Watchmen lunged towards me to protect the Dark Widow, but it was too late. Before I could be stopped the sword had pierced through her chest. I left the weapon where it had struck. She staggered back, and then dropped, a light smile on her face.

The Watchmen who had tried to save her seized me and held me to the ground. Aida rushed to my aid but was held back by other Watchmen. She was screaming and kicking in a violent struggle to free herself, pleading with them to let me go. Sobo Ha-ha rushed to the fallen Dark Widow and raised her head. He was in visible pain and sadness at her impending death.

"My end is here at last," the Dark Widow managed to say, gasping for breath.

"No, High Lady," Sobo Ha-ha said. "I will help you."

"No, High Eeid," the Dark Widow responded, her voice growing weaker. "Even you cannot help me now. The wound is deep."

I shrugged myself free of the Watchmen who held me and I slowly walked over to the fallen widow, my mother, and knelt beside her.

"Mother," I said to her, addressing her as such for the first time, an attempt to ease the pain of her passing, "my rage got the better of me."

She looked into my eyes, saying, "It pleases me that I fall by the hands of my own flesh and blood, and not by another's."

Then my mother stopped breathing. Her smile remained on her face and her gaze remained, looking straight into my eyes. It suddenly dawned upon me the depravity of the deed I had just committed.

I had killed my own mother.

***

WHAT CAN ANY MAN, WHO had committed an act such as I had, feel or think? Was there a worse crime that one could commit in this world than to kill one's own mother? I tried to convince myself that she had deserved no better, but it was hard. No words exist that I could put to paper to suitably make you understand the depth of my despair.

Aida slowly walked up to me as I knelt next to the fallen high lady of Tera-Hool, my mother. I fell into Aida's arms and cried like a baby. She held me tight before she noticed that Commander Malouda and his men, the Watchmen of Tera-Hool, were slowly closing in on me, swords drawn.

There were over fifty Watchmen loyal to Malouda in the room, along with about seventy Horsemen. Outside the palace, about 200 Watchmen stood guard, along with about 400 Horsemen loyal to Lord Elcan, whom the high lady had kept back to help secure her palace. Had it not been for Aida, I would have had no desire to fight or live on. Yet there was little I could do to avert our impending doom, for in addition to being greatly outnumbered, I had no sword on me, for it had been seized upon my capture.

Commander Malouda and his fifty Watchmen in the room closed in. I closed Aida's eyes to spare her the face of death that was about to meet us.

"I beg of you to let the girl go," I pleaded with Commander Malouda. "She no longer poses a threat to you. It is me you want."

The Watchmen closed in further on Aida and me, thirsty for our blood and ready to hack us to bits, a price well paid for the slaying of their high lady. Then Commander Malouda raised his sword high above my head and

153

struck. The sword came down and landed between my hands, breaking the ropes that bound me. I was baffled. The commander further puzzled me by his subsequent action. He gave a signal to his Watchmen, who all raised their swords and got down on one knee facing me.

Then Commander Malouda said, "We, the Watchmen of Tera-Hool, hail thee, Gyvan Drabo, High Lord of Tera-Hool."

High Lord of Tera-Hool?

"What is this?" I asked, completely confused, wondering why the Watchmen of Tera-Hool had just sworn loyalty to me, the murderer of their high lady.

But Aida, always the one with the answers, was quick to understand it all.

"Mai-Fatou, the high lady of Tera-Hool, is dead," she said. "And you, her only child, are now heir to her throne, High Lord Drabo."

"And the Watchmen? They intend no vengeance for their lady?" I asked Aida.

"Had you not been her son," Commander Malouda responded, "you would have been dead the moment your sword ran her through."

"And the Horsemen?" I asked.

"We heed the call of the Dark Widow and of Lord Venga, our lord and master," Lord Elcan bellowed, his dismounted horsemen ready to fight and continue the evil cause of the Dark Widow and Lord Venga.

Then Commander Malouda turned to Lord Elcan and said, "Then that makes thee my enemy, Horseman."

"And thee mine, Watchman!" Lord Elcan roared.

Undeterred by the death of the Dark Widow, the Horsemen of Diaghan decided to stay true to her cause. They were going to aid the fugitive raw-breed general, Lord Venga, in his quest to turn the people of Earth into a slave army to be used in a war in Eartholia Proper, a war that was certain to doom humanity. The Horsemen stood prepared to attack all who stood in their way—Aida, the Watchmen, and me.

"As high lord of Tera-Hool, successor to the high lady, Mai-Fatou, I command you, Lord Elcan, to stand your men down and lay down your weapons." I attempted to prevent an impending battle in which those on my side were heavily outnumbered.

"No, High Lord Drabo," Lord Elcan defended. "Our allegiance lay with Mai-Fatou, not with her title as high lady. And today you and all who are with you shall perish!"

So the battle lines were drawn. Only one side could emerge the victor. Being many times our number, the Horsemen attacked the Watchmen and me. Several Watchmen immediately surrounded me to protect me, their high lord, from harm, for I was weaponless.

The swords of Horsemen and Watchmen clashed, the Watchmen who surrounded me keeping me away from the fighting. But seeing my desire to join battle, Commander Malouda walked up to me.

"Your sword, High Lord," he said, handing me my sword, the same killing tool my father and his father before him had wielded. It felt good to hold it again, and I wasted no time in joining the thick of the fight against the Horsemen, while keeping Aida close and protected. We were a team again.

Word of the skirmish quickly spread to the outside of the palace, whereupon the Watchmen and the Horsemen stationed there turned on each other too, as instructed by their commanders. I wondered if we were going to survive this, for the Horsemen still were more than twice our number. But we fought on.

I shoved Aida into an empty room and closed the door behind her. Then I made my stand outside that door, making certain no Horseman could get in. But my presence alone did not stop many a brave but foolish Horseman from trying. My shiny blade or wrist knife, which had remained concealed, was the last thing many of those brave souls saw.

The Watchmen and I fought as best as we could manage, trying to secure the palace grounds, yard by bloody yard. Even Commander Malouda, my former enemy, showed no misgivings about disposing of his former allies, the Horsemen. At one instance during the melee I spotted him fighting four Horsemen single-handedly. Believing his moments on Earth to be few, I lamented that I could not get to him in time to save him from his numerically superior opponents. But when I took a second look towards him after a minor distraction of my own that involved two Horsemen who ceased to exist shortly thereafter, three of the four Horsemen who had battled him were lying on the floor, bleeding and screaming in pain, with the fourth one taking a nasty cut from him across the chest and dropping down lifelessly.

But bravery and skill alone could not bring victory to us, for our low numbers could finally do us in. As I scanned the battleground within the palace hall and outside of it, I noticed the numbers of Watchmen steadily dropping. It was only a matter of time before our final destruction.

But then something happened, something which I can only describe as a miracle. It was something that would solve one mystery and open another. Puzzles, mysteries, secrets—these had lately become the norm of my life. Why, for example, had a Red Sentinel we had spotted in Do and Djedeba been following Aida and me from the moment we had departed Timbuktu to search for the second orb? Now I was about to find out why this had been so, but would also encounter another mystery in the process.

Just when I believed we were about to be overrun and butchered by the Horsemen, and I was hoping for a miracle, one occurred indeed. I suddenly heard the galloping of horses from outside. I looked out through the window and to my eternal gratefulness I saw hundreds of imperial cavalry troops—Red Sentinels—charging at the Horsemen of Diaghan.

Reinforcements had arrived.

Now we had the advantage in numbers. Many of the Horsemen, realizing their impending doom, scrambled to flee the battle. These feared warriors had been taken so completely by surprise that the fear they had previously inflicted upon their enemies was now nonexistent, at least not in these crack imperial troops—Red Sentinels—who made up the emperor's personal guard, the best-trained force in the army. But how had the Red Sentinels gotten here just in the nick of time?

The fighting continued for a short while longer before ending in an imperial victory. Seventy-one Horsemen were captured and the rest had been slain or had fled, most likely to Djenné, one of the last rebel strongholds and where most of the Horsemen were already stationed. Lord Elcan and Sobo Ha-ha were nowhere to be found. Even Sobo Ha-ha's spy owl was gone, the piece of flesh it had been eating left lying on the floor, mixed with the blood of the dead and the dying.

I opened up the room in which I had kept Aida safe from the fighting. She was curled up against a wall, holding her doll, Naya. She was terrified, having excruciatingly endured the sounds made by the clash of arms and the screams of men as they uttered their last breaths on this Earth.

But as I walked into the room, a most bizarre and inexplicable event occurred. This was when I suddenly heard a desperate cry from behind me. I quickly turned around and noticed that it had come from a Red Sentinel who had been ambushed and was about to be killed by two Horsemen whose hiding spot in the hall he had just stumbled upon as the hall was being cleared of any remaining hostile forces. Neither I nor any of the Watchmen or Sentinels were close enough to aid the beleaguered Sentinel. But before the two Horsemen could make their kill, they were suddenly and inexplicably violently lifted off the ground by some unseen force, smashed against the ceiling, and flung to the floor, their bones crushed and their bodies rendered lifeless. I was dumbfounded. And so were the Watchmen. But the Red Sentinels, on the other hand, simply looked at me, not too surprised at what had just occurred.

What force could have killed the Horsemen so? By all accounts it had to have been extremely diabolical. But why had the Red Sentinels not been surprised? Did they know something that the rest of us did not know? Was there an eeid in our midst who had used his Third Shadow to aid us? I looked around but could see no sign of an eeid. I looked at the terrified but still very intelligent Aida to inquire if this had been some deadly incomprehensible trick of her making, but she shook her head before I could even say any words. All were silent, preferring to let the matter be, thankful that the ambushed Red Sentinel had at least been saved.

But the funny thing was that at the moment when I had laid eyes on the two Horsemen about to kill the ambushed Sentinel, I had wished that I could seize them and throw them against the ceiling before they could make their kill.

Like all in the room, I, too, chose to forget about the inexplicable and bizarre event of the two flung Horsemen. Whatever it was, it was sure to be revealed or explained to us at some point. I again turned my full attention to Aida.

"The fighting is done, child," I said to her, carrying her in my arms. Then I stroked Naya and said to it, "I thank you for looking after Aida." Aida smiled.

We walked out of the room. All was surprisingly quiet. Too quiet. Hundreds of Watchmen and Red Sentinels stood in the hall, waiting for me. I put Aida down and waited for the leader of the Red Sentinels to come forward and explain the circumstances of their timely arrival. Even more importantly, I wanted to understand the reason for their arrival. As I waited, I looked down, near my feet. Before me lay the body of Mai-Fatou, the Dark Widow. I was instantly reminded of my pain. Life would never be the same again.

I had slain my own mother.

The Words Of The Child Eeid

chapter 46

EVEN THOUGH GYVAN DRABO SAID to me, "We are okay now, little girl," I knew it was not okay, at least not for him. He had just killed the mother he had spent most of his life searching for. In his eyes I saw that he could no longer live with himself, the vigor and life of those wild, excited eyes were now gone—forever. I felt his pain, the one that bites and sticks, never to go away. The one that would creep up every time he tried to laugh or smile, and fill his heart with regret. Yes, that was the end of the always spirited Gyvan Drabo, the only thing keeping him going now being his regard for Lili and me.

I held his hand as he looked at the Red Sentinels for an accounting of their timely appearance. A feeling of strangeness filled the air, for while the Watchmen of Tera-Hool had all sheathed their weapons, waiting for instructions from Gyvan, the Red Sentinels who still had their swords unsheathed and dripping with the blood of battle were slowly closing in towards Gyvan, led by their commander, Gans, who was a bitter rival of Gyvan. Something was terribly amiss, and whatever it was, was bad. What was happening here? As yet no one had said a word to bring to rest this mystery. Neither had Gyvan, nor Gans, nor any of their men. Gans, who had always cared for my well-being, walked up to me. He pulled out a scarf and dried the tears already flowing from my eyes amidst all the horrors I had just endured.

"Cry not, little one," Gans said to me softly. "Save your tears for the horrors that may befall us yet."

The horrors? What was Gans's meaning? Then he turned to face Gyvan.

"Commander Gans," Gyvan called calmly. "The enemy is vanquished. Yet your men do not sheath their swords."

"The Dark Widow is slain," Gans responded.

"My rage got the better of me," Gyvan said regretfully. "My wits failed me. But at least she is dead."

"The Table instructed you not to kill her. She was needed alive."

"Lord Venga is sure to find another host," Gyvan whispered to Gans, so only he could hear. "With the last orb, the raw-breeds at the Table can spin a charm to enable them to capture his White Shadow from the new host. The Dark Widow's death makes little difference."

"The last orb? Are you in possession of it?"

"If your men will sheath their swords and let me through, I will get the orb."

"Where is it?" Gans asked.

"At the watchtower."

"My men will accompany you to retrieve it," Gans said.

Gans signaled his men, and six of them quickly surrounded Gyvan, their pikes and swords trained on him, the tension and suspense rising rapidly. No one knew what would happen next. Commander Malouda and several of his Watchmen drew their swords and were about to rush to their high lord's defense against the flanking Red Sentinels.

"Stand down!" Gyvan ordered the Watchmen. "Sheath your swords. The Sentinels act under the authority of the emperor." The Watchmen reluctantly sheathed their swords and withdrew, understanding that Tera-Hool was again under the dominion of Mali.

The flanking Red Sentinels, led by Gans himself, led Gyvan and me to the watchtower. Gyvan looked at the watchtower's bell for a short while. He must have been thinking the same thing I was thinking—was the orb hidden in the bell as I had determined?

Gyvan put his hand inside the bell and pulled it out. It was empty. No orb. He put his hand inside the bell again and then pulled it out. An object wrapped in a thick brown cloth came out with it. He unfolded the cloth. The orb lay neatly within it—the last orb of Tichiman, its glow unmistakable. Gyvan looked at me, pulled me closer, and kissed me on the forehead, a solemn reaction to success.

We had found both orbs. Now what?

"All the orbs are found," Gyvan said to Gans. "What happens now?"

"I take you to the Table. To Timbuktu." Gans replied.

"As a hero or as a prisoner?"

"You killed the Dark Widow, Commander Drabo."

"Why is that so important to you?"

"Not to me, Commander Drabo, but to the Table."

"Explain yourself, I pray."

Gans then explained how the Table had instructed him to have some Red Sentinels follow us as we searched for the second orb, partly to see that we stayed clear of as much danger as possible, and partly to see that the Dark Widow was not harmed by Gyvan upon their meeting, which they believed was very likely. This solved the mystery of the Red Sentinel we had spotted a few times during our travels, the same one we had spotted in Do and in Djedeba. But I felt there was more to this.

By following us and by consulting the imperial officials Aida and I had interacted with, such as the iron mine officials and the garrison commander at Wagadou, the prying Red Sentinels had been able to determine that we were traveling to Tera-Hool. In the process an important discovery was also made, that the defenses of the city were thin, with most of its defending Horsemen having been dispatched to aid the Dark Widow's besieged troops at Djenné and some other sectors along the frontlines. As a result, some three days before our arrival at Tera-Hool, our trackers had sent word to the Table, informing them to send troops to Tera-Hool to capture the Dark Widow, as had been the intention of the Table. And so it was that the Sentinels, the only imperial troops daring enough to fully engage the Horsemen of Diaghan, had made their timely arrival and were allowed into the city by the Watchmen of Tera-Hool, whose allegiance had switched to Gyvan Drabo, a soldier in the service of the emperor.

But upon the arrival of the Red Sentinels, the Dark Widow was found slain, and as instructed by the Table, should such occur, Gyvan was to be seized by any means necessary and brought to the Table—the real reason for the surveillance the Table had kept on him.

But why?

With a signal from Gans, a heavily armed detachment of Red Sentinels carrying monstrous-looking chains approached Gyvan, obviously with the intention of using them to restrain him. Commander Malouda's attempt to challenge this move against his high lord was quickly put on hold with a single look from Gyvan, demanding that he stand down. What manner of terror did Gyvan instill on the Table that he was to be restricted and humiliated with chains?

It was disturbing. All we had to do was to get to the Table, where I hoped answers could be provided. So together with Gans and his Red Sentinels, we all departed Tera-Hool for Timbuktu along with Gyvan, as a prisoner mounted on a horse that was harnessed to five other horses that were also harnessed to the monstrous chains that bound Gyvan.

At the behest of Gyvan, Commander Malouda and the Watchmen stayed behind, yielding to the greater authority of the emperor and reluctantly allowing their master and high lord to be carted away like a man-eating beast of fearsome monstrosity. My heart saddened to see Gyvan, a soldier who had endured untold hardship for his emperor, treated as such.

What did they really fear from him?

Sobo Ha-Ha Speaks

chapter 47

THE LOSS OF THE ORBS and the death of the high lady, the host of Lord Venga's White Shadow, was a devastating loss on our part, perhaps even setting us back by many months. Was I displeased? Yes. Was I discouraged? No. We had lost a host before—Fadiga—but had gotten another—his wife, Mai-Fatou. Lord Venga would soon find another, I knew, but who? That, I would soon learn on my next visit to him in his fortress on the Island of Ten Devils, where no unwanted being would dare to tread.

But first I had to see about the progress of the blood dripper, the final element needed to bring to fruition our designs for this Earth and Eartholia Proper. Thus I returned to the caves of Mount Koulikoro to attend to the mysterious creature or being of which I still knew very little. I was hoping that the mist around its cave would have cleared further by now, possibly allowing me to catch a clearer glimpse of the being.

Upon my arrival there I was delighted that the mist had indeed cleared as I had hoped, though not enough to allow me that ever elusive glimpse of the mysterious creature. I administered the sacred potion prepared by Lord Venga himself as I always did. The blood dripper hissed, and then it roared. I had never heard it roar before. This meant only one thing—it was maturing, soon to be ready for our use. I trembled, a joyous tremble, knowing that our goal was close at hand.

But still, we needed a new host for the White Shadow.

And who was this host going to be?

The Soldier's Tale

chapter 48

Poor Aida. This little angel was more worried for me than I was for myself. Like me, she could not comprehend why I was being dragged to Timbuktu in chains monstrous enough to restrain even the dragons that plagued our nightmares. I was, however, allowed a brief moment to update my journal.

But I worried little about my situation for there existed more to worry about, like the fate of my soul in the afterlife upon my demise. How could I explain that my mother had been slain by my own hand? Regarding this, Aida had attempted to put some ease over my mind and explained that the Dark Widow had been a woman I barely knew. But the truth is that I did know her, from the moment our eyes laid upon each other when I was brought before her by her rebel soldiers. I had felt a connection, the type which only a mother and son could feel. Yet I had committed an act so heinous and vile by slaying her with my own hands. My guilt was unbearable.

I had slain my own mother!

The Traveler's Account

last words

I HAD SLAIN MY OWN MOTHER! With these words the soldier's account of his deeds ends, a work unfinished, and his journal closed. Gyvan Drabo, a man buried in guilt, a valiant soldier torn apart. As you read further, you will learn for yourselves what became of so tormented a soul.

The Words Of The Child Eeid

chapter 49

THE DEATH OF THE DARK Widow had done little to slow the progress of the dark clouds, which continued to grow as before. Evil remained at work. Lord Venga, Sobo Ha-ha, and Lord Elcan were still alive, no doubt plotting some wicked revival and likely searching for a new host. Who could this host be? Could he or she succeed where Fadiga and the Dark Widow had failed?

The journey to Timbuktu, which should have taken three days, was going to take seven, for we were slowed down by repeated rebel attacks on our convoy, all of which were fended off by the hardened Red Sentinels, though quite a few men among them were lost. We also had to make use of alternate routes, the rebels having destroyed several bridges which could have shortened our journey.

As at all times during the few months past, death and misery existed everywhere. The plague continued to spread, the famine continued, the war continued to take its horrible toll, and the fate of man remained uncertain. We passed through a village where most of the adults were dead and the children were dying, in a world that was itself dying, where the farms no longer flourished and the cattle that remained no longer produced milk. What little food the people had left in their stores had been looted by rebel forces. To ease the suffering the Red Sentinels provided half their rations to the young ones so they could breathe the air for a few days more.

Timbuktu as I knew it had ceased to exist. When we arrived in the city few people were to be found in the streets, most staying indoors, afraid of all and trusting no one. Many more had left the city, searching for better fortunes elsewhere, though it was known to me that none existed anywhere else.

During better days a military convoy entering the city would have attracted huge crowds of cheering onlookers, but not now. The people of Timbuktu had nothing to cheer about. The few people who could be seen on the streets simply walked on, and in some cases right through our convoy, not caring that it was the emperor's own guard or that they could be run over by our horses. The soldiers who guarded the city were in no better shape than the city populace. They had lost their vigor and tenacity, and only did their duties because there was nothing else to do. It was said that half of them had deserted anyway.

There were several dead and dying around the city wells where the water had dried up. Here, children had once played, using the water to stay cool during the intense dry season heat. At one of the wells was a boy trying without success to draw some water. All he could get in his pail was dust. He collapsed of exhaustion, just waiting to die. I went to him, and from my gourd I poured some of my rationed water on his lips, forcing some down his throat. He drank heartily and found the strength to get up, whereupon I gave him some yam from my rations. He thanked me and told me he was not going to eat the yam, but take it home to his little sister, who had had nothing to eat in days. Then Gans came along. He asked the boy to eat the yam himself. But that was not all. The Red Sentinel commander then gave the boy his water gourd and some more yam from his own rations, asking him to take those to his little sister.

Lord Venga and his dark forces seemed to be winning this battle between good and evil. Even the imperial forces were said to be losing at Djenné, where they had been unable to seize the city, and faced endless harassing attacks from the Horsemen and other forces previously dispatched by the Dark Widow. Conditions for the imperial forces was getting bleaker by the moment. Reports even surfaced that some soldiers, to avoid starvation, were boiling their leather shoes and clothing to eat!

***

GYVAN REMAINED IN THE HEAVY chains upon our arrival at the emperor's palace. Desolation and despair had not spared the palace either. About twelve members of the Emperor's Poor stood outside the palace gates, hoping for any scraps of food that could come from within its walls. During better days, these Emperor's Poor, the handicapped, mostly blind people, had had an edict passed in their name, allotting revenue and lands for their sustenance and well-being. Today no sustenance was to be had, not even from the emperor himself, who was their champion and

166

benefactor. He had none to give. He had no way to help his people, save to destroy the dark forces that plagued the land.

Misery also showed its ugly head on the palace buildings themselves, the glass windows having fallen into disrepair, those few still in place having even lost their shine. Even the once-vicious guard dogs had lost their ferocity and all semblance of viciousness. Their spiked gold collars as well as the gold swords and shields carried by the palace guards had also lost their color and sharpness.

As we walked towards the Table there was complete silence, as most were not concerned about talking unless it was good news worth talking about, and good news was scarce in these times. The only noises that could be heard were our footsteps and the clanking of the chains that bound Gyvan, the high lord of Tera-Hool.

I took note of a rather disturbing sight as we walked. There was an unusually large number of guards present, as if they expected an attack from the rebels. But I knew these extra guards were not there for the rebels. They were there to guard against Gyvan. What was it about him that made the Table fear him so? It could not be just because he had disobeyed their orders and killed the Dark Widow. It had to be something else, something the Table was hiding from us.

Only Gans, Gyvan, four Red Sentinels guarding him, and I were allowed into the room where the Table waited for us. Upon our entrance, the Elders and the two raw-breeds, Shokolo-ba and Tin-zim, said nothing. They simply fixed their gaze on Gyvan for quite a while. Dressed in their white robes, except for the Tuareg representative dressed in the blue robes of his people, the Elders sat motionless. I bowed to them as I always did. Except for the emperor, who threw a quick smile at me, there was little reaction from the Table, who hardly noticed me but continued to stare at Gyvan as if he were some fiendish beast that needed a constant eye to be kept on it.

After the long silence, the emperor spoke, addressing me.

"Child eeid," he began, "first, I thank you for healing me of the night blindness. The night is as clear to me now as it is to any other."

"I am honored, Your Highness," I said. My prescription that the emperor eat the raw liver of an ass every week had indeed helped to heal his night blindness.

I was pleased for the emperor, but still I waited for him or any Elder to explain why Gyvan had been dragged to the Table in chains.

"Your Highness," Gyvan asked respectfully, "why ever am I brought before you so bound, in chains fit only for a reckless criminal?"

"If you stand before me so bound, Commander Drabo," the emperor responded, "then I must assume that the Dark Widow lives no more."

"That is so, Your Highness," Gyvan said. There was a disturbing murmur from the Table as the Elders expressed their disappointment at the death of the Dark Widow, and strangely seemed more terrified of Gyvan than even just moments before.

"We commend you, Gans, for bringing in the commander as he is," the emperor said.

"For the empire, Your Highness," Gans responded.

"You may unchain him," the emperor instructed Gans.

At this, the Elders and the two raw-breeds vigorously protested the emperor's decision to have Gyvan unshackled. The emperor stood by his decision and several Red Sentinels reluctantly and very cautiously approached and removed the chains from Gyvan, terror visible in their eyes and in those of the Elders as Gyvan was unleashed from his bonds.

A signal from Gans sent all the Red Sentinels away from the room, who did so very willingly and in great haste. I also noticed that the raw-breeds and every Elder, except for the emperor, had their hands placed on their swords as a precaution against some inexplicable danger from Gyvan that they perceived was in the making. Gyvan was just as surprised as I was.

What was it about him that made him so terrifying to the Table in this particular instance? Then it hit me. It was the Cross of the Paipan. No, that could not be. The cloth he had worn around his head to conceal the Paipan's cross was still there. But then again, perhaps Gans's spies might have informed the Table of Gyvan's duel with the Paipan. No, that too could not be, for yet again, not even the Paipan could inflict such fear upon the Table, for all knew that she could not dare to attack the emperor's palace, a fortress that was protected by Red Sentinels, the elite imperial soldiers who had used their skill and superior numbers to help crush the Paipans at Assassin Hill. So the terror had to be caused by some other entity. But what?

"I hear you have been crossed by the Paipan," Musa the Elder, the emperor's brother, addressed Gyvan.

Gyvan untied the cloth from around his head, revealing the dreaded mark of death. All in the room gasped, though I knew not whether it was in fear or in admiration for the soldier.

"Is she dead?" the Tuareg Elder, who wore blue, inquired.

"She lives, my lord," Gyvan responded.

Tin-zim, one of the raw-breeds, spoke next.

"Do you have the orb?" he asked Gyvan.

"I do," Gyvan replied.

He pulled out the orb from his bag, which he had been allowed to keep. But as he moved forward towards the Table to hand over the orb, the Elders, with the exception of the emperor, suddenly leapt off their seats and scurried farther away from him in absolute terror, pulling out their swords as if they believed Gyvan was about to inflict some cruel manner of devilish injury upon them.

"Hold still, lords of Mali," the emperor scolded the Elders, obviously disappointed with their reaction. "You need not fear the soldier. He means no harm." The Elders reluctantly and guardedly replaced their weapons and assumed their seats again.

"My lords," Gyvan pleaded with the Table, "I beg an explanation for the manner of my reception."

Would the Elders explain to him why he was being treated like some fiendish creature intent on causing harm, or would they make it another mystery with deep secrets known only to them? I waited. The emperor looked at the raw-breeds, apparently seeking their approval as to whether to present Gyvan with the answer he sought. The raw-breeds nodded. The emperor looked at Musa the Elder and nodded. Musa the Elder looked at Gyvan and took in a deep breath.

"There is something different about you now, Commander Drabo," Musa the Elder began, "something that changes everything."

"I am the same man that was dispatched from here many weeks past," Gyvan defended his person, "to seek and bring before this Table the orbs of Tichiman, and the orbs of Tichiman I have brought forth."

"You slew the Dark Widow, did you not?" Musa the Elder asked.

"My lords," Gyvan addressed the Table, "my rage was my weakness, and that weakness failed the empire as I slew the Dark Widow." Then he got down on one knee. "I now ask of the Table if any avenue remains whereupon I may redeem the situation we face, even if such an avenue calls for my death. All you have to do is ask and I will gladly obey."

The emperor asked Gyvan to rise, then said, "I know, Commander Drabo, High Lord of Tera-Hool, that you will do whatever it takes to save the empire, and that is why I asked that you be set free of your bonds. I do not question your loyalty to the empire."

"Your Highness, I will do anything to correct my error."

Then the Elders threw quick glances at each other, and then at Gyvan. They were about to reveal to him something major, something monumental, something that he could do to correct his error, something hair-raising, something that had to do with the fourth riddle, something that even I could never have foretold.

I waited. Musa the Elder again took in a deep breath before speaking.

"There is one thing you can do, Commander Drabo. One thing you must do, and in doing it, your very existence will be brought to an end." There was a frightening pause. "You will die."

Gyvan's life would end? Why did they have to end his life despite all he had done for the empire? Surely there had to be another way out of our predicament. He looked up at the Table, dismayed, but accepting his fate as he had promised.

Then he said truly, "I am prepared to sacrifice myself for the empire, if that would remedy my error and destroy the evil that plagues the land. But I have one condition."

"Your condition?" Musa the Elder asked.

"That Aida be spared any blame. Whatever it is I must do must not involve putting her in further danger."

"Aida has served the empire well. What it is you must do involves you and only you."

It was so unfair. Why did Gyvan have to die?

"No, Gyvan," I protested, tears streaming from my eyes. "You do not have to do this."

Gyvan looked at me and said sweetly, "For you, child, I will sacrifice anything, so that you may see the land returned to what it was before the evil that now rips it apart took hold."

"No!" I sobbed. "We can go to the Island of Ten Devils and find Lord Venga. We can capture and destroy the White Shadow from him. Ask the emperor to send his army!" I sobbed out of desperation to save the man who had risked his own life many a time to protect me.

"No, Aida," he responded softly. "It ends here. Now."

My plea was one that could not be heeded, for I knew, the Table knew, everybody in Mali knew, that no army would put a foot on the cursed Island of Ten Devils for any reason.

"Child eeid," the emperor turned to me, "The soldier has to do what must be done to save us all."

"She is not an eeid, Your Highness," Gyvan said. The Table went silent, waiting for Gyvan to explain himself. This he did, telling them how my vast knowledge of all things earthly and non-earthly came from my excessive reading and inquisitiveness, and how I had even defeated Sobo Ha-ha, the high eeid of Tera-Hool at his own game. The Elders and the raw-breeds looked at me in quiet disbelief. I believed they felt a little dim-witted that I, only a little girl, had been able to outwit them too. But in the end, as hard as it was for them to believe that I had carried out this deception for so long, they came to terms with the facts, for after all, I had solved the riddles and helped deliver the sacred orbs of Tichiman.

"We have no quarrel with you, little one," the emperor said to me. "You have served us well. But you must understand that the soldier must now do his part to finish what was begun."

"And must he die in order to finish it? It was you who failed to inform him that the Dark Widow was his mother."

"His knowledge of his kinship to the Dark Widow may have led to tragic consequences for us all, child," Tin-zim the raw-breed said.

"I fail to comprehend how," I said.

Shokolo-ba pulled out the small box that contained the scrolls that had the riddles of Tichiman. He pulled one out and said, "The answer to your many questions, Commander Drabo, lies in here, in the fourth riddle of Tichiman, the only one he had made easy enough for us to solve."

Finally, the mysterious fourth riddle was about to be revealed to us. What was it, and what did it have to do with placing Gyvan in chains? What did it have to do with the terror the Table felt in Gyvan's presence? How would it explain why Gyvan had to die in order to remedy the error of slaying the Dark Widow?

Sobo Ha-Ha Speaks

chapter 50

My spy owl, Noo, stood on my shoulder as Lord Elcan and I stood before Lord Venga at his court on the Island of Ten Devils. We trembled before him, uncertain of what action he would take against us for not preventing the murder of Mai-Fatou, the host of his Third Shadow, the White Shadow.

This fugitive raw-breed general was perhaps the most unpleasant of things one could lay eyes on, perhaps the most grotesque and ugly being in all creation. Raw-breeds were ugly, but this one must have been the ugliest there was. His eyes were small and one of the two horns that protruded from the back of his head had been halved by a blunt object. His face was awash in what appeared to be pus-filled boils, and he had a mouth that drooled some foul, disgusting greenish liquid of an almost indescribable nature. In short, this extraordinarily ugly creature presented a sight that would ruin even the appetite of a starving toad.

The slaying of the high lady had severely physically weakened Lord Venga, for the force with which the White Shadow from the slain widow had returned to him had taken a ruthless toll on his physical being. He appeared old, weak, frail, and diseased. He could barely hold himself up, and had to be assisted by servants. Even his meals had to be fed to him. But I was not discouraged. I understood that in a few weeks he would recover his strength and find a new host to help continue our effort against the empire and the raw-breed government in Eartholia Proper.

Lord Elcan and I had come to the Island of Ten Devils to consult with Lord Venga in order to know what we could do next, for though the high lady was no more, thousands of rebel soldiers stayed true to her cause. We stood in front of Lord Venga as the imposing and frightening creature sat in his court, his own network of spies and agents having already informed him of the death of Mai-Fatou and the fall of Tera-Hool long before our arrival at the Island of Ten Devils.

"They say you were outsmarted by a little girl," was the first thing Lord Venga said to me. "A little girl who was not even an eeid, they say."

"Lord Venga," I pleaded, "her knowledge is beyond that which any eeid can challenge or destroy."

"And you," Lord Venga turned to Lord Elcan. "You are yet to prove your worth to me. I do not pay you to fail, Lord Elcan."

Lord Elcan looked down in shame. We were both terrified of what Lord Venga would do to us. However, what was strange about him was that even with the death of the Dark Widow, he was not as worried as I thought he would be.

"My lord," I dared to say, "a new rebel leader will emerge to take Mai-Fatou's place. Whoever he may be can make a new host for your White Shadow."

Lord Venga looked at me and smiled, pus dripping through his fangs. It was a smile meant to reassure me, I know, but it appeared to me chilling and frightening, made more so by the odd and terrible contortions of his sickening facial features.

"We already have a host," he said, "one ten times more powerful than all the eeids on New Eartholia and me put together and doubled. All we have to do is get that host to our side."

"Who is he?" I asked, surprised at the speed with which Lord Venga had been able to obtain a new host.

Then he told me. I was horror-struck. It was a most unexpected person. Looking back, I should have known. The high lady had known, but I had not. And you will not believe who this person was.

The Words Of The Child Eeid

chapter 51

THE FOURTH RIDDLE OF TICHIMAN was about to be revealed to me and Gyvan, putting to rest the unexplained happenings of recent days.

"'It moves with the moon and the stars,'" Shokolo-ba began to read the riddle, "'with the sun and the blue sky, for its birth had brought death, and the death had brought lifetime upon lifetime which is equal to none, and a lifetime which has no end. What is it?'"

"The half-green crow," I said. "The answer is the half-green crow."

To explain the riddle for Gyvan, I began by telling the tale of the half-green crow, a tale lost in time and only very recently retrieved from old manuscripts hidden in private collections. A long time ago, a half-green crow promised to do a great favor for an eeid on condition that the eeid grant him a single wish. After the favor was done, the crow demanded that his wish be granted as promised. It was a terrible wish that the crow be granted the eeid's Third Shadow and all its powers. Not wanting to part with his Third Shadow, yet bound by his honor to grant the half-green crow's wish, the eeid placed his Third Shadow in the soul of the half-green crow's mother. The eeid could still use his Third Shadow as needed, but it could only be transferred to the half-green crow if it killed its own mother, a deed the eeid knew the crow would never do. But the eeid failed to understand just how badly the half-green crow wanted to obtain the powers of the Third Shadow, for soon after, the half-green crow did kill its own mother, and the Third Shadow and all its powers were transferred to it. The half-green crow became the most powerful crow in its realm, feared by all and knowing no fear itself. But the torment of slaying its own mother haunted it day and night, for to this day it is said that it wanders the sky aimlessly, knowing no rest and searching for a way to forgive itself for its abominable deed.

After telling the tale of the half-green crow, Musa the Elder explained how it related to the fourth riddle and to Gyvan's predicament, why the Table now feared him so, and most regrettably, why he had to die.

"Gyvan Drabo," began Musa the Elder, "you and the half-green crow are alike. When it slew its own mother, it obtained for itself powers beyond belief. Your own mother was the host to the White Shadow of Lord Venga just like the half-green crow's mother had been to the eeid. When you slew the Dark Widow, your mother, Lord Venga's White Shadow was transferred to you, along with all its powers. Because you inherited the White Shadow from your own mother, it is ten times more powerful than it was even with Lord Venga."

"Would it have mattered if another had slain my mother?" Gyvan asked.

"No," Musa the Elder continued. "It would have mattered not. When a host to the White Shadow dies, regardless of the means of passing, it is transferred to the nearest blood kin, its power increasing ten-fold should the transfer be from mother to son, as was the case with the half-green crow. As is the case with you, Commander Drabo."

So that explained it all.

Gyvan Drabo was now the host of the White Shadow!

But his mold of the White Shadow was not dormant as had been the case with Fadiga and the Dark Widow. His was active, ten times more potent than it was even with Lord Venga, on account that it had come to him from his birth mother, as had the half-green crow's.

Gyvan was now the most powerful being in the land. This explained the bizarre occurrence that had taken place in the Dark Widow's palace just before Gyvan's arrest. That was when the two hidden Horsemen who had ambushed and were about to kill a Red Sentinel were suddenly lifted off the ground by some unseen force, smashed against the ceiling, and flung to the floor, crashing to their deaths. This had been done by Gyvan without his knowledge or control, the subconscious of his all-powerful White Shadow having already started working in him, for he had wished those two Horsemen dead.

Gyvan could now destroy the Table and save himself if he so desired!

But though the Table stood imperiled in Gyvan's presence, it was still the duty of the Elders to do what had to be done to save the empire and man.

So Musa the Elder continued, "So we stand upon this piece of Earth, left with only one manner of dealing with the threat of Lord Venga and his White Shadow. That means capturing it from you, Commander Drabo, using the orbs which you have so dutifully placed into our hands."

"Could capturing Lord Venga's White Shadow from me enable you to destroy it once and for all?" Gyvan asked.

"No, High Lord," Shokolo-ba answered. "Though the permanent destruction of Lord Venga's White Shadow is our ultimate desire, it cannot happen without the presence of its primary host, Lord Venga himself.

"May we not then send troops to the Island of Ten Devils, aided by Gyvan and the powers of his newly acquired White Shadow, to capture Lord Venga and bring him to the Table?" I inquired, considering how Gyvan could use his new powers to save himself and permanently bring an end to the peril that loomed over Eartholia Proper and New Eartholia.

"Though the high lord now be ten times more powerful than Lord Venga himself," Shokolo-ba continued, "he at the moment lacks the experience of the White Shadow's use and would present no match for the experienced Lord Venga. We face no other choice now but to capture the White Shadow from you, Commander Drabo. When the process is done your body will sleep but will wither and die in the coming days."

Gyvan stood speechless.

He was now an eeid. But he was also about to be killed.

He was the host to the most powerful mold of Third Shadow, the White Shadow, now ten times more powerful than even Lord Venga. That was why he had been brought to the Table in chains. That was why he was so feared by the Table, the same Table which had just told him that he would have to die to save the empire, the Table Elders whom he could now destroy faster than any of them could even blink, if he so chose.

Yet Gyvan remained silent. Would he destroy the Table and join Lord Venga, or would he allow himself to be killed so that Eartholia Proper and New Eartholia could be saved? I understood his dilemma. How could he end his life at the peak of his power when he could choose to destroy those who wanted to destroy him?

The two raw-breeds, Tin-zim and Shokolo-ba, walked guardedly towards him with the orbs of Tichiman in their hands, ready to capture his White Shadow and end his life with it. Gans did not bother to call in his Sentinels, for he knew that if Gyvan wanted to destroy them all there would be little they could possibly do to stop him, not even with a hundred Red Sentinels. As for me, I knew not which way to turn. For the sake of man I wanted the White Shadow captured, but even more I did not want

Gyvan to die. But the thinking of the Table was clear: Gyvan had to go. But the problem was that nobody knew for sure what Gyvan wanted. He had not given his permission for his White Shadow to be captured, nor had he protested such a deed. He could destroy the Table and become the most powerful person in Eartholia Proper, or he could let himself be captured and his life be ended.

Which was it going to be?

The raw-breeds drew closer to him. No one was at ease, uncertain of what Gyvan would do. The tension rapidly built up, sweat running down the faces of several Elders. Only the emperor remained calm, confident of what he believed would be the outcome. Gyvan remained still, silent as a rock, giving no hint as to his thoughts or his actions that would follow. The raw-breeds continued to draw closer to him.

I held Naya tightly, frightened by the uncertainty of the situation, not certain whether I was for Gyvan or for the empire. Then, as if he sensed my dilemma and pain, he turned to me to put my mind at rest. He smiled at me and nodded, as if asking for my approval for whatever decision he was going to take. I had seen that smile before. It was one of peace and grace. He was letting me know that peace was going to prevail. I rushed to him and threw myself at him. He hugged me dearly and patted Naya's head.

"Tell Lili I thought of her every single day," he said to me. He then instructed Naya, "You take care of Aida, you hear?" Then he let me go. He turned to the Table and faced the raw-breeds, who closed in with the orbs.

The two raw-breeds began the eeidic chants to trap Gyvan's soul and capture the White Shadow. These chants were incomprehensible to all, for they were in Breed. Gyvan stood still, facing and accepting the fate that had come to pass for him. As the raw-breeds continued, Gyvan slowly began to lose his strength. There was a bitter agony in his eyes as he staggered and struggled to breathe. Then the orbs glowed and shrank. Gyvan dropped to the floor. I ran to him. He was not breathing, his lifeless body pale as a corpse. The tears streamed down my face.

I had been thinking relentlessly of what I could do to save him before he fully succumbed to the endless abyss of death. I clutched my only friend, Naya, hoping it would console me in my grief. Then a hand touched me from behind, softly, on my shoulder. I turned around and looked. It was the emperor himself. He had actually left his seat and come down to me, a most unexpected honor.

"Weep not for the soldier, child," the emperor pleaded with me. "He did what he believed had to be done. Allow him to rest in peace."

I cherished the emperor's kind words, but as he spoke an idea struck me. I faced him, the Elders, and the raw-breeds. I was going to try to do the impossible, to appeal to the emperor's sense of justice and duty to save Gyvan Drabo.

"Your Highness," I began, desperately trying to rescue my guardian soldier, "the Table declares that it is more desirable to capture the White Shadow from Lord Venga himself, for in doing so his White Shadow can be destroyed, completely ending forever his threat to Eartholia Proper and New Eartholia. I insist then that we take it upon ourselves to do as such—to seek out Lord Venga and destroy his Third Shadow."

The Table was briefly silent.

"But that would mean going to the Island of Ten Devils," Musa the Elder argued.

"It would also mean completely destroying the White Shadow, so it never again threatens man or raw-breed," I defended.

"You are right, child," Shokolo-ba said. "But you know, as we know, that no human army will ever again set foot upon the shores of Ten Devils."

"Gyvan Drabo has brought us this far," I insisted. "He can also find a way to recruit men willing to go to Ten Devils."

"The Island of Ten Devils is only one thing he has to worry about when recruiting men," argued Musa the Elder. "He also bears the Cross of the Paipan. No one in his right senses will be in his company."

"He has brought forth the orbs, my lords," I pleaded. "Surely he deserves a chance to save himself and capture Lord Venga, a more perfect and permanent solution to the troubles that plague us all."

"No, child," Tin-zim said. "The soldier cannot help us now, for he is no longer in possession of his White Shadow, his current entrapment by the orbs having caused the powers to be lost from him. Should he be released now he will be just a man again—fully human. And that is not all. The White Shadow trapped in the orbs would also return to Lord Venga, giving us no other means of capturing it, save from Lord Venga himself. Please, child, try to understand."

"Give Gyvan a chance."

"I am sorry, child," the emperor said. "We have to make do with what we have. As much as I wish we could, we are unable to destroy the White Shadow. All we can do is capture it from Commander Drabo."

Then I fell upon another idea. There was still one trick I could play, one I had not used before. "My lords," I addressed the Table, "Commander Drabo, High Lord of Tera-Hool and envoy of His Highness Emperor Abubakari II of Mali, is the only one I have left in this dying world. I have solved riddles for you, and now I must ask you to solve one for me. Should you solve it, I shall leave the soldier to his fate and trouble you no more. Should you not solve it, I must implore you to release him, to give him a chance to *destroy* the White Shadow!"

The Table remained quiet, taken aback by the boldness of my request.

"You do know, child," the emperor broke the silence, "that for the White Shadow to be destroyed, Lord Venga will have to be captured alive from the Island of Ten Devils and brought here to the Table. Do you believe capturing a raw-breed who is guarded by pray-devils, the most horrid creatures on this Earth, to be an easy task?"

"I also read from the Breed Legends, Your Highness," I began my response, "that should the Third Shadow of a raw-breed or eeid return to its primary host, as has just happened to Lord Venga, this primary host would be severely weakened, unable to properly defend itself or use its powers until a period of about thirty days has elapsed."

"And did you not also read, child, that the eeid or raw-breed will therefore have to depend upon the protection of others to protect itself during such a period of weakness, such as Lord Venga now relies on the protection of the pray-devils at Ten Devils, over whom he has absolute control?

"I did, Your Highness. But still I only wish to ask of you one riddle, a single riddle."

"A single riddle, eh?"

"A single riddle, Your Highness."

There was silence as the Elders pondered my proposal. I did not like this silence, so I decided to give some of the Elders something else in exchange for their cooperation. It had to be something they needed, and two of them were in need of something. So I addressed them directly.

"Magool the Elder," I addressed one of them, "you are in pain. I can help you."

"Indeed I am," Magool the Elder responded. "How did you know?"

"I can see. You have a severe case of stomach ulcers and the stomach flu. It has only gotten worse since I first appeared before this Table." I had indeed noticed his illness. He had usually spoken in agonizing pain and had frequently excused himself from the Table, and whenever he left he was holding his belly. "I can cure you of whatever ails you, Lord Magool, if you agree to consider my proposal."

"I am a sick man, yes," the Elder responded, "but will the others here agree to endanger humanity because of one sick man?"

I then turned to another Elder, Tehan. He was not actually sick, but what plagued him was, for many, worse than illness—chronic bad breath!

"Lord Tehan," I began, "I have noticed the reluctance of the other Elders to sit close to you. And those that sit next to you flinch and turn their faces away from you in disgust whenever you open your mouth to speak. Even you know that, and that is why you sometimes cover your mouth when you speak. I can heal you of whatever ails you, my lord."

The elder's face lit up. He said nothing.

"You can heal him?" another Elder asked me.

"That I can. All I wish is to ask of you just one riddle, and in exchange I will heal their ailments whether you answer the riddle or not."

There was silence again. No one said anything. I waited. We waited, until the emperor broke the silence.

"The girl shall pose her riddle," the emperor declared.

The Table and the raw-breeds protested vigorously, determined to see Gyvan and the White Shadow captured and sealed. Magool the Elder and Tehan the Elder said nothing, mindful that I had promised to help them in return for their support.

"But, Your Highness," Kouyaté, the Tuareg Elder began to protest, "why should we risk releasing the soldier when the White Shadow is finally within our grasp?"

"Because, Kouyaté," the emperor responded, "it is hard to find men like Gyvan Drabo anymore. He had the power to destroy us all and reign supreme, but he chose to control that power, setting it aside for the greater good. Such men are few. He deserves another chance at life."

Then the emperor turned to Tehan the Elder and added, with a chuckle, "Besides, you can smell Tehan's breath halfway across Timbuktu when he speaks."

"But how do we know Commander Drabo can bring Lord Venga before us, as the girl says?" Musa the Elder asked the emperor.

"Because the girl has given us her word," the emperor responded.

"Your Highness," Shokolo-ba protested, "you put the fate of two realms in the hands of a girl who has seen ten summers and no more on this Earth."

"This little girl you speak of, ten summers and no more, gave us the orbs. If she says Gyvan Drabo can bring forth Lord Venga from the Island of Ten Devils, then I trust it will be so. We will let her pose her riddle."

"But, Your Highness," Tin-zim protested, "we cannot release the soldier now."

"Answer the child's riddle and the soldier remains trapped. Answer it not, and the soldier goes free." This was the emperor's final decision. The matter was no longer for debate and the Table resigned itself to his decision, and then waited anxiously for my riddle.

So I began the riddle. "What is the dark creature that turns blue when unclothed, the creature that uses the eternal holes in the heavens to make night become day, the creature that is man in his land, but woman in another?"

The Elders discussed my riddle among themselves for a few minutes, the emperor not involving himself with them, for he was on my side. After pondering for a short while among themselves, Kouyaté the Elder, the Tuareg representative and the most boisterous against giving Gyvan another chance, spoke up.

"I have heard that riddle before," he began. "I remember hearing it as a boy. The answer, though, I do not remember."

"Maybe you have, Lord Kouyaté," the emperor said to him. "But the answer, you must remember, should you desire that the soldier remain trapped in his abyss."

The Elders continued conferring among themselves, until Musa the Elder spoke.

"The answer to your riddle escapes us, child," he declared, quite displeased.

The emperor smiled, pleased with my victory. I then provided the answer, which turned out to be much simpler than any of them expected.

"The answer, my lords," I began, "is the *Tuareg* man!"

"Oh?" exclaimed Kouyaté the Elder, the Tuareg representative. "Yes, now I remember. I am the dark creature, the Tuareg man. I turn blue when unclothed because the blue dye of my blue garments remains on my skin." He pulled back the sleeves of his blue garments, revealing the layer of blue dye on his skin. "The holes in the heavens are the stars and the moon, which my people use to navigate through the deserts at night." He paused, trying to remember more.

"What about the part of the riddle which states that *this person is man in his land, but woman in another?*" asked Musa the Elder.

"Most of us Tuaregs are Mohammedans," Kouyaté the Elder continued. "In most of the lands of the Mohammedans the women are the ones who are veiled, but in our Tuareg lands, the men are the ones who are veiled."

There was silence at the table. The Elders and the raw-breeds now had to release Gyvan per the emperor's word.

"Now will you release the high lord?" I asked.

"The Table gave you its word," the emperor said. Then he turned to the raw-breeds. "Release the high lord."

"As you wish, Your Highness," Shokolo-ba said, frustrated and disappointed.

After some incomprehensible eeidic chants in Breed by the raw-breeds, Gyvan was released from his ghostly gloom. He stood up, rising slowly, dazed and mystified. I ran to him and held his hand as he collected himself.

***

GYVAN DRABO WAS FINALLY FREE, returned to us where he belonged. Delight once again returned to me, my mind brought back to ease. Yet there was one person who was most displeased, who was angry at what had just happened, disappointed with Gyvan's return to an earthly presence. It was not Musa the Elder. It was not any Elder. It was Gyvan himself. He was not pleased at all.

"What is the meaning of this?" he roared. "My silent abyss had freed me from my guilt, but now I have been brought back into this cruel world to again face its torment."

He was right. He had been freed from the guilt of slaying his own mother. But I explained why he had been returned into this cruel world, into an even crueler one now to face Lord Venga himself. He was terrified.

"You expect me to go to the Island of Ten Devils?" he asked, a tremble in his voice.

"I do," I said.

"And you expect me to somehow get past the pray-devils and get to Lord Venga?

182

"I do."

"And you expect me to simply capture Lord Venga, again get past the pray-devils, and somehow bring him before the Table?"

"Yes, I do," I said again, confidently.

"Why are you so stubborn?" he stormed.

"Because that is how little girls are."

"Were we not in the presence of the Table I would give you a spanking so severe you would hate the word 'sit.'"

I simply looked at Gyvan and smiled, happy to see him again. He was happy to see me too, no matter how much he wanted not to go to Ten Devils, and no matter how much he said he had preferred his silent death trap.

"Okay, Ten Devils it will be," Gyvan said to me. "Pray for me while you stay in the palace."

"I am not staying here," I scolded. "I am going with you to Ten Devils."

"Don't be silly. Your duty to the empire is done. I can no longer risk your life, child."

"You will need someone to solve the riddle of the Keeper of Ten Devils."

The riddle of the Keeper of Ten Devils was known to be presented at the gates of the island, by an entity known only as the Keeper of Ten Devils, to all unknown parties who dared and wished to enter the island's interior. Solve the riddle, it was said, and passage would be granted into the island, where a most gruesome and certain death awaited you at the hands of the pray-devils, the ferocious creatures that inhabited the island. Solve the riddle not, it was also said, and a fate worse than death awaited you—banishment to Demon's Pit. You will soon learn more about this riddle of the Keeper and the Island of Ten Devils.

But even the riddle of The Keeper of Ten Devils could not convince Gyvan to let me accompany him to the Island of Ten Devils.

"I will find another eeid to help with the riddle," Gyvan tried to convince me. "The Island of Ten Devils is no place for a child."

"And if you do find another eeid, would he be willing to go to Ten Devils led by someone who bears the Cross of the Paipan?"

"The child is right, Commander," an Elder said. Gyvan reluctantly gave in, but was still tremendously worried for my safety.

The emperor soon dismissed Gyvan and me to be fed and be rested before returning to the Table to talk about the Island of Ten Devils. But before we could leave, I was reminded of some unfinished business I had started.

"You had your riddle, child," Magool the Elder said. "Now you must help me with my stomach pains."

"Chew two parts of ginger root each day until the pains stop," I prescribed, having learned of this remedy from a doctor in Gao.

"What about me?" Tehan the Elder eagerly asked, eager to end his chronic bad breath.

I hesitated a moment. Then I gave him my prescription.

"Wash your mouth every day."

Gans led us to our quarters, clearly bitter at Gyvan and despising the fact that he had been released. As we walked through the courtyard into our quarters, I looked at the sky growing ever darker, increasing the misery of man and beast alike. The flowers no longer bloomed, the crops no longer grew. The city's granaries, which had contained enough food to feed the city for ten months, had been completely emptied. Even the emperor and his officials were not immune to the misery around them, for even they had been reduced to eating fodder that was meant for cattle and other beasts of burden during the dry season. Everything had lost its vigor. Even the salt in the food served to us by the emperor's cooks had lost its taste.

It was dusk before Gyvan and I appeared before the Table again, and this time there were fewer guards present, for after all, Gyvan was no longer a threat to the Table and the safety of its Elders. We were here to discuss how Gyvan could possibly recruit soldiers to go to the Island of Ten Devils. This was a near-impossible task, for no soldier could be ordered, even by the emperor, to go to the island, just as no soldier could be ordered, ever, to take his own life.

"Your Highness," Gyvan said to the emperor after being asked whether he could be sure of getting any volunteers for his enormous task, "as of now I know of three men and a woman who, should they still be alive, would not hesitate to undertake this task for the empire." Gyvan was referring to his four army friends: Shang, the female scout; Jeevas, the cavalry officer and Shang's suspected lover; Babayaro, the migrant infantry officer; and One Eye, the albino caravaneer and archery officer.

"And why may they not be alive?" Musa the Elder asked.

"Because the last I saw of them they were on their way to Djenné, dispatched to help with the siege."

"Djenné," the emperor lamented. "Many an able soldier we have lost in that cursed city. Even after the death of the Dark Widow the city still stands."

"The city's defenders no longer fight for the Dark Widow," Shokolo-ba said. "They now fight for Lord Venga and the high eeid, Sobo Ha-ha."

"Then you must go to Djenné, Commander Drabo," the emperor continued, "and find the four souls who would follow you into certain death upon Ten Devils."

"That would make only six of you," one of the Elders said to Gyvan. "You, your four battle-weary soldiers, should they be alive, and the girl child. Six people to go to Ten Devils, answer the riddle of the Keeper, fight the pray-devil army, kidnap Lord Venga, escape from the island, and somewhere along the way possibly fight against the Paipan, who surely searches for you as we speak. The end of man has truly arrived. Six!"

"Six it may be," Gyvan asserted. "But we will make it work."

"Wrong!" yelled Gans, the commander of the Red Sentinels whom Gyvan believed was violently jealous of his important status with the Table. Gans drew his sword and rushed towards Gyvan. Completely taken by surprise, Gyvan could not react fast enough to Gans's aggressive move, for Gans, too, was known for his skilled swordsmanship. As we all gasped at what was about to unfold, Gans raised his sword, threw it in the air, and caught it by the point of its blade, his hand protected by the thick leather gloves he wore. He held the sword in that position, facing Gyvan. What was this Red Sentinel up to?

"Only six of you to go to Ten Devils," he said to Gyvan, "but I say seven, my lord. Commander Drabo, High Lord of Tera-Hool, I beg of you to accept my sword into your service. It has seen many battles for the empire and has bested many, and it will serve you on this most difficult quest you undertake. It would be an honor if you would allow me to serve one so noble as yourself, who was willing to give up his life for the sake of many. Please, my lord, accept my sword into your service."

All were awestruck, especially Gyvan, who had always believed this Red Sentinel to be a potential enemy.

"No, commander," Gyvan said to Gans. "It is you who do me the honor by offering your services. Stories of your exploits and deeds were what influenced me to join the army. The empire survives because of men like you. Gans of Selegugu, Commander of the Red Sentinels, I humbly accept your services."

Gans, perhaps the person most hated by Gyvan, and perhaps the person who hated Gyvan most, had become the first volunteer to follow Gyvan and me to the Island of Ten Devils—to certain death.

"Unto their deaths you send these men and the girl child, Your Highness," Kouyaté the Elder lamented, still disgruntled with the release of Gyvan, "to the Island of Ten Devils, a place we know little of, and where we can send no scout or agent."

"Wrong, my lord," Musa the Elder said. "There is one woman who knows more about the Island of Ten Devils than any human known to exist."

"How could she?" Kouyaté the Elder wondered aloud.

"She has been there."

"Where do I find her?" Gyvan eagerly inquired.

"Go to the Valley of Voices," Musa the Elder continued. "Ask for the Truth Teller."

Musa the Elder told us nothing further about the Truth Teller, other than that she was said to have seen at least a hundred summers. How could she have gone to the Island of Ten Devils and returned alive? We certainly hoped we could learn from her.

But first Gyvan decided to begin his recruitment for Ten Devils. It was better to start early, he said, increasing our chances of getting volunteers or whoever would be brave or foolish enough to follow a man crossed by the Paipan into the most dangerous piece of land on Earth.

Before Gyvan, Gans, and I left the palace, Gyvan sent a hasty dispatch to the Watchmen of Tera-Hool. Gans said that that was not going to help us, for the Watchmen could not be asked to go to Ten Devils, for their duty lay in Tera-Hool. Gyvan responded that his dispatch had not been a call for the Watchmen to follow him to the Island of Ten Devils. He proceeded to explain to Gans the purpose of his dispatch, but I did not stay to hear him, for I was called upon by the palace maids to be bathed and have my braids redone. When they finished with my hair, Gans told me I looked like a queen. Gyvan told me I looked like a squirrel.

Before our departure to recruit volunteers for Ten Devils and find the Truth Teller, Gyvan had another task to complete, one that was very dear to him. This was to visit his beloved Lili and to again inform her that he could not yet return to marry her on account of a most dangerous undertaking on the Island of Ten Devils. How would Lili react to all this?

***

"Ten Devils?" Lili screamed when Gyvan informed her of our next task. "Why would you go there? You should spare yourself the pain by falling on your own sword right now. At least that would be an easier death. And to think that you are taking little Aida with you—shameful!"

Poor Lili, her livelihood had been shattered in these dark times. The trade caravans that had traversed the northern desert, transporting the goods she had depended on for her trade, had ceased to exist. Nothing but skeletons—human, camel, and other beasts of burden—lay across that vast wasteland, they said. No markets remained for trade, for no farmer or craftsman had much left to trade. And gold, they said, had even lost its value. Even though the death, famine, despair, and desolation that ravaged the land had not touched or damaged her beauty, there was sadness and hopelessness in Lili's eyes, the same that lurked in every man, woman, and child, the same that made all know that death was near, the same that had only one meaning: we were the walking dead.

Though Lili was finally made to understand the necessity of our expedition to the Island of Ten Devils, she believed the venture doomed to failure, and she vainly insisted on its immediate abandonment.

But before our departure Lili brought us some food, what little she could scrape up. It was pounded pork brains, dried goat cheese, and millet.

"Where on Earth did you get food like this at a time like this?" Gans asked, puzzled.

"I had saved it for your return," she said, referring to me and Gyvan.

"Then you must join us to enjoy this meal," Gyvan responded.

"No," she said sadly, "I've had my share. Now is your turn."

The meal was a luxury not even the emperor could afford, and even though the salt in it seemed to have lost its taste too, we enjoyed our meal, during which time Lili cleaned and fixed up my Naya, making her look as new as she had been when Feidi gave her to me.

Gyvan had also been given a note for 100,000 gold dinars by the Table to help him recruit men for his expedition to Ten Devils. But you need not have been a cataract-removing doctor to know that this would do us no good. There was very little left to buy in the markets and no one would exchange his life for gold. Yet we were going to try to get volunteers by any means necessary.

First, Gyvan stopped at his regimental garrison to begin recruiting soldiers from there, but I think he also wanted to show off his new status to his former commander, Tigana, the friend who had discharged him from the army after his episode with the wild women, and whom he now terribly despised.

"I hear you are now the high lord of Tera-Hool," Tigana said to Gyvan as we all met in the garrison, along with Gans.

"So they say, General," Gyvan said.

Tigana was feeding his tits with some insects. He could no longer afford to feed them grain, their regular diet, though only a few grains per day would have sufficed. Tigana was truly glad to see Gyvan, and even though Gyvan claimed he despised the commander, he, too, was happy to see him. They set their differences aside and talked about the good old days, their adventures together, and about Gyvan's adventures, past and coming.

"So," Tigana asked at one time, pointing at Gans, "where does this snitch fit into all this?"

"Watch it!" Gans snapped back at Tigana. The only hatefulness here was between Tigana and Gans, for many high-ranking officers had never liked Gans, believing he held his position as the emperor's chief guard in too high a regard, frequently telling on other officers and influencing the emperor's decision on many matters. Yet not a single person could be found to prove these allegations true.

Tigana was most impressed with Gyvan when he learned that Gyvan had fought the Paipan and survived, but when Gyvan revealed his Paipan's cross, admiration quickly turned to fright for a short while, before it turned again into even greater admiration.

When Gyvan told Tigana about his intentions to recruit men for Ten Devils, Tigana, like Lili, believed the venture doomed, but told Gyvan he could try to recruit the soldiers. We all waited for the men to return from a training exercise just before nightfall. There were about 400 men in the regiment, the ranks having been replenished with many desperate souls who now flocked to the army hoping to gain free rationed meals. Understanding that the men had the lawful right to know the perils of his expedition, Gyvan revealed his Cross of the Paipan, causing quite a stir among the troops, made even worse after he asked for volunteers to go to the Island of Ten Devils on promises of rich rewards from the Table. But for all his pains, Gyvan got not even a single volunteer, with one man even stating that he would rather die of the misery here than live ten times the misery that existed in Demon's Pit or face a pray-devil or the Paipan. Another said he would rather get into an argument with his mother-in-law.

Gans, Tigana, Gyvan, and I then retreated to a room to discuss our options.

"None of your men would follow me to the island, General," Gyvan said to Tigana, who was now busy stroking his great tit.

"All but one. Me."

"You?" Gyvan asked, quite surprised.

"I, General Tigana, will join you on your quest."

A smile appeared across Gyvan's face. There now were four of us daring enough to set foot on the Island of Ten Devils—Gyvan, Gans, Tigana, and myself. But we needed at least 50,000 men if we hoped to stand a chance against the evil that lay in wait on the island. I was pleased that Tigana had decided to come with us, for he was a good soldier from what I had learned. Among his weapons was his throwing knife, a weapon designed with multiple blades in order to increase its chances of hitting a target when thrown. It was a weapon capable of chopping a man's leg off from a hundred paces, a weapon he had made to use on an old enemy he hoped to encounter, an enemy he only usually referred to as the traitor of Sihili Pass.

Our next stop was Djenné, to learn if Gyvan's battle companions were still alive. These were Shang, Jeevas, Babayaro, and One Eye, the one-eyed albino archery officer who had pulled out his own eye with a hot fish hook to prevent a blinding disease from spreading to the other eye. If they were still alive, would they be willing to follow us into certain death on Ten Devils?

As we journeyed to Djenné, one thing was clear. Gyvan was no longer the happy, talkative person he had been; an invisible torment lurked beneath his skin. He had lost some part of him. Deep within he was saddened, deeply distraught, not for the desolation that gripped the land, not for our impending and certain deaths on Ten Devils, but for the death of his mother, and the manner in which she had passed—the mother he had spent his whole life searching for. I tried to comfort him as much as I could, but still he seemed to withdraw into himself every day, becoming more and more of a recluse as the days went by.

***

JUST BEFORE OUR ARRIVAL AT Djenné I caught a glimpse of a familiar fiend. It was Sobo Ha-ha's spy owl. Had it spotted us? Would it again afflict us with some misfortune as it had in Tera-Hool? Gyvan had promised to destroy this spiteful creature should he again lay eyes upon it. But this did not to happen, for no sooner had we spotted the fiendish bird perched on an acacia tree than it locked eyes with us and dashed away before any harm could be brought upon it, and no doubt to inform Sobo Ha-ha and Lord Venga of our movements.

Sobo Ha-Ha Speaks

chapter 52

Tsing-tsing, Lord Venga's devoted raw-breed accomplice, attended to the raw-breed lord, who lay in bed, barely conscious. The raw-breed lord was drinking blood soup, a broth made from his own blood mixed with crocodile tail and spiced with baobab leaves and chameleon liver. I had concocted this medicine to help him recover his strength and the use of his Third Shadow much more rapidly, strength which he had lost when the White Shadow from Mai-Fatou and her dim-witted son had returned to his body. The medicinal blood soup, which had always worked well with eeids who had found themselves in similar predicaments, was not working as well with Lord Venga, perhaps because I had never before used it on a raw-breed. But still I held out my hope for him, especially since victory seemed to be finally within our grasp. The emperor and his raw-breeds had failed to capture Lord Venga's Third Shadow, the White Shadow, and it had had three human hosts, long enough for the dark forces to make a solid presence on Earth, and almost long enough for the still mysterious blood dripper to approach maturity. All we now had to do was wait for this blood dripper, whatever it was, to mature, and then this Earth and Eartholia Proper would be ours.

Neither Tsing-tsing nor Lord Venga was yet aware that Gyvan Drabo, his White Shadow's last host, had been lost to us. Lord Venga still believed his weakness to have been caused solely by the return of the White Shadow from Mai-Fatou, the high lady. Though victory was close at hand, I trembled as I brought the information of our loss of Gyvan to Lord Venga, for the loss could slow the maturity of the blood dripper, the only segment of his whole design which I still did not fully comprehend.

"Lord Venga," I called, a slight shiver running through me. "We lost the host."

The bowl of blood soup he been drinking from fell from his hand.

"Tell," he said weakly, frail from his recent ordeals.

I then proceeded to tell him about Gyvan's capture and the subsequent loss of his Third Shadow at the hands of the Table.

"So the Table will need me in order to destroy the White Shadow," he managed to say. "It is their only option."

"No army will follow the soldier here to Ten Devils," I emphasized. "In a few weeks the clouds will fully darken, the blood dripper will mature, and this world, and yours, will be ours."

"What makes you so sure we are so safe here from the soldier and the raw-breeds at the Table who support his every move?" Tsing-tsing asked.

"He has only the girl and two soldiers who follow him as we speak," I responded, having only very recently been provided this bit of information by my trusty eye in the skies, Noo.

"With himself and only the girl, he killed Mai-Fatou and has almost destroyed me," Lord Venga scolded weakly.

"We have the riddle of the Keeper, my lord." I tried to dispel his fears. "To get into this island they will have to answer the riddle, or be damned to Demon's Pit forever."

"And if by some miracle this little girl, who answered the riddles of Tichiman, should also answer the riddle of the Keeper, what happens then, eeid?" Tsing-tsing shot back.

"My lord," I said, "they will not even get that far, for I have a surprise waiting for them should they even succeed in setting foot upon this island."

The Words Of The Child Eeid

chapter 53

"WHY ARE THEY CALLED PRAY-DEVILS?" Gyvan asked me. "I've always wondered about that name. How can the devil pray?"

"The Breed Legends provide no answer for that," I responded. "But legend says that when man was enslaved in Eartholia Proper, he prayed to God for help. But God was unhappy with man because of his arrogance and disregard for all other creatures. So God did not respond to the prayer. But the devil did. To spite God and man he assisted the raw-breeds by giving them the creatures we now know as pray-devils."

Gyvan chuckled, obviously not taking the account seriously.

Upon our arrival at Djenné, where imperial troops continued to lay a desperate siege to the heavily fortified city, we found the situation even much worse than had been reported in recent dispatches. There were now more wounded than unwounded soldiers in the imperial lines. The city showed no signs of succumbing to imperial troops, thousands of whom had fallen, with no gains having been made against the rebels. Supplies were low and help was naught, men deserting by the hundreds daily, it was said. Even the war horses were starving, many having been let go by their officers because they could no longer be fed or provided for. Those were the unlucky horses. The lucky ones were simply killed and eaten by their owners and soldiers, sparing the animals the torturous nature of a slow and painful death from starvation and disease.

We made our way to the tent of the general in charge of the imperial forces.

"Ah," he greeted, referring to me as we walked into his tent, "what is an eeid doing in Djenné? It would take more than your Third Shadow to root out the rebellious scum holed up in the city."

I recognized the general. Mhal Cancid was his name. He had once been a teacher at the University of Gao, but like many, he had left to join the army when the war had broken out. He was a member of the Dogone tribe, the people who lived around Mopti, known for building their houses and towns on the faces of cliffs. He was more than a soldier and teacher. He was also a writer on scientific matters. My family had had in its possession one of his essays in which he helped to convince me, and almost all scientific minds in the empire's universities, that the sun, and not the Earth, was the center of all that lay here and beyond the universe. It was a fine piece of work, backed up with illustrations that showed all the planets circling the sun. I was pleased to see the old man. A far cry from his old days as the charming but controversial teacher, he was now a walking war zone. He had lost an eye to an arrow, it was rumored that he was slowly going blind in the other one, he limped on one leg as a result of a fight with an axe-wielding rebel, he had battle scars on every visible spot of his face and body, he had a huge bandage over his right palm, and an arrowhead was said to be buried deep within one of his thighs.

Eeid or not, Mhal Cancid thought Gyvan an especially cruel person to expose me, a child, to the horrors of a war zone. I assured the general that I had seen and been through worse, and would soon see, go through, and hopefully survive even much worst. He said he had a set of twin girls, about my age, and hoped that he would survive to see them again.

His next reaction was to Gans.

"What is this snitch doing here?" he asked disapprovingly of Gans. Perhaps Gans was responsible for him being sent to Djenné, I thought.

"Let old problems rest easy, Mhal," Gans responded.

I decided to quickly change the subject before it could get ugly.

"What is the nature of your wound?" I inquired about the wound on his right palm that was covered with the bandage.

"Pulled a flaming arrow out of the shoulders of one of my men," he said. "It gave me quite a nasty burn. The rebels still have so many resources in the city that they can afford to make entire arrows out of iron."

So the general was suffering from a burn. I could help him fix that.

"Ask your doctors to find some castor beans," I said. "Have them extract the oil by grinding and sifting the seeds. Soak a piece of cloth in the oil, then wrap it around the burned palm and hold another piece of cloth that has been soaked in hot water until the hot cloth cools down. Do this twice a day until the burn heals."

"You better do as she says, General, if you want any relief from that burn," Gyvan enforced.

"I know," the general said. "Her sister was one of the best eeids I ever knew. My wife has lost quite a few of my books to her, paying her for her services. How is that sister of yours, by the way?" he asked me.

"She is dead," I said softly.

While I helped the general with his burns, I decided to also apply what little I knew of medicines to aid in another grave illness that had befallen many an imperial soldier on this damned battlefield. This was gangrene, the dreaded infection that had led to the amputation of many a limb among many a soldier on this battlefront, both friend and foe. For many others, it had been too late, for they had succumbed to the infection after holding onto dear life for many a feverish and miserable day. So to aid with the war effort and to save many a life and limb, I also instructed the imperial doctors as to how to treat a wound and prevent gangrene from setting in. This amounted to the application of onion juice on the wound, finished with a coat of wild honey, if it could be found, and covered with a clean bandage.

Gyvan later explained to the general the nature of our mission. He then had the general summon the soldiers he had come to Djenné for— One Eye, Jeevas, Babayaro, and Shang. Sometime later, One Eye, Jeevas, and Babayaro arrived at the general's tent. Though they looked healthy and strong, you could see in their eyes the despair and fatigue that plagued this seemingly endless battle that had destroyed many.

"Where is Shang?" Gyvan asked?

"She took a patrol to scout a weakened area of the city's defenses we think we can make a push through," Jeevas said. "But not to worry. She'll be back. She always gets back."

"Yeah, you would know, eh?" Gyvan teased, touching on the suspicion that Jeevas and Shang were lovers.

Then One Eye turned to Gans and asked Gyvan, "What is this snitch doing here?"

"Watch your mouth!" Gans snapped back at Jeevas.

Had Gans, a close confidant of the emperor, upset the entire army? It seemed every soldier had something against him.

"We can deal with our personal problems later," Gyvan warned both men. "But for now let us work on the big problem that we all face."

"Good," Babayaro said to Gyvan. "I know you did not come here just to see our beautiful faces."

Just then an officer walked in and asked the general for permission to lead the next day's attack against any weakened positions on the city's defenses. Before the general could respond, two stray arrows burst through the tent. One hit a wooden tent pole and the other hit the officer straight through the neck. He dropped instantly, choking in his own blood and dying just moments later. Had that officer not been standing in front of General Mhal Cancid, the arrow would have hit him instead, putting an immediate end to his worries about his numerous battle injuries and pains.

The general did not seem disturbed or panicked at all. He simply called in some guards, who removed the body of the unfortunate officer. That was life as usual in the frontlines of Djenné. When Gyvan asked where the arrows had come from, the general said that they were from rebel hit-and-run soldiers who often sneaked into the imperial camps and shot random arrows into tents because they knew that those inside could not see where the arrows came from.

"That is just one more hazard we have to put up with in Djenné," he said.

A short while later, some soldiers brought in the severed heads of two rebels they said had shot the arrows. They had been tracked down and caught just before they could make a getaway.

Gyvan soon explained to One Eye, Babayaro, and Jeevas the purpose of his mission, causing quite a stir among them at the mention of the Island of Ten Devils. Though terrified, these true warriors dared show no fear. Within a short while they managed to live with the idea of going to the island, and even became quite enthusiastic about the venture.

And then Gyvan pulled off his headband, revealing the Cross of the Paipan etched on his forehead. The room immediately went silent. General Mhal Cancid was so terrified he almost ran out of the tent until he was reminded by Tigana that he was just as likely to get killed here in Djenné as at the hands of the Paipan. One Eye, Jeevas, and Babayaro were shaken too, but maintained their calm. This did not stop their commitment to Gyvan's venture.

"I have always wanted to feel the rush of fighting the greatest swordfighter known to exist," Jeevas commented, referring to the Paipan.

"I have always wanted to know what a pray-devil really looks like," Babayaro added.

"And what could be so bad about Demon's Pit? Well, this is my chance to find out," One Eye joined in.

"Fools, all of you!" General Mhal Cancid scolded. "You are all fools!"

***

By nightfall, Shang was back from her scouting assignment, reporting her findings to General Mhal Cancid. The weakened position she had gone to scout had been hastily rebuilt by the rebels, who had also sent out reinforcements to the area, expecting an attack there. She had lost two good men to the enemy during this assignment.

Shang was a beautiful woman whom I came to admire greatly. Gyvan had told me that she was the only woman in the army, accepted because of her great scouting abilities, a skill she had learned from her father, a famed hunter from the fabled hunting grounds of Do.

After reporting her findings she acknowledged Gyvan and welcomed him to Djenné, which she described as the rear end of a pregnant hippoptamus. Gyvan informed her of the purpose of his visit, and true to her warrior spirit she too, chose to show no fear, pray-devil or no pray-devil, Paipan or no Paipan.

"If the Paipan wants to get you, Gyvan," she said, "she'll have to go through me. And as for the pray-devils, it is about time they feel the rage of man."

As Gyvan, his recruits, and I left General Mhal Cancid's tent that evening, Shang, who had yet to acknowledge Gans's presence, turned to Gyvan and asked, "What is this snitch doing here?"

***

The following day, as we rode to the Valley of Voices to speak to the Truth Teller, it was clear that we could never find the 50,000 men needed to invade the Island, for how could one ask 50,000 men to walk to their deaths? The task at Ten Devils would have to be completed by only eight daring and senseless souls—Gyvan Drabo; Gans, the commander of the Red Sentinels; General Tigana, Gans's former commander; Jeevas, the cavalry officer; Shang, the female scout; One Eye, the albino archery officer and part-time caravaneer; Babayaro the infantry officer who hailed from lands beyond the southern forests; and me, Aida of Traoré, no more than ten summers on this Earth. So there we were, eight and no more, hoping to do what we believed could only be done by 50,000.

As we journeyed to the Valley of Voices, Gyvan decided to at least try to recruit soldiers from several military dungeons along the way, including one which housed some of the empire's most dangerous criminals. The dungeon commander believed Gyvan to have lost his mind by wanting to go to the Island of Ten Devils. Even those in the dungeons scheduled to be put to the axe, but offered a chance of freedom if they joined Gyvan's cause, preferred the relatively easier death of the axe man's blade than a chance at freedom only to meet a more gruesome end at the Island of Ten Devils, or sustain an even more miserable existence at Demon's Pit. And Gyvan did not even mention the Paipan.

In another dungeon two men who were scheduled to die on the same day we arrived there in fact readily volunteered to follow us to Ten Devils, but after Gyvan rightly informed them of the possibility of a Paipan attack, they very politely backed down, preferring the relatively swift and less horrifying death by the axe man. These two ignorant men, who had murdered their children for marrying each other because they belonged to different clans, walked themselves to their executioners and were put to the axe.

***

SOME DAYS LATER WE ARRIVED at the Valley of Voices. This village, which had once welcomed many a stranger, was now, like many a town and village, cursed by the evil that plagued the land. It now was desolate, unwelcoming, and mistrusting of strangers, its ragged inhabitants gawking at us through their windows as we rode into the village. Its chief came out to talk to us, no doubt unsure of our intentions.

"We search for the Truth Teller," Gyvan said to him after he inquired as to the reason for our visit.

"Go away," the chief warned us. "No one can help you here."

Gyvan displayed the imperial ring, convincing the chief that our visit was a matter of state and therefore of the utmost importance. The chief took us to the home of an extraordinarily aged woman, where we were all seated on stools under a huge, dead fruit tree in her yard. A young man the woman introduced to us as her grandson served us some bean cakes and corn beer. These were rarities during such times as these which we dared not turn down, out of respect for this old woman whose reputed knowledge of the Island of Ten Devils we so desperately needed.

"So," the Truth Teller began, with a cheerful expression and a smile that concealed beneath it a rare beauty that had been lost to time, "to what do I owe this royal visit?"

"The Island of Ten Devils, madam," Gyvan said.

At this, the Truth Teller's cheerful smile faded. She stiffened, as if some demon in her memory had suddenly been awakened. She said nothing.

Gyvan continued, "They say you are the only one known to have ever been to the island and returned, and the only one alive known to have ever seen a pray-devil." The Truth Teller said nothing. Gyvan pulled out a small sack of gold from his pouch and placed it in front of the Truth Teller. "Gold we offer you," he continued, "to tell us what you know of the island."

"And more gold to add to your fortunes," Gans added, placing another sack of gold in front of the Truth Teller.

The Truth Teller looked at the gold. She slowly picked it up and returned it to Gyvan and Gans. "Keep your gold," she said softly. "Your families will need this more than I will, for you will all perish at Ten Devils."

Gyvan and Gans reluctantly took back the gold, embarrassed for having thus dishonored the lady.

What the Truth Teller then told us about the Island of Ten Devils is an incredible story of horror, death, courage and survival, a story that reaffirmed many a tale that already existed about the accursed island, a tale that caused my blood to freeze and my bones to crackle in terror.

***

To FULLY UNDERSTAND THE STORY of the Island of Ten Devils, it important to go back into history, to know how the pray-devils that gave the Island of Ten Devils its horrendous reputation came into being.

According to the Breed Legends, during the Breed Wars of long ago, the pray-devils were a species created by the raw-breeds to aid in their enslavement and control of the human species. They were the guards of the human slaves on New Eartholia, the slave colony in the outer world dimension—our Earth. When the key to the portal of Gorgida was lost, the pray-devils trapped on Earth with the human slaves hastily abandoned their duties and escaped into the unknown to seek their own fortunes. No one knew where on Earth they had settled. They had simply vanished, it seemed. But many thousands of years later, as man greedily settled all corners of this Earth, some ventured too close to the hidden Earth-home of the pray-devils, the Island of Ten Devils, located in the middle of Moon Lake. That was when the dreaded monsters resurfaced, some eighty summers past, during the reign of the Sossos.

Seeing their Earth-home threatened and unable to control the growing number of human settlers, who closed in ever more rapidly, the pray-devils decided to send a warning to humans to keep away from their island. Their message was one never to be forgotten—a massive and devastating raid on the surrounding towns and villages to let man know that they, the devils, were to be feared and not to be trifled with. But even that did not stop man. It only worsened and confirmed man's fear of these man-eating creatures, whose presence presented an everlasting threat unless they could all be destroyed.

So in response to their raid, the Sosso king dispatched a huge force of about twenty thousand strong to the Island of Ten Devils. All were slaughtered by the pray-devils, down to the last man, within moments of their arrival on the island. To prevent another invasion by the humans, the pray-devils invoked Mory Tipp, a famed eeid they had kidnapped, who before he was eaten by them, was coerced into protecting the island with the mystical Gates of Ten Devils. These gates led trespassers either further into the island or into the eternal damnation of Demon's Pit, a place worse than death. Any man or woman wishing to set foot upon the island had to stop at the gates to answer a riddle posed by the ghostly spirit of Mory Tipp, the gatekeeper now known to all as the Keeper of Ten Devils. Answer the riddle, it was known, and passage would be granted into the island where death was certain at the hands of the man-eating pray-devils. Answer it not, it was also known, and damnation of your soul into the abyss of Demon's Pit was the result. Demon's Pit—a place where even devils and demons feared to tread, which even devils and demons considered hell.

After the failure of the first invasion of the island, the Sosso king gathered an even larger army of 30,000 men, which he led himself onto the island. They never got past the Gates of Ten Devils, for their failure to answer the riddle of the Keeper condemned them to Demon's Pit, where even then, eighty years since, their undying screams could be heard, pleading for death to come, to ease the agony that they endured, an agony worse than anything words can describe. This account of the second invasion was told by two men who had stayed ashore to watch over the emperor's fleet of boats, but had been close enough to witness the events. These men were long since dead.

That is how the pray-devils had protected their Earth-home for all those years since their discovery by the humans, using fear and intimidation to keep humans away from their island, for no one, not even an army, could set foot on the island for fear of facing the same fate as had befallen the Sosso king and his 30,000 men, who continued to lament in eternal damnation in Demon's Pit. Hideous creatures they were, those pray-devils, immortal creatures immune to the natural hazards of disease and age that plagued man and animal alike.

***

BUT HOW HAD THE TRUTH Teller survived on the Island of Ten Devils?

"Eighty summers ago," she began to tell her tale, "I was only eighteen summers on this Earth. People had been disappearing. Some had gone to the farms and never returned. Many children had gone to the learning houses and never returned. No one knew why, until the Earth-home of the pray-devils was found in the middle of Moon Lake. Those who had disappeared had been caught and fed upon by pray-devils. Then one night the horrors took a turn for the worse, when the pray-devils decided to send man a message to make sure we stayed away from their island. They raided the surrounding towns and villages, killing hundreds. Those were the lucky ones, for their deaths were instant. Others, thousands of them, were taken away. Those were the unlucky ones. They were to be fattened and eaten at a later time.

"The devils are flesh-eating beasts that eat at least a small part of their victims immediately after the kill, when the flesh is still fresh. They fight with two weapons each, a broadsword and a flesh hook—a fork-like weapon used for sticking, holding, and devouring in a single gulp the body part of their enemy that has been sliced off by the sword. I saw a devil chop off and eat a man's arm right before the man's very eyes."

The Truth Teller's account was truly terrifying, but what she had imparted to us so far was common knowledge to all. Gyvan, however, chose to let her talk on. Perhaps it made her feel better, believing that she could possibly dissuade us from throwing away our lives.

"When the Sosso king learned of the pray-devil raid he was furious," the Truth Teller continued. "He called on soldiers and volunteers throughout his empire and from neighboring kingdoms, to come together and put an end to the pray-devil menace. 20,000 turned up, 20,000 healthy and strong fathers, brothers, sons. Among them were also a few mothers, sisters, and daughters, including me, who followed this army to support our fathers and sons.

"Onto the Island of Ten Devils we marched, under the leadership of the emperor's only son, Prince Chelé, bold and boastful, ready to end the pray-devil threat. We made our landing on the island without incident, whereupon patrols were immediately dispatched to seek the positions of the beasts that inhabited this vile place on Earth. But all the patrols reported no sightings upon their return. It was a ghost island, it seemed, the silence noticeable, with nothing in the winds to warn us of the troubles that lay ahead. It was so tranquil that poor Prince Chelé even suggested that the beasts must have fled after laying eyes upon his enormous army, a suggestion with which all the officers agreed. But escaped or escaped not, the emperor's son vowed to hunt them down to the last one. So the army marched on, further and further inland. Still nothing was found, that is until such time as we came upon a crudely constructed fortress. It was a deserted looking building surrounded by a single high wall with an iron gate. The army stood in front of the gate while the prince and his generals pondered how best to proceed. Yet no pray-devils came out to engage us. They were cowering, in fear of our army. That is what we believed.

"Then everything suddenly changed. We started to hear screams among our men. We would hear a scream and reports would get back that a man had simply vanished without a trace. Then we soon learned that somehow our men were being snatched and dragged away by the very quick, stealthy, and cunning pray-devils, whom we could not as yet see. The screams were getting closer to me each time, my heart pounding faster and faster as panic and confusion began to take hold among the troops. The screams and disappearances continued for a few minutes more. Then there was complete mayhem. The devils then emerged from hiding places behind every tree and rock, swarming us from every direction, many others charging out from the fortress. The next few moments came to pass very quickly, moments that lasted only a few unbelievably terrifying moments, yet claimed the lives of twenty thousand souls.

"Twenty thousand perished that day on Ten Devils, all killed and eaten along with their horses too. Twenty thousand brave souls who had come to destroy the evil that resided on the bedeviled island. Even the emperor's son, Prince Chelé, was not spared. He invoked the emperor's name in vain as he was pulled off his horse and gobbled up, head first.

"It had taken two months to raise that army, but only a few minutes to destroy it, almost to the last person." Here the Truth Teller paused, the events that had transpired on that day too disturbing to bring to memory. "I know you want to know how I survived," she then said to Gyvan, directly.

"Please, tell," Gyvan urged.

"It was my sister's husband who saved my life," the Truth Teller continued her account. "He was a big man, but no match for the devil in a pray-devil. I saw his arm and left side hacked off and devoured by a beast. He managed to break free, crawl to me, and ask me to lie down, whereupon he laid on me, shielding me from the devils. He was in terrible pain, his wounds no laughing matter. He bled to death, right there, in my arms.

"Those devils never saw me under his body. When their carnage and euphoric butchery was done, they searched the bodies for fresh kills. One came over to my sister's husband, but he had been dead a long time, so he was left alone. During the night, when I thought it safer, I crawled from beneath his body into the safety of the surrounding forest, where I hid and rested until I could recover my strength.

"I was not the only survivor. There had been others too, but not for long. I continued to hear them plead for mercy throughout the night as they were tracked, hunted down, and eaten by those merciless beasts. When my turn came, I ran as fast as I could, with the devils in hot pursuit. I ran blindly, and soon after chanced upon a river into which I jumped. It was my every intention to drown myself in order to spare myself the terror of being consumed alive. But to my surprise, the devils ended their chase, stopping right there at the edge of the river bank."

"They cannot swim?" Shang asked, alarmed.

"No, child," the Truth Teller said. "Pray-devils cannot swim. They gave up their chase and I swam into Moon Lake and hastily rowed away in one of our boats, leaving that horrific place for good.

"The Sosso king was so horrified by the news I brought back that he raised an even larger army of 30,000 strong, which he led himself onto the Island of Ten Devils, despite my pleas that he no longer try to invade the island. And of course you know the rest. Today those 30,000 men, including the emperor, languish in Demon's Pit, their souls trapped forever in torment in a place where neither man nor demon dares to tread."

We all knew the account of what had happened to the emperor and his 30,000 men. They had failed to answer the riddle of the Keeper of the gates of Ten Devils, installed there by the famed eeid, Mory Tipp, on the forced command of the pray-devils, after the first attempted human invasion of their island.

It was after the failure of the two invasions of the Island of Ten Devils that the next Sosso king decided that the pray-devils could not be defeated on their territory. He embarked instead on a policy of containment, whereby he stationed thousands of troops in the lands surrounding Moon Lake, where the Island of Ten Devils rests, hoping to make the pray-devils unable to escape or launch another raid on the humans. This strategy of containment, continued by the Malian emperors after the takeover of the Sosso kingdom, proved successful, for during the eighty years since the last attempted human invasion, not a single pray-devil had left the island to lay a hand upon a human creature.

"Why do you think," the Truth Teller asked us, "that eight of you with one child can do what 50,000 men failed to do?"

"Because," Gyvan began, "we now have one thing that those 50,000 men did not have—advance knowledge of our enemy and its weaknesses—thanks to you."

"And how do you intend to answer the riddle of the Keeper at the gates?"

Gyvan looked at me and smiled.

***

Meeting Mhal Cancid, the imperial general at Djenné, reminded me of a book his wife had given to my dear sister as payment for services performed on her. The book was titled *Book of Routes and Kingdoms,* and in it was the citing of a somewhat clever trickster of an animal said to reside in Arabia. This animal was a harmless hooded serpent known to the Arabians as the false cobra, for it mimics the look and behavior of the very dangerous and deadly cobra, putting to fright and to flight any foe that may lay eyes on it. I told Shang about this interesting snake as we conversed on a variety of subjects during our journey. Little did I know that this seemingly meaningless conversation with the scout would save our lives in the days to come.

A few days into our journey to the Island of Ten Devils, I noticed that Shang had begun carrying a small bag slung across her back. No one knew what was in it, and no one cared to ask. That was her affair. But I would later learn that it had to do with my mention of the Arabian false cobra.

Most of the talk as we rode to the Island of Ten Devils was about its damned pray-devils. There was also talk about the Paipan, who we knew was out there, watching and stalking, waiting for the right moment to strike her marked target and all who were with him.

"Can you fight her?" Babayaro asked Jeevas one afternoon as we grazed the horses.

"I do not know," Jeevas said. "But all I know is that no person, save Gyvan, has ever fought a Paipan in single combat and lived to tell of it."

"What about you, Gans?" Shang asked the Red Sentinel. "Perhaps if the Paipan attacks, you should be the one to fight her. After all, you have fought and defeated Paipans before, at Assassin Hill. You were there, eh?."

"True," Gans said softly. "But I was with an army, fifty-nine times the number of Paipans."

Shang was referring to the Battle of Assassin Hill some fifteen summers past, when the confederation of fourteen kings had treacherously attacked and destroyed the Paipans in order to end any potential threat they may have posed to their own power. Gans had been among the two thousand Red Sentinels called to join that battle that had seen the demise of the Paipans.

Eight days after we left Djenné, we came upon a river where huge boats usually ferried travelers across to the other side. But upon our arrival at this location, only one boat remained. It was the last for the day, we were told, and it was already packed with travelers venturing elsewhere to seek better fortunes. No room existed on the boat for all eight in our party and our horses. We needed the entire boat, including the three crewmen who sailed it, if we intended to cross the river. Because we could not wait until the next day for another boat, Gyvan offered gold to the travelers in exchange for their places on the boat. But, in a hurry themselves, the offer was turned down by them all. Our negotiations failed to persuade any of them to change their minds. So I took the only option left to us. I climbed onto a nearby crate, reached for Gyvan's head, and pulled off his headband, revealing the Cross of the Paipan. Within the blink of an eye, not only was the boat somehow miraculously cleared of passengers, but also the entire area. Some of the passengers had even jumped overboard and swam away. The boat's crewmen were only stopped from leaving when

Gans held them at sword point. They then involuntarily volunteered to sail us across the river. Gyvan promised to pay them twice what the escaped passengers were supposed to pay. While delighted that they were at least to be compensated for their forced discomfort and endangerment, they never stopped staring at Gyvan and looking over their shoulders, expecting the Paipan to suddenly appear and silence them forever.

As we crossed the river, there existed an eerie feeling about, eerie because we knew something was quite amiss, something horrible in the making. But what? What had suddenly caused the hairs on our backs to stand on their ends? What had suddenly sent a chill through our spines? Then the answer came from one of the crewmen.

"My lord," the crew chief yelled at Gyvan. "We are being followed!"

It was a fast boat. A boat just like the ones the rebels had used for months to patrol and terrorize fishermen along the rivers they controlled. This one was teeming with Horsemen, only they were dismounted, of course, unable to fit all their horses on the boat.

"Faster," Gans yelled at the crewmen as the rebel boat chased on, drawing closer to us.

"No," Gyvan ordered, "let the Horsemen come. We will make an example of them."

The crewmen reluctantly brought our boat to a stop as ordered by Gyvan. Gyvan and his soldiers then stood on deck in a column and at the ready with their swords drawn, while the crewmen hid behind crates, terror-stricken at the horror that was to come. I stood behind Gyvan and his soldiers. Shang, who still had the mysterious small bag slung across her back, winked at me reassuringly. I should have been frightened, but I was not. I was with the finest soldiers in the empire. I felt safer with them than I could have felt with an army of ten thousand.

Tigana pulled out his throwing knife and checked it for its sharpness, then returned it to its sheath, perhaps hoping soon to use the weapon of vengeance on the old enemy he often referred to as the traitor of Sihili Pass, the enemy he said he had made the knife to use on.

The rebel boat drew nearer, eager to make its kill. There were about twenty Horsemen in it, determined to face Gyvan and his six soldiers— hardly a fair match for the rebels, the poor unfortunate souls. What were these Horsemen thinking? I asked myself. Did they have any idea who they were up against?

"Our fight is not with you, Horsemen," Gyvan shouted towards the rebels as their boat got within hearing range. "The Dark Widow is dead. Go home to your families." No response came from the Horsemen. They were eager to draw blood. You could see it in their eyes.

As soon as the rebel boat got close enough to our boat, the Horsemen in it all lined up on the side of their boat. Swords drawn and spoiling for a fight, they all made a unified jump into our boat. At that same instant I flashed a glance towards our crew to see if they were doing anything to help. They were not. They were cowering in a corner to save their skins. When I looked back towards Gyvan and his soldiers, they were cleaning blood off their swords. The rebels all lay in a neat line in front of them, slain.

What happened had been too fast even for me to describe. The Horsemen had simply been obliterated before I had even had time to understand what Gyvan and his soldiers were going to do to them. It was as if they had all been killed while in midair as they jumped into our boat, before they had even landed on the deck.

"That wasn't so difficult," Shang said, sheathing her sword.

"Look!" one of the crewmen suddenly yelled.

Heading towards our boat were more rebel fast boats—five of them. That meant there were about a hundred Horsemen in all on these boats. It had been quite easy for Gyvan and his soldiers to handle twenty Horsemen on the first boat. A hundred would have been no crisis either, but Gyvan and his soldiers needed more room to maneuver and fight, or risk being surrounded in the confined space of our boat and slaughtered.

Tigana turned towards the boat's captain and barked, "To land! Quick!"

Gyvan threw a small sack of gold dinars at the boat captain. "There is enough gold there to buy you another boat and pay for any expenses," Gyvan said to him.

The captain picked up the sack. "All hands!" he screamed at his men.

I have never seen men work harder for their pay. They raced for the nearest section of land as the rebel boats gave chase, getting ever closer. Our boat soon arrived on land, on the edge of a swampy forest. The crew gathered the gold Gyvan had given them and quickly disappeared into the surrounding forest. This was not their fight, and for good measure they had done the right thing. Gans picked me up with one arm and threw me across his back.

"Hold tight, little girl," he said to me, "and don't you let go."

We all jumped out of the boat onto land, an extremely swampy piece of terrain where the soldiers were sunk in the mud up to our knees. The rebels were now even closer since we had come to a stop. We made a dash for dry land, where Gyvan and his six soldiers could more readily combat the 100 men after us. It was a dash for survival. As we ran through the swamp we could hear the Horsemen behind us. They, too, had gotten off their boats and were hot on our tails.

Running in the swamp reminded me of two pieces of information I had once read about the swamp. The first was that in the land of the pyramid builders beyond the great northern desert there existed a most unusual cat, known to the locals as the swamp cat, for it lived in the swamps. But what made this cat unusual is that it did not mew like other cats. It barked like a dog. The second piece of information I had read about the swamp I will reveal to you in a short while, for it would play a crucial role in events that were yet to unfold.

As we ran through the swampy forest, searching for a clearing dry enough and wide enough to enable Gyvan and his soldiers to make a successful stand against our pursuers, we heard a cry from Babayaro. We turned towards him. He was sinking.

Quicksand.

"Quick!" Gyvan ordered. "Let's get him out!"

This was not good. None of the soldiers could get close enough to Babayaro to aid him, for fear of ending up in the same quagmire. We had to think quickly and do something fast if we hoped to save him as he struggled to free himself. We had no rope to throw to him and pull him out. He struggled to reach out to some of the lower branches of a baobab tree he was sinking next to, but to no avail. The branches only got farther and farther away from his reach as he continued to sink. He was soon down to his neck in the glop. This brave soldier was about to meet a gruesome end, a most miserable demise. Poor Babayaro. Had he come to Mali all the way from the kingdoms beyond the southern forests only to drown in a puddle of mud like some wild animal?

But as quick as the devil can be, quick-thinking Jeevas pulled out his sword and leaped onto the nearby baobab tree, where with a single swoop from his sword he chopped down the longest branch he came upon. The branch fell to the ground, whereupon Gyvan immediately picked it up and ventured as close to the quicksand as he could and threw the branch to Babayaro, who grabbed it eagerly, just as his mouth was about to be engulfed by the mushy, slimy, slushy, muddy puddle. Gyvan and the others grabbed the other end of the branch and pulled. Babayaro came out, safe at last.

There was no time to relish this triumph; no time even for him to thank his redeemers, for the Horsemen remained in hot pursuit, getting ever closer to us. Jeevas leaped down from the tree. We had to keep moving. But whatever was in the slush into which Babayaro had just sunk all the way to his mouth must not have been pretty.

He stank.

We finally chanced upon some dry land wide enough to make a stand against the Horsemen, but not before Babayaro had sunk himself into a pool of water to rid himself of some of the mud, and thankfully, the stench that had clung to him.

Gyvan and his soldiers then stood their ground, awaiting our pursuers. Gans pulled me from his back and gently placed me on the ground, upon which time he and his surviving companions quickly formed a defensive circle around me. The Horsemen soon emerged from the swamp and immediately surrounded us, none daring enough to come close to within sword range of Gyvan and his soldiers. The leader of the Horsemen leader emerged. He stood in front of his men and smiled, likely believing that his numbers intimidated the imperial soldiers.

Tigana was the first to speak, recognizing this leader as Lord Elcan, the Dark Widow's military commander. The two knew each other.

"Lord Elcan," Tigana began. "I never thought I'd see this day, when I can finally put you to the sword."

"General Tigana," Lord Elcan responded, "you ought to be dead, killed at Sihili Pass with the rest of your wretched bunch."

"You were always a sloppy officer, Lord Elcan. That's why you never made general. You were careless, that's why I remained alive. You never could do anything right."

"No, I never made general because I did not know the right people, like you did."

"Well, Lord Elcan, today you will pay for your crimes at Sihili Pass."

I had heard about Sihili Pass before—an incident of the utmost betrayal and treachery. It had happened in the opening days of the civil war, when a small company of imperial soldiers had been sent to a small village to build a well so that the people there would no longer have to venture into dangerous rebel territory for much-needed water. A large rebel detachment caught wind of this design and attacked the village repeatedly in order to discourage them from cooperating with imperial authorities. Every rebel attack was repelled by the much smaller imperial force stationed in the village, whose success lay in its occupation of strategic ground which gave it a great advantage, preventing the rebels from entering the village. However, the resources of this small imperial force were dwindling, and even though reinforcements had been sent for, they had not arrived. The rebels had become desperate in their search for a way to enter the village but knew of none. Running out of supplies and desperate to save his own life, the commander of the imperial force did the unthinkable.

He betrayed his own men, and the village.

In exchange for his own life, he secretly met the rebels and showed them a hidden route into the village, a pass previously concealed by the village's defenders. It did not end there. He led the rebels into the village and instructed them to kill everyone, his men and every living soul—the men, women, children, and even the dogs and cattle. He had wanted no survivors left to reveal the evil he had committed. That imperial commander joined the rebel army and became one of its leaders.

The next day imperial reinforcements arrived at the village. They found only one survivor—an officer of the imperial force. He was barely alive. His name was Tigana. The commander who had betrayed him was none other than Lord Elcan.

Today both men would settle old scores.

"Now, General Tigana," Lord Elcan began, "I finish what I started at Sihili Pass."

"No, Lord Elcan," Tigana responded. "Now we make the souls at Sihili Pass rest easy." The general readied his throwing knife.

The Horsemen charged. Gyvan and his soldiers stood their ground, maintaining their circle around me, a human fortress created for my protection. Lord Elcan lunged at Tigana.

The ensuing battle was intense, Gyvan and his soldiers moving in unison, leaving a pile of dead and dying Horsemen around them, the bodies forming a barrier of sorts against other attacking Horsemen. The numbers of the Horsemen dwindled as the moments went by in this fight which the Horsemen were going to lose. Those among them who ventured too close to Gyvan had the unpleasant surprise of encountering his wrist knife across their throats, ending with an "urghh" and a gush of thick red blood shooting from them. Tigana and Lord Elcan were at it as well, their own fight of vengeance and retribution in progress.

While the fight was going our way, it was clear that Gyvan and his men were slowly losing their breath, tiring from the overwhelming numbers they faced. These were no ordinary soldiers they were fighting. These were Horsemen—the best soldiers in the rebel army. Yet in a short while the rebels were soon reduced to about thirty, still more than three times our number. Gyvan and his soldiers could hold their ground for barely long enough to eliminate these thirty. Then we heard more noises coming from the surrounding forest. Who else was coming?

More dismounted Horsemen—about sixty of them.

Gyvan and his soldiers sank in despair at the sight of the Horsemen's reinforcements, tremendously increasing the difficulty the imperial soldiers now faced. They had already been engaged heavily in this battle for longer than they would have wished. But even the strength and stamina of these soldiers had its limits, and they could not now possibly hold out unendingly against a relentless foe of about ninety that surrounded them.

"Give up the fight and I promise you that your deaths will be swift," Lord Elcan gently said to Gyvan and his soldiers in absolute confidence of his imminent victory. "Give up not, and you will still die, eventually, slowly." Lord Elcan laughed eerily, with a seriously and dangerously threatening undertone of the pains he was capable of inflicting upon some unfortunate victim, if given the right opportunity.

Then just when it seemed our circumstance could get no worse, more Horsemen arrived, joining the thick of the fray. About forty of them. And these were mounted! We had to do something, and very quickly. There was no way the imperial soldiers could now survive this vastly increased number of Horsemen without a miracle. We now faced about 140 Horsemen in all, including cavalry. How could we get out of this? There was only one way out—to run. But how could we even do this? We were completely surrounded. Yet we at least had to try. While maintaining their circle around me, the imperial soldiers and I slowly inched away from the clearing, making a break for the surrounding forest and hoping to use its thick vegetation to cover our escape, hacking our way through the hordes of Horsemen. And behold, we did manage to get to the thick of the forest, leaving a trail of dead and dying.

But alas, something went horribly wrong. I got cut off from Gyvan and his soldiers. I immediately began desperately running away as about fifteen Horsemen took after me in hot pursuit. I was screaming as loudly as I could, knowing that Gyvan and his soldiers could hear me. I looked back and saw them chasing after the Horsemen following me. And behind my protectors were the rest of the Horsemen, itching to slice them to bits, like hounds on a blood trail. While I was slightly comforted that the imperial soldiers were coming to my rescue, something else disturbed me.

Shang was missing.

Had she been cut down? Had she met her end?

The Horsemen on my tail were quickly catching up to me, though I ran as fast as my legs could carry me. But my run was not blind. I had a little surprise planned for my pursuers. I was looking for the baobab tree, the one next to which Babayaro had almost sunk into the quicksand. I soon spotted the tree and I came to an abrupt halt, waiting for my pursuers to get closer. They got closer in no time, their swords eager to shed my blood. I looked at the quicksand, desperately hoping that what I was about to do was not ill-planned. If it failed it would be doom for me. It was a risk few would take, but one I had to take, for I was left with little choice. It was a gamble with my life, which had to do with the second piece of information I had read about swamps, the first being the existence of the swamp cat that barked like a dog.

I looked again at the quicksand, and then back at my ferocious pursuers, who were getting ever closer to me, their razor-sharp swords hungry to slice me to shreds. Then I did what I had to do. I plunged myself into the quicksand. My pursuers came after me. They had me. That is at least what they thought, until they realized what I had known for some moments now—

We were all sinking.

I could see the shock on the faces of Gyvan and his soldiers when they realized what I had done. They were too occupied with the other Horsemen to find the time to assist me. More Horsemen attacked them, once again surrounding them, leaving absolutely no chance for my rescue or escape for them.

My pursuers and I continued sinking in the slimy slush, the pursuers struggling violently to free themselves and desperately calling on their fellow Horsemen to help them. But that help was not coming, for the other Horsemen at that moment solely concerned themselves with destroying Gyvan and his men.

Lord Elcan and his Horsemen closed in on the terribly fatigued imperial soldiers, ready to make their kill. The imperials had all but given up, with Shang already dead or captured, and me sinking and soon to be up to my waist in the quicksand.

"As I said, General Tigana," Lord Elcan said to Tigana, ready to put him and his party to the sword, "now I finish what I started at Sihili Pass."

Then something happened.

At first, I was not quite certain of what was happening, until it became obvious that the Horsemen were suddenly screaming for their lives and scattering in all directions. Something, or someone, had appeared on the other side, putting the fear of the devil in their very souls. Whatever this thing was, it meant death for them if they stood in its way. Lord Elcan stood his ground, waiting for the Horsemen along this creature's path to clear out so that he could see for himself what had terrified them so. And soon the creature was revealed.

My pursuers and I kept sinking.

This thing which had so terrified the Horsemen was not a thing at all. It was a human, a woman, the Paipan, the quickest and deadliest swordfighter there was, the most feared assassin.

The battle assassin had finally come to make her kill.

An enraged Lord Elcan aggressively scolded his men as they fled in all directions. "She is on our side!" he screamed at his men. "Get back here! The Paipan is with us!"

Some of his Horsemen returned, their brief escape having given Gyvan and his men just enough time to catch their breath.

I continued to sink to my death, Shang was dead, and Gyvan and his fatigued soldiers were surrounded by Horsemen. Now the Paipan, no doubt in the service of Lord Elcan and Lord Venga, had chosen this moment to terminate her marked target, Gyvan Drabo. Did her sudden arrival make our already bleak situation even worse? It should have.

But the Paipan's next actions brought a puzzle to us all that one expected. Almost as suddenly as she had appeared, she swiftly extracted her single-edged blindingly sharp sword from the sheath slung diagonally across her back and struck at a mounted Horseman. The rider's horse jerked underneath him as the force of the assassin's blow flung him into the air, leaving much of his blood and a disgustingly nauseating chunk of his decapitated entrails on his spooked horse. What was left of the man's body then splashed violently into the swamp, his torso and legs held together only by his spine and the narrow portion of his skin that covered the back of the spine. The assassin then proceeded to attack more unsuspecting Horsemen in her path, making it known that she was not on their side.

But whose side was she on, and why?

Lord Elcan hid himself behind a tree, coming to grips with the inexplicable turn of events. Why had the Paipan changed sides? Did she want to fight Gyvan by herself? The Horsemen were fighting the seven toughest soldiers in the empire, and it was proving to be no simple task. Having the Paipan join the conflict against them, as was seemingly the case, did not exactly help their situation. This sudden turn of events so confused the Horsemen that many of them took flight once again.

But would all these do me any good? My pursuers and I continued to sink, our deaths drawing ever closer. Yet there existed a major difference between how we were sinking. While the mud was up to the necks of my pursuers, it was only up to my waist, even though I had plunged in before them. They continued to struggle and cry for help from their comrades, who now were busy fleeing away from the Paipan, their task of killing Gyvan and his soldiers now made enormously more hazardous to their health.

I glanced towards Lord Elcan. He was trying to understand the happenings with the Paipan. As his men fled in all directions, he understood that he alone could not stay and fight Gyvan, his men, and the Paipan. He struck down one of the mounted Horsemen from his horse and was about to mount it, when to his shock an object came flying through the air towards him. Before he could react, this object crashed against his ankles and violently sliced off both his feet. It was Tigana's throwing knife, his weapon of vengeance he had kept all these years for the day he would meet the traitor of Sihili Pass. A grisly vengeance was exacted at last.

Lord Elcan plunged into the swamp on his knees and with a loud splash and a piercing cry, and in incalculable pain and agony. The mud was up to his chest. He could not stand. He no longer had any feet to stand on. Abandoned by his Horsemen, there was no escape for him. Gyvan and his soldiers left him there for now, giving him a moment to experience the same agony he had impacted upon many a man, woman, and child at Sihili Pass and elsewhere.

Gyvan and his soldiers ran towards me, my pursuers having disappeared beneath the swamp, sunk in the quicksand without a trace. The imperial soldiers were surprised to see that I had only sunk to my waist. They quickly used the same branch that had been used to pull out Babayaro during his own near demise to pull me out, bringing a welcome relief to us all. I was out and they were now safe from the Horsemen. Then they turned around. Someone was standing before them, sword drawn and bloodied.

It was the Paipan.

What were they to do now?

Or was it the Paipan?

At least that was what Lord Elcan and his Horsemen had thought. But standing before us was our very own Shang, in all the semblance of the Paipan, dressed like her, pretty as she, and just as viciously bloodthirsty.

"How did you think of that?" I asked her.

"The false cobra," she responded with a smile. I smiled too. Gyvan and the other soldiers were at a loss at Shang's words, but I understood. She was referring to the information I had imparted to her about the false cobra, the hooded Arabian snake I had read about, which pretends to be a cobra so as to frighten away predators. Yes, that piece of information had saved our lives.

Shang had saved our lives by becoming the *false Paipan*.

What she had carried around in that mysterious bag that had been slung across her back were items of disguise to make her appear in the semblance of the assassin. We were all elated that Shang was not dead, Jeevas more elated than all, for there was that look between the two of them that showed a great deal of care for each other, such as only lovers could manifest. She threw herself into his arms and he held her tightly. We let them have their moment, the rumors about them being lovers very likely true.

Soon the attention focused on me and how I had managed to keep afloat while my pursuers had sunk. Whatever was in the slush into which I had partially sunk must not have been pretty.

I stank.

"As for you, little girl," Gyvan said to me as he picked up and dipped me into a pool of water to rid me of some of the mud, and thankfully, the stench, "Whatever caused you to plunge yourself into the quicksand, knowing death was imminent?"

"There is a lesson many swamp-dwelling people have learned about quicksand," I responded. "The more you struggle to get out of it, the faster you will sink. But if you remain calm, you could stay afloat longer because the body is not as heavy as quicksand. The Horsemen did not know this. I remained calm, they did not." This was the other fact I had read about swamps, in addition to the existence of cats in some swamps that bark like dogs.

"What if Shang hadn't appeared to save the day?" One Eye asked.

"We would have been killed anyway," I responded. "All I did was delay my death."

Then we all turned towards the badly injured Lord Elcan, his screams cutting through the newly found silence in the swamp like a pig on the way to slaughter. Tigana walked up to him and stood over him.

"Your wounds bleed under the swamp," Tigana said to him as he reached into the swamp and retrieved his throwing knife, his weapon of vengeance used upon the traitor of Sihili Pass at last. "That's good, because I'm not going to kill you."

"Be sensible, Tigana," Lord Elcan pleaded, a desperate desire for survival in his eyes. "Gold! I could give you more of it than you can imagine."

"Soon it will be dark," Tigana continued softly, indifferent to Lord Elcan's pleas. "There are all kinds of nasty creatures in the swamp that come out to feed at night. The tiny ones are attracted to blood. They will begin by feeding on your wounds and will slowly work their way up, feeding on you from the inside. If you are lucky it might only take you three days to die."

"No," Lord Elcan pleaded, "you cannot leave me here like this!"

"Take this time to think about the pass at Sihili. Farewell."

The imperial soldiers and I began to walk away from the area, almost deafened by the violently desperate cries of Lord Elcan as he pleaded for our help.

***

SHANG EVENTUALLY RID HERSELF OF the Paipan disguise lest she scare away ordinary citizens or set an army against us, or even worse, lest the Paipan stumble upon us and find the scout in her semblance.

As we traveled to Ten Devils, Gyvan and his soldiers chiefly engaged themselves in planning strategies they intended to use on the island. At one time while we rested I asked Gyvan if he also had planned a strategy to counter the Paipan's skill. He simply requested that I have faith in him. I had faith. But I also believed in the practical. Faith alone could not vanquish the Paipan and whatever hordes of pray-devils awaited us on Ten Devils. If Gyvan and his soldiers had struggled to defeat the few hundred Horsemen encountered in the swamps, then what about the thousands of pray-devils that inhabited the island? Faith alone could not bring us victory. We needed something more practical, something to strengthen our faith. Something that could toughen Gyvan and his soldiers, that could help protect them from harm.

Armor!

I had put this to thought for quite some time. What could I do to protect Gyvan and his soldiers from the broadsword, flesh hook, and bite of the pray-devils; from the arrow of any Horseman; or worse, from the deadly blade of the Paipan? The answer soon came. It was steel, cold hard steel, the very metal used in making the best swords for the army. But steel was too heavy and hard to get. Gyvan and his soldiers needed something lighter, for they had to be able to maneuver, and quickly too. Then I thought of iron. But it was not as tough as steel, and it was heavy too. It could be cumbersome. Wood perhaps, I thought. It was light and could stop sword slashes and arrows from long ranges. But it would be no defense against the powerful jaws of a pray-devil and could break easily under a heavy blow from a pray-devil's blade. What else could there be?

I could think of nothing else to protect the soldiers, no other form of armor that could be quickly put together to aid them. I was about to settle for tin plates, the type used by some special units in the emperor's army, when something happened. It was something very simple, which to the ordinary eye was just another element of life. Yet to a walking library like myself, it was something more, one that was about to answer my questions on armor.

It was the simple human action of spitting.

Gyvan had just spat out a piece of mango he had been chewing after realizing that the mango in his hand had half a maggot in it. But how did the simple act of spitting help me to answer a question about armor? It reminded me of a tiny creature we know as a spider, of which there exists many a species that have been observed and written about by curious minds. There are some that can kill a man, some as small as ants, some as big as mice, and some whose females kill and eat the males after mating. And most importantly, there are some that immobilize their prey by spitting on it, paralyzing, and eating it. Spitting out the mango had reminded me of the spitting spider.

But what had spiders to do with Gyvan, his soldiers, Horsemen, pray-devils, the Paipan, and the armor I needed? The answer is spider webs. Though he never had the chance to prove his theory because he got killed in a horse racing accident, a mathematician in Timbuktu with an interest in animal products had argued that the silk from a spider's web was five times stronger than iron and steel if measured pound for pound. In addition, it was more flexible. That meant I could use spider silk to build armor for Gyvan and his soldiers that was stronger, more flexible, and much lighter than steel.

"Spider silk?" Gyvan mocked me after I informed him of my intention to build such armor. "Is this your idea of a joke?"

But he knew I could not be joking. He consulted with his soldiers about my intention, all of whom decided that it would be a waste of their time to build armor out of a substance as feeble as spider silk. But after I reminded them that according to my calculations the average pray-devil bite could inflict four times as much damage on a man as that of the biggest crocodile ever spotted on the Sankarani River, they wasted no time in helping to gather all the spider silk I needed, by paying some locals five pounds of hard-earned dried beef to collect as much spider silk as they could possibly find. The locals had refused to accept gold, understanding its near worthlessness during these rough times. After many hours they brought back about ten bales of spider silk. For another six pounds of beef, I hired three weavers who worked day and night to weave the silk into suits of armor. After three days of collecting and weaving, compressing and weaving again, we had eight suits of armor, one for each of us, each suit only big enough to cover the torso and back. Gyvan tested his armor by placing it on a tree, and then having One Eye shoot one of his arrows at it. The arrow stuck in the armor for about half a second, and then fell off with a bent tip.

The armor worked.

So the mathematician of Timbuktu was right. I had proven his theory. I was the first to create armor out of spider silk, armor that was stronger than iron or steel, much stronger than what the army used, yet much lighter and more flexible. In better days, without a doubt I would have been the talk of the universities. But now nobody cared, save those who were about to use the armor. We were now better ready to deal with whatever obstacles lay ahead, whether they were of this world or another.

***

SEVEN DAYS LATER, WE ARRIVED at the shores around Moon Lake. Around this lake thousands of garrisoned imperial troops were strategically positioned, as had been the case for many a decade, making sure that the pray-devils remained contained on their island of death. The commander of the troops, though thinking us insane and trying to dissuade us from setting foot on the island, showed us the best location to land on the island should we still stubbornly decide to proceed as we intended. Needless to say, we found not a single soldier among the thousands here who would follow us to Ten Devils. The commander believed that that would dissuade us, but it did not.

However, the commander's greatest weapon, which he hoped would totally dissuade us, came at nightfall. He walked us to the shore of the lake, where we heard the most disturbing and terrifying sounds one could ever desire to hear. They were the screams of the Sosso king and his 30,000 men trapped in Demon's Pit, pleading for death to come and relieve them of their unending anguish. But there was no death, only misery. Truly, Gyvan's soldiers and I were petrified. Gyvan alone remained unshaken, informing us that he had absolute confidence in my ability to answer the riddle of the Keeper, just as I had done on many an occasion past.

The truth is that I had no such confidence myself. What if I failed?

At dawn, after readying our weapons and new suits of armor, we were ready to depart for the island itself. The garrison commander gave us a boat to sail to the island. He and his officers knew so well that only certain death awaited us that they even asked us if they could keep our horses which we had to leave behind.

The lake was as calm as death itself, but we sailed on. Every few moments a few screams were heard from Demon's Pit, causing me to shake violently each time. I held Naya tightly.

"Don't you worry, little girl," Shang consoled me at one time. "Those devils will have to get through us all before they can get to you."

Then Gyvan said to Naya, "You be a good girl. You will be fine."

Then I noticed that Gyvan's soldiers were staring at him as if he had lost his mind by speaking to a doll. Gyvan and I smiled at each other. We alone understood Naya.

Shortly afterward, we reached land and disembarked.

We now stood on the most perilous spot on Earth—the Island of Ten Devils.

Sobo Ha-Ha Speaks

chapteR 54

"Eight humans pose little threat," Tsing-tsing the raw-breed said, referring to Gyvan, his soldiers, and the girl child. "They'll make quite a tasty snack for the devils."

"The humans won't get that far," I added. "The riddle of the Keeper will condemn them to Demon's Pit before they can get through the gates."

"They have the little girl," Tsing-tsing said. "I will therefore not trust our security to the riddle."

"There might be no need for the Keeper's riddle or the pray-devils," I said. "I still have a pleasant surprise I've arranged for our unwelcome guests."

Noo had reported the presence of Gyvan Drabo and his team on our island. What folly for such brave men and women to walk headlong into certain death or damnation.

The Words Of The Child Eeid

chapter 55

THE ISLAND WAS SILENT, A silence so loud it was deafening, interrupted only occasionally by cries of lament from the tormented souls doomed forever in Demon's Pit. Would we meet the same fate as Prince Chelé and his 20,000 men who were ambushed and wiped out within minutes, or would we meet the same fate as the prince's father and his 30,000 men who were now damned to eternal torment in Demon's Pit?

Much of the island was rocky and dry, with a heavily forested area we could make out some distance away. It was in the same forest where the Truth Teller had hidden during her dreadful day on the island of death and sorrow. Birds chirped in the sunny weather. Colorful flowers and tasty looking fruits hung from the few plants and trees that dotted the rocky plain just before the forest. It was an inviting scene such as had not been seen anywhere else in the empire for many months now. Yet behind all this dazzling beauty lay death and damnation, the worst of each that anyone could not possibly desire even upon an enemy.

We proceeded silently inland with Gyvan and his soldiers moving stealthily, their swords drawn, watching every step they treaded and expecting an ambush as had befallen Prince Chelé and his men.

Then we came to a sudden stop. I held Naya tightly with one hand and held Gyvan with the other. We froze, staring in absolute horror at the person who stood before us. We very carefully stepped back, the terrifying being that stood before us causing this immediate but careful retreat. At first I thought Gyvan and his soldiers were about to turn back and flee, but this was not the case. They were only taking a moment to determine how best to manage the deathly peril that stood before them.

"What now?" asked One Eye, the albino.

No one responded. They all had the same question as One Eye.

Standing before us and ready to deal a quick death was the battle assassin—the Paipan. The real Paipan. I managed to throw a quick glance towards Shang who, while as terrified as the rest of us, must have been thankful that she had rid herself of the Paipan's disguise. Had she not, none can say what manner of unthinkable retribution she may have received from the merciless assassin. The Paipan stood still, neither uttering a word nor budging from her position as Gyvan and his near panic-stricken soldiers scrambled to make a hasty defense against this unbeatable foe. I stared at her, attempting to comprehend how a woman so wronged in her past could choose to right her wrongs by wronging so many others. She was as cold as death itself.

As I feverishly stared at the assassin, I noticed something very different about her this time, something no description of her had ever mentioned. It was her clothing. It appeared we alone had not thought of armor. She too, had been at it, for like us, she was now clad in armor, a notion quite new, for Paipan's were not known to have used armor. She must have learned that Gyvan, her marked target, was now accompanied by six other soldiers, six very good soldiers. That was the only reason I could fathom that she had armored herself in a fine suit of breastplate armor that fittingly showed her fine curves, revealing the full woman of her. But what might her armor have been made from? Bronze, iron, steel, wood, padded cotton, or even spider silk? No, not at all. It was made with the hardest bone in the human body.

Teeth. Human teeth. Thousands of them.

The Paipan had had two layers of teeth attached together to make her armor, reinforced by a thin sheet of iron in between the layers of teeth. Her armorer was superb, making me quite jealous, for very few weapons could penetrate that armor. I could see the despair in the eyes of Gyvan and his soldiers upon setting eyes on her armor. It was hard enough to fight the Paipan, and now she was not only the Paipan, but an armored Paipan. How much harder could a battle against her be?

There were seven professional soldiers in all, yet together they still dreaded the Paipan. And still she just stood there, watching them, her demeanor calm and focused. She waited for the first one among them with a death wish to move against her. The soldiers stood in a row, with me having been pushed to the rear of them to keep me clear of the assassin. If she wanted to get to me, she would have to go through all seven soldiers first.

221

"Assassin," Gans called daringly, "we seek entrance through the Gates of Ten Devils. In the name of Emperor Abubakari II and all things dear to man and to Mali, we ask that you step aside and mind your own affairs."

We all waited for a response from this harbinger of death whose face expressed no emotions and whose sword still rested in its sheath that was slung diagonally across her back. We waited for what seemed an eternity, hoping to avoid a fight that we were likely to lose. No response came from the cold-hearted assassin.

"Then I'm afraid you have made your choice, assassin," Gans continued, attempting to sound brazen in the face of certain doom. "Death for you it will be."

What unfolded next was perhaps the most startling display I had seen in all my months of observing combat. At the very instant of Gans's last word, an arrow from One Eye's bow sliced through the air and headed straight for the Paipan's eye. It was a lightning-quick and unexpected shot which none had expected and which no target could cheat. Yet as easily as a four-wheeled cart on the downhill, the Paipan, with her right hand moving quicker than a wench can curse a common thief, snatched the arrow in midair inches away from her eye and very instantly sent it flying back at the unsuspecting albino archery officer with a deadly speed and accuracy equaled only by that of a spitting cobra. One Eye's life was only saved by his equally quick reflexes, which enabled him to swiftly step aside, letting the quick arrow fly past him just inches away from his own good eye. It all happened so fast I thought I had dreamt the whole thing. I just gawked at the assassin and the archer in speechless amazement.

But that was only the beginning.

In a flash, and faster than I could even think, all seven soldiers and the Paipan sprang towards each other, eager as the devil can be, colliding in the middle, with the assassin drawing out her sword only at the very instant of their collision. She moved faster than anything I had ever seen, fending off her attackers quite easily, attacking and defending when necessary, and sometimes even gaining the upper hand and putting her opponents on the defensive. She was spectacular. She was magnificent. She was a marvelous swordfighter, repelling attack after attack and launching attack after attack of her own, which also were repelled by the soldiers.

The soldiers grew desperate and frustrated as the moments went by, moments that only seemed to make their foe stronger. The soldiers tried every fighting trick they knew, only to see it crumble in the face of the

Paipan's vastly superior swordsmanship. They tried everything, except the throwing knife of General Tigana, his weapon of vengeance with multiple blades, which could chop off a man's feet or rip his head off his shoulders from a hundred paces. It was the same one that had doomed Lord Elcan, the traitor or Sihili Pass. Now it was time to again put it to use. The general quietly withdrew from the fighting while the other soldiers kept the Paipan engaged. General Tigana soon stood still, watching the assassin closely, waiting for the right moment to strike with this deadly weapon. It had never failed him. It could not fail him now.

Soon a precise and perfect opportunity arose. The Paipan's back was turned away from Tigana as she easily defended an attack from Shang and Gans, who attempted to flank her. Then, swiftly and without a moment's notice, Tigana's secret weapon flashed out of the hidden sheath beneath his tunic and whizzed towards the battle assassin.

There was a deathly whizzing sound in the air as the vicious throwing knife rapidly spun towards its target. This time it wasn't heading for her legs as had been the case with poor Lord Elcan. It was heading for her neck, to make a quick and certain kill. Her back was still turned towards Tigana and his weapon, which was rapidly closing in from behind her, perhaps a fitting end to the Paipan. She would not even know what hit her. Her death would be swift.

But alas! Yet again the battle assassin, as easily as a swallow can glide, swiftly spun around and snatched the weapon in midair—a feat none had ever done before, not to the general. But before the general had time to think about his mishap and absorb the shock of his failure, his own weapon suddenly came flying back towards him, heading for his neck too. What he had meant for another's doom was now destined for him. He just stood there waiting for his end as his own weapon, which on many an occasion had saved his life, was now about to take it on account of the Paipan's insurmountable skill.

It is often said that a man who builds a house knows it best. So it may be said that a man who builds a weapon knows it best. Perhaps that is what accounted for what Tigana did next. Just as easily as the Paipan had caught his knife in flight, so too did Tigana. He caught it and replaced it in its sheath, resolving that while it had vanquished many an enemy, it was useless against the Paipan, the greatest fighter in the empire. And as quickly as the eye can blink, Tigana was back in the fight, throwing blow after blow at the unshaken assassin. I had observed the Paipan and Tigana in astonishing bedazzlement as each had displayed a fighting skill very few in the entire army could ever come close to matching.

The Paipan was now fighting against seven again. It seemed not to matter to her whether she was fighting seven or seven hundred. There were times during the fighting when she attempted to break free and head for me, but each time, she was swarmed by the soldiers who watched over me like bees around their hive.

Many moments of fighting elapsed and I noticed that Gyvan was no longer fighting. He had withdrawn from the fight and was watching it intensely. He was studying something. He was watching the assassin's every move. Then he walked up to me.

"How do you stop an undertaker from dancing?" he asked me.

"The Dance of the Undertaker," Jeevas said, referring to Gyvan's question after having stumbled close to us in the midst of the fighting and overheard his question. "The Paipan uses the Dance of the Undertaker. I thought that fighting style was only a myth."

"No, Jeevas," Gyvan said. "With a Paipan, everything with the sword is possible."

"Her skill gives her the strength of a hundred soldiers," Jeevas said.

"So," Gyvan turned to me again, "how do you stop an undertaker from dancing?"

"Simple," I said. "You stop the music."

Gyvan smiled. He had finally found a way of besting the Paipan. During their first encounter he had begun to study her moves and fighting technique. Now, at this moment, he understood that she used the legendary Dance of the Undertaker, a technique believed to be lost in time and known only in myth. With this technique the Paipan moved according to how her opponent moved. Her opponent's foot movements, which determined his next body movements, told her what to do next. The Paipan's "dance," or her next move, was in response to the opponent's "music," or his foot movements. All Gyvan had to do now to stifle the Paipan was to stop the music, or his foot movements, a move that would therefore stop the Paipan from "dancing," or knowing what his next move would be.

Gyvan was now ready to rejoin the fight. But first he attempted to again negotiate with the battle assassin.

"Assassin!" Gyvan called out.

The fighting stopped immediately. The assassin and the soldiers turned towards Gyvan.

"This fight is between you and me, assassin," Gyvan said. The Paipan offered no response, save her already familiar cold, blank stare.

Then to his soldiers Gyvan said, "This is my fight. I alone will battle the assassin."

Shang attempted to dispute. "That—"

"No, Shang, the assassin is mine."

Reluctantly the other soldiers backed off. Gyvan alone stood in front of the Paipan.

"Assassin," he called. "I again ask of you to stand down and let us be. I, too, know how it feels to slay one's kin by one's own hand."

And behold. There was a reaction from the Paipan this time, Gyvan's last words having awoken the bitter memory in the assassin of when she had been forced to slay her young in order to spare them a most painful and torturous death. Gyvan had likened her experience to the slaying of his own mother. We all waited to see or hear what she would say or do. She looked at Gyvan square in the eye, as intensely as never before. A single tear drop rolled down her left cheek. Gyvan had brought the Paipan to tears. Would she at last come to reason and let us be?

She lowered her sword, walked close to Gyvan, fixed a deathly gaze upon him and said, "Fall on your own sword and die."

That was the only time I ever heard the Paipan speak, offering Gyvan mercy by giving him a chance to kill himself.

"Then to battle it is, assassin!" Gyvan said.

I then saw again one of the most spectacular fights I have ever seen. Gyvan and the assassin attacked each other and collided in the middle with a thunderous clash of death-dealing swords, whereupon Gyvan stood his ground, not moving his feet, leaving them still, but fending off attack after attack, and throwing offense after offense of his own. The Paipan watched Gyvan's feet, but they produced no "music" for her to dance to. And though she soon became disoriented, she still fought on, narrowly missing a few death jabs against Gyvan.

After a few but extremely intense moments, the Paipan stepped back and stared at Gyvan, puzzled, wondering how her opponent had so suddenly turned his fortune.

"I offer you one more chance, assassin," Gyvan pleaded with the Paipan. "Sheath your weapon and let us be."

The Paipan, in a rage fueled by her displeasure of meeting a worthy challenger for perhaps the first time, charged at Gyvan. But her rage violated a prime rule in the Dance of the Undertaker: the dancer must always be mild-tempered, and fight with the sword, not with anger. In her rage she got careless, and in her carelessness, she exposed herself to the point of Gyvan's sword. Gyvan did not fail to seize this opportunity that may not have again arisen. He stabbed the assassin right on her right shoulder, leaving a gaping hole there that instantly spat out a thick gush of red hot blood. The Paipan fell back in disbelief as she felt the blood dripping from the wound, her right arm completely disarmed. It was the one she had used to wield her sword.

To everyone's disbelief she promptly snapped up her sword with her uninjured hand and instantly charged at Gyvan, just as ferociously as before, and without a moment's delay. She fought just as well with this hand as she had with the other. Gyvan stood his ground, his feet motionless. Even with only one good arm, there was no doubt that the Paipan could still make quite a "dancer" if "music" was provided. Gyvan took no chances. With some sudden and blindingly quick moves he struck at the good shoulder and both legs of the Paipan in ultra-quick and easy succession, puncturing and immobilizing the respective limbs.

Gyvan had done the unthinkable. He had bested the Paipan!

We stared at the assassin in utter disbelief. First her sword dropped. She tried to pick it up but failed, her injured arms too weak to be of any use to her. Then she dropped, falling against a dead tree. Gyvan sheathed his sword. He very guardedly walked over to her and looked at her straight in the eye. I knew she still had a lot of fighting in her, only her body could not support it. Blood oozed from every limb of her body.

I, too, walked to the Paipan and looked her straight in the eye. She was still spoiling for a fight. I pitied her. A woman so wronged by this cruel world, a woman who also had wronged many in this cruel world, a woman like no other, now bested. What would her fate now be? That was for Commander Gyvan Drabo, her conqueror, to decide.

"Let her live," Babayaro urged Gyvan. "She is the last of her kind."

The other soldiers mumbled in agreement.

"As you see, my sword is sheathed," Gyvan said. "I have no intention of taking the life of the last Paipan."

Sobo Ha-Ha Speaks

chapteR 56

"So the Paipan is beaten?" the still ailing and fairly weak Lord Venga managed to roar at me as I fed Noo with horse flesh, a reluctant reward for having reported this piece of devastating news to me.

"So much for your unpleasant surprise, eh?" Tsing-tsing scoffed.

"I did what I could," I defended myself. "The soldier is good. What can I say?"

"And where do they head now, the soldier and his team?" Lord Venga asked.

"Right towards us. They have left the Paipan wounded," I said.

"Will she live?" Tsing-tsing asked.

"Who knows?" I said. "It's a pity. She was the last of them."

"So," Lord Venga continued, "what options are left to us now?"

"Not to worry, my lord," I reassured Lord Venga, who remained worried about his inability to use his White Shadow and the weakness he still suffered from the return of his White Shadow from Mai-Fatou and Gyvan Drabo. "The Keeper's riddle will see that the soldiers never get past the Gates. The terrors of Demon's Pit await them."

The Words Of The Child Eeid

chapter 57

As we approached the Gates of Ten Devils, the cries from Demon's Pit grew louder and more horrifying. These were cries from the tormented victims of the riddle of Mory Tipp, the Keeper, all damned eternally to this abyss of no return.

We approached the gates guardedly, the weight of the entire world resting again upon me. I had solved the riddles of Tichiman; would I solve the Keeper's riddle, a more hazardous riddle in which failure meant immediate and eternal damnation? The cries from Demon's Pit only increased my worry. I held Naya tightly.

Just before we reached the gates, a high-pitched voice not different from that of a boy child pierced the air around us.

"Listen to the cries from the pit of demons and choose now whether to proceed or return from whence you come!" the voice warned.

We looked around for the source of the voice but saw nothing, save the gates. Then an apparition of a boy child, some ten or eleven summers, about the same age as me, slowly formed in front of the gates. He seemed pleasant and cheerful, yet deadlier than a black mamba on a foot trail, for death and untold terror were hidden behind that boyish and merry face of his.

"I welcome your visit, strangers," the ghostly apparition of Mory Tipp, the Keeper, addressed us. "What may your purpose be?"

"We seek audience with Lord Venga," Gyvan said, "the one who rules here, fugitive in Eartholia Proper, the land of the raw-breeds, and architect of the misery and doom that plague the lands beyond this island and further beyond."

"My sympathies to you, soldier. But first you must answer my riddle, one to which I have sought an answer for a hundred seasons and longer."

"Ask your riddle," I urged.

"And you, fair maiden," the ghostly child eeid addressed me, "will you be the one to answer my riddle?"

"I will, good sir," I responded, showing unto him the same courtesy he had shown unto me.

"And understand, fair maiden, that should you not answer my riddle you and your party shall with immediate effect be condemned to the pit of demons for all eternity."

"And understand, good sir, that should I answer your riddle my party and I shall with immediate effect be granted passage through these gates of devils."

"That shall happen, fair maiden. But understand that I cannot speak for whatever ills lie beyond these gates of devils."

"The ills that lie beyond these gates are well known to me and my party, good sir. Now, your riddle?"

"Where the North Star leads, and where my brown is blue, they call me Kalabi Dauman, and my nine roars can be heard from here to the ends of the seas and back again. What is my destiny?"

What was his destiny? I asked myself. The riddle was brief—too brief. There was not enough information for me to use. I thought for a while, trying to make use of whatever information I had. The soldiers were still, eager to hear me, the horrifying cries from Demon's Pit echoing in their ears.

"I cannot say the answer to your riddle, Mory Tipp," I said.

The soldiers froze in a piercing silence, so silent it could be heard, and the cries from Demon's Pit more audible now than ever. Gyvan gently placed a soothing and encouraging hand on my shoulder.

"You cannot say the answer to my riddle, fair maiden?" Mory Tipp asked.

"No, Mory Tipp. I cannot say the answer to your riddle."

The eerie silence continued. Mory Tipp said nothing. I said nothing either. I had said enough. But this was not enough for Gyvan and his soldiers, their souls soon to be damned forever in Demon's Pit, condemned to never know peace either in this life or in any other.

Then Mory Tipp broke the silence. "So, fair maiden," he addressed me, "you cannot make the answer to my riddle?"

"No, good sir," I responded rather cheerfully. "And neither can you."

The soldiers were stunned that I took our impending damnation into Demon's Pit quite lightly. But they were even more stunned when I told Mory Tipp, the Keeper, that he could not answer his own riddle either.

"Neither can I?" Mory Tipp asked me.

"Correct, good sir," I responded confidently. "The riddle you ask is that of Gong Shé, set a hundred generations ago. It is that of which no one dares to say the answer."

Mory Tipp was silent. I was silent. The soldiers were silent.

Then Mory Tipp again broke the silence. "You, fair maiden," he began, "and your party shall with immediate effect be granted passage through these Gates of Ten Devils as was my word to you. Whatever lies beyond the gates is not within my power to control."

Gyvan and his soldiers, who had already resigned themselves to the cruel fate of Demon's Pit, breathed heavy sighs of relief, a most severe damnation spared them. Sighs of relief were all they could manage, for they could not cheer yet for this victory, knowing that more troubles lay beyond the Gates of Ten Devils.

I had answered the Keeper's riddle without stating an answer. Though pleased with the outcome, Gyvan and his soldiers found it a rather curious resolution, and inquired of me as to what the answer to the riddle really was. To this I told them as I had told the Keeper, that the riddle *is that of which no one dares to say the answer.*

The cries of lament and torment from the 30,000 damned souls at Demon's Pit continued to fill our ears as we walked towards the Gates of Ten Devils. How I wish it could have been within my power to release them from their anguish and ease their pain so that they could find rest in death.

"Mory Tipp," I called out. "What about the damned in Demon's Pit? What might it take to release them from their ordeal?"

"Lord Venga now holds the force that keeps us so tormented. Capture or destroy his White Shadow, and we, the damned, will be free and our souls will rest."

"*We?*" I asked.

"I, too, am damned, fair maiden," Mory Tipp said solemnly, "for my soul was caged here to guard these gates with my riddles. It is not of my own free will that I perform this task."

Then there was a sudden cry from Babayaro.

"The owl!" he screamed.

It was daylight, yet perched on a branch looking down at us was the sinister spy owl of Sobo Ha-ha that had brought great calamity upon us before.

"Hide yourselves before it spots us!" Gyvan screamed at us.

"Too late," One Eye the albino archery officer said. He was already aiming at the bird with his bow and arrow, which he promptly shot, releasing a deadly accurate missile that hit the bird right in the chest before it could make a hasty escape. But this was no ordinary owl. It was a spy owl trained and strengthened by a high eeid. So it did not surprise me that with an arrow stuck in its chest it leapt off the branch and flew away, likely again to inform the high eeid and Lord Venga of our travels.

"The bird won't last long," One Eye said.

"The high eeid will be most unpleased," Mory Tipp warned softly. "You may all pay dearly for that."

Sobo Ha-Ha Speaks

chapter 58

Noo died right in my hands. I had tried everything I could to save it—summoned all the charms and powers of my Third Shadow, both dark and good. None had worked. Now the bird was gone, the arrow having hit its mark. I had trained this bird from the time it was in an eggshell and it had served me faithfully since, even to its last breath, informing me that the little girl had answered the riddle of Mory Tipp. I kissed Noo on its beak and I cried at the loss of the only friend I had ever had—a dear friend whom only I could understand, a dear friend who alone could understand me. I was lonely again.

"The bird is dead," Tsing-tsing spat out harshly. "Now we know not how the soldiers move about."

"The pray-devils will find them," Lord Venga said, his strength slowly returning to him. "I hope those beasts have not lost their taste for human flesh."

"They have spent the last eighty years waiting for a chance to satisfy that hunger, my lord," I said, fuming and eager for vengeance against those who had killed my Noo.

I was not happy. I was going to make Gyvan Drabo, his soldiers, and the little girl pay for what they had done to my little Noo. It was now a very personal matter. I was going to use a spell I had not used before, one I had not used on account of the colossal amount of energy it required, and also on account of the fact that it could only be used once in a lifetime. This power was lightning. I was going to destroy the damned imperial soldiers and the girl child by using bolts of lightning. I left Lord Venga and went forth to my chamber to prepare my lightning spell.

The Words Of The Child Eeid

chapter 59

THE GATES OF TEN DEVILS led to a narrow passage bordered by steep cliffs on both sides. We crossed the gates and walked through the passage and were surprisingly met by a scene of wondrous and astonishing beauty. The rivers were blue; the ponds sparkled; the grass was low, level, and green; and the trees were tall, elegant, and arranged in nature's own way of assuring its own magnificence. Yet no one among my party failed to understand the danger that awaited us beyond this rare and exquisite splendor.

We advanced into the island slowly, heading towards the forest that lay quite a distance away. From the Truth Teller's account we knew it could conceal us for at least a short while. Shang walked in front of us, leading the way and using her scouting skills to guide us through the safest routes, for she could tell the routes that were less traversed by the pray-devils, using tracks left behind which only she seemed to recognize. A while later, she suddenly signaled us to stop. She examined the ground thoroughly, getting more nervous and frightened with every passing moment.

"What is the problem?" Gyvan asked, whispering.

"Sshhh!" Shang cautioned as she studied our surroundings. Then she put her ear to the ground and listened. A short while later she whispered to us, "There is a pray-devil patrol in this area."

"How did you do that?" Jeevas asked, referring to how she had obtained the information by putting her ear to the ground.

"I can hear the vibrations inside the Earth that their feet make. I have attempted this skill many times before but this is the first time I have actually been able to hear anything."

"Then let's get out of here," Gyvan said. "We take another route."

"No," Shang said, pointing at several directions. "There are much larger patrols there, there, and there. We have to stay here and face the beasts that are coming this way."

"How many come our way?" Gyvan asked.

"About fifty."

"Fifty?"

"And that is not all."

"What else?" Tigana asked.

"A raw-breed walks among them."

"Raw-breed?" Gans asked.

"Must be Tsing-tsing," Gyvan guessed.

"Whoever it is," Babayaro said, "we have got quite a fight coming up."

"We leave no beasts alive," Gyvan said to his soldiers.

Babayaro tore a huge piece of cloth from his garments.

"I will use this to carry you on my back," he said to me. "It will be rough out here once the swords get to work." I nodded and mounted his back, whereupon he used the torn-out cloth to tie me up there, much like a mother carries her infant.

"No matter what happens, do not let go," he said. I held tightly onto him.

The soldiers and I split into three groups. Two groups dashed up the two hills that bordered both sides of the valley we stood in, waiting for the pray-devils they knew would come through the valley beneath. Gyvan, Babayaro, and I were on one hill, concealed behind some rocks. Gans, Tigana, and Jeevas were on the other, concealed behind some bushes. Shang and One Eye stayed in the valley beneath. Shang again placed her ears close to the ground, listening for any vibrations caused by approaching pray-devil footsteps. A moment later she gave a signal. The pray-devils were coming.

Shang sprinted up the hill and joined me, Gyvan, and Babayaro. One Eye, with his bow and arrows, remained in the valley and in full view of any pray-devils that could appear. What was he doing? He would be seen by the beasts and digested before anyone could help him. No one else seemed to worry about him but me. But I knew the soldiers knew what they were doing, so efficient in the art of soldiery that they had needed no words or directions from their leader to effect this plan to engage the approaching pray-devil patrol.

A few moments later the pray-devils, some fifty of them as had been estimated by Shang, appeared, looking at and heading directly towards One Eye, their flesh hooks, broadswords, and fangs glittering menacingly in the sunlight that showered this island.

The beasts no doubt had seen One Eye, the human creature who stood in the valley some distance away from them, looking straight at them. The human creature was not intimidated, neither wavering nor moving from his position. Then the devils started racing towards him, eager to make a tasty appetizer out of him. But the one-eyed albino archery officer and part-time caravaneer stood his ground fearlessly. The beasts got closer and closer, then close enough.

That was when the caravaneer reached for his bow and his quiver, which held about twenty arrows. With the speed of a spitting cobra he suddenly began letting his deadly arrows fly towards the approaching pray-devils. He was so fast that I hardly noticed any arrows in his bow. The arrows were in and out of the bow almost faster than I could even notice them. I only caught glimpses of them in flight, heading towards their targets, each one hitting its mark and dropping a devil. In no time at all, all twenty arrows were exhausted, and so were twenty devils. Now only about thirty devils remained for Gyvan and his soldiers to face.

Unfortunately, Tsing-tsing, the raw-breed, had not been struck by one of the caravaneer's arrows. Now it was time for close quarters combat— swords. One Eye pulled out his sword and charged at the pray-devils, who focused mainly on killing the lone archer, unaware of the ambush that been set up against them. Suddenly, Gyvan and his group, composed of Shang, Babayaro and me, still strapped to Babayaro's back, charged on the left flank of the pray-devils, yelling like demons on the loose. It was a good surprise, for the devils had believed One Eye to be alone. We raced down the hill and into the midst of the devils, throwing them into confusion. Gyvan and his group slashed and struck their way into their midst. His arrows gone, One Eye joined the fray with his sword, a weapon he could handle as skillfully as he could handle the bow. While he fought the devils from the front, my group fought from their left flank. The brief moment of confusion for the pray-devils had given the soldiers a chance to put to eternal rest a good many of the beasts.

Just when the pray-devils were about to recover from the ambush and regroup, Gans, Jeevas, and Tigana came running down the hill, attacking the devils from the right flank, creating more mayhem among them. Again the beasts found themselves in confusion, and again the soldiers used this brief opportunity to put to eternal rest a great many of what was left of the beasts, with each soldier putting to use the best of his or her skill.

As the fighting between man and beast raged, I dangled on Babayaro's back, with Shang protecting his rear, so that I could not be harmed. Many a pray-devil attempted to get to me but wound up in little pieces from the quick sword of Shang. During much of the fighting, Gyvan faced the raw-breed, Tsing-tsing, with neither of them gaining the upper hand against the other. Many minutes of fighting elapsed before we could count all the pray-devils dead, Tsing-tsing having escaped to fight another day.

That was our first encounter with the pray-devils, and success had been ours. I felt lucky to be among these soldiers. Only a select few could accomplish a deed such as had just occurred. Not even a hundred soldiers in any other army could have performed such as these seven soldiers had just performed. But would success such as this always be ours? What would we do if we mischanced upon a beastly army larger than that which we had just destroyed?

***

AFTER THE BATTLE, SHANG BEGAN to guide us to the forest, where we planned to hide during the night. But trouble awaited us. It was shortly after we came across a river at the top of a hill and began heading downhill that Shang suddenly came to a halt. We halted too. What was amiss? All I could see was a grassy area in front of us, along the hill we were about to pass through, heading downwards. Then I understood the scout's concern. The grass was high, likely harboring some pray-devils hiding within it, lying in wait for our arrival.

"If those beasts can hide in there," Gyvan whispered, "then so can we."

At this, it was concluded that we proceed downhill through the grassy area. I could see the bottom of the hill, which was rocky, with hardly any vegetation. It was very likely an old riverbed. Babayaro got me off his back so that I could walk on my own, to make the journey downhill easier for both of us. We proceeded quietly and cautiously into the grassy bush, the only noise being that of the rushing river at the top of the hill. Some seconds elapsed without incident. But all was not right. I felt the danger, and it was close.

Then Shang again motioned us to stop. We were a quarter of the way down the hill. Shang's eyes were cold. Trouble was finally upon us. She went down on her knees and placed an ear to the ground as before, and listened. We waited anxiously, the swords fidgety in the hands of the soldiers, with Gyvan even inspecting his wrist knife to make certain it was securely bound around his wrist and ready to be put to instant use if need be.

"What is it?" Jeevas asked Shang.

Shang stood up. "More devils," she responded. "About 200 of them."

"Where?" One Eye asked.

"We are among them!"

Sobo Ha-Ha Speaks

chapter 60

MY LIGHTNING POTION WAS READY. In its most potent form I could dispatch lethal lightning bolts to strike Aida and everyone around her wherever on this Earth they were. But my potion lacked one very important ingredient—a lock of Aida's hair. Without it, I could not direct my lightning bolts directly at her. But that worried me little. I still had the garments I had worn when I visited her and the soldier in their tent during my vain attempt to destroy her Third Shadow. That meant I now had part of her spirit, an ingredient that could also serve the same purpose as a lock of her hair. While a lock of her hair mixed into my deadly lightning potion could undoubtedly seal her fate by enabling me to swiftly and precisely target and strike her dead with only a single attempt, my garments, which only contained her spiritual presence, could only allow me to create a potion not quite as precise and efficient as a potion that contained a lock of her hair. My current potion required several attempted strikes before a bolt could finally strike her dead as I desired. I could, however, only send four lightning bolts at her and hope that one would hit her and all who walked with her. That was all I could do in this lifetime.

I was doing this for Noo so that its soul could rest easy.

The Words Of The Child Eeid

chapter 61

WE NOW STOOD IN THE bush, in the midst of some 200 pray-devils as we headed downhill towards the rocky dried out riverbed that lay at the bottom, and yet again we found ourselves imperiled. Was it the pray-devils who lay in waiting ready to make a quick afternoon snack out of us? No. It was the fact that it was somewhat sunny, yet there occurred the sound of thunder. It was a lightning strike which headed our way, landing very close, missing me by only a few paces. The soldiers and I all looked at each other in puzzlement. Then we heard a cry of pain within the surrounding bushes. It had come from a pray-devil, an unfortunate one that had sneaked close to Babayaro only to find out that rather than Babayaro being surprised by it, it received the surprise instead, and was struck dead by a bolt of lightning.

We continued downhill. Then there was another lightning strike, the sound deafening as it crashed through the air. We all fell down, lying flat, attempting to man some defense against this bizarre occurrence on a hot, sunny day. The lightning bolt had struck closer than before, closest to me. I was terrified, and so seemed the soldiers. We could not afford to sit back and understand why lightning strikes were occurring in the middle of a sunny day, for there were pray-devils trying to eat us. So we leapt to our feet and continued downhill. I heard an "urrgh" sound from behind me. I turned around and saw a pray-devil on the ground, its head separated from its body, its blood fresh on Jeevas's sword. As we progressed several more devils strayed into our midst but were quickly cut down.

We continued downhill silently, the only other sounds being the rushing river at the top of the hill and the occasional clash of swords and the shrills of dying pray-devils falling victim to Gyvan and his soldiers as they encountered and engaged each other in this bush of death. A few times, we ourselves strayed into small groups of pray-devils, quickly disposing of them and disappearing within the tall grasses and thickets, only for other devils to catch up with us again and only to be yet again disposed of.

We were not quite halfway downhill when something grabbed me from behind, something non-human. I immediately felt its hot breath closing in against my neck. I turned around. It was a bloody pray-devil, its mouth wide open, its foul breath blowing over my neck and some unsightly and disgusting liquid from its open, salivating mouth dripping onto my face and mouth as its sharp teeth and fangs closed in. The soldiers could not react fast enough against this beastly creature. I closed my eyes. I did not want to witness my own demise.

Then there was a third lightning strike. The soldiers again fell to the ground attempting to man some defense against the deathly lightning bolt. But I could not fall to the ground, for the bloody pray-devil continued to hold on to me. But almost as soon as the lightning struck, however, the salivating beast shrieked and collapsed, the air reeking of his burnt flesh as smoke rose from his body. He had unwittingly saved my life. The lightning bolt meant for me had gotten him instead.

The nearness of this last lightning strike to me made one thing clear: the lightning occurrences were not by chance. They had a diabolic source, no doubt from the Dark Widow's high eeid, his attempt to rid this world of me. The next lightning strike could be even closer, perhaps even finding its mark.

I had to think quickly!

Think, think, I urged myself. There had to be a defense against lightning. Then it occurred to me that I had recently chanced upon some related information in a book said to have once belonged to a Persian of some four hundred years past named Abdul Kassam Ismael. He was a Grand Vizier of Persia, who was said to have always carried his entire library with him wherever he traveled, a library of 119,000 volumes which had required four hundred camels to carry. The information in the book was about an Arabian dabbler in the sciences who attempted to power a seafaring craft with energy he believed could be harnessed from lightning. It was said he created a mechanical device of some sort on which he placed an iron pole some eight feet tall, facing the heavens. He placed this device on his sea craft, believing that the iron pole would attract a lightning strike from the heavens and deliver its energy, which would be directed by the pole into his mechanical device, which contained machinations of his creation that would power his craft. Indeed, a lightning bolt did strike his pole as intended, but his machinations failed to work as intended, for the bolt set his craft afire, causing it to sink to the bottom along with the poor scientist. No one was known to have attempted a feat such as that since. But on that day, on a death hill on the Island of Ten Devils, I resolved to attempt part of the experiment as had been attempted by the unfortunate Arabian, for it was the only way I could save our skins. Though I lacked all the materials needed to construct the device I had in mind, I could almost make anything out of nothing. So I turned to the soldiers to give them instructions.

"Take five swords from the slain devils," I instructed. "Break off the hilts of each and then tie the swords together, end to end, so that they form a long pole."

The soldiers did as I instructed, tying five pray-devil swords end to end, using the belts of the pray-devils that held their sheaths. Soon they had the five swords joined together, forming a long pole.

I continued my instructions to Babayaro, who now held the improvised pole. "Stick the pole to the ground so that it stands upright, facing the heavens." Babayaro did as instructed.

"Now what?" Babayaro asked me.

"We run!"

We hurriedly continued our descent downhill, moving as far away from our pole as possible, until it was no longer in our view. The soldiers wanted to know what purpose the pole would serve and I informed them that every bolt of lightning striking our vicinity would be attracted to our pole now, not towards us. That is what I hoped, for that is how the Arabian had attracted lightning bolts to his sea craft.

Then we heard it—the thunder. This time with a deafening din louder than all the previous strikes combined. Again we crashed on our bellies, another attempt to man a defense. But this time was different. The lightning had struck nowhere near us. It had struck some distance away, where we saw a streak of lightning that seemed to lead from the sky to the Earth, exactly to our pole. My device had worked. But that did not end our peril. It only led to another, perhaps a worse one, as had been met by the Arabian.

Fire!

That was the result of my experiment. That had been the result of the Arabian's. The lightning strike on the pole had set the surrounding bush on fire, which was now sweeping rapidly across this grassy area. The entire hill would soon be in flames, I knew, engulfing us in its rage. Within moments the pray-devils that had been hiding within the bush began piercing the air with deathly screams and lamenting in pain as the merciless inferno caught up with them.

"Quick," Gyvan screamed at us. "We go back uphill, to the river."

This was a logical order for Gyvan to give. There was a river at the top of the hill which could shield us from the flames, and it was a much shorter distance to the top of the hill than to the bottom of the hill. Yet I objected to his order.

"No," I interjected. "We go downhill. Fire moves faster uphill than it does downhill."

"Do as she says," Gyvan ordered his soldiers.

Gyvan quickly tossed me on his back as we raced downhill towards the old seabed where the fire was surely going to burn out on account of the lack of vegetation there. As we raced we heard the continued screams of the pray-devils as the raging flames caught up with them as they raced uphill, hoping to shield themselves with the river. We barely made it to the safety of the bottom of the hill, collapsing in exhaustion as the flames fizzled away after reaching the bottom, just moments behind us. I looked at the hill. No sign of living pray-devils existed, all having burned before reaching the top of the hill, a rather fitting end to the creatures that only moments earlier had been hoping to be nibbling on us. They had wanted a taste for human flesh. Maybe we could also try to see if humans could have a taste for cooked pray-devil flesh, I thought. No, that was a rather sickening thought.

We quickly leaped to our feet and crossed the dried-out riverbed, leaving the area, a precautionary move against any lingering pray-devils. Before long, we came upon a forested area, the same where the Truth Teller had hidden during those years past, a temporary refuge from an already chaotic day. Here we rested and ate from our rations, which consisted of honey-sweetened yam bread, smoked ostrich meat, and salted locusts. One Eye also used this chance to make more arrows out of tree branches and arrowheads out of sharpened rocks.

Soon it was dark, a night only interrupted by the occasional cries from the restless souls of Demon's Pit pleading for death. We understood that it was only a matter of time before the devils would stumble upon our hideout and pounce on us. But still we needed rest. We could not hide forever, but the forest gave us a reprieve from the fighting and a chance to do what friends do when they have nothing better to do—talk about a wide range of things, from fishing in the Bani River to the siege of Djenné, and even about the suspected love affair between Jeevas and Shang, which they neither confirmed nor denied.

But as we rested and joked around, we knew that there was one important problem which had to be solved: how to get into the fortress the Truth Teller had said was on the island. Surely it was there that Lord Venga hid, his inability to use the powers of his White Shadow requiring him to protect himself so.

After a short rest, we stealthily walked through the forest towards the direction of the fortress, which we soon spotted from the safety of the surrounding forest. It was a roughly kept place built entirely of stone, surrounded by pray-devil guards expecting us at any moment. Tsing-tsing, the raw-breed, was instructing the guards, no doubt warning them about us. We withdrew deeper into the forest, avoiding pray-devil patrols, until we found an area secure enough to plan a strategy for infiltrating the fortress. Every plan conceived and suggested by the soldiers was found to be flawed when put to discussion, leading them to conclude that this was a task too impossible to be carried out under our circumstances.

Would this Earth have been better off with simply capturing Lord Venga's White Shadow as had been done before? Had I done wrong to convince the Table to release Gyvan Drabo from his deathly slumber? Was I therefore to be blamed for our current predicament and the imminent doom of man?

Yes, we were facing a task so impossible that even the devil himself would cringe at the very thought of carrying it out. How could seven soldiers and a little girl infiltrate the pray-devils' fortress and kidnap Lord Venga, a powerful raw-breed guarded by thousands of flesh-craving beasts?

"Perhaps we should just charge the fortress," Shang suggested in playful frustration.

"Right, woman," Jeevas scoffed. "Perhaps you intend for the beasts to chew your bones and drink your blood, but they are having none of mine. I do— "

"That's it!" I cried, cutting off Jeevas. "That's it!" A brilliant idea had suddenly struck me after Jeevas mentioned the blood drinking.

"That's what?" Babayaro asked.

"Drink," I said.

"Drink what?"

"Drinking water. That is how we get into the fortress."

"We are going to drink water to get into the fortress?" Gyvan asked, puzzled.

The soldiers gawked at me, eager to know what I had in mind. How could drinking water help us get past thousands of pray-devils, infiltrate their fortress, kidnap Lord Venga, extract him, once again get past the thousands of pray-devils, and get him to Timbuktu?

I then proceeded to explain that because there were many rivers on the island, the walled fortress was very likely built above one to supply the devils with a very near source of drinking water. If we could find the river that supplied the water, we could swim underwater through it and into the fortress, undetected.

The soldiers were silent for a short while, no doubt impressed and weighing the feasibility of my simple but ingenious plan.

"Why did I not think of that?" Jeevas asked.

"Because you are stupid," Shang jokingly responded.

"May they choke you," Jeevas shot back.

First we had to find the river that ran through the fortress. From where we were we could not see all the corners of the fortress walls, the night hindering our visibility. Shang instantly went to work, placing her ears close to the ground and listening for vibrations made by running water.

"There are at least two rivers that run towards the direction of the fortress," she said, rising up. "I'll look around to find out which one best suits our purpose."

She was about to leave when Jeevas stopped her.

"I'll come with you," he said, "to help protect you from the pray-devil patrols."

"No, Jeevas," she said sweetly. "It would be faster if I work alone."

"Be careful," Jeevas said softly, a genuine concern for her in his voice.

Shang nodded, smiling sweetly at him. There was no hiding it. They really cared for each other dearly.

Shang disappeared into the darkness to do what she did best—scouting. She reappeared a good while later, her sword in hand, dripping with pray-devil blood.

"I found a river entrance," she said excitedly. "We need to go now while the devils believe we are all in here. I engaged several patrols, but left a few devils alive so they could report our presence here in this forest. While they distract themselves looking for us here we can swim into the fortress."

Shang led us through the pray-devil-infested forest and towards the river, a trek during which we encountered a few patrols which the soldiers quickly disposed of. During each encounter, however, a few devils were left so that they could again report our presence in the forest, hopefully drawing many of the fortress's defenders towards the forest to search for us. Eventually Shang brought us to the river, a fairly narrow strip of water that ran straight into the fortress by way of a canal that ran underneath a section of the fortress walls.

All we had to do was swim into the fortress. But as we stealthily walked closer to the river we realized we had a problem. It appeared that the pray-devils had anticipated our intentions, and had stayed one step ahead of us. On the wall that stood above the river at the spot where it flowed into the fortress there stood a guard tower manned by two pray-devils, who had with them a huge bell to sound an alarm if an intruder was spotted. And just below the wall, standing on both sides of the river, stood one guard on each side with access to ropes connected to the bell, which could also be used to sound the alarm. Getting to the river would have exposed us to the pray-devil guards, who no doubt would have wasted no time in sounding the alarm, dooming us for good.

How then could we get into the fortress?

"Only one way to deal with this," Babayaro said. "We have to destroy the guards."

"They will spot us and sound the alarm before we even get close enough to kill them," Shang said.

"No need to get close," One Eye said, pulling out some arrows from his quiver.

Believing that shooting at the pray-devil guards was a terrible idea, Gyvan said to One Eye, "By the time the first guard drops dead from your arrow the others will have noticed his injury and will immediately sound the alarm before you can kill them too."

"Let me worry about that, Gyvan," One Eye responded, readying his bow and sticking four of his newly made arrows into the ground in front of him. He got down on one knee, licked the fingers on his shooting hand, and pulled one of the arrows from the ground.

Sobo Ha-Ha Speaks

chapter 62

"BRING ME THEIR HEADS IN a pot," Lord Venga softly but sternly ordered Tsing-tsing, who had just run into Lord Venga's war room to inform him that the soldiers and the little girl had been spotted in the surrounding forest, quite close to the fortress.

"The heads, you shall have, my lord," Tsing-tsing responded quite confidently. "This time they will not escape us."

"Talk is of no use, you imbecile. Get them. Now!"

Tsing-tsing ran out of the room. Lord Venga was furious, his anger growing by the moment as Gyvan only continued to draw closer and closer to him, despite all the obstacles that had been sent his way during the many months past.

"I am surrounded by incompetents!" Lord Venga screamed. "Had I not lost my powers from that woman…eh…what do you call her?"

"Mai-Fatou of Tera-Hool, my lord," I said nervously.

"Yes, Mai-Fatou. Had she not gotten herself killed I would have had the powers to crush those soldiers simply by desiring it. And now I have them right at the gates of my fortress, hoping to send me back to Eartholia Proper in chains."

"Tsing-tsing will kill the soldiers and you will regain your powers, my lord, completely restored to you even before the blood dripper matures and before the darkness of the clouds is complete. Then Eartholia Proper and New Eartholia will be yours for the taking."

The Words Of The Child Eeid

chapter 63

WE ALL STILL WAITED AT the edge of the forest to see what One Eye had in mind regarding the swift silencing of the four pray-devils that guarded the alarm bell stationed on the part of the wall that stood above the river entry point which was our access into the fortress. He knew exactly what he had to do. He had already pulled out one of the arrows he had earlier stuck into the ground before him. Now, still on one knee, he carefully placed the arrow in his bow, took aim, and let it fly.

Then the rest happened so quickly I can hardly describe it, save to say that at that moment the one-eyed caravaneer displayed a skill with the bow and arrow that I can only describe as dazzling and equaled by none. Before the first guard even realized that he had been hit by an arrow, One Eye had pulled another from the ground and sent it flying towards the second guard. The last two guards met the same deadly fate as had the previous two. One Eye's speed and accuracy was so remarkable that it had taken less than three seconds for the entire event to come to pass, happening so fast that the four unlucky guards seemed to drop dead at the same time, and as noiselessly as a slumbering newborn. We all looked at One Eye in awe, astonished by his unbelievable command of archery.

He turned to Gyvan and said, "Now, Commander, the river is yours to take."

"Show off!" Babayaro teased One Eye, who simply smiled.

With the guards eliminated, we began tiptoeing towards the river, One Eye ready with another arrow to fly in an instant should a pray-devil surprise us and attempt to expose us. We eased ourselves into the cold river and swam completely submerged towards the fortress, with Gyvan leading the way. We surfaced moments later, following Gyvan's lead.

We were now in the fortress at Ten Devils, the heart of pray-devil territory.

There were no pray-devils in sight, except for the three that manned the gates into the fortress walls, our presence barely visible to them in the surrounding darkness. The gates were locked, ensuring that no one from the outside could get in, unless, of course, they could do what we had just done—swim. We stealthily crawled out of the river and to a dark corner of the wall where the pray-devils at the gates could still not possibly see or hear us.

"Jeevas? Gans?" Gyvan whispered. "We need that gate to remain locked."

Jeevas and Gans nodded, understanding their commander's wishes perfectly. They stealthily high-crawled towards the gates, and in only a sprinkle of a moment all three pray-devils manning that position became nonexistent. Jeevas and Gans sheathed their daggers and returned to us. We had to act fast to infiltrate the main building that the fortress walls surrounded, somehow kidnap Lord Venga, and somehow extract ourselves before the thousands of pray-devils locked out of the fortress and still searching for us in the forest tried to get back in; or before any other beasts discovered the dead guards and raised an alarm.

The door into the main building itself had no guards, the pray-devils obviously believing this additional measure of security unnecessary since they expected no one to be daring enough to attempt to attack their fortress. They were wrong. We tiptoed towards the main building's door. The soldiers had their swords drawn, except for One Eye, who still had his sword sheathed but was ready with his bow and arrows, ready to be put to instant use should the need arise. Upon our arrival at the door, Gyvan lightly pushed it in. To our amazement, it slid quietly open. Security within the fortress was somewhat nonexistent, a fact we took a welcoming yet apprehensive delight in. After all, for thousands of generations since these beasts had first set foot upon this island, none, save perhaps the soldiers of the ill-fated expeditions of some eighty years past, had presented any real threat to the devils, and none in the eighty years since.

We were now in the building where we believed Lord Venga rested. What else lay within it, no one was certain. But what we were certain of was that we had to get into the building if we intended to find out. Gyvan very cautiously inched his way into the building, the sweat of anxiety and uncertainty streaming down his face. The rest of us soon followed upon his signal. We emerged in a corridor, a quiet and deserted area dimly lit by a few torches. Several huge stone pillars also lined the corridor, keeping the roof from tumbling in.

"We know not what manner of peril may dawn upon us in the moments to come," Gyvan whispered to us. "But we stick together and search every room in this vile building until Lord Venga is found. May luck be upon each of you."

First, we cautiously looked into the first room along the corridor, slightly pushing the door open and peeking inside. Here, some thirty to forty pray-devils were feasting, too drunken and crazed to notice us as they enjoyed a meal consisting of what I made out to be hippopotamus flesh—raw! We left them alone to enjoy their meal, too stomach-turning to keep watching. It reminded me of an account I had read about a far southern people who lived way beyond the southern grasslands, in a land some chroniclers called Buganda. It was said that the widows of a dead king in this land had to drink beer from a bowl in which the entrails of the dead king had been cleansed.

The next room we peeked into was empty. We were about to approach the next room when Shang suddenly stopped.

"Shhh," she warned. "Footsteps approaching."

We heard nothing, but trusted Shang's extraordinary senses.

"How many?" Gyvan asked.

"Eleven or twelve. Possibly heading outside."

"We can't let them do that!" Gyvan warned. "They will see the dead guards and may open the gates." Then he ordered us, "Behind the pillars, quickly!"

We all hid behind the huge pillars that lined the corridor. Jeevas pushed me behind him, keeping me out of sight and danger. As the footsteps of the pray-devils grew closer, I saw the soldiers readying not their swords, but their daggers. They had to make their impending kills close and quiet.

Then the pray-devils appeared, twelve of them, their razor-sharp fangs, flesh hooks, and humongous slashing swords visible and gleaming in the dimly lit corridor. If anything went wrong we were sure to join the hippos on the eating table. We did not want that. And so the soldiers leaped out from within the darkness, from behind the pillars. They were now the pray-devils' devils.

Have you ever seen a pray-devil scared?

Some of the completely shocked beasts dropped their weapons and tried to run, while others, though terrified at the impossible situation they now faced, stood their ground and tried to fight. It all mattered little, for within a split second the twelve devils were all dead—by the points of merciless and swift daggers. The soldiers quickly hid the bodies behind the pillars and continued to search the next rooms.

Sobo Ha-Ha Speaks

chapter 64

LORD VENGA WAS CONFIDENT THAT his troubles would disappear on that same night. New Eartholia and Eartholia Proper would soon be his to rule. By now the soldiers should have been killed by the pray-devils who searched for them in the forests. But why had no pray-devil returned to inform us about it? I therefore informed Lord Venga that I was going to determine for myself what had become of the soldiers. I left him in the room with five pray-devil guards and walked outside, heading for the eating room to assemble and dispatch a team to go out to the forest and report back with the progress on the hunt for the soldiers and the girl child.

I was thinking about Noo, my slain spy owl, as I walked down the dimly lit corridor. Had he been alive I would have dispatched him to bring back the information I now desired, a task he would have performed more efficiently than any envoy—human, raw-breed, or pray-devil. Noo had been a special bird. I had obtained him from an egg forced out of its deceased pregnant mother, which I had torn out from the belly of a python I had destroyed in order to extract its bile for use in a potion I would prefer to remain undisclosed. I trained Noo from the time he was in an egg. It would take me an eternity to find another like him, I knew. But then again, I thought, I might never again require the use of a spy bird, for what was left of this world was about to fall to Lord Venga, who would give me more powers than any king or emperor on this Earth could ever dream of. When such a time arrived, I assured myself, I would certainly concern myself with more important matters than spy birds.

My disheartening thoughts about Noo gradually drifted away into optimistic thoughts of all the powers and riches that were soon to befall me in a world under Lord Venga. But these thoughts abruptly came to a very uncomfortable halt—interrupted unbelievably, as I felt a cold, sharp object against my throat.

"Well, well, well, Sobo Ha-ha, High Eeid of Tera-Hool," came a voice I instantly recognized as that of Gyvan Drabo.

I was stunned. Gyvan and his bunch were in the fortress. But how? How had they managed it? What was I to do now? One wrong move and the soldier was going to bury his dagger deep into me.

"So we meet again," I said, uncertain of what was going to happen to me.

"And this time I brought some friends along," Gyvan Drabo said. "They are not very nice people, so I really do not want you to get to know them. Trust me. It is for your own good. But for us to keep it that way I am going to tell you this and tell you only once. Take us to Lord Venga!"

Gyvan Drabo wanted me to betray my lord and master. How could I do that? And how could I not do it with the cold dagger threatening to dig deep into my throat? The dagger was a weapon more potent than any force any eeid could command, for death dealt by it was certain, instant, and ghastly.

"Walk!" Gyvan Drabo ordered me.

I did not want to do as he had ordered, but the thought of a dagger hole in my throat commanded such an invincible, nonnegotiable, and convincingly threatening force that I had to comply, walking towards the room where Lord Venga rested. Have you ever seen a man with a hole punched through his throat? I have seen it before. Even I can tell you that it is not a pretty sight, especially when the blood you see gushing out is your own.

As I reluctantly led the imperial soldiers towards Lord Venga, I was hoping the pray-devil guards with him would pounce on the soldiers before any harm could be brought upon my lord. Even without his powers, Lord Venga, or any single raw-breed, could crush ten human soldiers in combat. But alas, these soldiers were no mere soldiers. They were well-skilled in the art of deadly combat and swordsmanship, as I had learned these many weeks past.

When we came to the door of the room where Lord Venga rested, I stopped.

"Is this it?" Gyvan asked me, whispering.

"It is," I said feverishly.

"If this is a trick, eeid, my dagger will see that you make a tasty meal for the devils. I hear they are especially attracted to eeid flesh."

"The raw-breed you want is in that room," I whispered back.

"Who else is in there?" Gyvan asked.

"When I left the room, Lord Venga was alone," I lied, hoping the five pray-devils in there would destroy the unsuspecting soldiers.

"Shang?" Gyvan called out to the female soldier in his outfit. She walked to the door, placed her ear on it, and to my amazement and horror, she was able to tell who else was in the room with Lord Venga.

"A raw-breed, Lord Venga, sits directly in front of where we stand," she began. "There are three pray-devils to the right side of the room, and two more on the left."

She was a tracker, I realized in utter disappointment.

The Words Of The Child Eeid

chapter 65

HERE WE WERE AT THE door that separated us from the fugitive creature that had caused so much death and misery in the land. All we had to do was seize him and take him to Timbuktu, where Tin-zim and Shokolo-ba could destroy his Third Shadow. According to Shang, he was in the room with five pray-devils, the devils being of minor concern to the soldiers. The main concern was Lord Venga. Even though he had temporarily lost much of his strength, he was still a raw-breed, physically capable of destroying ten human soldiers on his account alone. But surely Gyvan and his soldiers could stand a fighting chance against the raw-breed, I prayed.

"Shang," Gyvan began his orders, "take the two pray-devils to the left. Jeevas, you engage the three to the right. One Eye, watch Aida and keep an eye on the eeid. Babayaro, Tigana, Gans and I will engage Lord Venga."

With that, One Eye strapped me to his back. Then the other soldiers all burst into the room, surprising Lord Venga and the devils with him. Though eager to join the fight, One Eye could not, for he also had to watch over me and keep guard over Sobo Ha-ha. Jeevas and Shang wasted no time in dispatching their pray-devils, after which they joined Gyvan, Gans, Babayaro, and Tigana in the fight against Lord Venga, a fight that was already proving quite strenuous for the four soldiers assigned to engage the raw-breed lord. He was a skilled fighter, a terrifying creature, huge and monstrous, with the right dose of swiftness and agility to accompany his excellent swordsmanship. Gyvan could in no way ever single-handedly duel against Lord Venga as he had done with the Paipan.

The fight against Lord Venga was extreme, the raw-breed fighting all six soldiers using a force and skill perhaps equaled only by that of a small army. I did not even want to fathom the possible outcome of the fight had Lord Venga had the command of his White Shadow at that moment. His sword and flesh hook moved as quickly as the six swords fighting against him. Then in the midst of the melee there seemed to come a point where all were fatigued, pausing only briefly to catch their breaths.

"So you are the soldier who gained powers to control the land but threw it away," Lord Venga said to Gyvan.

"This land was never mine to control, Lord Venga, and neither is it yours."

"You are an ignorant fool, boy," Lord Venga scorned. "This world and my world have always been made up of men who have tried to control the will of others."

"That is not exactly true," I interrupted. "Actually, about 1,233 years ago in a place called Greece, which lies very far to the north of here and even farther beyond the land of the great desert lion, the rulers were not always despots but governors elected by their people."

Lord Venga, Sobo Ha-ha, and all the soldiers forgot their fight for a moment and just stared at me, wondering what on Earth I was talking about, with an attitude which, without words, simply implied that at that particular moment nobody really cared about Greece or whatever in the world I was talking about.

"And you, little one," Lord Venga then said to me. "When I am finished here I'll see that the pray-devils have you. They love little bites between their meals."

With this threat, Gyvan and his outfit renewed the offensive against Lord Venga. As the fighting raged, at one point, Sobo Ha-ha tried to move away undetected, but One Eye simply looked at him and shook his head. One Eye did not even have to threaten the eeid with a weapon, for the archer's bow was slung over his shoulder and his sword remained in its sheath. The single look was enough, for Sobo Ha-ha understood that that sword could be drawn out a hundred times faster than he could even think or summon a spell.

The fighting with Lord Venga was getting nowhere. He was resilient in his resistance and was prepared for every blow that came his way, until he made a fateful flaw. He jumped onto a chair to avoid a sweeping cut from Jeevas that was aimed at his legs. But as soon as the raw-breed landed on the chair, Gyvan swiftly cut off the chair's legs with a single swoop of his sword. The chair came crashing down, along with Lord Venga. Before the fugitive raw-breed could regain his balance, Gyvan picked up a huge block and dropped it on his head. Lord Venga's weapons dropped. His eyes closed. He became still.

"Is he dead?" One Eye asked. Gyvan daringly put his ear on Lord Venga's heart.

"He breathes." Gyvan said.

We were relieved, for we needed Lord Venga alive. Gyvan and his soldiers immediately used the block to break the hands and a foot of the unconscious raw-breed lord, a safety measure to ensure he could neither battle nor flee upon his recovery.

"What do we do with him?" One Eye asked, pointing at Sobo Ha-ha.

"Hold on to him," Gyvan said. "He may have information to help us escape this island."

We all began to head out very cautiously, hoping our exit would be as quiet as our entry had been. Gyvan, Gans, Babayaro, and Tigana carried the unconscious Lord Venga, each man holding him by a limb. Shang, One Eye, and I were in front, along with Sobo Ha-ha, our hostage. Jeevas protected the group from the rear. We walked through the corridor, hoping to avoid the thirty to forty pray-devils enjoying a hippo meal in the eating room.

As we neared the eating room we all stopped dead in our tracks. Standing right in front of us was a pray-devil licking the blood on a hippo bone he had in his hand. He was as shocked as we were to see each other. He looked at the unconscious Lord Venga, then at Sobo Ha-ha, then at us. In a flash One Eye was onto him, but it was too late.

"INTRUDERS!" the pray-devil roared before he was cut down by One Eye.

Then it was mayhem.

The pray-devils poured out, seemingly from every room we had not searched, as well as from the eating room. They were in the hundreds, a frightening sight. One of them looked at us and commented in a rough gruff voice, referring to us, "Isn't it something when your dinner suddenly gets up and tries to fight you?"

We raced out of the building and towards the river as the hordes chased after us. We could not risk going through the gates, for it would have taken quite some time to open it. Our only option was again through the river, the same way we had come in. We raced on, and soon realized that Sobo Ha-ha had slipped away amidst the chaos.

With Lord Venga we could not run fast enough to beat the pray-devils behind us, so the soldiers decided to make a stand for it, though by that time we had been cut off into two groups. Shang, One Eye, Tigana, and I were in one group. Gyvan, Gans, Babayaro, and Jeevas were in the other, trying to protect themselves as well as trying to stop the determined pray-devils from retrieving the unconscious Lord Venga, whom the soldiers had dropped on the ground and formed a well-defended circle around, making it a death trap for pray-devils that tried to get through. Getting to the river was in no way an easy task, for between us and the river were new hordes of devils. On my own corner of this little hell on Earth, the hordes were relentless in getting to Shang, One Eye, Gyvan, and me.

And then another problem arose.

We soon heard some pray-devils just outside the gate trying to get in. But they were unable to do so, for the gate was locked from within. The pray-devil guards whose task it would have been to open it up had already been silently daggered by Jeevas and Gans upon our entry into the fortress. Now some of the pray-devils inside the fortress were desperately struggling to get to the gate to let in the thousands of their fellow beasts trapped outside. And that was not all. Other beasts also attempted to get to the alarm bell so as to warn all the surrounding devils of our intrusion. Should they be allowed to open the gate and sound the alarm bell, we would be facing thousands of pray-devils, we knew. We were doomed. It appeared it was only a matter of time before we would be hacked to bits and added to the eating menu, for hordes of pray-devils began running to sound the alarm bell while others bolted towards the gate to open it up and let in the thousands of fellow beasts who were out there. What could we do to alter our grim fate?

This was where One Eye stepped in again with his miracle skill. He sheathed his sword, unstrapped me from his back, licked his fingers, and pulled out his bow and an arrow. Then one by one, and as rapidly as only One Eye could perform, he started spitting out arrows with deadly and devastating precision at the pray-devils that dared to head for the gate or the alarm bell. It was therefore no surprise that in only a short while, pray-devil volunteers for these tasks became more and more scarce, realizing the severe health hazard posed to them by the albino archer. But still a few unhindered braves among them continued the hazardous attempts, only to end up with arrows stuck in their bodies. One Eye's actions strengthened our determination and increased our confidence of a possible positive outcome.

Tigana protected me from the pray-devils that got too close and Shang protected the arrow-spitting One Eye from the pray-devils that were stupid enough to approach him. All around us, the bodies of pray-devils piled up, an arrow in many. But One Eye's arrows could not last forever. They were running out, and fast. We had to make a run for the river before he ran out.

"Take Aida and run for the river!" Gyvan ordered Tigana, Shang, and One Eye.

"What about you?" Shang asked him.

"We'll be right behind you!"

But we knew there was no way Gyvan, Gans, Babayaro and Jeevas were going to be able to be right behind us. They were receiving the brunt of the pray-devil assault, the beasts bent on retrieving their master. Gyvan and his group needed major reinforcements—us—before they could make a successful breakaway. I did not want Gyvan left behind, and Shang certainly did not want Jeevas left behind. We all wanted to leave no one behind.

Then One Eye ran out of arrows.

Tigana lifted me and threw me onto his back. "Hold tight, little girl," he said. "We are all getting out of here."

Shang, One Eye, and Tigana, with me clinging to his back, quickly dispatched the much smaller force of pray-devils attacking us and charged to the rescue of Gyvan, Jeevas, Gans, and Babayaro, who were about to be overrun. When we got them, Gyvan was so relieved to see me that he quickly pulled me from Tigana and placed me on his back.

Tigana, Jeevas, Gans, and Babayaro then picked up the unconscious Lord Venga with one arm each, while fighting with the other. Our mad dash for the river began. Shang and Jeevas protected our outfit from the front, with One Eye and Gyvan, with me clinging to his back, protecting the outfit from the rear. The pray-devils remained in hot pursuit. I was not sure if they were after their lord or after a delicious meal they saw in us. Anyway, it mattered not. We would be dead either way, I thought to myself.

Then some pray-devils started heading for the gate and the alarm bells. One Eye had no more arrows to stop them now. We had to get into the river quickly. If the gate was opened we could still get to the river before the incoming pray-devils could catch up to us. But if the alarm bells were sounded, Heaven help us. There could be thousands of these vile beasts waiting for us outside, alerted to be on the lookout for us as we exited the fortress. One of us had to stay back and prevent the pray-devils from getting to the bell. It was our only chance of survival.

"I will stay!" Jeevas declared. "I'll keep the devils from the bells for as long as I can."

"And I will stay with you," Shang declared, realizing that this could be the last time she saw Jeevas, her lover.

"No, dear," Jeevas protested. "You must go on. You all must go on! We will meet again, dear one, I promise."

This was a daring suggestion from Jeevas, one that we all understood could spell his doom. But there was no time for any heartfelt goodbyes at that moment. One Eye quickly took Jeevas's place in carrying Lord Venga. Shang wanted to hold and hug Jeevas on this parting, but she could not, for the devils continued their relentless pursuit. Gans and One Eye yanked her away as we continued to race for the river. Gyvan, though, was able to shake arms with Jeevas.

"We'll meet on the other side, wherever it may be," Gyvan blurted while chopping down an intruding pray-devil. Jeevas nodded.

"Stay a nice little girl," Jeevas said to me.

I waved at him. He smiled. Then he ran towards the bells to hold back and delay the pray-devils that ventured towards it. The rest of us ran towards the river to take advantage of the opportunity Jeevas was providing to us. Just before we plunged into the river, I was able to look back and see him facing and holding back hordes of pray-devils. There must have been about forty of them trying to get to the bells. The gate had already been opened and more devils had poured in.

"Sound the alarm!" Tsing-tsing, the raw-breed, screamed at his monsters.

With the gates of the fortress opened, even more pray-devils bolted in. But it was too late for them to catch up to us now. Their only hope lay in sounding the alarm and alerting the others outside the fortress of our presence. But Jeevas was there to delay that process for as long as his strength could allow him, felling many a devil that rushed to the bells as the hordes converged upon him. I saw him take two sword stabs from the devils, but still he fought on, his spider silk armor helping to protect him from many a blow that went his way.

Then we plunged into the river. I was still clinging to Gyvan's back. Babayaro, One Eye, Gans, and Tigana still held on to Lord Venga. A very short moment later, we all emerged from the river, safely outside the fortress. Lord Venga regained consciousness as a result of his contact with the cold water from the river, but a quick blow from Babayaro's sword hilt sent him right back to sleep. We got out of the river and One Eye, Babayaro, Gans, and Tigana picked up Lord Venga again.

The alarm bell had still not sounded, Jeevas still holding his ground. We began sprinting into the safety of the forest, hoping, but knowing it to be quite impossible that Jeevas would soon be joining us. We were relieved when we got into the forest, but still we did not stop. We continued running, still needing to pass the gates of Ten Devils and get to our boat. We knew the pray-devils would end their pursuit as soon as we hit the lake, not daring to follow us on land because of the presence of the large imperial force that had kept watch on the island some eighty years since.

Our hasty flight continued, going in our favor so far. And then something happened, something we did not want to hear, but knew we would. It was the alarm bell. It was ringing. This time we stopped. It was an instinctive stop.

It was an honorary stop.

Jeevas, the cavalry officer, was dead!

***

JEEVAS HAD DONE WHAT HE could for us, what he could for the empire, what he could for those he loved, what he could for this Earth. The bell continued to ring, alerting every beast on the island to our whereabouts. Did we resume running then? No, we remained standing in silence, a moment of silence for the one who had so honorably sacrificed for us all. We knew there were pray-devils behind us but still we stood. This homage to the fallen soldier was due.

The bell kept ringing.

The other soldiers patted Shang on the shoulder to show their condolences, for we all knew Jeevas's death affected her most, the alleged romance between them never having been confirmed or denied.

"He sacrificed himself so that you could live," Gyvan consoled Shang.

"I never even had the chance to tell him that I carry his child," Shang said. "We had been secretly married."

It did not surprise me that Shang was with child. I had suspected this after she had said that for the first time she had been able to place her ears to the ground and hear the vibrations from the approaching pray-devil patrols. That was because pregnant women have heightened senses.

Gans held Shang's hand and said to her softly, "We must go on."

Shang nodded and smiled as a tear drop rolled down her right cheek.

Then the running continued towards the Gates of Ten Devils. It was a narrow exit. By this time there were hundreds, maybe thousands, of pray-devils behind us. The ground trembled as the hordes thundered frantically, aggressively towards us. We could not run fast enough, for we, of course, were burdened with the unconscious Lord Venga. And those devils were fast! We began to hear the cries of torment from Demon's Pit as we got closer to the gates. As soon as we got to the narrow passage through them, Shang stopped and put her ear to the ground. She stood up and looked at Gyvan.

"Commander," she said to Gyvan, "The devils will overrun us before we get to the boat."

"We'll pick up our pace," Gyvan said, breathing heavily. "Let's hurry while we can."

"No use. We stand no chance. I'll stay back and hold them to buy you time to get to the boat. The passage is narrow. I can hold them for a while. But you must hurry."

Shang was right. The pray-devils were bound to overrun us before we could even get to within halfway of our boat that awaited us at the lake's shore. The passage towards the gates was quite narrow, allowing only for one or two people, or pray-devils, to stand or walk across it at a time. A trained fighter could hold his or her ground for a long time against much greater numbers, given those circumstances.

"We can all try to make a run for the boat," Babayaro pleaded with Shang, aiming to convince her to abandon her plan.

"No, Baba," Shang said. "You all must go. This is where my journey ends."

"What about the child you carry?" One Eye asked.

"The child and I will meet its father on the other side. He calls us."

Gyvan, Gans, Tigana, Babayaro, and One Eye shook arms with Shang, a deep and sincere farewell that needed no words. She patted me on the head, briefly stroked the braids on my head, and smiled at me. Then we parted, leaving her behind to hold the narrow passage and protect our escape. We raced for the gates, the cries from Demon's Pit growing louder as we drew nearer. When we reached the gates I looked back. There was not a single pray-devil in sight, Shang undoubtedly doing a magnificent job of holding them back, delaying their progress.

We crossed the gates of Ten Devils and raced towards the shore, where we instantly boarded our boat, along with Lord Venga. We immediately set sail for land towards the imperial garrison on the mainland that kept watch over the island. We were safe at last. Those devils would never dare set foot in human territory. As we rowed away my mind suddenly went to Mory Tipp, the boy eeid who had been trapped in Demon's Pit and doomed forever, unless, of course, we could safely deliver Lord Venga and have his Third Shadow captured or destroyed.

My thoughts were suddenly interrupted when only a moment later we saw the pray-devils emerging from the gates of Ten Devils.

Shang, the scout, was dead!

***

SHANG'S DEATH HAD NOT COME as a surprise, a sacrifice she had deemed worthy of honoring Jeevas, her true love.

Not much was said upon the realization of her passing. We continued rowing away from the island, our mournful silence a mirror of how we felt about the passing of two exceptional soldiers and their unborn baby.

Then we saw something that quickly turned our sorrow into incredible terror, almost pounding our hearts into a pulp. It was something more terrifying than we would have wanted to believe.

"This cannot be!" One Eye blurted.

"That is not possible!" Gyvan said.

"This changes everything," Tigana added.

"The devils only bluff," Babayaro suggested.

"I don't think so," I corrected.

Behind the thousands of pray-devils that had just emerged through the Gates of Ten Devils were hundreds more, carrying boats. They intended to sail to the mainland, determined to retrieve their master at all costs, even if that required engaging the imperial garrison that was thousands strong.

"What do we do now?" Babayaro asked.

"We row!" Gyvan yelled, and this we did, as vigorously as a market thief can run.

The next time I looked back towards the island, many of the pray-devils had already taken to their boats and were now rowing in the lake after us, led by Tsing-tsing, whose boat was in the lead of the pursuing fleet.

We were rowing towards the military garrison on the mainland that had been stationed around Moon Lake for eight decades to contain the devils, a successful measure so far. There, we knew, deprived of the protection of their familiar island, the pray-devils would meet their end and be slain by the thousands of imperial troops who had been trained and prepared for just this moment. But as we rowed closer to the garrison, we noticed something else that troubled us, the racing of our pounding hearts increasing.

"What is the meaning of this?" Gans roared, troubled by what we saw on the mainland.

The garrison, our protection, our sole hope of survival, the first line of defense against a pray-devil raid, was completely deserted. Not a single soldier was in sight. Only earlier that day the place had been teeming with soldiers determined to stop any pray-devil that dared to set foot upon the mainland. Now the devils were heading for the mainland, yet not a single soldier could be seen anywhere at a time when they were needed most. Had they all fled in terror at the sight of the advancing pray-devil army? These men had been trained specifically for fighting pray-devils, their importance so highly valued that they had been kept away from all the fighting that ravaged the land in the destructive civil war that raged in the empire. But now, at the hour when duty called, they had fled, unwilling to fight and die in a battle that many would agree would have led only to certain death. Perhaps, then, they were not to be blamed for their escape. It had been the only logical thing to do.

Gyvan, his surviving soldiers, and I were alone once again. What were we to do now? We continued rowing, soon arriving on the mainland right in the garrison grounds. There was no sign of a struggle or disaster, displacing Babayaro's theory that the garrison may have been attacked and wiped out by a large rebel force. There just were no soldiers there, not even inside the hundreds of military tents that dotted the garrison grounds. We decided to head for the surrounding bushes, with a painful understanding that our cause was lost. Gyvan again placed me on his back as he and his soldiers started running towards the bushes after the pray-devils also began to land their boats on the mainland, relentless in their pursuit.

But before we could make it to the bushes, Gyvan abruptly signaled his soldiers to stop. He had come to the grim realization that our continuing flight served no purpose, the devils being only just a few hundred paces behind us.

This was the end.

Gyvan gently pulled me off his back and led me into a nearby tent.

"Don't you come out until there is absolute quiet," he instructed me.

Then he looked at me right in the eyes, smiled, and patted me on the head, a sort of silent farewell from a hardened soldier going to his death. He turned swiftly around and dashed outside before I could say anything.

It had been hard for him to part with me. I think I had noticed his eyes water as he had turned around, not wanting me to lose hope by learning of his own despair. I remained in the tent as he had instructed, holding Naya tightly, the only friend left to me now.

"It has been my honor to serve with you all," I heard Gyvan address his soldiers outside. "May each of you find peace in the afterlife, should such a thing exist."

I was a stubborn girl. Hoping desperately for a miracle, I peeked outside of the tent to see Gyvan and his soldiers make their last stand. They had dropped the unconscious Lord Venga and formed a defensive circle around him.

The pray-devils closed in.

Gyvan kissed his sword as he readied it for a final showdown. My heart sank in despair and sadness. The pray-devils, eagerly craving the flesh of man, swarmed the imperial soldiers from all sides. There were thousands of them. Gyvan and his men numbered only five. The first five pray-devils that were privileged to be the first to get closest to the soldiers were quickly separated into two pieces each.

And then the remaining hordes converged on the soldiers.

But then there was a mysterious order.

"Attack!" came the order.

But it had not come from Gyvan.

It had not come from the pray-devils.

So where had it come from?

The order was instantly followed by thousands of wild cries of excitement—human cries! But where were the humans? Gyvan's team and their pray-devil pursuers suddenly stopped in their tracks, just as puzzled as I was, trying to determine the source of the human cries, whether they were from friend or foe.

I continued to listen carefully and was soon able to tell from where they hailed—the surrounding bushes. Yet no one could be seen in the bushes, and no one emerged from them. A brief moment of deadly, frightening, and uncertain silence among the soldiers and the pray-devils elapsed as they all wondered about the source of the cries.

Then in a very abrupt instant, thousands of arrows from the surrounding bushes came raining down on the pray-devils, causing a panic among their ranks as an untold number among them began dropping dead. For a brief moment the pray-devils seemed to forget about Gyvan and his men, whom they had completely surrounded, and were about to devour. Perhaps they had realized that with thousands of arrows from an unknown source raining down death upon them, they were not that hungry after all. Rather than wait for the arrows to come to them, and to maintain some order among his ranks, Tsing-tsing, like any good military commander, ordered his devils to charge into the bushes to engage the unseen archers. The pray-devils charged as ordered, screaming viciously and erratically, eager to deal a quick death to the unseen foe. A few of the devils, however, stayed back to attempt a rescue of Lord Venga, but were also divided into two pieces each.

Still I wondered about the mysterious archers. Who were they?

Responding to the charge of the pray-devils towards the bushes, the mysterious archers emerged, their swords drawn and ready to engage the pray-devils at close quarters and at equal measure. Many were on horseback, but most were on foot. They, too, numbered in the thousands.

Then I realized who our rescuers were. It was of little surprise to me. I should have known. They were the imperial soldiers who had manned the garrison on whose grounds we now stood. Now they were doing what for many years they had trained and prepared for—stopping the pray-devils. Their lookouts had seen the pray-devils take to the water after us, and so they had feigned desertion, lying in wait in the surrounding bushes, ready to spring an ambush on the pray-devils, briefly causing some confusion and disorder within the pray-devil ranks.

The clash of both armies was thunderous, with man and beast battling to the death; with shrills and screams of pain and death emanating from both beast and man alike, the numbers among each reducing as the carnage raged on.

But sadly, as I watched the battlefield, more humans were falling to the swords, flesh hooks, and fangs of the pray-devils than devils were falling to the swords and spears of the humans, who were almost disastrously outmatched by the pray-devils. Many a soldier fled the battleground after witnessing another eaten in an instant. And to make matters worse, there existed an endless supply of flesh-craving pray-devils rowing from the Island of Ten Devils. The fight could not last much longer this way.

I then came to a sudden, terrifyingly disturbing realization. For the pray-devils, this was not just a fight to retrieve their master, Lord Venga.

It was an invasion.

***

MY BLOOD WENT COLD WHEN a hand unexpectedly yanked me from the relative safety of the tent and threw me into the air. I closed my eyes and stiffened. I was going to land in the large disgusting mouth of a pray-devil and make a tasty snack for it. But I landed on Gyvan's back. He winked at me.

"We are getting out of here, little one," he said to me.

It was good to be back with him and his men. While the fighting raged on between the army and the beasts, we managed to find a safe area where we could rest awhile and determine how best to proceed with Lord Venga amidst the ongoing butchery occurring around us. Gyvan explained that the garrison soldiers could not be expected to hold out against the pray-devils for more than a day. He believed the pray-devils were very likely to break through the defenses and attack Timbuktu, where Tsing-tsing knew Lord Venga was likely to end up. We therefore had to use this opportunity to make a speedy escape to Timbuktu while the army here kept the devils engaged.

Obviously the commander of the garrison must have already dispatched messengers to Timbuktu with word of the pray-devil attack. But Gyvan wanted to reinforce that message by dispatching another messenger, this time with more thorough information on exactly what to expect—a full-fledged pray-devil invasion. He therefore stopped a mounted soldier.

"I am Gyvan Dra—" Gyvan began to introduce himself to the mounted soldier.

"I know who you are, Commander Drabo," the soldier said.

"Good," Gyvan responded. "Ride to Timbuktu and inform the Table of what you see here. Tell them to prepare the city's defenses for a long siege. Also tell them that I bring the package they await."

The rider nodded and immediately departed for Timbuktu. Alone, he could get there in one day. But for Gyvan and his group, burdened by Lord Venga, the same journey could last up to two days.

Gyvan also dispatched several riders to the villages and towns that were on the way to Timbuktu, bidding its residents to evacuate their homes and flee farther away from the road to Timbuktu, or into the relative safety of fortified Timbuktu, lest they fall victim to the devils during their march to besiege the city.

Babayaro found seven horses on the battlefield for our party, the previous owners of the horses having most likely been eaten by those monsters who seemed to have an insatiable and voracious appetite for man flesh. There were blood stains on the horse for Lord Venga, who at this time was awake but had been bound, gagged, and strapped to the horse.

Just as we were about to ride away, we heard the hooves of hundreds of horses heading to the battlefield. Finally the humans had reinforcements of their own. They were Watchmen of Tera-Hool, over whose dominion Commander Gyvan Drabo was now ruler. Riding in front of them was their commander, Malouda, Gyvan's former enemy. Though small in number, these soldiers provided additional reinforcements badly needed by the imperial troops.

"How did the Watchmen know we were here?" I asked Gyvan, pleasantly surprised.

"Before we left for the island I sent word to them, requesting that they deploy here to reinforce this garrison."

This additional help, though they only numbered about 900 cavalrymen, was perhaps enough to help slow down the pray-devils for an additional day. While the Watchmen immediately rode into battle, Gyvan sought out Commander Malouda and the garrison commander, explained to them that we were headed for Timbuktu, and bade them delay the devils long enough for us to get to the city.

We rode to Timbuktu in all haste, taking special care to conceal the raw-breed in our charge from prying eyes. The riders Gyvan had dispatched to warn villages and towns of the approaching pray-devils had done their jobs well, with some villages having already been completely deserted only hours after being warned, while others were in the process. Not a single village or town had failed to heed to the message, the dread of the pray-devils very evident. The man-eating beasts were not to be trifled with.

In just over two days we arrived in Timbuktu, the Table having clearly received the message of the approaching man-eating beasts. Only one word can perfectly describe the scene in the city.

Mayhem!

Chaos, confusion, panic, and near disorder—that was the scene in Timbuktu. It was packed to capacity with people from surrounding villages and towns trying to get in with all the belongings they could carry. No space existed for all those possessions and belongings. Worst of all, the granaries remained empty. How were all these people to be fed? But they were subjects of the empire, and as such they had to be allowed into the city.

There were soldiers both inside and outside the city walls working frantically and feverishly to bring some semblance of order to the process of entry into the city, where the only items allowed in were weapons, food, and livestock, the last two of which were desperately going to be needed for the siege that was sure to follow, of which no one knew how long it was going to last. The weapons too were of utmost importance, for this was going to be a fight for survival in which it was certain the other side would take no prisoners, except maybe to fatten them up to be fed upon later—fresh!

Because Gyvan and his men were recognized by the city's soldiers, we entered the city without much hassle, easily avoiding the pains faced by the screaming thousands who had to be inspected by the soldiers. We immediately went to the emperor's palace, where chaos also reigned. Panicked officials and guards were running around left and right, some trying to make hard decisions, others trying to find information about their own families, some trying to get to their families, others trying to bring their families into the greater safety of the emperor's palace, and some simply driven insane by the prospect of an exceptionally horrific death.

In the midst of all the pandemonium and disarray, we managed to make our way to the room where the Table held its ground, still trying to maintain a semblance of a functioning government. The Table Elders remained surprisingly undisturbed and calm, a complete opposite from the happenings outside the walls of that room.

"We asked for one raw-breed, and you bring us thousands of beasts!" Emperor Abubakari said to Gyvan as soon as we walked in.

"Not my intention, Your Highness," Gyvan defended. "Hopefully reinforcements from other garrisons and fortresses will be here before the devils can overrun us."

"If we can hold out for that long," Musa the Elder said. "Messengers have already been dispatched. It will take at least thirteen days for the nearest sizable force to get here."

"We got word that you have a package, Commander," Shokolo-ba said.

Gyvan then exposed the concealed Lord Venga. Shock and disbelief seized the Elders and the raw-breeds, Shokolo-ba and Tin-zim, as they saw a now helpless Lord Venga brought before their very own eyes.

"No wonder the pray-devils risk all to invade the mainland," were the only words the emperor could say.

Shokolo-ba removed the cloth that gagged Lord Venga, their loathing for each other apparent in exceptionally scornful manner in which the two eyed each other.

"So, Lord Venga," Shokolo-ba addressed, "this is what you come down to?"

"This won't be over for a long time, Shokolo-ba," Lord Venga scoffed. "This is not yet the end."

"For you, it is."

"Shokolo-ba," Musa the Elder interrupted, "I bid you to make haste with what must be done before further harm is brought upon us all. You may at a later moment handle your quarrels with the villain. But for now, sir, time is not on our side."

Shokolo-ba agreed. He signaled Tin-zim, who brought in some potions and items of Breedish design. He stood them in front of Lord Venga and began uttering some eeidic chants in Breed, the language of the raw-breeds. Realizing that his demise was near, Lord Venga made one last attempt to gain a recruit for his cause and save his skin.

"Listen, Tin-zim," he said, "it is not too late. Join me. Eartholia Proper is still ours for the taking!"

"Your designs for Eartholia Proper, and this Earth," Tin-zim began responding, "are part of a dream that should never be allowed to see the light of day. How many more lives must be lost before you come to realize the folly of your ways?"

Lord Venga said nothing, understanding that the raw-breeds could not have come all the way from Eartholia Proper only to give in to his whims. Shokolo-ba continued his chants, and as he progressed, Lord Venga began to scream louder and louder, tormented by some unseen force that brought him untold agony, a force that could only possibly be understood by raw-breeds or eeids. Then the screams suddenly stopped. Shokolo-ba discontinued his chants. He calmed himself, relaxed, and took in a deep breath. The great raw-breed general, Lord Venga, his gaze now just a blank stare, slowly closed his eyes, dropped to the floor, and passed out.

"Is it done?" the emperor asked.

"Not yet, Your Highness," Shokolo-ba responded. "The White Shadow now weakens in him. Tomorrow night it will be ready for capture and eventual destruction."

"Tomorrow night?"

While in his spellbound sleep, Lord Venga was strapped to a chair and kept under the ever watchful eyes of the raw-breeds, waiting for the morrow when the grand act of our task would be completed—the capture of Lord Venga's Third Shadow, the all-powerful White Shadow. It was then that it could be permanently and completely destroyed, ending forever Lord Venga's threat to Eartholia Proper and New Eartholia, and the torments that plagued the land. No longer would we live in fear and distrust of each other. No longer would we fear the still mysterious blood dripper. Earth was soon to be safe at last from Lord Venga's evil.

But would Timbuktu be safe from the approaching pray-devils?

***

MOMENTS AFTER LORD VENGA WAS put into his deathlike slumber by the raw-breeds, the Elders, despite the dire situation Timbuktu now faced, took it upon themselves to express their condolences for the loss of Jeevas, Shang, and their unborn. But more notably, though they expressed an admiration for my answering of Mory Tipp's riddle, they found it incomprehensible why I could not disclose the answer of the riddle to them, just as I had not disclosed it to the tormented boy eeid, Mory Tipp, himself. I dared not disclose to the Table what its answer was, just as I had declined to do with Gyvan and his soldiers, informing them, and Mory Tipp himself, that the answer was one too disturbing to divulge.

The emperor insisted that I stay in his quarters under the protection of his guards during the upcoming siege, but I respectfully declined, letting him know that I felt safest with Commander Drabo. The emperor understood my position and had no quarrel with it.

Help for Timbuktu was said to be on its way from other military outposts and from the neighboring states and kingdoms, the earliest of which could only arrive to aid us in thirteen days. Thirteen days was an awfully long time to hold out against a pray-devil force that was very likely to smash and break through the city walls in only a few days, two or three at the most, according to Babayaro's determinations. Gyvan saw things differently. He believed the city could still do more to assist with its own defense and improve upon its chances of holding out and ultimately surviving the pray-devil onslaught. He therefore approached the emperor.

"Your Highness," Gyvan addressed the emperor, "outlasting this siege for thirteen days will be no small feat. Our defenses, as they are, cannot be expected to hold out in that regard. There is much more that can be done to strengthen our defenses."

"Does it matter, Commander?" the emperor asked calmly, readying his sword and iron plate armor for battle. "Death is but a day away. But if you believe that there is more you can do to make a difference, then you have my permission to do whatever you may require to strengthen the defenses of this city and save us all."

With this authority, Gyvan called all the generals together and informed them of his intentions. Together with all the men, women, and children they could muster, they were all to spend all night and all day building two more walls to surround the city. There was also to be an outer moat filled with all manner of sharp and prickly objects to deter the attackers from attempting to scale the walls. Gyvan's defensive plan was intended to give the city three walls, each one constructed with parapets and serving as a line of defense. The city's defenders were going to man the outer wall as the first line of defense, and if it fell, they were to withdraw to the second wall. And if that fell too, then they were to withdraw to the third and innermost wall to make a last stand. And if that wall fell too, then...*Good luck* was all Gyvan said about that.

Gyvan divided the defensive perimeter into five zones, each one commanded either by himself, One Eye, Babayaro, Gans, or Tigana, angering some of the officers in the upper echelons of the army, seeing themselves placed beneath lower-ranking soldiers. Yet Gyvan made them come to understand that his choice of commanders was so chosen because they had the most experience battling pray-devils, and were therefore best suited for the operations at hand.

The work on constructing the defensive walls began without a moment's delay, with the commanders making use of every man, woman, and child who could carry a tool, taking advantage of the unlimited amount of labor provided by the endless supply of panic-stricken people still pouring into Timbuktu. Though this labor supply was of a great advantage to the ongoing construction, we knew we would run out of something extremely critical, and of which the city already had a very limited supply—food.

As the construction progressed, Musa the Elder managed to convince Gyvan, Gans, Tigana, One Eye, Babayaro, and me to rest awhile amidst the chaos and near collapse of civility occurring all around us. It was a well-deserved reprieve after our ordeal and services to the empire, he insisted. Our meal, though extremely meager, was all that could be scraped up from the emperor's kitchens. It included a rare delicacy, most likely preserved for us for just this occasion—spiced chicken intestines topped with goat testicles and fish eyes. As I devoured my meal, which was more delicious and appetizing than anything I had eaten in weeks, I began to wonder whether a pray-devil might also judge my flesh to be the most delicious and appetizing meal it had eaten in weeks.

Even a brief rest after our rare meal was not for Gyvan, and at my stubborn insistence, after I learned of the visit he was about to make, it was not for me either. So together we departed the palace, battling through the chaotic streets that were choked with hordes of panic-stricken people, and visited Lili, the woman he was to marry. It seemed so long since my last parting with her.

We found Lili not far from her house, helping to sharpen wooden spikes that were to be used in the moat around the city. She had grown pale and sickly, the trouble in the land having taken a toll on her, though her smile revealed the rare beauty hidden beneath the look of gloom and doom on her face.

"I am afraid," she said to Gyvan after they had hugged and kissed each other, a rather incomprehensible act which only adults seemed to understand, and one during which I distracted myself by looking away towards the continuing pandemonium on the streets of Timbuktu.

"No harm will come to any of you as long as I breathe," Gyvan said of Lili and me.

He insisted on spending the remainder of the siege with Lili and me, fighting by us or dying by us should it come to that. We joined Lili in the preparation of the city's defenses, for if we all hoped to live, those two extra walls and a moat had to be built. So it was that throughout the night every able-bodied man, woman or child, lowborn or highborn, worked on the construction almost without rest. Even the emperor and the Elders did not spare themselves, for the emperor, the night no longer a problem for him, could now see at night as well as the next man or woman, on account of my prescription of a weekly dose of an ass's raw liver. Lili and I worked right beside Gyvan, who occasionally rode off on his horse to supervise the construction in other parts of the city.

By midday on the following day, most of the construction had been completed, with only small segments of the outer wall unfinished, their construction of which was abruptly interrupted when everyone suddenly stopped working, a dead silence falling over the city. Something was amiss.

Something undesirable. Something terrifying that could be heard some distance away outside the city. An eerily uneasy mood filled the air as the terrifying sound grew louder and louder as it drew nearer. Very slowly, heads began to turn towards the direction of the sound, apprehensive of what they would see, the loudness of the frightening silence terrifying to the core. What was approaching the city?

Then, slowly, from the direction of the sound, something began to surface—rising dust. That could only mean an army was approaching, the sounds having been produced by this approaching army. But was this army friend or foe? The frightening silence over the city held still. Those outside the city walls working on the construction were frozen where they stood, too terrified to run into the city.

Then there was a cry. "It's the army!" yelled one of the city's lookouts manning a watchtower. "It's the army!"

A wild jubilation ran through the city. Loved ones hugged each other and shouts of joy rang out to all directions. Our reinforcements were finally here, enough men to stop and destroy the pray-devils. We were saved at last.

But how had the reinforcements arrived so quickly? It was supposed to take at least thirteen days for the nearest to arrive, even under the best of conditions. But as this army got closer, the answer to my question was answered as a sad realization began to slowly come to bear upon all, the joy and elation slowly petering out. Hope rapidly turned into despair once again. This approaching army was not part of the reinforcements we were expecting. This was a fleeing army, fleeing to the safety of fortified Timbuktu as had many a man, woman, and child. This army was none other than what was left of the thousands of garrisoned soldiers and Watchmen of Tera-Hool whom we had left to fight the pray-devils at the Moon Lake garrison. Now only a few hundred of them remained, fleeing from the pray-devils in all haste, making an escape from certain death, disaster and annihilation. This was a harbinger of the doom soon to meet us all.

"Inside the city! Quick! Lock the gates! The devils approach!" many of the beaten soldiers shouted at us as they scrambled into the city.

"The devils will be here by dusk," a haggard and battle-weary Commander Malouda informed the emperor. "They are right behind us. We couldn't stop them, Your Highness. There were too many."

"You did what you could," the emperor assured him. "Your efforts bought us time to better our fortifications."

"Fortifications?" Commander Malouda asked. "Useless. The devils will tear them down before we are through fighting their first assault."

"Where is Commander Habé?" Gyvan asked of the Moon Lake garrison commander.

"Eaten," came a reply.

These survivors numbered some six or seven hundred. They had been a force many thousands strong. Their arrival only renewed a sense of fear, despair and mayhem in the city, leading many of the panic-stricken civilians working on the fortifications to hysterically flee to their homes and abandon the work on what was left. Others even tried to flee from the city, believing it to soon become a death trap. These were stopped by the soldiers, who had no desire of letting anyone fall into the hands of the pray-devils.

The remaining work on the fortifications was hastily completed by soldiers, after which they manned the defensive positions on the outer wall, our first line of defense. Now we waited. That was all there was to do. Every male, civilian or soldier, low born or high born, who could be armed, even the emperor, was sent to the outer wall and given a quick course in the ways of combat if need be. Even those in the Emperor's Poor who could hold a weapon asked for and received some. The emperor's guard dogs, though now reduced to scavenging scraggy-looking beasts, were readied for battle by their handlers. Shokolo-ba and Tin-zim, whose existence within the city remained secret, stayed within the emperor's palace to watch over Lord Venga and to capture and destroy his Third Shadow by nightfall.

The outer wall was too dangerous for Lili and me to be with Gyvan, and upon his insistence, we remained within the inner wall along with all the women, children, the sick, the very old, and the very young. Lili found a rooftop next to the emperor's place where she and I could sit and watch all the happenings as they unfolded. We stayed on the rooftop along with a few others, all frightened like never before of the fate that awaited us in the coming days.

Then we waited.

Dusk was approaching, the moment Commander Malouda had warned we should expect the pray-devils. I watched the civilians, who by this time had calmed down, the mayhem and chaos having just recently given way to a quiet resignation and acceptance of the horrors to come. All was quiet now. The soldiers manning their defenses on the parapets built along the outer wall watched the horizon, observing every happening outside the walls. Everyone watched, waiting for the rising dust from the direction the pray-devils were expected to come.

But what we saw next was not just the rising dust from an army approaching the city. What we saw was a dust storm. Thundering towards the city were thousands upon thousands of pray-devils armed with their slashing swords and flesh hooks, their terrifyingly sharp fangs gleaming threateningly, ready to kill in battle and instantly devour those unfortunate enough to cross their paths. The number of pray-devils far exceeded the number of troops in the city. The beasts seemed hungry too, and were sure to find plenty of food within the city.

Their appearance and the violent noises they made were so terrifying that many within the walls, including a few soldiers, simply could take it no longer and simply fainted out of fear. But I felt secure with our city's defense, for it had been planned by Gyvan. The thorn-filled moat surrounding the outer wall would definitely stop the pray-devils, of course, I knew. There was no way they could possibly get through it. And I was right. The pray-devils, upon coming within a short distance of the city, stopped in their tracks to consider how to best proceed with their assault. Within a short while, though, they surrounded the entire city, ready to digest its inhabitants. They began threateningly screaming, yelling, and making noises of all manner, all designed to sow further fear and terror into us and weaken our will to resist. Children were crying, their parents were terrified, the archers were nervous, their fingers holding arrows against their bows and itching to let the arrows fly upon the command of their officers. But we waited. That was all we could do.

And then the devil attack began.

The beasts came head on from all directions, falling onto the city like a swarm of locusts on the lone tree along their path. Our archers sent their arrows flying, wave after wave of deadly missiles, bringing down the devils by the thousands. The damned beasts were not deterred, for still their attack continued as before, with each charging pray-devil wave more ferocious than the one before it. The beasts were throwing themselves towards the city faster than our archers could cut them down. Before long the beasts were on the edge of the moat that surrounded the city, making the task of our archers almost a useless intervention, for it appeared there were more devils than we had arrows.

But I was comforted, knowing that these beasts could not possibly cross the moat, which was filled with all manner of death-dealing objects such as pikes, sharpened sticks, broken glass, and even ferocious vipers and other types of poisonous serpents and scorpions dropped in there by some of our more imaginative citizens. Yet again I was wrong. The damnable beasts did not stop at the edge of the moat. They simply charged on, straight into it, where many perished, each one more ready to die than the one before it. Did they not understand that entry into the moat meant death? Were they not afraid to die? Then I understood. Those who were jumping into the moat were sacrificing themselves for their comrades, filling up the moat with their bodies so that their living comrades could safely tread over them to deal us death at the walls. Whether that was bravery or some ghoulish lunacy, I'll allow you to be the judge of that. But within minutes the entire moat was filled up with the bodies of pray-devils, presenting a horrifyingly disturbing sight and effectively neutralizing the defensive purpose of the moat, for it had failed miserably to stop the damned devil army.

Now it was time for them to breach the city walls.

Our problems were just beginning. The next wave of pray-devil attackers advanced, bearing ladders—instruments to scale and breach our walls—each ladder carried by a team of five beasts. Our archers continued shooting their deadly volleys against the devils, aimed this time at the ladder-bearers. And while many a ladder-bearing team was destroyed, it soon became obvious that their untold numbers and endless supply of reinforcements guaranteed their eventual success. So it was that before long, these ladder-bearers soon reached the wall, quickly followed by wave after wave of sword and flesh hook-wielding devils ready to retrieve their master and have a human dinner in the process.

As the devils placed their ladders against the wall, the city defenders, including the emperor and the Elders, hurled everything they could at them—rocks, arrows, knives, boiling water, hot oil, and even a putrid mixture of dog vomit and weather-stewed cow manure, all vain attempts to prevent the entry of the beasts into Timbuktu. Wave after wave of them continued to attack, some making it to the top of the ladders only to be cut down by the defenders as soon as they stepped on top of the wall and onto the parapet. The defense was ferocious, perhaps even more so than the devil attack. I saw the emperor himself cut down two pray-devils and save three soldiers who were about to be slashed and eaten. Yes indeed, our defense of our beloved city was fierce. Every soldier, nobleman, or boy able to wield a weapon was engaged in the desperate stand against what was sure to end in our doom.

The fighting continued for many hours, and then the unthinkable happened.

The pray-devils began to withdraw!

***

THE WILL OF THE PRAY-DEVILS had been broken. We had defeated them. Loud cheers of victory erupted throughout the city as the word spread from end to end of the cessation of the devil attacks. Some families even emerged from their underground hiding quarters. We had beaten back the pray-devils.

At least that is what we thought.

Little did we know that more was still to come.

Euphoric rejoicing quickly turned into hysteric terror as word again quickly spread that the devils were regrouping and were once again assaulting the city with an even larger and more fearsome force. Amidst the current hysteria, many in the city quickly scrambled back to their hiding places. I saw three women who, unable to take the torment any longer, simply dropped dead out of fright and disbelief.

Many of the soldiers, now familiar with combating pray-devils and their fear of the beasts somewhat diminished, maintained their calm and waited for the beasts to reach the walls, while the archers, as best they could, continued raining death upon many a devil who got within shooting range.

The second phase of the attack with fresh pray-devil troops was more devastating against the defenders. Many more of these defenders, already fatigued from the relentless fighting, began falling to the swords, flesh hooks, and fangs of the beasts, many of which were now succeeding in climbing over the wall and into the city, although most of these were cut down by defenders. As tenacious as the defenders were, the countless numbers of the devils were too great to be held back for much longer. The number of human casualties began to grow at an alarming rate, enabling the devils to bring in battering rams which they used against the wall, attempting to knock down sections of it through which their forces could pour into the city.

For hours the battle raged, and for hours fear and courage, death and destruction reigned. And then I heard the order no one within the city wanted to hear.

"Fall back! Fall back!" Gyvan ordered.

The first defensive wall had fallen.

All the defenders of the first wall, including Gyvan and the emperor, hastily abandoned their positions and began a mad dash towards the second wall, hotly pursued by pray-devils, who savagely overran and instantly devoured a few of the unfortunate soldiers. Among these poor souls I recognized an Elder who went by the name of Kirit the Elder. After losing his left leg to the belly of a hungry devil, the poor man lay in a pool of his own blood and bled to death. The remaining soldiers, including Gyvan, the emperor, Musa the Elder, One Eye, Babayaro, Gans, Commander Malouda, and Tigana, were now running for their lives towards the second defensive wall as the pray-devils were very quickly catching up to them. But these devils, before they could make their kills, were themselves quickly and easily cut down by archers who had been stationed behind the second wall for just this purpose. The survivors of the first wall safely retreated into the second wall, where they again manned defensive positions on a parapet built behind the wall. The pray-devils were once again locked out, and we were once again trapped in, hoping to hold our position for thirteen days until reinforcements could arrive. But how could this happen, when in only a few hours the damned devils had breached the moat and broken through the first wall?

The existence of the second wall did not hinder the devils, their attacks continuing ever more ferociously, though many among them had fallen. The fighting raged on, with screams of man and shrills of devil all around as death engulfed both. The pray-devils, their numbers seeming only to increase, continued to be emboldened by their success over the first wall. The defenders, their numbers only dropping, but with now a smaller perimeter to defend, also seemed no less emboldened as the necessity for keeping this second wall defended at all costs was recognized.

Nightfall was fast approaching. Lili and I rushed to the emperor's palace where I intended to learn of the progress being made towards the capture and destruction of Lord Venga's White Shadow. We were soon granted access to Shokolo-ba and Tin-zim after I had prepared Lili for the raw-breeds and made her promise to maintain her calm upon setting eyes on them. But as soon as she laid eyes on the creatures she let out a cry so loud that Red Sentinels guarding the building rushed in with swords drawn, believing that pray-devils may have somehow gained entry into the palace. I calmed Lili down and the Sentinels withdrew.

"The White Shadow?" I asked Tin-zim. "Is it ready to be captured?"

"Soon," Shokolo-ba said. "I am dispatching guards to request the presence of the emperor and Gyvan for the event."

"We will inform them," I suggested.

"As you will, child," Shokolo-ba said. "But please do mind your steps out there."

Lili and I exited the palace and headed towards the gates of the second wall. But I knew that for our safety the guards at the gates could not let us through. So how could we convince them otherwise? We certainly could not tell them about Lord Venga and the two other raw-breeds present within the city walls, lest we cause more panic that would do more harm to a city already on the brink of annihilation. Then Lili came up with a clever suggestion. We filled two water gourds with water and took them to the gates, where the guards stopped us.

"Where do you think you are going?" one guard asked. "Want to get eaten?"

"We have water for the soldiers," Lili said, showing them our gourds. "It will help them."

The guard hesitated a moment, smiled, and let us through, bidding us to be careful. We gave the water to the first few soldiers we came across, who gulped it down heartily.

There was death everywhere, death of human and devil alike, but mostly of human, for most of the devil dead lay outside the first and second walls, cut down by archers or hacked by sword- and spear-wielding soldiers before they could climb over either wall. Lili and I walked along the base behind the second wall, searching for Gyvan or the emperor. We soon saw the emperor and his brother, Musa the Elder, slashing, stabbing, and cutting at attacking pray-devils attempting to get over the wall. We climbed over the parapet amidst great risk to ourselves and went to them.

"What are you doing here?" the emperor asked, surprised, and gasping for breath.

I informed him that it would soon be time to capture the White Shadow, at which he was only slightly relieved, knowing that it would do little to spare Timbuktu a harrowing fate.

"I'll get word to Commander Drabo and the others," his brother said.

We were about to walk away with the emperor and his brother when two pray-devils jumped over the wall and onto the parapet. Believing Lili and me to be easier targets, the beasts quickly grabbed us and were about to pull us over when the emperor, Musa the Elder, and some nearby soldiers fell on them like a swarm of angry bees. Within seconds the pray-devils were transformed into bits and pieces by the sharp and quick swords of the human warriors.

As the emperor, Musa the Elder, Lili, and I approached the gate of the third wall as we hurried towards the palace, we saw many women and children coming out of the city carrying gourds filled with water. They were taking them to the soldiers. Lili and I had set an example to be followed.

All the relevant persons were soon in the palace to witness the capture of Lord Venga's White Shadow—Commander Gyvan Drabo, Emperor Abubakari II, Musa the Elder, twelve other surviving Table Elders, and I. Lili was respectfully asked to wait outside.

"Four Elders are missing," a surprised Tin-zim commented.

"Eaten," Gyvan responded simply.

Shokolo-ba took the orbs of Tichiman and laid them on the unconscious Lord Venga. Then together with Tin-zim, he began chanting some words in Breed which made no meaning to anyone else in the room. A moment later, the orbs changed color into a bright green and Lord Venga's dark complexion changed into a dark yellow. He now looked like a completely different creature, even uglier and more grotesque than he already was.

"That is the look of a raw-breed that has lost its Third Shadow," Shokolo-ba explained. He picked up the orbs of Tichiman and put them in a bag he slung across his chest.

The Third Shadow of Lord Venga, the White Shadow, was captured at last.

But still it had to be destroyed.

Sobo Ha-Ha Speaks

chapter 66

"LORD VENGA!" I HEARD MYSELF scream, as I sensed the painful capture of his Third Shadow, the White Shadow. The death of my lord, Fadiga, and his widow, Mai-Fatou, now all seemed for naught. Now Lord Venga too was almost no more. What would I do with myself now? The numbers of my kind—reduced. Our days—few. And our only hope, Lord Venga, was now a powerless prisoner soon to wither away into death at the hands of those bent upon his destruction. I sat down and put my face in my hands.

I wept.

The Words Of The Child Eeid

chapteℝ 67

THE WHITE SHADOW WAS A threat no more. What would happen next?

Man was finally safe from the throes of Lord Venga and his White Shadow. But still we were not safe from the pray-devils.

All the parties involved in the capture of the White Shadow, save the raw-breeds, went outside to the roof where we could view the battle and hope that the capture of the White Shadow had released the pray-devils from the spell in which Lord Venga had held them. But nothing had changed. The devils continued their attack as viciously as before. But an event of another sort soon occurred, an event perhaps just as relieving as a hopeful withdrawal of the pray-devils.

It was the color of the sky. It returned.

The dark clouds that had haunted this Earth all these many months past soon faded. Life returned to the sky. Darkness now gave way to light. The bright blue color of the sky and the sun's rays beamed down and bathed the Earth with its wondrous beauty once again, a dazzling spectacle finally returning to us during our last moments on Earth.

But still the battle raged on, the fighters oblivious to the changes around them. The fangs, swords, and flesh hooks of the grisly pray-devils gleamed even more terrifyingly in the bright sunlight—the beasts, salivating for that delicate taste of human flesh, the rare delicacy they had so missed for many a decade.

"What now?" the emperor asked Shokolo-ba and Tin-zim.

"Now the threat to Eartholia Proper is no longer," Tin-zim said. "When this battle is over we will return there, along with Lord Venga, so that he may be tried for his crimes against peace."

"And the destruction of the White Shadow?"

"It will happen upon our return to Eartholia Proper, and after his trial. By our laws Shokolo-ba and I are not authorized to take it upon ourselves to destroy the Third Shadow of another."

Then Shokolo-ba asked the emperor, "Can your forces hold the pray-devils until your reinforcements arrive?"

The emperor shook his head. "We will all be dead by morning."

"Then the moment the first pray-devil shows its head in the palace we will destroy the White Shadow. Our present circumstances dictate that we act as such."

"Do I have your word?"

"You have my word."

With that, the emperor, Musa the Elder, Gyvan, and the other twelve surviving Elders left for the walls again to continue the battle. Lili and I joined the other women and children in supplying water to the thirsty soldiers fighting for us all.

The battle raged on, getting more and more bitter as the hours went by. As I observed the savagery erupting all around me, one thing about it delighted me, however, and this was the realization that there now existed some other creatures that had found the flesh of the pray-devils particularly tasty, and desirable. These were the emperor's **guard** dogs, having been thrown earlier into the battle by their handlers to help with the city's defense. Individually no dog on its own could subdue a pray-devil, but their handlers had quickly trained them to attack in packs, wreaking havoc among the pray-devils that succeeded in climbing over the wall.

Lili and I, along with many other women and children, continued to make countless rounds to deliver water to soldiers who requested it, a necessary duty with sometimes unpleasant aspects. For example, many an instant, a harrowing trip was made to deliver water to a soldier who had requested it, only to find him slumped against the wall, dead—missing an arm, leg, or sometimes even a head, having had it bitten off by a damned devil. Such was the nature of a war such as this.

Lili and I restricted our water delivery to the section of the wall under the command of Gyvan, who continued to fight tirelessly, trying to minimize the loss of life among the men under his command. He saved many a life that day among his men, and many a man gave his life to save him.

***

SOME HOURS LATER, A RED Sentinel ran to Gyvan.

"I bring word from the emperor," he said. "He says the raw-breeds and Lord Venga have vanished."

"What do you mean?" Gyvan asked, startled.

"Shokolo-ba and Tin-zim have escaped, Commander. Escaped and left us to die!"

Why had the raw-breed peace agents escaped? Why had they not informed the emperor before taking their leave? But these questions mattered little now. After all, the raw-breeds could have made little difference in the defense of Timbuktu.

"And Lord Venga and the orbs?" Gyvan asked the Sentinel.

"Gone."

"Did they escape with Lord Venga or did Lord Venga escape with them?"

"No one knows. The guards say they heard a loud noise in the room and when they went in there, the raw-breeds had vanished."

"The Portal of Gorgida," I said.

"How?" Gyvan asked.

"It is the same way the raw-breeds came here. Shokolo-ba or Tin-zim must have had the key to the portal, and that is what they used to open the portal."

"Good," Gyvan said. "It means that the raw-breeds are out of here for good. Now we must continue to defend our city."

Was it really a good thing that the raw-breeds had escaped? I was not sure. But for now we had to deal with our own troubles at hand—the attacking pray-devils. So Lili and I dashed away and continued our water rounds, while the city continued to defend itself against overwhelming odds.

Hours later, in the middle of the night, came the call no one wanted to hear. Again it was from Gyvan.

"Fall back! Fall back!"

The second wall had fallen. Now only one wall was left.

The wild run then started towards the third and only wall left between survival and death. The run to this wall was not as organized as had been the run to the second wall, for there were now hundreds of women and children involved who had been delivering water to keep the soldiers strong enough to defend the city. They were now among the thousands of soldiers running from their positions along the second wall into the city to make a last stand against the devils.

But once again, the archers already stationed on the last wall were there to rain down arrows on the few pray-devils who had breached the second wall and were now giving chase to the soldiers, women, and children now running into the city. The fleeing soldiers only let themselves into the city after the last of the women and children had been let in, having stayed behind to slow down the advancing beasts, at great cost to themselves. Within a short horrifying moment the surviving humans were all within the protection of the city and the gates were closed.

This was our last stand.

This time Lili and I stayed with Gyvan. If this was our last moment on Earth, we were going to spend it with him. It made me think of Shang, Jeevas, and their unborn child, and how they must now be together on the other side of life in peace and quietness, smiling down on us and wishing us the best. Many a faithful woman and child, along with many a brave soldier, had fallen along the second wall. Soon it would be our turn, the thousands of us trapped within the city walls of Timbuktu.

The pray-devils had breached two heavily defended walls in less than two days, and it was not rational to believe that the last wall could be held for eleven more days until reinforcements could arrive. We just had to wait to die, it seemed. For some people this was too great an ordeal to bear. They took their own lives by falling on their swords. Others simply stood above the walls and jumped into the hordes of pray-devils below them. The slow wait for death had been too unbearable for these poor souls.

The pray-devils, despite their heavy casualties, continued launching more and more vicious attacks, each one more devastating than the one before it. After all, they only had to breach one more wall. They attempted to batter it or scale it with their ladders, as had successfully been achieved twice before. But still our soldiers stood their ground, defiantly holding off wave after wave of assaults as they made their final stand.

Most of the defenders were determined to fight to the last man, with one soldier even tying himself to his post, stating that under no circumstances would he flee or withdraw, but would rather die fighting there, if only that action could help his daughter live a little longer. I admired his determination, though I privately deplored his method, for tying himself to his post could seriously impede his ability to engage the enemy in close quarters. Gyvan understood this too, but chose to say nothing to the soldier, noting to me that if the soldier's action could help him die happier, then so be it. I agreed.

Before long, almost all in the city, and most of the women and children who had been delivering water, were in close proximity to their loved ones doing the fighting. These women and children were assisting in any way they could, using anything that could be wielded as a weapon—sticks, rocks, pestles, pots, pans, and even shoes —dropping them on the hordes of pray-devils congregating outside the wall below. The fighting raged into the night, our defenses still holding strong, though barely. For almost two continuous days, our badly outnumbered soldiers had already been fighting. Their strength could not hold out for a third. Yet they had to keep fighting until they could no longer fight.

Later during the night, a soldier ran to Gyvan.

"General Tigana reports that a section of his wall has been breached," he said to Gyvan. "For now, his men keep the devils at bay, but they cannot hold on for much longer."

Gyvan dispatched twenty of his men to help Tigana defend the breached wall, knowing that his now reduced number of defenders compromised the defense of his own wall. A short moment later, we also learned that One Eye's wall had been breached, and that the emperor had dispatched some of his men to help defend the wall. Not long after, the emperor's wall was also breached, leading Babayaro to dispatch some of his men to help defend it. Minutes later, it was Commander Malouda's wall, breached with battering rams, forcing Gans to dispatch some of his men to help reinforce its defenses.

Everything was now going wrong. Our defense was falling apart.

Though several sections of the final wall had been breached, the defenders were able to keep the pray-devils from pouring into the city by filling the breached sections with bodies of slain devils. But at dawn our situation grew even more desperate. A section of the wall under the command of an Elder was also breached by a reinforced column of devils bearing a concentrated number of battering rams. Before the defenders could receive any reinforcements, those already there were completely overrun and killed, a pair of razor sharp fangs biting into the Elder's right thigh before another bit into his left ribs and devoured that entire section of his body almost in a single gulp.

The pray-devils poured in through this breached wall.

They were now inside Timbuktu!

For two days and one night we had fought tirelessly to defend Timbuktu. We had failed. Now it was time for a reckoning with the devils. Lili and I stayed close to Gyvan as he and his men tried desperately to fend off the attackers. Then his wall got breached. More devils poured into the city in droves. More sections of the wall began to fall to the devils in quick succession, enabling the beasts to pour into Timbuktu in numbers uncountable. I held Naya tightly.

The end was at hand at last.

***

IT WAS A HIGH-PITCHED WHISTLE, whose source no one could determine. It was an unusual sound the likes of which I had never before heard. I looked towards the direction from where it had come, outside the city, far away beyond the endless sea of pray-devils, many of whom were now within the city and continuing to pour in. Then, behind the devils, from where the sound had come, emerged thousands and thousands of another type of enemy, an even deadlier enemy, even more destructive and more dangerous.

Raw-breeds, thousands of them.

Lord Venga was back to exact deadly vengeance upon man. The raw-breeds were all on horseback, armed to the teeth, bringing with them the scourge of this Earth. How had they arrived so suddenly? There was only one answer: through the Portal of Gorgida.

"The blasted, treacherous raw-breeds," Gyvan roared. "Now they come to finish what Lord Venga started!"

"I don't think so, Gyvan," Lili said. "Look!"

Lili pointed to the farthest point of battlefield. The raw-breeds were charging. But they were not attacking us. They were attacking the pray-devils.

"They come to help us," Lili cried euphorically. "They come to help us."

Gyvan then started yelling to panicked soldiers and civilians, "They are on our side! The raw-breeds are on our side!"

During ordinary times, most people, whose knowledge of raw-breeds only went as far as the frightening stories told in the Breed Legends, would have rather swallowed their own vomit than believe in any such thing as raw-breeds helping humans. But at this desperate hour, all were willing to believe in anything that presented itself in the form of help. And so it was that word of raw-breed assistance quickly spread throughout Timbuktu, a renewed sense of hope and survival quickly gripping the city in the face of a most brutal death at the hands of the pray-devils.

It was a rescue so timely that even the pray-devils were completely taken by surprise. Now caught between the raw-breeds and human soldiers bent upon dealing down deadly and merciless vengeance upon the vile, monstrous creatures, the devils were thrown into utter mayhem. The tables turned, and now desperate to survive themselves, the devils suddenly shifted to attack the more formidable foe—the raw-breeds. Most now started pouring out of the city and began charging at the approaching raw-breeds, who themselves had the pray-devils surrounded.

Emboldened, enraged, and thirsty for bitter vengeance, the city defenders, who now saw that the pray-devils were in retreat, left the city walls and took after the beasts, determined to exact a hefty retribution worth its weight in blood. A few pray-devils who still remained in the city were now the target of rapidly organized special cleanup units Gans had tasked with staying within the city walls and destroying any lingering devils found within it. And I tell you, many a devil did they gruesomely destroy, and without the slightest prick of conscience. Two beasts, for example, after having their eyes and fangs forcibly and brutally gouged out, were hanged by their tails in the city center and provided as sport for children, who viciously pummeled them to death with rocks and missiles of all kinds.

The pray-devil army was in a rout.

Gyvan, Commander Malouda, and the surviving Watchmen of Tera-Hool mounted their horses and raced to join battle outside the city walls, along with the Emperor, the surviving Elders, and a few hundred surviving soldiers. Lili and I, along with many other civilians, stayed on the parapets along what was left of the city walls, and watched the battle as it unfolded. I watched Gyvan fight his way through the sea of pray-devils, seeming to seek out someone.

Tsing-tsing.

Tsing-tsing himself was fighting a combined force of raw-breeds and humans. Gyvan caught up with him just in time to save a raw-breed who was about to be butchered by the rogue raw-breed. Gyvan swung his sword at Tsing-tsing, but it hit one of his horns, the blow easily bouncing off. Gyvan then dismounted his horse and faced the raw-breed, who himself was not mounted. Both warriors battled each other, a duel in which each was the match for the other. Allies who came to the aid of each were quickly cut down by the opponent.

The battle for Timbuktu raged on endlessly. The number of pray-devils left on the battlefield was dwindling as the moments went by until only a few were left. Many that had tried to escape were hunted down by human cavalry and hacked to bits. Not a single one could be left alive. It would have been like leaving a lion alive in a goat farm.

Tsing-tsing was the last of the enemy still standing after the battle had long been over. A crowd of raw-breeds and humans quickly formed around the dueling Gyvan and Tsing-tsing. Some had tried to interfere on Gyvan's behalf but he had asked them to stay away. He wanted to destroy the raw-breed himself. The duel between the two continued, each still proving to be the equal of the other at arms. And then Gyvan suddenly stepped away and stopped fighting. All wondered what was amiss. He stared at Tsing-tsing briefly, and then as suddenly as he had broken off, he dove back into the fight. But this time Gyvan was launching no attacks against the raw-breed. He was defending the raw-breed's attacks, yet observing and watching every move the creature made. I smiled and assured a highly concerned Lili that she had little to worry about, for I understood perfectly what Gyvan was doing. He again suddenly stepped away and stopped fighting. Then he looked at Tsing-tsing and winked.

Then, as suddenly as he had broken off, Gyvan dove back into the fight, this time launching a hyper vicious attack against the raw-breed. There was one difference this time about the nature of the duel: Tsing-tsing was almost no match for Commander Drabo. But what had given him the sudden edge over the raw-breed? Where had his skill suddenly come from? I knew the answers to all these. That was why I had assured Lili that she had little to worry about. I knew perfectly well what commander Drabo, the high lord of Tera-Hool, had been working up against the rogue raw-breed.

It was the Dance of the Undertaker!

Gyvan had learned not only how to defeat the Dance of the Undertaker of the Paipan, but also how to use it. But soon the crowd had seen enough of the fighting and demanded its end. This only further enraged the frantic Tsing-tsing, who then lunged at a briefly distracted Gyvan, hoping to catch him off guard. But Gyvan was one step too quick for the irate raw-breed. The high lord, as swiftly as a striking black mamba, used his sword to knock Tsing-tsing's into the air. The raw-breed's sword flew up, then began its descent, its point facing straight downwards, heading straight towards Tsing-tsing's head. The baffled raw-breed looked up at the weapon, but it was too late. It went straight through his head, right between his horns, the point of the weapon exiting through his neck. A cheer erupted from the crowd, from human and raw-breed alike. The battle was over at last.

Lili and I ran to Gyvan and threw ourselves at him.

"The Dance of the Undertaker," came a coarse voice from behind us. We turned and looked. It was Shokolo-ba, standing next to Tin-zim. They were dressed in raw-breed battle gear, their swords bloodied.

"How do you know of the Dance of the Undertaker?" Gyvan asked Shokolo-ba.

"I've been around a bit," Shokolo-ba responded.

"We thought you had run out on us," the emperor said to Tin-zim and Shokolo-ba.

"No, Your Highness," Tin-zim said. "We are peace agents. We went to obtain help, to finish what we had started—the pray-devils."

"What about Lord Venga?" Musa the Elder asked.

"He is a prisoner of the Committee—the body of officials who govern Eartholia Proper. He will be tried for his crimes against the Committee and will most probably be twined after his White Shadow is destroyed."

"Twined?" the emperor inquired.

"It's a method of execution in which the criminal is turned into a rope."

"How does that happen?" the bewildered emperor inquired.

"The criminal's skin is peeled like an orange while he is still alive, and dried off to form a hard, durable kind of rope. Should he still be alive by the end of the process, he will be soaked in a solution of salt and dumped in a fire ant colony to live out the rest of his hours."

"Interesting," was all the emperor said about that.

Sobo Ha-Ha Speaks

chapter 68

My dreams of becoming a great lord under Lord Venga had been destroyed. Upon his demise, I swiftly retreated to the Island of Ten Devils, where surely very few humans would want to set foot, even with all the pray-devils destroyed, for its reputation remained too horrific to endure. But I was mistaken. The humans were determined to end the pray-devil threat for all eternity. So only a few days after the Battle of Timbuktu, an army of man and raw-breed landed upon the island. There was no riddle of Mory Tipp to protect it any longer, and there were no tormented cries from Demon's Pit to frighten away the soldiers. The anguished souls of Mory Tipp and the tormented of Demon's Pit had been released into the peaceful abyss of death, their souls now resting, unbothered, upon the capture of the White Shadow. No pray-devils remained to protect me either, for they had all gone to Timbuktu, and there all had met their end.

I was found in the fortress at Ten Devils. I was spared an axing, but my Third Shadow was destroyed and I was confined for the remainder of my days to this dungeon in the middle of Gao, where I now reside, not far from the Dunes of Roses.

The days of eeids are few. Only a small number of us remain now, they say, for the world is changing, being peopled by those who rely not on the mysterious dark arts of the Third Shadow, but on reason, knowledge, learning, and experience. They rely on people like the girl child, Aida of Traoré.

The Words Of The Child Eeid

chapter 69

Eight days after the siege of Timbuktu was broken, the Table, which now included seven new Elders to replace those slain in battle, met with the governors of the twelve provinces of Mali, and with ambassadors from many a kingdom near and far. In this meeting the emperor expressed his gratefulness for the return to relative peace in the realm, to the resumption of trade between the empires, kingdoms, and states, to the return of peace. For all these, the emperor said, this Earth owed an eternal gratitude to one person, a girl child—me. But all that glory I could not claim for myself alone, I said, for many a man and woman had fallen for the cause; many a man, woman, or child, highborn or lowborn, would have done as I had done, had they knowledge and power such as I possessed. And to the officials I gave seven more names that deserved the gratitude of this Earth: Gyvan Drabo, Tigana, Gans, Babayaro, One Eye, and most importantly, Shang and Jeevas.

Magool the Elder thanked me for curing his stomach ulcers, even though he had faced an unending barrage of nagging from his wife for eating all the ginger in her kitchen. Tehan the Elder, with the stinky mouth, informed me that he now regularly cleaned his teeth. No longer did people suddenly find excuses to leave a room every time he opened his mouth to speak.

***

Twenty-nine days after the lifting of the siege went by and life in Timbuktu and the empire only got better. The unhappy times and vicious war of the many months past were but a distant memory now, too painful to remember and too undesirable to mention. The empire again lived in the glory of its former self, where justice and prosperity reigned, where the farms thrived and the granaries were packed, though small pockets of rebel resistance remained, chiefly in Djenné.

Yet there was one man I knew, one man who seemed lost and unaffected by these gains, one man who retreated into a dark, gloomy state of his own making. He was my dear guardian soldier, Commander Gyvan Drabo, the high lord of Tera-Hool. Distraught by his slaying of his birth mother, he had slowly withdrawn into a dark world of his own, keeping to himself even during the festive moments hailing our victory, and avoiding his friends and companions, including Lili and me, the closest companions he had. Not even the officials from his newly acquired dominion of Tera-Hool could gain an audience with him concerning matters of governance, as he locked himself away in a room in Lili's house for three days and three nights, some say weeping for the unforgivable deed he had committed, as had the half-green crow.

Poor Lili. I worried for her. She knew not what would happen to her dear husband-to-be. Fearing for his life, and fearing that he could bring harm upon himself, she had some soldiers break down the door of the room in which he had imprisoned himself. Gyvan Drabo was found pointing his dagger at his own throat, but lacking the courage to proceed with the unthinkable.

Upon his rescue, Gyvan finally emerged from his pitiful isolation and bid Lili and me follow him to the tomb that housed his dear grandmother and aunt. And true to his word, and to my eternal delight, my father and sister were entombed right next to them. Perhaps it was fate that had brought Gyvan Drabo and me together, for the day I had lost my father and sister was the day I had met him and Lili, who by now had become the two people I loved the most in the world.

In my sleep during that night, someone came to my dreams, someone I had given thought to on many an occasion, and whose fate I had worried about since our encounter on the Island of Ten Devils. He was Mory Tipp, the boy eeid who had been the Keeper of Ten Devils and whose soul had also lamented with 30,000 other tortured souls in Demon's Pit until our capture of the White Shadow from Lord Venga himself had released them from their suffering into the eternal rest of a peaceful death. In my dreams Mory Tipp thanked me for the peace his soul now enjoyed. My actions, he said, had helped free a hundred thousand other tormented souls in this world and beyond. Then he vanished. I awoke with a smile. I walked to Lili's room, where I tucked myself under her arms as she slept.

Mory Tipp had also brought greetings from some people I knew—a man, a woman, and a baby boy child named Pii.

***

I SPENT SOME TIME WITH Tin-zim and Shokolo-ba before they made their exit out of this outer world dimension into their inner world dimension, through the Portal of Gorgida, some thirty-one days after the battle for Timbuktu. The White Shadow was safe with the Committee, the governing body of Eartholia Proper. It was ready to be destroyed upon the trial of Lord Venga, and upon a time of their choosing, a notion that disturbed me, but one which I chose to dwell little on, for nothing by me or the emperor could be done to influence the decisions of the Committee.

My time with the raw-breeds was spent learning about their ways and manners, and even Breed, the language they spoke. I believed it to be in the best interests of both our worlds to learn and understand more of each other, for even though the Portal of Gorgida was to be sealed for eternity and the key destroyed upon the return of the raw-breeds, my short experience of ten summers on this Earth had taught me one lesson:

Nothing was absolute!

The day after the raw-breeds made their exit, Commander Gyvan Drabo, the high lord of Tera-Hool, was due to return to his dominion of Tera-Hool to govern his subjects as was his duty, in the name of Emperor Abubakari II of Mali. But that was not to be. Our dear tormented soldier had designs of his own. Tera-Hool was not his to govern, he said. And so before the emperor and before the Table, he abdicated his throne as high lord of Tera-Hool and named his successor—me, Aida of Traoré!

And so I became the high lady of Tera-Hool, somewhat reluctantly, with Lili as regent, and counseled by advisers with knowledge of governance dispatched by the Table, until I could come of age to assume my duties as was expected of my subjects. That was the decision of Gyvan Drabo, and nothing existed on this Earth that could have caused him to change his mind.

And to Tera-Hool, Lili and I moved some weeks later, along with my family's private library, where I now have exactly 2,208 volumes, finally surpassing my father's old friend and teacher in the University of Timbuktu, Ahmed Baba, who boasts only a meager collection of 1,419 volumes.

***

THAT WAS A SAD DAY, when I became the high lady of Tera-Hool. That was the day Gyvan Drabo left us. He had spent a lifetime seeking the mother he never knew, and now he would spend another seeking absolution for slaying her—the woman who had birthed him—as had the half-green crow. He was going east, to the Dunes of Roses, he said, to reflect on his sin. Then he would head south, across the great southern forests and beyond, to the lands where few had been. Perhaps there, he said, he could find release for his sin and free himself of the guilt that so haunted him. As to when he would return or whether he would ever return he could not say. I gave him my Naya to comfort him and help ease his pain as it had done for me in my own times of need, fear, and uncertainty.

Poor Lili, tears rolling down her cheeks, understood not what to make of it all, for Gyvan even said unto her that she would be doing no wrong if she found another. There could be no other, she responded to her beloved, for she was going to wait for his return until the end of time.

She was going to wait eternally for her dearly beloved.

Gyvan Drabo never finished the written accounts of his adventures, for by his own assertion he had come to realize that there was more to life than the fortune and glory of oneself.

There was pain.

The Traveler's Account

chapter 70

The Keeper's Riddle

I am Abdel el Maliki. It is I who brought to you the accounts that you have just read. It has been four years since Commander Gyvan Drabo went into the unknown wilderness beyond the great southern forests. He has not been seen or heard from since. All inquiries made by the emperor or the high lady of Tera-Hool about his whereabouts have yielded nothing. Today they only wait. Maybe he wanders the world like the half-green crow does in the sky, searching for a way to forgive itself for killing its own mother.

Peace exists in the empire today, except in Djenné, which the rebels still control. After the death of Mai-Fatou and the capture of the Third Shadow, the fight of the rebels became a fight to govern themselves, all attempts by the emperor to subdue them proving unsuccessful. The siege was finally abandoned by the emperor, and Djenné was left to its own fate. Ninety-eight times armies of past and present had tried and failed to take Djenné. It had been no different with Emperor Abubakari II of Mali.

The city was never taken.

This brings me to the emperor and the Keeper's riddle, placed at the Gates of Ten Devils, which Aida had solved but had given no answer to, stating that it was the riddle of Gong Shé, set a hundred generations ago, with an answer none dared to say, for it foretold an event none dared to foresee. The riddle was the prophecy of the emperor, Abubakari II, a prophecy that foretold the day some three summers past when the daring emperor left his throne to his brother, Musa the Elder, and set sail with a fleet of a thousand ships into the vast western sea and into the unknown. It was his own quest for adventure, a quest to satisfy a curious mind, a quest to learn what lay beyond the world we knew, perhaps a quest to understand more about the horror that had just been spared this world.

The Keeper's riddle had said, "Where the North Star leads, and where my brown is blue, they call me Kalabi Dauman, and my nine roars can be heard from here to the ends of the seas and back again. What is my destiny?"

"The place where the North Star leads" is the great desert to the north which travelers use the North star to travel through, yet it is blue because this brown desert, known to most as the Great Sandy Sea, is, according to this riddle, the sea of water in the west, and that is why it is blue. Kalabi Dauman is the ancestor of those who value adventure over the troubles and torments of government and statesmanship; the nine roars heard "from here to the end of the seas and back again" represents the ninth lion king of Mali, Abubakari II, who, preferring adventure to government, left his throne and took to the uncertainty of the sea for its adventures.

Neither word nor sight has been made of the emperor or his fleet of a thousand ships since. Neither word nor sight would be made of the emperor or his fleet of a thousand ships ever. So foretells the prophecy of Gong Shé, a prophecy too disturbing to mention.

THE PORTAL OF GORGIDA

There is an event which Aida of Traoré, the high lady of Tera-Hool, failed to mention in her account. Perhaps it was true forgetfulness, perhaps it was a lack of knowledge of the event, or perhaps it was a deliberate omission, the possible consequences of the event too troubling to bring to light. I came upon knowledge of this event from Gans. He was there when it happened.

Eight days after the raw-breeds helped to break the siege of Timbuktu, they were ready to return to Eartholia Proper through the portal of Gorgida, the same way they had come to our world, when another raw-breed suddenly came running to Shokolo-ba, whispering a message in his ear. Shokolo-ba erupted in rage at the message.

"Trouble?" Emperor Abubakari II asked.

"Your Highness," Shokolo-ba called, "Lord Venga has escaped."

"And the White Shadow?" the emperor asked grimly.

"Still safe with the Committee."

"Then there is naught to fear, eh? The White Shadow can be destroyed now."

"No, Your Highness. It cannot be destroyed without Lord Venga's presence."

"Still there is naught to fear, right? Without his White Shadow, he is powerless."

"I know," Shokolo-ba said grimly. "But there is another problem."

"Please tell."

"The key to the portal is missing."

So that was it. The Portal of Gorgida was open. The key to close and seal it was lost.

Who knew what else could come through?

THE BLOOD DRIPPER

It has been four years since the occurrence of all you have just read for yourself, and it has been seven days since I last met the parties involved, save Gyvan Drabo, whose fate beyond the southern forests remains unknown. But today, a rather strange event occurred whose circumstances I have yet to comprehend. Whether this event relates to those of four years past or not, I as yet cannot determine.

It all happened on my way to a horseracing tournament in Timbuktu when I was informed that it had been cancelled. That was because most of the riders, who were members of the cavalry units that supported the city's defense, had hastily scrambled for a crisis in the village of Bohama, a few days ride from Timbuktu. It was then that I noticed at least three cavalry regiments riding out of the city, fully armed and ready for battle. I approached the leader of one of the regiments, inquiring of him the nature of the unfolding crisis.

"Something is happening in Bohama," he said. "We do not know what, but something is happening. Something bad!"

"Rebels?" I asked.

"No, not rebels, not pray-devils. A rider from Bohama came to the palace. All he said to the Sentinels was, 'Run away! Let the people run away! This kind of evil you have not seen before! Run away!' Then he dropped dead."

The regiments then rode away, knowing not what to expect. A short moment later, another rider came to town. This time he was looking for me, bearing some correspondence from Sobo Ha-ha, dispatched by way of a trusted emissary the former high eeid secretly maintained in his service while he languished in his confinement deep within an imperial dungeon in Gao. The correspondence reads as follows:

"My lord, el Maliki, this hasty correspondence relates to you certain events that occurred some three days since. It regards a near forgotten undertaking that was put in my charge by Lord Venga during those troubled times long gone. I regret to inform you that those troubles are set to return to this Earth, perhaps more terrifyingly and worse than anything either you or I could ever imagine. It all concerns the creature referred to by the Table and Lord Venga simply as the blood dripper.

"No one but Lord Venga himself knows the blood dripper's designs or manners. Even I know very little of it, save to say that if unleashed, no word yet exists that can appropriately describe the carnage that it would heap upon this good Earth and beyond.

"I wish now to relay to you, sir, that the blood dripper has recently matured, and its horridly expected results have come to fruition, its effects already being felt in the village of Bohama not far from where I author this note. Before it is six days from the time you read this correspondence the horrific effects of the blood dripper will be felt by you too. Before it is twelve days after you have read this correspondence the horrific effects of the blood dripper will be felt by the empire. Before it is twenty days after you have read this correspondence the horrific effects of the blood dripper will be felt by every living soul that inhabits this doomed Earth!"

Sobo Ha-ha, former high eeid of the dominion of Tera-Hool and
prisoner eternal of His Highness Mansa Musa of Mali.

www.facebook.com/timbuktu.chronicles

www.timbuktubook.com

LaVergne, TN USA
16 May 2010
182746LV00004BB/10/P